THE ORACLE OF DUSK

AN EPIC FANTASY ROMANCE

ELYSE THOMSON

TWO LAURELS PRESS

The Oracle of Dusk

CONTENT NOTES

For my readers who prefer not to read the content notes, please feel free to skip this section and dive right in.

For my readers who would prefer a list of content notes before proceeding, I've provided what I hope to be a fairly substantive list below.

Content Notes: death, animal death, grieving, blood and gore, maiming, torture, emotional abuse (historic), threat of sexual assault (never carried out), kidnapping, swearing, consensual on-page sex.

THE WORLD OF
TRISIA
◇ CAPITAL CITY
• • BORDER
ROAD
NIVEAN CAPITAL
NIVEUM
THE BETWEEN
DRAGON'S SPINE MOUNTAINS
THE DRAGON'S TONGUE
QUEEN ROAD
COLONNADES OF THE COLOSSUS
HERE ENDS THE DIVINE TRIAD'S PROTECTION
ALTANUS
CANYON TRADE ROAD
AUREUM
DRAGON'S TAIL MOUNTAINS
THE DRAGON'S FLANK
ALTANUS NOVUS
DRAGON TALON HARBOR

ROSEUM
ROSEAN CAPITAL
THE FAIRY WOOD
GIANT'S JAWBONE
VIRIDIS
BOREAS
GILVIAN CAPITAL
GILVUS

Glossary

Terms associated with the Temples

Cleric – All those associated with the temple, from the lowest acolyte up to the high priestess.

Acolyte – First order, someone who has chosen to serve a temple, and is in training to rise through the ranks.

Initiate – Second order, someone who has chosen to serve a temple, and has either fulfilled part of the divine mandate of the temple and/or received divine magic from the goddess.

Priestess – Third order, someone who has chosen to serve a temple, has divine magic, and can administer sacred rites and rituals. If their blood is spilled, their goddess will punish the guilty.

Paladin – Third order, someone who has chosen to serve the temple in a militaristic fashion, granted divine power, sometimes a criminal granted a pardon and divine power in return for strict adherence to a divine mandate.

Head Priestess – Fourth order, the priestess in charge of the administration of the temple in the absence of the high priestess, administers sacred rites and rituals. If their blood is spilled, their goddess will punish the guilty.

High Priestess – Highest order, a woman chosen by their goddess to serve as the head of their goddess' worship on the physical plane. If their blood is spilled, their goddess will punish the guilty.

Religious Terms

Divine Triad – The trio of goddesses responsible for the protection of Trisia (Knowledge, Passion, Justice).

Sinister Triad – The trio of goddesses held responsible for the cycles of chaos and calamity in Trisia (Lies, Death, Vengeance).

Dualist – People who worship both aspects of the Triad, considered heretics by the temples and believed to be responsible for instigating cycles of chaos and calamity.

Cult of the Elder Gods – People who worship the tangible deities and refuse to worship the Triad. Blame the temples and dualists for causing the cycles of chaos and calamity. Considered an insignificant, fringe cult.

Cycle of Chaos – A period of destruction heralded by the alignment of the planets associated with the sinister triad, where monstrosities plague the land of Trisia.

Cycle of Calamity – A period of massive destruction heralded by both the alignment of the sinister planets as well as the rebirth of Drakon, The Beast of Old.

Tangible gods – The gods associated with the physical plane of existence (sky, sea, land, cattle, fire, water, etc).

Intangible gods – The gods associated with intangible characteristics (Knowledge, Lies, Passion, Death, Justice, Vengeance, etc).

The Loom – The afterlife, where souls wait to be spun back into the Tapestry of existence by the weaver goddess, Fate.

The Tapestry – The metaphysical plane of existence representing all living things in the universe and their lives, connections, and fates.

Avatar – A person possessing wild magic who is chosen by a goddess to fulfil a specific divine mandate and given divine magic. If their blood is spilled, their goddess will punish the guilty.

<u>**Magic Terms**</u>

Wild Magic – Magic gifted by the tangible gods to the chosen people of Trisia.

Wellspring – A place that can only be found by those possessing wild magic, or those who are meant to possess it. Where people chosen by the tangible gods are called to receive wild magic.

Divine Magic – Magic gifted by the intangible gods to the chosen people of Trisia.

To Kyle,
For all the fond memories of watching you play Zelda games.
(Because let's be honest, I was never going to be able to beat the water
temple.)

Chapter 1
Aurora

Aurora had never been happier in all her life, crouched as she was beside the skeletons of the ancient damned in a temple once lost to the sands of time. With only a few brush strokes more, achieving her lifelong dream and paying the ultimate reverence to her patron goddess was in sight. Years of gruelling study and fervent prayers had all led to this moment. It was, she would later learn, the last moment of blissful normality before her world turned upside down.

"You missed a spot," the princess of the Viridian Empire whispered with an irreverent grin.

Aurora flicked her gaze back to her task, delicately brushing the last layers of debris off the globe-like relic before her, tucking errant blonde strands behind her pointed ear.

"You're full of shit," Aurora replied.

The greatest upheavals of history made for the most interesting of studies, but were the most wretched of times to be alive. A truth borne out by the bones of her forebearers, their final screams lost to the ages. Now, as their skeletal remains saw the waning light of dusk for the first time in millennia, the only sounds were the soft hush of brushes on sand and bone and the quiet grunts of her fellow clerics adjusting to the physical demands of their tasks.

"Careful, or High Priestess Orithyia will scold you for your unladylike language in the presence of my exalted self."

Aurora scoffed.

"I'd tell her it's your fault. That's a valid legal defence in at least three provinces."

"I *am* terribly infamous." The princess patted her brilliant russet hair as she reclined in the recently uncovered alcove, a smile quirking up the corners of her full lips, her warm brown eyes sparkling with humour. She brushed an errant grain of dirt from her green and pink peplum jacket and crossed her legs at the ankle where her green leather boots complimented the rich brown of her tight trousers. Always the epitome of current fashion, no matter that she sat amongst lowly scholars. "Probably more so because they're always hoping your virtues will rub off on me."

"Goddesses forbid. The perfect Princess Phaedra has led a faultless and quiet life."

"Yes, quite the opposite of the wild, wicked life of my dearest friend. Why, I caught you dog-earring a page last year. Wars have been fought over less."

Aurora bit back a snort as her colleagues politely coughed.

"Hush, Your Highness."

"Bore."

"Brat."

Aurora fought back a rising tide of impatience. What she did today would mark the turning point in her life. She would graduate from acolyte of Knowledge to a fully-fledged initiate—a scholar of note. From the moment she'd walked the halls of the obsidian temple's museum, she'd been enthralled by the ancient past. Her first steps into the temple library left her in awe at all there was to learn. Knowledge, the goddess to whom Aurora had pledged herself, expected her followers to uncover the mysteries of the world, and as Aurora carefully freed the small, globe-like artefact from its pedestal, she could confidently say she'd begun to fulfil the goddess' divine mandate.

Aurora's heart soared as the last of the relic was fully uncovered. Pride swelled in her chest as she placed the freed relic onto the hovering tray beside her shallow trench. The culmination of a lifetime of study, hard work, and the favour of her goddess infused every stroke of her pencil as she catalogued the details of her find in the pages of the dig's journal at her side. Her first ancient relic. Aurora was a true scholar now. She couldn't wait to discover its secrets and share it with the world.

"You did it," Phaedra whispered.

"I did." Aurora's breath hitched.

She owed Phaedra much. The princess had come into her life like a tempest and had never seen fit to leave. It was thanks to Phaedra's influence that Aurora's department was flush with the funds for this dig. Some might treat her achievement as lesser for that friendship alone, but that would be simple jealousy.

Phaedra wrapped her arms around Aurora's shoulders.

"Is my baby initiate crying?"

"N-no."

"Liar." Phaedra kissed her head.

"Pest." Aurora touched Phaedra's hand and squeezed.

There was no truer friend in all of Trisia than Phaedra.

Aurora wiped her eyes, squinting as the setting sun's last light bled into the flickering torchlight in the inner chamber. Soon, the site would be too dim to safely work in. During the day, the light from the ancient temple's entrance gave enough light to work by. Now, they all risked ruining their eyesight in the encroaching dark. Groaning as her back protested, Aurora stood fully, wincing as blood flow returned to her legs and feet. Dusting off the faded black fabric of her trousers and black and grey brocade peplum jacket, she stamped her leather boots, willing the pain of pins and needles away. Her fellow clerics were similarly attired in shades of deepest grey, though few were as sensitive to the whims of fashion as Aurora. A bell announced the end of the day, and her colleagues put their equipment aside, covering the site with thick fabric tarps. Phaedra hooked her arm through Aurora's and led the way along the raised wooden platform to the exit.

There would be a celebration tonight. As the most junior member of the dig, and in honour of discovering her first relic, Aurora would be expected to drink and carouse all night long. She fairly skipped along the platform.

"Have you heard from your family?" one of the initiates asked another.

"They fled to the city in time, thank the merciful Triad."

"And the farm?"

"Went up in flames. Whole countryside has been plagued by monstrosities."

A bitter reminder that Trisia was not at peace, and to count her blessings that her family lived safely within the walls of the Viridian capital, Boreas. As they passed by the bones of those lost long ago in times much like these, Aurora fought down a shiver. At least Aurora wasn't on the front lines, or responsible for the welfare of the people of the empire.

Aurora squeezed Phaedra's arm in sympathy. The Viridian empire had been beset by a plague of monstrous entities, and the imperial family was quickly losing the war. As the youngest princess, Phaedra's role was to keep morale up, but even her façade of boundless cheer was beginning to slip. Joining Aurora on the dig was the only rest Phaedra had allowed herself in months. Aurora hoped for her sake that this cycle of chaos would soon be at an end.

"Sometimes I wish I had divine magic," the initiate sighed.

Phaedra squeezed Aurora's hand in sympathy then. She needn't have. Aurora had long ago come to terms with the fact that she had been abandoned by magic in all its forms. There was magic in the discovery of ancient secrets and that was enough for her.

"There's nothing you could have done, even if you did," the other initiate reassured them.

Only those with divine magic could dispel the monstrosities that formed when the sinister planets aligned. Outside cycles of chaos, monstrosity infestations could be put down rapidly, but during such a cycle was another story altogether. The beasts that spawned now were vicious, intelligent, and required martial training to deal with.

The clerics of Justice, the swords of the Triad, had been run ragged and spread thin for half a year now, putting down infestations that came back threefold. It was a true blessing that this dig had been allowed to happen at all. Phaedra being at the dig ensured that at least a few of Justice's initiates remained on site for her protection, and ostensibly, the safety of the whole dig team.

Luckily, High Priestess Orithyia CLXI was also of the opinion that one never knew when or how the pursuit of greater knowledge would prove to be what turned the tide in a crisis, just that, oftentimes, it had proved thus. No one knew what recovering an ancient artefact would allow them to do. The last had inspired the hovering surfaces for trays and carriages. Maybe the one Aurora had just unearthed would help grow crops or beat back monstrosities.

The sinister planetary alignment wouldn't last forever, but in the meantime, people suffered. Aurora could only pray it would end soon.

When they stepped outside, the breeze brought the mouth-watering scent of spiced meat. A treat in times like these. The hum of chatter grew louder the closer they got to the dining tent, a long, wide canopy of black felt opened to the outdoors, the cooks working over spits just outside. In the fading light, the rocky desert of the ancient site glowed rosy gold, a few prickly cacti the only bit of green. Much had been buried in the millennia since the ancient capital had been in use, with their current dig site shifting through the rubble of the ancient temple of Knowledge. In the far ancient past, this was the capital of the long-gone kingdom of

Aureum. The city, Altanus, must have been stunning before the repeated cycles of chaos and calamity had rendered it into rubble. Today, it was a desert far from the only habitable strip of the Aurean province.

As a queue quickly formed, Aurora and Phaedra expertly slipped themselves in near the front, to the grumbling of those less nimble.

"I'm going to enjoy watching you get tipsy."

"You say that as if you aren't going to join me." Aurora smiled and raised a brow.

"Oh, I will, once I make sure you've loosened up enough to flirt with that initiate you've been eyeing all season," Phaedra whispered.

"Shhh!" Aurora blushed.

"What was his name again?" Phaedra teased.

"Fae, don't you—"

"Hmmm, can't quite recall. But I did hear his nickname had something to do with having a very talented tongue." Phaedra's smile was savage.

Aurora placed her hands over Phaedra's lips, glaring. If she kept this up, the man in question would surely overhear her, and potentially run scared. Most were already intimidated by Aurora's relationship with royalty, and the last thing she wanted was to miss her chance with the man and his rumoured tongue just because Phaedra couldn't help being a pain in her ass when the whim struck her.

"I should have sewn your mouth shut as a child."

"Mother would have thanked you for that, I think."

"I could still do it. I'm sure I could find a rusty needle somewhere."

"Will that be before or after that silver-tongued young man puts his reputation to the test?" Phaedra asked, staring tellingly at Aurora's nether regions before slowly returning her gaze back to Aurora's, fluttering her lashes like some coquette in a play.

Aurora grabbed Phaedra in a headlock and mussed up her crown-like braids

"Not the hair! Not the hair!" Phaedra squawked.

A thread of panicked gasps jolted through the line of clerics. Aurora released Phaedra and they both looked around to find out what it was that had startled the dinner line. Perhaps they were shocked that Aurora had manhandled the princess? But they weren't staring at the two of them, their gazes were off in the distance. Hopefully, no one had spilled the beer cask. Now *that* would have been worth gasping over.

"Don't tell me something happened to the beer!" Phaedra cried theatrically.

The laughs were half-hearted at best.

Understandable.

Not even Aurora could find her humour as a heavily armoured initiate of Justice made his way up the path to the dig site. It didn't help that he was accompanied by a swarm of fearsome soldiers, all wearing imperial green. Yet Aurora knew none of these warriors, despite being friendly with many of Phaedra's bodyguards.

Phaedra straightened instantly, setting Aurora on alert.

"Stay here," Phaedra whispered.

"Who are they?"

"Paladins."

Aurora sucked in a breath. Often plucked from the gladiatorial pits, they were men and women who had committed grave crimes and had chosen trial by combat. If they survived, they were pressed into service in the temples of Justice as an elite fighting force, knowing if they strayed from the righteous path, the goddess Herself would not only revoke the divine magic She'd given them, but curse them to fates much worse than death. While initiates of Justice granted divine magic were thick on the ground these days, paladins were rarely seen unless the situation was truly dire.

Sick dread curled in Aurora's gut. No doubt they were here for Phaedra. Only royalty warranted such drastic protection, and they all wore the imperial green of Viridis. Searching the eyes of her fellow clerics, it was clear that they had all come to the same conclusion—evacuation was imminent. Aurora spared a glance to the ancient temple ruins. It had survived thousands of years intact, but if some epic battle were about to take place, it could be destroyed for good. Their careful excavation had revealed some of its secrets, but had also left the site open to unprecedented destruction. Merciful Triad, what a tragic waste.

Aurora desperately tried to commit every detail of her precious ruins to memory. They'd uncovered the weathered friezes and the roof first, gradually creating an opening into the temple interior. The ancient fluted columns were visible now, some cracked, others scorched. Maybe, if she were lucky, she would have a chance to sketch it, so that future generations might know what it once looked like before it was lost. The whispers of her peers grew quiet. No doubt they too were taking one last look. It was only when one of her fellows elbowed her in her side that she turned away from her ruins.

And was faced with the sight of paladins towering over her.

Aurora swallowed down a shriek. They must all have had a drop of giant's blood in them, to be able to loom over her so ferociously.

Only Justice's initiate was made of sensible proportions, being only a hand's width taller than she. The muted grey of his tunic and leggings was indistinguishable from the mail shirt atop it. His simple breastplate, vambraces and greaves were unadorned, unlike the armour of the imperial guards or any lord's soldiers.

"Aurora Tintori, acolyte of Knowledge, from the Boreas temple?" His voice was smooth, a pleasing baritone. His steel helmet protected his head and face, save for the T-shaped opening for his eyes, nose and mouth. From the part of his face she could see, he appeared to be her age, in his late twenties. Trivial details her mind latched on to as her legs turned to jelly.

"Initiate," Aurora said. Another trivial detail. It was easier to focus on those.

"Pardon?" he asked, bewildered.

"Aurora Tintori is an initiate," Phaedra clarified, returning to Aurora's side with a protective arm around her shoulders. Gone was her commoner's speech and easy mien. Here stood the princess of an empire.

He cleared his throat.

"Initiate Aurora Tintori, from the Boreas temple of Knowledge?"

"Y-yes?"

He frowned, scanning the faces of her fellow scholars. The silence was as piercing as the bright, icy blue of his gaze.

"Please, come with us."

Aurora's eyes widened, her heart leaping up her throat. Oh goddess, what could they possibly want with *her*? The other warriors levelled her with looks ranging from stoicism to bewilderment, boredom to outright disdain. Aurora looked to Phaedra. Surely a princess would know what was going on?

Phaedra skillfully inserted herself between Aurora and the warriors.

"My dearest paladins, you are meant to direct your overwhelming hostility towards monstrosities, not my confidants. Aurora, come with me. We will hear what they have to say in my tent." Phaedra hooked her arm in Aurora's and led her to the imperial tent, a large, rounded, home away from home covered in thick green felt and containing more comforts than any initiate could dream of. Plush, decorative rugs, a copper tub for bathing that one of the guards heated to perfection each night with their wild magic, fresh fruit and excellent wine on the carved wooden dining table, soft beds with silk sheets, and giant trunks full of clothes, shoes and books. Comforts that were incapable of appeasing Aurora's rising panic.

Aurora snuck a glance behind her. She wished she hadn't. A pack of armoured beasts stalked her steps.

"Fae, what's happening?" Aurora whispered, her hands shaking.

She'd never been in real trouble her whole life. She'd abided by every tenet of the law both secular and divine—she'd never even returned a book late! Had her family done something? No—impossible. They were honest cloth merchants in Boreas. They had nothing to do with trouble-making, paladins, politics, or battle. Not even her youngest brother, the little beastie that he was, would get himself in trouble this big—would he? He'd been approached once by one of those heretical cultists, but surely he hadn't gone and joined them... right?

"I don't know yet, which is concerning to say the least. Let me do the talking. I won't let anything happen to you. They may be paladins, but royal blood trumps glorified temple gladiators every time."

Sometimes it was hard to say which had the greater power—the temples, or the monarchy. If trouble were in the offing, Aurora hoped her goddess wouldn't be too upset with her that she was rooting for the monarchy this time.

Some prey instinct made Aurora look back again.

She tripped, her feet suddenly leaden.

That furtive glance had cost her her last shred of hope that the whole thing was simply some kind of mistake, or the empress being especially cautious about the safety of her youngest daughter. Phaedra helped her to stand and urged her onwards, but Aurora no longer felt the ground beneath her feet. The world was swallowing her whole between frantic heartbeats.

There, in a nondescript sheath at the blonde initiate's side, was a hilt any true Trisian would instantly recognise.

"He has the holy sword of Justice," Aurora pronounced as blood drained from her face.

Phaedra stiffened, redoubling her pace as if they could outrun the truth. But if Aurora's eyes had not deceived her, there was nowhere to hide.

"No. It's not possible."

"Fae, if he has the holy sword—"

Aurora's step faltered, her heart threatening to burst from her ribs. The holy sword could only be called upon when Drakon, the Beast of Old, resurrected—when a cycle of chaos became the cycle of calamity. A cycle of horrifying suffering, destruction, and despair. But the goddesses always gave Their people the means to triumph...the holy sword, and a hero to wield it, an avatar of Justice Herself, granted both divine power and protection in addition to whatever wild magic they already wielded.

"No. It was a trick of the fading light." Phaedra's voice hitched. "I refuse to accept that. It can't be *that* bad."

Aurora thought back to the skeletons in the temple ruins—lives snuffed out in an instant in a cycle of calamity thousands of years ago. Would initiates a thousand years in the future be prizing her remains from the rubble, determining her grisly final moments from the marks on her bones? The heroes of cycles of chaos past rarely lived long lives. The avatar born of the cycle of calamity fared little better—and neither did those whose fates were bound with his.

"Why do they know my name?" Aurora could hear the hollow desperation in her own voice. Would knowing the answer be better than the terror threatening to consume her?

"Anyone who is anyone knows of you through me. Mother is probably just being thorough, you'll see. If there is some danger or other, they know I wouldn't agree to go anywhere without you." Phaedra's voice was tight and high, her feet moving faster than ever.

That much was true. Aurora might as well be adopted family at this point. But that meant they were here for Phaedra after all. And that meant Phaedra's fate was in danger of being caught up in the middle of the cycle of calamity.

Aurora wanted to will it all away, to wake up from this nightmare. Her dreams had come true today, but she would give it all up in a heartbeat.

The frightened animal in her clawed at her heart. She needed Phaedra like she needed air. A world without her friend was a wasteland not worth contemplating.

When the flaps to the imperial tent were opened to reveal Orithyia, the one hundredth and sixty-first high priestess of the temple of Knowledge, and the look of abject pity in her wrinkled eyes, Aurora fell to her knees. Gentle hands helped her to a seat as a steady voice instructed her to breathe. Nausea threatened as all eyes in the tent were trained on her.

Every stare felt as threatening as a blade pointed at her throat. Why were they looking at her? She was no one. Nothing. Just a hysterical little initiate contemplating a world without its brightest, warmest light.

"You recognised the holy sword, didn't you?" the high priestess asked, her voice calm.

How could she not? Its likeness had been carved into reliefs since ancient times. Its depiction lived on as an essential ingredient of every heroic statue. Textbooks had its image lovingly painted across the leaves at every opportunity.

Aurora nodded her head, just then noticing the wielder of that sword on bended knee before her, his gloved hand on her shoulder, steadying her. Blue eyes searched her green ones with concern. He'd removed his helmet, long strands escaping his braid and framing a handsome face with hair as pale as moonstone. Why was he at her side? Why was the avatar looking at her like that, a mixture of pity and wariness pinching his features?

Aurora turned to Orithyia, a woman she would know anywhere. Naturally tall and slightly stooped with age, the high priestess' hazel eyes were calm. Her long white hair was styled up in intricate braids, reminiscent of the ancient styles, her gown of the deepest black was the same, a midnight brocade peplos with sleeves, complimented by her veil-like himation and silver diadem decorated with obsidian jewels. High Priestess Orithyia CLXI had been present at every milestone, from her first steps into the temple's library to her first day as an acolyte. From her first perfect score to her first academic failure. She'd been a benefactor, a stern tutor, a role model, as quick with a kind word as with a remonstration. Orithyia was the grandmother Aurora had never had.

And now she was here again, heralding a new, terrible chapter in Aurora's life. She was here to shepherd her through a trial which would surely tear her in two. If something happened to Phaedra, Aurora's heart would simply perish.

"Is Phaedra going to be alright?"

Phaedra scoffed as though such a thing were a given. But there was nowhere in Trisia that was safe during a cycle of calamity.

"Why were you asking after Aurora? What has happened?" Phaedra demanded.

Orithyia ignored the princess.

A very bad sign.

She took a seat by Aurora's side and took her trembling hands in hers. Soft, papery skin, bony and veined. They were the hands of aged wisdom. Safe details for her mind to latch onto.

"Yes, Aurora, the princess' fate remains untied to the current cycle."

Aurora nearly collapsed again, relief flooding her. Phaedra was going to be alright. *Maybe this won't be so bad.*

Her relief was short-lived.

"But yours has been woven into the very centre of it."

Chapter 2
Aurora

Aurora's screams of denial were trapped in her throat. She froze, paralysed by terror. But as her voice failed her, Phaedra roared in her stead. The princess marched over to the high priestess and smacked her hands away from Aurora's.

"No! This is unacceptable. I will not allow it. You have clearly erred in the reading of the signs," Phaedra accused her.

"There is no mistake," Orithyia replied, her voice grave as she returned Phaedra's glare.

Orithyia's authoritative tone only goaded Phaedra on. Like grease and fire.

"Get out! All of you! And *you*!" Phaedra all but hissed at the avatar of Justice. She gathered her wild magic and shoved him away. He recovered quickly, glaring, yet saying nothing in his defence. "Stop touching her! You will never have her. The world will burn before I let you take her!"

"If you don't, it may very well come to that. The goddesses have given us the means to end this cycle of calamity," the high priestess replied, standing to her full height and adjusting her robes and veil, entirely unfazed by Phaedra's outburst.

"Fuck the cycle! And fuck the goddesses! We'll go to the lands where their power is weakest!" Phaedra screamed, slipping back into a commoner's affectation.

Beyond the lands protected by the divine Triad, there were many other realms, but the goddesses' power and influence were weakened away from Their temples, leaving Their adherents at the mercies of rival, foreign gods and the caprices of fate. Even worse were areas entirely unprotected by any deities—the between, where monstrosities thrived. If Phaedra took Aurora and fled Trisia, there was no guarantee for their safety.

"Hold your tongue! Blasphemy is a crime, even for a princess," Orithyia retorted.

"The *crime* here is demanding an academic stand on the front lines of a damned cycle of calamity! She has no martial training, no magic, and you plan to what—throw her at The Beast of Old? Use her as bait? Fuck you! Fuck this! I won't let it happen!"

One of the paladins, a lean woman of uncommon height, sighed in irritation.

"Permission to remove the princess? Her tantrum is delaying our mission."

The high priestess nodded.

"You have no authority over me! This is *my* empire!" Phaedra turned an outraged glare on the paladin in question.

"Why do you think the paladins are wearing the imperial colours? Empress Neverita has already given us leave to do what we must," Orithyia said.

"Her Majesty would never stand for this!" Phaedra hissed.

Distracted by the high priestess, the paladin picked up Phaedra, tossed the shocked princess over her shoulder, and strode outside. Phaedra's screeches of indignation were barely muted by the thick felt of the tent. Aurora was alone, her protector dismissed as if she were a mere servant rather than a Viridian princess. Nausea threatened anew.

"Give us some space, please. Ready the lopers for the journey," the high priestess commanded the paladins, gesturing to the flap of the tent.

"We don't take orders from Knowledge's hags," the tallest warrior huffed.

"And we're not thrice-damned servants," the brawniest added.

"I, for one, would like to see how the little temple mouse responds, now that she can't hide behind the princess' skirts," the last warrior said, her dark eyes raking Aurora with disdain. "Best to figure out just how much of a burden she'll be on this quest."

The avatar of Justice put himself between the paladins and Aurora, his back to her. He was not the brawniest of warriors, nor the tallest, but his very presence demanded attention. As he spoke, his voice was soft but no less commanding.

"But you *do* answer to me, and to Justice. Do as the high priestess has asked."

"Swinging a holy sword won't earn you my respect," the tallest warrior hissed. "Bloody Nivean swine. I was earning accolades while you were suckling at some barnyard teat in your backwater province!"

"I don't require your respect, only your compliance. Now go," the avatar replied, unfazed by their hostility, his head held high.

In the battle of wills, the avatar was the winner. The paladins took their leave, grumbling the whole while.

"Thank you, Silvanus. Justice chose wisely when She made you Her avatar," Orithyia sighed.

"We shall see." He nodded, turning his attention back to Aurora. "I apologise for their rudeness. Allow me to introduce myself. I am Silvanus, avatar of our goddess, Justice."

He bowed, as deeply as one might to a princess. Taking her hand, he bent his head over it and kissed her dusty knuckles. Aurora's insides squirmed. What in the goddesses' good graces was going on? Aurora swallowed down her fear as best she could. Her voice was barely above a whisper when she managed to speak.

"What do you want from me?"

Phaedra had not misspoken when she'd described Aurora. More mouse than warrior, her only magic was that she knew the temple's main library like the back of her hand and had an uncanny ability to assist Phaedra in all manner of mischief. She was no one. An acolyte who had only just become a true initiate.

"You know that the sinister planets are aligned, correct? That their influence has created the plague of monstrosities?" Orithyia asked, as though teaching a lesson to a particularly slow student.

Aurora nodded. It was a basic religious teaching, one especially well-known in times such as these.

"And you know very well that sometimes, these alignments have heralded a cycle of calamity and the rebirth of Drakon?"

Aurora nodded again, biting her lip, lest the screams trapped in her throat break free. The Beast of Old was a fearsome horned serpent that slithered through the skies on a bank of malevolent clouds, raining down death and devastation. Nowhere was safe from its wanton destruction.

"Then you must also know that in such dire times, the goddesses give us the means to end the cycle—a holy sword and a hero gifted both wild and divine magic to wield it, an avatar of Justice."

"Yes," she whispered.

So what in the world did that have to do with her? She was neither a holy sword nor an avatar of Justice. While her research focused on the earliest recorded cycle of calamity, she was hardly the most learnèd on the subject.

"Silvanus is that hero, that avatar of Justice. High Priestess Nerio has confirmed as much. But there is one last piece to ending the cycle of calamity. A piece we keep hidden from view, whose existence is never publicly revealed, for fear the heretical cults might bring them harm." Aurora swallowed down bile, clammy hands gripping the fabric of her trousers. "The sinister aspects of the goddesses—Lies, Vengeance, and Death—may not be worshipped openly in Trisia, but they have their followers, those who will rise up for their champion, their avatar—the Beast of Old. But Drakon rises only when his prey has been reborn. A devoted follower of Knowledge, one who awakens the magic to seal the beast. You are its prey. And we need you to awaken that magic. I'm sorry, Aurora."

Merciful Triad, they were all doomed.

No, no, this was simply not possible.

"That can't be. I have...I have ruins to uncover. Artefacts to catalogue. We've only just excavated the inner hall. There's so much left to be done."

Orithyia sighed.

"I read the signs again this morning. Our goddess has spoken."

The goddesses Knowledge, Passion and Justice often sent signs for their high priestesses to interpret, but this was simple madness. There must be another explanation for the signs.

"But, there must be some mistake! I can't be this person. I'm...I only just became an initiate..."

"Do you doubt my expertise?" Orithyia raised a white brow.

"I—no—but you must think—"

"I do not *think*, Aurora, I *know*. Knowledge sends Her signs for us to interpret. Thanks to Her divine guidance, I have never once been wrong. Do you suppose I would not be absolutely certain before I presented this to you?"

Tears stung her eyes then. Despair began overwhelming denial. She would surely die. They all would, if the conclusion of this divine mission rested on her shoulders. She was no more capable of being a hero than a fish was of flight. The only weapons she'd ever wielded were her wits and her pen. Anyone who claimed the pen mightier than the sword had never been asked to face down the Beast of Old holding naught but a quill and a pithy remark in their defence.

"But I can't—"

"You can, because you must, Aurora. Knowledge has spoken. The divine Triad wills it. Your fate has been spun," Orithyia said, the stern disciplinarian once more. Aurora's heart sank. Orithyia's pale grey eyes softened then, a look that had Aurora biting her lip as it threatened to tremble. "You would not be given this role if you were incapable of seeing it done. In that, I have absolute faith. You may believe yourself unworthy of this great task, little dove, but I have watched you your whole life, and *I* believe in you."

That proved to be the final fissure that ensued she crumbled. Aurora sobbed openly then. Orithyia hobbled to her side and wrapped her in a bony embrace, petting her hair as the enormity of what lay before her swallowed her whole.

Outside the tent, Phaedra's voice was raised in command and a commotion ensued. Screams and a great clash accompanied howling winds. Phaedra's wild magic. Wrenched out of her own despair by fear, Aurora straightened. Had the monstrosities already come for them? Was Phaedra alright? The flap of the imperial tent whipped open, the snap of the fabric drowning out Orithyia's curse.

"Which one of you made her cry?" Phaedra howled as she stormed inside, her russet braids a windswept mess and her dark brown eyes burning like hot coals of hatred. Just as Aurora recovered from one fear, another arose. In this state, Phaedra was a true danger.

"Your tantrum is unacceptable, Princess. Leave at once!" Orithyia shouted above the din.

"Ah, so I'll be courting Knowledge's wrath then." Phaedra grinned with malice. "I'm not surprised. Never liked you, and it seems She has poor taste."

Aurora's heart seized. She'd never seen Phaedra so furious. Would she truly risk a goddess' wrath over a coward's tears?

Silvanus stepped between the high priestess and Phaedra.

"Please reconsider, Your Highness. No one here has harmed Aurora."

"Oh, will I be courting Justice's wrath as well? Perhaps we should find one of Passion's priestesses so that I can cover all my blasphemous bases."

"Fae, stop!" Aurora pushed past them to get to her friend. Phaedra was too hot-headed for her own good. If she harmed either the high priestess or avatar, Knowledge and Justice would severely punish her.

The moment Phaedra wrapped her arms around Aurora, the wind died down. She could feel Phaedra's heart beating wildly, her breathing unsteady. Phaedra was one of those whose wild magic made them more prone to let their magic have free reign in states of heightened emotion. Aurora was one of the few who could calm her. Crisis averted, Aurora's legs trembled. Neither her heart nor her body would be able to withstand much more of this.

"Say the word, and we leave Trisia," Phaedra whispered.

Goddesses, how she wanted that. To simply run away from everything she'd just been told. Some small part of her still believed it was all a mistake. Maybe if she left, the Beast of Old wouldn't rise. It would be better for everyone that way.

"You would only bring Drakon with you," Silvanus said, crushing her hopes. "He comes for her and her alone." Silvanus turned to Orithyia. "We'll be on our way shortly. I believe I know enough to answer any other questions Aurora or the princess might have. It would be best if you're safely ensconced in the Boreas temple."

"Very well. Aurora, do you have any other questions you would like me to answer before we part ways?"

Her mind was scrambled, her heart a jumbled mess. How was she supposed to think clearly in a situation as unprecedented as this? There were too many questions for her mind to hold at that moment, too many screams she was holding back. But one question in particular came to the fore.

"How am I to awaken magic when I've already failed to do so?"

If saving Trisia hinged on her awakening magic, then there was a deep and abiding issue with the threads of fate.

Magic flowed across the whole of Trisia. Some even awakened the power to see it. But in Trisia, there were only two ways to awaken magic—through listening for and answering the call of a wellspring, and through prayer. Wellsprings of wild magic rarely stayed in the same place for long, while the holy sites of divine power were more fixed in the landscape and temples built atop them.

As a child, Aurora had heard the call of the Viridian wellspring, answered it even, but had walked away empty-handed. She'd been rejected by wild magic, no matter that she'd heard its melody. And so, she'd rejected wild magic and devoted herself to the temple, to Knowledge.

And yet, no matter that she'd prayed for three days in front of her goddess, she did not receive divine magic. Half submerged in icy water as clear as crystal, wearing only the thinnest of linen dresses, her muscles had burned from cold and tortuous stillness. Tears had stopped streaming from her eyes after the second day of that ritualized torture. There had been no point to them. For three days she'd bent her head and clasped her hands in front of the statue of Knowledge. Only silence had met her mind's pleas.

Orithyia knew all of this.

Silvanus cleared his throat.

"The high priestess mentioned that you had heard the call of the Viridian wellspring. Clearly you have some affinity for wild magic. If you heard it, you'll be able to hear the other wellsprings, as I can. As luck would have it, I heard the call of Aureum's wellspring while travelling here. If we leave quickly, we might catch it before it moves." His smile was gentle. "I know this has all come as a great shock to you, and any right-minded person would be terrified, but there is hope, Aurora."

"Fae?"

Having awakened her magic at the Viridian wellspring, Phaedra was more versed in these matters than Aurora. After all, wild magic was the pride of the imperial house of Trisia. Aurora had been so devastated by her failure as a child that she'd refused to learn much about the subject. Yet another glaring error.

"Technically, yes. There is a wellspring in every province of the empire. Though I'm surprised the temples would allow one of their own to admit as much openly."

"You belittle the Triad and their devotees at your own peril, Princess." Orithyia sighed.

"The temples have long suppressed wild magic rites in the empire. Don't insult me by feigning ignorance," Phaedra retorted.

"I'll not have this debate again, Your Highness. Nevertheless, I can see Silvanus has you well in hand, Aurora. I will take my leave, and pray for your safe journey." Orithyia nodded at her before leaving the tent.

"Good riddance," Phaedra muttered.

"We should be on our way as well, Aurora." Silvanus offered her his hand.

Phaedra slapped it away.

"If she's going anywhere, then I will be coming along. In which case, she doesn't need you pawing at her like some stray dog. And while we travel, keep your paladins in line. The next one who so much as breathes impolitely in her direction better hope they die at the beast's hands, and not mine."

Aurora's heart stuttered in her chest.

"Fae, no! You can't! What if you get hurt?"

"What if *you* get hurt? If I come with you, Mother will be forced to send along *real* warriors." She eyed Silvanus with disgust.

"If something happens to you because of me, I'll never forgive myself!"

"Then the solution is simple. Don't let anything happen, and we'll both be fine. Which will be easier to accomplish with imperial guards."

More people who might be sacrificed if Aurora failed.

"Ooh!" Aurora pushed Phaedra away, fuming. No one could be as infuriating at Phaedra when she wanted to be, or as stubborn. But this was no prank, where the worst that could happen was a scolding. "You're such a stubborn ass! I won't let you risk yourself. Go home!"

"No. I'm a princess, this is my empire, and I go where I please. You can't get rid of me."

"I'll... I'll tell your mother about the gladiator last spring!" Aurora claimed, reaching for anything to get Phaedra to back down.

"Resorting to blackmail? Try harder. That's barely a scandal."

"I'll tell her you replaced the gemstones in her crown with crystals!"

"I'll tell her you helped. As if anyone but you would have the patience to pry them out so delicately. And if she hasn't already noticed, that's on her."

Merciful Triad, she needed to threaten something really drastic then.

"I'll tell your sisters where you hide your favourite shoes!"

Phaedra gasped, truly horrified now.

"You bitch! You know they'd steal them all on principle!" Phaedra grimaced. "No, I won't give in. Do your worst!"

"I'll tell her you were the one who slathered the poison oak in your ex-fiancé's clothes!"

"He deserved it for being a mouth-breather and nothing you say will make me leave you. And if you leave me here, I'll... I'll mislabel all your artefacts and contaminate the dig site!"

Aurora gasped.

"You wouldn't!"

"I would!"

"Damn it, Fae! I'm trying to protect you!"

"I could always tie her up and leave her here," Silvanus offered.

"No!" they shouted in unison, glaring at the avatar.

Aurora turned back to Phaedra. She had to say something, anything, to make her leave. The whole world could fall to chaos, but as long as Phaedra was safe, Aurora's heart could be at peace. The only thing more terrifying, more horrifying, than her own fate being tied to the cycle of calamity was the thought of taking Phaedra down this dark and dangerous path with her.

"Fae, please, I—"

A slithering sensation stole up her spine, one so strong she could have sworn she felt fingertips trailing along her skin.

"My little mouse, I've found you once again. And you will pay in blood for your crimes."

The low, rumbling whisper caressed her ear with its sinister voice. Aurora spun. There was no one behind her, no one present but for Phaedra and Silvanus.

"Did you hear that?" Aurora asked.

"Hear what?" Phaedra asked.

"That voice, those threats. Tell me you heard them too!"

"I—no, I didn't," Phaedra replied calmly, eyes swimming with concern. "This has been a really trying day for you—"

"No one will save you, little mouse! End this now, and I will—"

Silvanus put his hands over her ears, his divine magic washing over her like the flow of crystal-clear water, dissolving the taint of the voice.

"Don't listen to its lies, or its threats, Aurora. The beast will do anything, say anything, to prevent you from sealing it away."

"How do you..."

Could he hear it too? Was it truly Drakon? Pity formed in his icy blue gaze.

"It's the last piece of proof. Only the one who can seal it away can hear the Beast of Old as it draws near. Whenever you hear Drakon's voice, tell me. It means we must make haste if we don't want to be caught by it before we're ready to face it."

Mind numb, Aurora allowed herself to be led from the tent and onto a waiting loper. While horses made excellent draft animals, lopers were smarter and built for speed. She should be riding her own, but it had run off in the night without anyone the wiser. Perhaps she should have taken it for the inauspicious sign it had been. Long-limbed and sturdy with pearlescent white horns curling atop its head, the avatar's pure white mount pawed at the ground with its hooves, eager to be running once more.

"This is Neptune. He's as fast as they come and strong enough to carry us both through the night to the wellspring," Silvanus said, patting the loper's graceful neck before he snapped the reins attached to its horns. Without another word, the loper sprang into action.

So this was it. The moment her life was sundered. Behind her, the life she'd fought for, the career she'd strived for, her sense of self and safety—all gone. She'd lived her heart's truest dream for less than an hour. Before her, threats of death and a fate she was wholly unfit to carry out. Silvanus seated himself behind her and urged them all to ride as swiftly as possible. Not long after, Phaedra caught up on her own steed, keeping pace beside Silvanus, the paladins not far behind.

"What did it say?" Phaedra asked as they rode into the cold desert night.

Aurora shivered as she relayed it, word for horrid word.

"What language is that?"

"The c—" She was about to answer that it had spoken to her in the common tongue. But it hadn't. It had spoken a language drilled into every scholar of the ancient past, one rarely spoken aloud, except in the ancient rites of the temples. Thanks to her studies, she knew it as well as the common tongue. "The ancient temple tongue," she answered.

She met Phaedra's eyes as the realisation sank in. There was no escaping it now, this dreadful certainty. Aurora was lashed to the cycle of calamity, her fate tangled and twisted with that of an ancient monstrosity. The beast had risen because of her, because of some magic she had yet to awaken or master, and it wanted blood.

Her blood.

*"Run all you like. I will **always** find you."*

CHAPTER 3
PHAEDRA

Phaedra was absolutely certain that both the high priestess and the avatar were full of shit.

The princess' blood boiled as she watched that boot-licking temple rat play the hero for Aurora, putting his hands all over her with unearned familiarity, whispering in her ear. He'd come riding up on a white steed, its curling horns glowing like mother-of-pearl, as he gifted them all with a smile on his pretty face. Lies, all of it. He had no right to hold Aurora as closely as he did, no matter that they were sharing a saddle. A good friend would have his hands cut off for the offence. It would be but a trifling matter. She'd ordered worse punishments for lesser crimes, after all.

Did they think Phaedra would just allow the temples to use Aurora in this way? Every last word that came from Orithyia's mouth was to be viewed with suspicion. The old hag was a leech plaguing the imperial family, whispering in the empress' ear since she was a girl, directing matters of state through her bloody signs and omens. She had her fingers in every pot.

Aurora was too indebted to the old hag to see that she placed people like pawns, as deliberately and cannily as an empress might. Now that the cycle of calamity was upon them, Orithyia was placing Aurora on the front lines, along with the supposed hero, no doubt three steps ahead of them all.

Phaedra eyed him, taking his measure. He was Aurora's type, and, if she were being honest, hers as well—at least when it came to men. Neither short nor hulking, striking features, an excellent smile and an air of confidence typical of those who had trained their whole lives in some martial skill.

Was it any wonder she suspected him? What better way to entice a woman to her death than to place a pretty face in her way to lure her? Because there was something Phaedra was absolutely certain of: Aurora was no warrior. Anyone who expected her to fight as one had only one true aim—to use her without a care for her wellbeing, or to kill her.

So was Aurora truly meant to save Trisia, or was she supposed to bait Drakon out of hiding so that someone else could? Had she been told of her vital importance, and then given the cruellest of false hopes, in order to keep her compliant until the moment of betrayal? Phaedra would be thrice-damned before she allowed anyone to harm her dearest friend, no matter if the whole of Trisia was at stake. What good was being a princess if she could not protect who was most important?

But perhaps she could help Aurora see this ruse for what it was. If she helped her friend truly question this madness, perhaps she would be less willing to do as she'd been told. Phaedra knew nothing of Aurora's supposed role in the cycle, but the boot-licker probably did. If she poked holes in his stories, would Aurora be convinced to let this hero do his job without sacrificing herself?

There was only one way to find out.

Phaedra urged her loper to meet their pace, digging her heels into its sides and slapping the reins attached to its horns. It raced across the hard-packed sand of the Aurean desert as the night stole the last rays of deepest dusk. Luckily, both beast and rider had excellent night vision, the full moon throwing pale blue light across the rocks and cacti. Her sturdy walnut met the frantic pace of the graceful white.

"What exactly is your battle plan?"

Silvanus barely spared her a glance.

"That will depend on Aurora's magic."

"What have the others in Aurora's place used as their magic?"

"I'm curious about that too," Aurora said.

"I wasn't informed of that."

"Oh." Aurora's face fell.

"I apologise. We'll send a messenger to the temple to contact the High Priestess on your behalf. If anyone knows something about it, she will," Silvanus offered.

"Do you have a plan for what to do if the beast catches us before she has magic she can use?" Phaedra pressed him, refusing to let him play the saviour for long.

"Run."

Aurora seemed as surprised as Phaedra to hear it.

"So you don't actually have a plan!" Phaedra accused him. Success.

"The *plan* is to safely escort Aurora to the wellsprings in Aureum, Gilvus, Roseum and Niveum to awaken her magic," Silvanus replied.

"And the holy sword?" Phaedra gazed at it tellingly.

"What about it?" He raised a pale brow.

"Isn't the sword supposed to seal Drakon? Isn't that why they call you a hero even though you haven't done anything?" she taunted him. Perhaps if she could show he was both incompetent and emotional, Aurora would see this for the farce it was.

"The sword is one piece of that, not the whole of it," he replied calmly.

She hated him for that false bravado.

"Apparently it's the smallest piece too, if you don't even have a plan to defeat Drakon without Aurora!"

Men always took the bait when their honour was at stake. Whether they admitted it not, shame ruled every single one of them. It was simply a matter of finding the right pressure point. Silvanus was putting on a good show, but he would crack eventually.

Except he ignored her outburst. It only made her angrier. None of these temple rats had any idea what to do. Scrabbling around in the dark, putting all their faith in omens and legends instead of sense. Their entire grand design seemed to be throwing Aurora at Drakon and praying. Useless, weak, short-sighted fools. They'd already bungled this cycle of chaos, their initiates running around from outbreak to outbreak, a day late and a step behind, no one organizing a proper response to the rise of monstrosities. Her own mother had been little better, allowing people on the periphery to remain in their unprotected, isolated settlements instead of demanding they evacuate to safer towns with temples where they could shelter during outbreaks of monstrosities.

"Just admit it! You don't have a plan! You're placing everything on Aurora's shoulders and you don't even have the decency to say it!"

Aurora looked up at the bastard as if pleading with him to deny it. For her, his mien was soft, comforting. But when he turned his gaze to Phaedra? She detected the barest hint of a glare in his cold blue eyes, the merest tightening of his hands on the loper's reins.

"Much rests on her, but she won't do any of it alone."

Aurora's worry eased a fraction, her shoulders loosening, the fear in her gaze lessening ever so slightly. Whoever this was, he knew well how to charm a woman. All the more reason to crush him underfoot.

"Save the horseshit, avatar. If you or any of the high priestesses want Aurora to survive what you have planned, then you'd have brought a whole damned army with you, not a handful of glorified gladiators and a single fucking sword."

"A smaller group moves faster, Princess."

"And a more organised one is safer."

"You're welcome to organize that fighting force, Princess. In fact, I hope you do. In the meantime, we make haste and reach the wellsprings while we know where they are." Silvanus pushed his loper to outpace hers as Phaedra swore under her breath.

She was *welcome to organize the fighting force?!* Triad's tits, she should strangle him for that alone. She'd spent months trying to force the sclerotic temples into organizing a larger fighting force, into training more martial initiates not just of Justice but of Knowledge and Passion too. There was no reason anyone with divine magic should not be fighting at this very moment, with the safety of Trisia at stake. But of course, the temples were resistant to change and moved at a snail's pace. Their excuses were always the same, and they always made her blood boil—that it had been this way for longer than anyone alive remembered, and things had always worked out. If Phaedra had been the crown princess, instead of the fifth spare, maybe they would have listened.

The man was a brick wall—just like his temple. She hoped she'd given Aurora something to think about though. It was clear they cared nothing for her safety, their supposed saviour. Phaedra swore she would get to the bottom of their ruse one way or another. She slowed her loper. Once she was next to one of her imperial guards, she tilted her head, motioning for him to break away from the main group. Who knew where the loyalties of the 'hero' or the paladins truly lay? They may wear her colours, but they showed no respect, no deference.

"Your Highness?" he asked as they broke off from the main group.

"Once you can relay a message to Boreas, contact my spies. I need to know what Orithyia knows about Drakon's fated prey and the hero. How Drakon was defeated in the past, what became of the heroes who sealed him away—*everything*. I don't like any of this."

Sure, there were legends and myths, but all of those were missing key details and embellished for the sake of plays and songs. She needed facts—quickly.

"It will be done," he assured her.

Whatever it took, Phaedra would protect Aurora. If that meant toppling temple lies and a certain high priestess, all the better.

She held onto that anger through the hours of gruelling riding that followed, her wild magic whipping up the desert sands as the night dragged on. By the time the sadistic, holy sword-wielding task master allowed their ragged party to rest, Phaedra didn't know who looked worse—the poor lopers, or their saddle-sore riders. Aurora nearly collapsed the moment her feet hit the ground. Once the much-reduced imperial tent had been pitched, Phaedra led Aurora inside, her friend's legs shaking the whole time. One of the guards helped her eat and wash up, her lids heavy and face pale. The second her head hit the ground and a blanket pulled atop her, Aurora fell asleep between one breath and the next. But while her friend slipped into oblivion, the princess' anger reached a fever pitch.

How dare that bastard pretend he didn't know the answers to her questions. No one stonewalled a princess of Viridis. He had to be a fool a hundred times over not to even inquire about the heroes of the past. He'd travelled with Orithyia from Boreas, and never once had the thought crossed his mind? Lies. It was time to get some real answers.

Phaedra gently extricated herself from Aurora's side, waiting until the sounds of the camps dimmed, the soft snorts of lopers and the snores of the guards and paladins competed with the crackle of the fire. She palmed the knife in her boot and crept out of the tent. The knife was just for show though. If she shed even a drop of his blood, Justice would punish her for it. But the avatar didn't need to know that. All he needed to know was that she was serious—enough that she would court a goddess' wrath. Soft as a whisper, Phaedra made her way to the false hero's tent. She'd partaken in many a midnight rendezvous, enough to know how to open the tent flap without a sound. But whatever else he might be, this man was a warrior. She would have to pin him before he woke.

"You're not my type," he said lazily, his eyes never opening as he turned away from her.

Her jolt of surprise was quickly replaced by fury.

"No, because your type is impressionable and imperilled, isn't it Sir Hero?" she hissed.

"Your words, not mine."

Goddesses, this man was infuriating.

"I came for answers. If you'd like to be anyone's type in future, you'll give me the truth."

He sighed and turned onto his back, looking at her with a baleful glare.

"Go to bed, Your Highness. Sunrise isn't that far off."

This.

Fucking.

Asshole.

Phaedra lunged at him then, blade in hand. But he was ready for her. Throwing his blanket at her, he moved with lightning speed. She barely managed to get one arm and her blade free before he trapped the rest of her body under his weight, wrapped and tangled by some filthy rag of a blanket. He reached over her, grabbing her wrist with calloused fingers, and pinched until her hand went numb and the blade fell from her grasp. He swatted it away.

"If I have to tie and gag you to get some sleep, I will, Your Highness. The choice is yours."

Phaedra fought his hold, bucking wildly, but it was no use.

"Get off of me, you wretch!"

"Bound and gagged it is."

She'd sooner allow herself to be torn apart by feral dogs. As he moved to carry out his threat, she reached for her wild magic. Woe to any who thought the air was the weakest element. She turned her head to see him better, and unleashed it. His eyes went wide, a hand at his throat. She threw him off her then, fighting her way out of his hold as he tried and failed to suck in a single breath. Retreating to the corner, blade in hand, she raised her chin as he doubled over. Point made, she pulled her magic back. And since she'd not spilled a drop of his blood, his goddess had no recourse to punish her.

He gasped, gulping in precious air, eyes watering. There. That's who he was. His glare of hatred was fully unmasked now. No more impolite brush-offs or evading. Phaedra smiled in triumph.

"What happens to the heroes of the cycle of calamity?"

"I don't know," he wheezed.

"Lies."

She stole his breath again, throwing up a barrier of wind when he lunged at her. She picked dirt from under her nails while he struggled. Once he was suitably exhausted by his vain efforts, she eased off.

"Do you really expect me to believe you travelled with Orithyia for what, ten days, and never once asked her? Do you have no interest in your future?"

"My fate is in the hands of the divine Triad."

"That's not good enough." She narrowed her eyes.

He chuckled darkly.

"Do you think I chose this, Your Highness? Do you think I had a say when a goddess named me Her champion? Don't be such a thrice-damned fool!"

"I couldn't care less what happens to you. Tell me what you know of Aurora's fate, and the fate of those who came before her."

"Only the High Priestess would know that."

"Don't insult me by implying you didn't ask her about it."

He rubbed a hand over his pretty face.

"I asked her about Aurora, her history, her personality, her martial capabilities or lack thereof. I asked about how to keep her morale up, about how best to protect her from Drakon, about all the ways in which that monster would try to harm her. I didn't ask about her future because I knew if we failed, then *no one* had a future."

"Then how do you explain knowing about her needing magic, hmm? The specifics of the past never once came up?"

"All I know is that whatever magic she awakens will be the one that will help us seal Drakon. It has always been thus."

He was just as bad as all the temple vermin who'd refused to embrace even the merest hint of change. They would all rather stick their heads in the sand than face the reality of their ignorance and inaction. Why must they be allowed such free reign to blunder across the face of her empire when lives were at stake? When Aurora's life was at stake?

"Which is as good as saying you know less than my fucking loper!" she hissed. He wasn't taking this seriously. None of the temple idiots ever did. Not unless it had something to do with their rites and rituals. Fae stood, raising her chin. She would make them take her seriously. "I swear on all the gods, tangible and intangible, that if you and the High Priestess plan to sacrifice Aurora to save yourselves, I will not rest until I've obliterated your very souls."

His eyes widened a fraction at her oath. She meant every word of it. Aurora had kept her sane, and given her a reason to laugh and hope and fight for a better Trisia. Without her, Phaedra would have become just another callous, ignorant, spoiled princess. If their incompetence or cowardice took Aurora from her, she would give in to every cruel, violent impulse she possessed—become a thrice-damned heretic if that's what it would take to destroy them. And she would start with this fucking idiot of an avatar.

The temple rat shook his head and sighed.

"If Drakon prevails, then it won't matter."

Phaedra held back the urge to spit at him. Barely. She doubted she'd get more from him this eve. Best to wait to confront him with the intelligence her spies would dig up.

"And another thing—stop fawning all over Aurora. Don't touch her. Don't flirt with her. Save your deceitful charms for someone else. Aurora is too good for you, and she always will be."

He quirked a brow.

"Are we trading in unsolicited advice, Your Highness? Then maybe you should focus on Aurora and how *she* feels, rather than forcing her to deal with your tantrums on top of everything else."

Phaedra gasped in outrage.

"How dare you?!"

"How dare I? You came into my tent to attack me when my divine mission is to save Trisia!"

"In my experience, the worst enemies are born in the guise of allies. And I'm not fool enough to trust some temple rat with a fancy sword to have Aurora's best interests at heart."

The bastard snatched his blanket back and settled in once more, ignoring her.

"Good night, Your Highness."

The gall of this nobody. The moment his divine mission was over, he'd no longer be an avatar. And if Aurora had so much as a scratch on her in the end, he'd pay in blood.

"When this is over, if Drakon hasn't killed you, then *I will*."

"You'll be welcome to try."

Phaedra exited his tent in a huff. That smug temple rat. She'd make him lick her filthiest boots before the end. And worse.

As she slipped back into her own tent and beside Aurora, his insidious remark rattled around in her head. Was she really not being the friend Aurora needed? No, that was just him trying to get under her skin. He'd found her weak spot and injected his poison.

True friends protected each other. What could he ever know about their friendship, aside from what that half-blind bitch Orithyia told him? Aurora had protected Phaedra's heart all these years and had been her solace and her sanctuary. There was no more loyal friend than Aurora. True to her name, she was the promise of light in the darkness. She deserved to shine as bright as the dawn, to smile and laugh and love. Now, when Aurora needed to be protected from the whims of fate and scheming temple dogs, Phaedra would be her sword and shield. In her darkest hour, Phaedra would be her light.

It was some time before she could shake off his words, despite her exhaustion. Eventually, her anger cooled enough for sleep to come.

Until Aurora woke with a panicked gasp.

Chapter 4
Aurora

Aurora raced through the cobbled streets, ignoring the panicked shouts of her mother, the shrieks of colourful birds trapped in wire cages, the cries of gulls overhead, and the crashing of waves against the piers. She ignored the medley of fresh spices, the stink of slaughtered fish and fowl, the perfume of ladies both high and lowborn, the tang of sweat, and the salt of the sea. None of it mattered. The only sound in Trisia that mattered was calling her. It sounded like citrus, it tasted like a cool breeze, it smelled like joy, and it felt like if she didn't find it, she would never be whole.

Half in a trance, she followed the music only she could experience. Wild magic was calling her, inviting her to awaken. Excitement pushed her faster. Past the market square, beyond the guildhalls and their imposing stone façades, through back alleys and over rusted gates into an overgrown, long-neglected patch of green. Aurora wriggled through thick brush and tangled, thorny bushes that hadn't seen a gardener's sheers in decades. Sticky blood ran in rivulets down her arms and the backs of her hands. Her scalp protested the sharp tugging of blonde tresses caught and snagged on twisted greenery. Yet still, she answered the call with nary a whimper.

Freeing herself from the nightmarish hedge, she came upon a small clearing with an even smaller depression in the centre. The music was loudest here, drowning out all else. Aurora stepped closer. From the centre of the depression, a sprig of green slowly wended its way upward.

As it reached higher, it grew in thickness, one coiling shoot becoming many. Two branches split outwards, a small, golden fruit growing and ripening on each. Aurora watched, transfixed, not even realising that another girl with russet hair, wild eyes and a tattered, stained silk dress had come into this hallowed sanctuary, heeding the same call. Not until that other girl had reached for the second fruit. They locked eyes then, and ate the gift of the wellspring, juices like liquid gold painting their lips, chins and hands.

As they devoured the last bite, the song that had called her dissipated.

"Who are you?" the girl asked.

"Aurora," she answered, wincing as the stinging pain of cuts and scrapes replaced the trance. "Who are you?"

"Princess Phaed—"

"*I am the one who will devour you whole!*"

The sanctuary burst into flames, once-living green turning to ash in seconds. Phaedra lay before her, broken and charred. Aurora screamed and screamed, hands shaking as she collapsed to her knees. She reached towards Phaedra, but the princess disintegrated into ashes, ripped away by the rising winds. Above, the sky darkened, taking on the crimson hue of a violent sunset. The winds whipped past, keening in her ears, dark clouds above swirling into a vortex. From the centre, the beast emerged, a great serpent with blood-red scales and countless, twisted horns, its eyes glowing like fiery gold, lit from within by a bone-chilling hatred. It opened a mouth full of fangs and dove from the sky.

Aurora woke with a start, her heart racing.

"It's okay. It was just a dream." Phaedra put her hand in Aurora's.

Aurora turned her head. Phaedra lay next to her, snuggled close in the tent they'd decided to share after they rode their mounts to near exhaustion. Aurora threw her arms around Phaedra. It had just been a nightmare. She held back her tears as Phaedra held her in turn.

Drakon's words had chased her nearly the whole way, subdued only by Silvanus' divine magic. Outside their tent, the pop and crackle of the fire, the calls of owls and the calm nighttime winds accompanied the grunts and snoring of their unlikely companions.

The beast's voice was silent. They'd managed to outrun it.

Aurora calmed her racing heart and pulled away, squeezing Phaedra's hand, a strange sense of déjà vu taking hold as she took in Phaedra's sleep-rumpled appearance.

"What was it about?" Phaedra asked.

"Hmm?"

"Your dream."

"Nightmare," Aurora corrected her.

"Whatever it was, tell me. You'll feel better once you've spoken about it."

Somehow, she doubted that.

"I dreamed of when we found the wellspring."

"Meeting me wasn't *that* bad." Phaedra smiled.

Aurora chuckled. No, it hadn't been.

"It started like that, and then everything burned. You...you died. It spoke to me in my dream, the beast, and then it was there, coming to devour me."

"Do you hear it now?"

Aurora shook her head. Thank the Triad for that.

"I won't let it hurt you."

"I wish you wouldn't promise something like that."

"Why?"

"Because you keep your word." Aurora grimaced.

"When it suits me." Phaedra winked. "You'll feel better once my reinforcements arrive. We're nearing a proper town, so once you awaken at this wellspring, we'll take a carriage back home where you'll be trained by the top tutors in Viridis and protected by the best defences in Trisia."

"*If* I awaken."

"You will."

"You can't know that."

She'd already failed once.

"You know how much I hate that old hag, but the high priestess was right. If your fate is to seal the Beast of Old, then you will. Ergo, you *will* awaken your magic. Besides, how many times has this cycle repeated? And every single time, Drakon is sealed."

But how many people would die? How many would suffer? What would be lost? Or more importantly, who? Phaedra meant everything to her, and she stubbornly insisted on putting herself in harm's way.

"She's not an old hag... and she didn't say I would survive it, Fae. Even our records of the most recent hero of the holy sword only speak of his deeds, not his life after the fact."

"If the previous hero was as tedious as Silvanus is, he probably bored his biographers into an early grave."

Aurora snorted.

"He's not that bad."

"You laughed. I know you agree with me."

The flap of their tent was opened then. Outlined by the flickering firelight was the man in question.

"Not giving in to your provocations doesn't make me tedious."

"Well, barging into a lady's tent makes you rude. So now you can be both," Phaedra hissed.

Ignoring her, he turned to Aurora.

"If you're awake, we should move. The wellspring is near, but there's no telling for how long." He held out his hand.

"We're sleeping! Go away," Phaedra moaned.

"Sleep is a luxury," Silvanus countered.

Aurora bit back a sigh and accepted Silvanus' hand. He pulled her to her feet, wrapped her in a cloak and quickly had her seated on his big, white loper. She felt like so much luggage as they departed the camp.

"Wait!" Phaedra cried as she scrabbled from the tent, russet hair in disarray.

"You and your guards can catch up with us after your rest, Princess," Silvanus said, urging their mount onwards. "Let the paladins know to follow."

Aurora winced as the graceful loper sped to a gallop. She wasn't the most accomplished rider, despite sharing Phaedra's tutors. Her inner thighs were chafed and her backside ached. She'd never ridden so hard in her life.

"Can you heal with your divine power, Silvanus?"

"If the wound was inflicted by a monstrosity, yes."

Aurora very much doubted she would ever ride a loper-shaped monstrosity. More's the pity, given her current predicament.

"Are you injured?"

"Just...sore."

"I would have thought you used to riding, being acquainted with the princess. And Neptune is quite the graceful racer."

Neptune could be the embodiment of grace and liquid speed but that wouldn't change the fact that hours of hard riding was injurious to one's backside. And it wasn't as though scholars did their reading and writing atop galloping lopers.

"We've led very different lives. It's not as though we're joined at the hip."

"Does *she* know that?" he asked, amused.

It was the first bit of dry wit she'd heard from him. Aurora risked turning her head to ensure she wasn't dreaming it. But there on his face was a smile.

"Great Goddesses, was that a joke?"

"Not a very good one, if you're asking." He frowned.

"Just a surprising one."

"Are prophesied heroes not supposed to crack jokes?" His lips curled upwards.

"I'm not entirely certain. You're the first I've met." Aurora found herself smiling back.

"Likewise."

"I'm not a—"

"Except that you very much are."

Aurora gripped the reins as her palms turned clammy. Even now, there were moments she slipped into comforting denial about that. It probably said as much about his soothing presence as it did about her need to escape her dread.

"How did you find out? How did you become Justice's avatar?"

"I was called to the Temple by High Priestess Nerio and asked if I could wield the holy sword for them. I thought it was some hazing ritual for the imperial guard, that the sword was a fake. You're probably the only other person in Trisia who can appreciate my surprise at finding I could actually hold it."

Quite.

The holy sword was said to incinerate any who attempted to wield it without Justice's permission.

"Were you scared?"

"Oh, absolutely. When I realised it wasn't burning me to a crisp, I puked all over the fancy marble floors. And myself. Not something I recommend doing in full plate. There's a good reason wild and divine magic only ever mix in an avatar."

Aurora barked out a laugh.

"Merciful Triad, I'm sorry."

"Not as sorry as my squire was, let me tell you."

Aurora suppressed a few giggles at the poor squire's fate. Some part of her eased, knowing that even a warrior of the hero's calibre felt fear at the prospect of what lay ahead. Perhaps that made her less unworthy for feeling the same.

"I had no idea you were training to be in the imperial guard."

"I was slated to become Princess Phaedra's newest guard, in fact."

"No," Aurora gasped.

She couldn't imagine the serious, staid Silvanus running around after Phaedra and putting up with her antics. All her current guards shared her sense of humour and had learned to pick their battles.

"Oh, yes. Empress Neverita wanted her youngest on a tighter leash."

"I mean this in the nicest possible way, but she would have made it her mission to chew you up and spit you out just to prove a point," Aurora said.

"Now I get to do battle against Drakon. Hard to say which is the more gruelling beast to subdue."

Aurora chuckled. No one won against Phaedra when she set her mind to something.

"You'd best be careful not to say that to her face."

"Duly noted."

"And Fae's not that bad."

"A resounding endorsement, clearly, given I received one just like it."

Aurora blushed and cleared her throat.

"I mean it! You'll never find another soul as loving or loyal."

"I've experienced the loyalty. I suspect the loving is something she saves for a select few."

In that he was correct. But it bothered her that he had a negative view of Phaedra. It wasn't anyone's fault that they didn't see the woman she truly was. After all, Phaedra was very good at crafting her public image and holding people at a distance. But she hoped Silvanus would see Phaedra as Aurora did. She deserved to have more people in her life who truly knew and cared for her.

"Everyone thinks being a princess is all parties and ballgowns and luxury. I used to think the same. But her fate was decided before she'd even been born. She never got a chance to have her own dreams, let alone pursue them. Her life is one of constantly being on display, of duty and sacrifice. Once I learned the truth, I have never once envied her that. Is it any wonder that she saves her true heart for those who've proven themselves worthy of it?"

"Fate rarely does Her chosen any favours," he murmured, almost too quiet for her to hear. Yes, she supposed they three had that in common now. There was little to envy in that. "Although there is something I'm curious about. How is it that a merchant's daughter turned acolyte becomes the princess' closest confidante?"

"Initiate," she corrected him, before realising it meant next to nothing now. Her whole life before this point mattered not a whit. It was strange to think that fate had robbed her of who she was.

"Apologies. Initiate."

"How did you know all that?"

"High Priestess Orithyia made sure I knew everything about you before I arrived. And you're quite the curiosity among the imperial guard candidates."

"Oh?"

"And the more I know, the better I can protect you."

"Oh." Aurora tried to push it from her mind. "Well, to answer your question, I punched her."

Everyone always asked that question, hoping for some secret key to worming their way into Phaedra's good graces. But hers was a friendship that had come roaring into Aurora's life like a gale. Silvanus was quiet for a long time after that.

The sun was just peeking over the horizon, a slash of bright pink and gold tinging the midnight blue. The loper cantered along the rocky desert path. Once, this would have been green and full of life. But much of Aureum had dried up in the ancient past, just as the rest of Trisia had, its mighty rivers reduced to a trickle, forcing the capital to move closer to the border with the still-verdant Viridian imperial centre. Her dig site had been at the ancient royal capital, Altanus, now buried beneath the sand and rock of thousands of years.

"No matter how many times I turn that over in my head, I can't picture you punching the princess," Silvanus said.

Aurora laughed. Neither could anyone else.

"I wasn't nearly so mild-mannered as a child. I was terribly jealous of Fae, and she of me. One day, I'd had enough of her prancing about the temple library with her sycophants in tow, praising her wild magic. I marched right up to her and gave her a black eye. She returned the slight, and from there it was a lot of hair pulling, biting, kicking and screaming."

"And you weren't executed?"

"Shockingly, no. Both the empress and high priestess already understood why we despised each other. I was furious that she had wild magic, pretty clothes, and a hundred friends, even though we'd both arrived at the wellspring at the same time. She was envious that I could be anything I wanted, do anything I pleased, and go where I wished without always being followed or being on display. I think Her Majesty thought it would be a good lesson in humility and compassion for Fae to understand a commoner's problems. I don't think anyone expected us to become friends after that, but for Fae, I was probably the only one outside her family who treated her like a normal little girl."

And for all their differences, Phaedra had proved to be the truest friend Aurora ever had. Where either faltered, the other was there to pick them up. When Aurora spiralled into gloom, Phaedra was ever her light. When

Phaedra thought to take one prank too far, Aurora was there to pull her back from her worst impulses.

"If you don't mind my asking, what drew you to study the past rather than become a merchant or the princess' lady's maid?"

"The last king of Aureum—King Theron."

"The one who attacked the avatar during the first calamity?" Silvanus asked, amused.

"The very same! His biography is our only written record of the first calamity. And he's so much more interesting than the playwrights make him out to be. My thesis focused on our interpretation of one of the ancient temple tongue words used to describe his bride. It turns out she was a princess!" Aurora gushed.

Oh, the older scholars tore her to shreds for that reinterpretation for months, but eventually a re-examination of the original text proved she'd been right. It was that academic victory which had persuaded Orithyia to let her prove herself on this dig—to become a full-fledged scholar.

"Well, as long as you don't intend to reenact certain parts of his story..." Silvanus smiled wryly.

"Best not bring it up with Fae." She laughed.

"Hmmm," he agreed. "Do you know the name of the first hero of the holy sword?" he asked quietly.

Aurora shook her head.

"No, only his title is mentioned in the king's biography. Nothing else that's survived the millennia bears his name."

But as the quiet hush of the desert began to fill with music, her moment of distracted happiness slipped away. She should have focused on her magic, not the past.

"We're close," Silvanus said.

Maybe this time Aurora would awaken the wild magic she should have awakened when she and Phaedra found the Viridian wellspring. She felt the pull again, the trance. This was different, though. It wasn't nearly as strong. It didn't warp and blend her senses. It sounded like sand slipping through her fingers, like the call of wild animals, like blood rushing to her ears.

"You hear it now?" Silvanus asked.

"Yes. But not as strongly as when I was a child," she answered.

He didn't comment again. Probably for the best, as the closer they got, the more insistent the pull was. Once more, the melody was a full-body experience unlike any other. Afternoon sun warmed her skin despite the early hour, sweet pomegranate tantalized her tongue, the scent of cinnamon filled her nostrils. Suddenly she was off the saddle, allowing the wellspring to pull her in, to seduce her. Aurora didn't know how long she walked, only that every step she took brought her closer, intoxicating her senses and filling her ears with a melody of the wild magic infusing this place.

It drew her to a large rock standing alone in the landscape. Aurora placed her hand on its cold, rough surface, but she knew this was different. The magic was not as compelling here as it had been in Viridis. The wellspring was entrancing, but she didn't feel as though some part of her needed it to be whole, as if it were some secret key to her soul. As Aurora stood there, hand to the rock, the music slowly faded, as did her hope.

She turned to Silvanus and shook her head.

"I'm sorry," she said.

"Don't apologise. We simply need to find the next wellspring."

"You make it sound so easy. They could be anywhere in Trisia."

"True, there is only one wellspring for each province, and they can be anywhere in that province at any given time. But Her Majesty began mobilizing scouts before I even set out from the capital. By the time we reach the province of Gilvus, I suspect someone will have already located it," Silvanus explained, leading her back to their loper. "Don't think just because we're expected to face Drakon, that we'll do any of this alone. I imagine it was much more difficult in ages past when Trisia wasn't united as an empire, but this age is different. Take heart in that."

She'd not known that about the wellsprings. Another glaring example of her cultivated ignorance.

"I...I will try. Thank you."

They mounted and headed back for the camp. The sun was now high enough to bathe the desert in a rosy glow.

"How did you awaken your magic?"

"I'm not sure I did. Once I visited the Nivean wellspring, all of a sudden, it was there. Not that I had much control of it, or any idea of what to do with it."

It was much the same for every person Aurora had ever asked about the subject. From one breath to next, magic was theirs, as tangible as a limb. She sighed. Another strange feeling of déjà vu crept up on her as she watched the loper's ears twitch as it trotted along the rocky path, rose gold rock interspersed with long, midnight blue shadows marking every pebble and dune.

"What was that?" Silvanus asked.

"What was what?"

"I..." He peered at her, blue eyes raking over every inch of her. "No, never mind. My apologies."

"The light plays tricks at this hour. It's almost easy to understand why the ancients thought the spirits were most active at dusk and dawn."

They weren't any longer, if they even still existed. If they'd ever existed. He smiled ruefully.

"I suspect a lack of sleep isn't helping."

"Maybe we'll get some when we return to camp."

"With the dulcet tones of the princess' insults and the comfort of the paladin's open contempt, how could I not rest peacefully?"

Aurora laughed. Perhaps Silvanus would have survived Phaedra's tests after all, had he become her guard. In another life, maybe they would have traded tips for dealing with her antics, rather than chasing hopeless leads and battling ancient evils.

Warm lips caressed her neck.

Aurora stiffened, turning to Silvanus with wide, fearful eyes, slapping her hand on her neck. What kind of hero accosted a woman?

Fingers trailed up her calves.

As panic threaded through her, Silvanus seemed just as surprised by her movements. He couldn't possibly be touching her, seated as he was behind her with his hands on the reins.

"Surrender yourself to me, and I will make your last moments worth dying for."

"It's here," Aurora said, swallowing down bile.

"You can *feel* it as well as hear it?" he asked, aghast.

"Yes," Aurora whispered.

"Filthy, fucking monster," Silvanus muttered darkly, washing her in divine magic, erasing the feel of the beast on her skin. "Well, it doesn't look like rest is in our immediate future."

"No," Aurora sighed. "Thank you. I don't... I don't know what I would do if you weren't here to—"

"Stop right there. I could be bleeding to death and I would consider it an honour to use the last of my strength to keep that thing from touching you. Never think you need to suffer through that for a moment, Aurora. Understood?"

"Yes. Tha—"

A loper shrieked in the distance. Shadows cast by the sunrise bubbled and congealed all around them. Their loper shied before stomping on the ground, sending the shadows scattering. She'd heard the steeds used by Justice's temple were imbued with the goddess' power and trained to fight as hard as their riders, but it was altogether another thing to see it in action.

"Monstrosities," Silvanus said, grimacing. "I need to find the centre of their eruption and destroy it or they'll spread."

He raised his hand and sent out a wave of divine magic, sparkling, pale light dissolving the monstrosities before they could take shape.

"Hold on."

Silvanus urged their loper to make haste as Aurora's heart was lodged in her throat. They made it to the next rise, the camp visible below. A sea of bubbling black circled their small camp, monstrosities rising from the shadows, their gruesome features hardening as they prepared for bloodshed. The camp was surrounded, hemmed in by tooth and claw, all of it dripping black shadow. Imperial lopers scattered and shrieked as monstrosities tore them down. Blood painted the shredded remains of tents quickly lost in a sea of roiling black. Imperial guards were devoured whole. The paladins and their mounts pushed back against the tide, but where their divine magic dissipated one monster, another three rose and took its place.

Aurora's eyes sought Phaedra in the slaughter. There, surrounded by imperial guards using wild magic to little effect, Phaedra stood bloodied, wide-eyed, and holding a small box in her hands. She was backing up as the monsters advanced, but one was rising behind her, its toothy maw wide open, ready to swallow her whole.

"FAE!"

Chapter 5
Aurora

Something swelled inside Aurora and snapped outward. The monstrosity looming with lethal intent behind Phaedra paused for a split second. It was enough. Phaedra clocked the beast and launched herself into the air with a powerful gust of air. Several of the monstrosities took flight after her. At Aurora's back, Silvanus pulled out a bow glowing with light, dispatching the flying monstrosities with arrows created by divine magic.

As she descended, Phaedra used another blast to keep herself aloft. Aurora's heart hammered in her chest as Phaedra dodged the claws and gaping maws of the monstrosities, continually escaping back into the air.

"Hold on!" Silvanus called as the loper surged forward.

Mount and rider raised a battle cry as they plunged into the madness. Leaning forward in the saddle, Silvanus covered Aurora's body with his, his bow transforming into a spear he angled forward. Its radiance cleaved a path in front of them, dissolving the bubbling mass of monstrosities before they formed and leaving the ground fully purified in their wake.

The paladins' lopers battled through monstrosities to follow behind, trampling the beasts beneath hooves blessed by the goddess Herself. In the centre of the camp, the remaining paladins and imperial guard fought back-to-back.

Phaedra descended in front of them and Aurora's heart leapt into her throat. Before Aurora could scream at Silvanus to halt the loper, Phaedra launched back into the air, twirling gracefully over them and landing in the saddle of one of the following steeds.

They circled the camp, cutting through monstrosities as though they were made of water. When the bulk were defeated, Silvanus handed her the reins.

"Take over!"

"What?!" Aurora squeaked as he leapt off the loper with the talent of a trained acrobat.

Aurora gripped the reins and kept her head close to the loper's neck, lest a stray claw-tipped paw take her head from her shoulders. Though given her steed's fierceness, she needn't have worried. The war-trained loper barrelled through the straggling beasts with ferocious ease, even without the holy weapon to help clear the way.

Phaedra urged her loper to race beside Aurora's, covering the side exposed to the inner ring of monstrosities.

On the edge of the camp, Silvanus stood as a lone warrior, his body glowing with divine power. She watched in awe as he planted his feet, twisted his hips and posed the holy sword as if to cleave the whole of the camp in two. Monstrosities bubbled up near his feet as he stood his ground, kept at bay as his inner radiance seared even her eyes. The lopers made another half-circle before he unleashed the power of the holy sword. An arc of light tore through the remains of the camp, sweeping away the monstrosities as though they'd been sculptures made of sand.

The lopers circled the camp once more, but the monstrosities were gone. The traces of their presence lingered in the cries of the wounded, in the blood soaking the hard-packed sand, in the torn and trampled tents. Only a single imperial guard remained alive, yet only one paladin had been wounded. A grim reminder that only divine magic could defeat the beasts.

Silvanus sheathed his blade, now resembling a regular sword once more, and rushed into the camp, using his divine magic to heal the wounded and consecrate the bodies of the fallen. The battle was over, but this was only the beginning of the calamity to come. A mere taste of horror.

Until now, she'd had a hard time understanding why so much history of the past had been lost, despite the continual presence of the temple of Knowledge. Now she knew why. Every cycle of calamity took its toll in blood, leaving fewer each time who could record that toll in ink.

Aurora had seen the remnants of villages sacked by monstrosities, the broken, burnt-out buildings, the dried blood flaking in the sun, streams of the dead-eyed wounded as they trudged towards the next town or village, the scraps of their former lives slung over their shoulders. She'd seen that, and yet she'd still believed that was the worst the calamity could offer, that the beasts were so easily defeated by those with divine magic and a bit of warrior's training.

She'd been so ignorant.

How much worse would this have been had it happened in the middle of an army on the march? One made up of mostly imperial soldiers rather than Justice's paladins? How much worse would it be if they attacked the capital, with its labyrinth of narrow streets and crowded buildings? Even trained warriors stood little chance against the beasts. What hope did the average merchant and labourer have? What hope did the elderly, the infirm, the youngest amongst them?

"We can't go back to Boreas."

"What?" Phaedra asked, her face drained of blood.

"We can't bring this with us back to the capital."

"We'll be safe behind the castle walls. Safer than anywhere else." Phaedra's brow knitted with concern.

Aurora shook her head. Drakon followed *her*. Everywhere she stopped would have a target painted on it. Everyone she travelled with would be similarly beset.

"No, I have to get to Gilvus. To the wellspring there."

Because she'd failed. Again.

How many more deaths would be on her head? How much more blood would stain her hands because of her ineptitude? She wished she could go back in time and shake her younger self. If only she'd been able to put her wounded pride aside and had learned more about the wellsprings, about wild magic, maybe she would have awakened her magic before the cycle of calamity had begun. Those guards would be alive now if not for her ignorance.

"What happened at the wellspring?"

"Nothing. I heard it call, but nothing happened."

Just like before. Tears stung her eyes.

"This isn't your fault, Aurora."

"Isn't it?"

"Oh no you don't! No. This isn't your doing."

"If I had wild magic—"

"Do you control the celestial bodies? The wills of all the gods, tangible and intangible? Did you create the monstrosities? No. Don't you dare blame yourself for this." Phaedra's lips pursed into a thin line, sweat rolling down her brow.

"But the guards—"

"Died protecting me. If anyone is to blame for their deaths, it's me. I chose to be here, and their duty was to follow. I understood the risks I was taking with their lives and mine when I followed you. That burden is mine alone." She raised her chin, her brown eyes flinty with determination. It was the look she wore when she assumed the role of imperial princess. Her armour against the pangs of her wounded heart.

Aurora looked away, only to catch the sight of blood pooling beneath Phaedra's mount.

"Fae, what happened?"

"Nothing. It's fine. It's just a light scratch."

Light scratch, her foot! Silvanus could heal wounds caused by the monstrosities.

"Silvanus!"

"For the love of the Triad," Phaedra muttered.

Aurora dismounted and hurried to Phaedra's side, which was most definitely not fine. The whole right side of her was drenched in blood, her clothes torn. Silvanus rushed over and they both helped her down from the saddle. Phaedra swore a blue streak, her face deathly pale by the time she sat on the ground. Aurora peeled the clothes away as best she could, allowing Fae to lean on her, her heart in her throat the whole while. Silvanus dispatched the rest with quick, business-like cuts from a hidden dagger. When he laid his hands atop the gory sight, Phaedra cried out.

"Fuck! Ah, goddesses. A-and here I thought I wasn't your type."

"If you can joke, you're not nearly as wounded as you appear," Silvanus assured her, his divine magic closing the wounds as if they'd never existed.

"Or maybe I *am* your type, now that I'm in distress," Phaedra hissed, eyes closed against the pain.

Whatever tension had kept Phaedra upright collapsed the moment she was fully healed. She slumped into Aurora's arms, the only evidence of her harrowing experience her tattered clothes and blood-stained skin, now blessedly free of grisly gashes.

Aurora tightened her hold on Phaedra, thanking the merciful Triad for sparing her friend.

"I'm so glad you're alright."

Phaedra placed a hand over Aurora's and squeezed back.

"I watched you get injured. What were you protecting that was more important than your life, Your Highness?" Silvanus asked.

"None of your concern." Phaedra's whisper held more venom than Aurora thought possible.

"Well, it's *my* concern, and *I* want to know," Aurora retorted, fear and anger making her tremble. Phaedra was often reckless, but how could she risk herself like this? Against monstrosities, no less.

Phaedra dug into her tattered cloak's pocket and produced a small box.

"It was supposed to be your awakening gift. But this temple rat ruined the surprise."

Aurora snatched it from Phaedra, the urge to throw it as far as she could coiling through her.

"How dare you?" Aurora choked on a sob, tightening her hold on Phaedra with one arm. "How could you think some trinket is worth your life?"

"My blood, sweat and tears went into this, so you'd better open it," Phaedra huffed.

Tears fell in earnest then as she one-handedly peeled off the crimson-soaked wrapping cloth. Aurora recognised the pattern. It was one of Phaedra's favourite silk scarves. The floral print was barely recognizable now.

"I'll never forgive you for this," Aurora sniffled as she tried and failed to undo a knot, wet and sticky and swollen from blood.

Silvanus reached over and cut through the silk without a word.

Beneath the wrapping, a familiar box greeted her. They were the ones used at the dig site to hold artefacts. Aurora remembered the numbers on the side—the very same ones she'd used to catalogue her artefact. With shaking hands, she opened the lid, revealing the small, damaged globe she'd unearthed at the ancient temple. Aurora's throat constricted with emotion, her vision now entirely clouded by tears.

"You stupid cow," Aurora cursed, closing the lid.

"Ugly crier."

"I h-hate you," Aurora stammered.

"Yeah? Well, your hair looks terrible."

"How could you do this?"

"With minimal effort. They left it out in the open."

"Phaedra!"

Phaedra reached up, her cold, clammy hand wiping tears from Aurora's face.

"You're more than just the shit hand that Fate has dealt you, and I was worried you'd forget that."

"Fae…"

She squeezed Aurora's arm, her voice suddenly fierce.

"You're a scholar. And after all the lectures about the long-dead King Theron and his long-dead bloody language you made me sit through, I'll never let you forget it."

Aurora choked on a teary laugh. Had it been less than a day since her whole life had been ripped out from under her? How quickly things had fallen away—her priorities, her pride, her sense of safety, of self. Yet even here, Phaedra lifted her up and out of the gloom. Aurora clutched the small box to her chest.

"You should have been more worried about yourself. If only for my sake," Aurora sniffed.

Phaedra waved off her concern.

"We're going to Gilvus next, right? Well, look forward to some pampering at my favourite beach houses while stuffing our faces with succulent seafood. If you're going to be concerned about something, be concerned for my waistline."

"No, actually, we won't," Silvanus cut in.

Both Aurora and Phaedra stared at him in bewilderment.

"What do you have against fun?" Phaedra asked.

"Nothing."

"Liar."

"Where else would we go?" Aurora asked.

"To the nearest major temple," Silvanus replied. "We'll find the most protection nearest powerful sites of divine magic."

"What about awakening?"

Had he already given up on her? Was she truly hopeless? Could it be that all that was left for her to do was to cower inside one of the temples and pray the goddesses sent someone else to save them from Drakon?

"You already awakened your wild magic. Long ago, I suspect," he answered.

"Did you hit your head in that fight?" Phaedra asked.

"I've never wielded magic before in my life. Nothing happened at the wellspring here! You saw it for yourself."

"What I saw was that you froze the monstrosity before it devoured Her Highness."

"But... I didn't do anything."

"Your Highness, did you freeze the monstrosity in its tracks?" Silvanus asked.

Phaedra shook her head.

Silvanus turned and called to the remaining warriors at the camp who were salvaging what they could and loading it onto the lopers.

"Who among you saved the princess from the monstrosity that was about to swallow her?"

No one replied, not even the imperial guard.

"It could have been one of the guards who were felled," Aurora insisted.

"It wasn't. I knew what they were all capable of. None of them had magic that could do that," Phaedra said.

"But then..."

If she'd used magic today, that meant she'd had it her whole life. A lifetime wasted as she'd allowed her magic to atrophy, thinking it didn't exist. How was she supposed to learn to wield it now, after decades of disuse? How had she managed in that critical moment?

"The closest temple is southeast, in Altanus Novus. We'll send word to Boreas to have the imperial tutors meet us there."

It was several days' ride to Altanus Novus, the capital of Aureum. There were a few towns along the main road where they could gather the supplies they would need, now that theirs had been reduced to tatters, blowing away into the great expanse of the western desert. But that would turn every town into another target, for both monstrosities and Drakon. Did they have another choice?

"How long do I have to master it?" Aurora asked.

"I don't know," Silvanus answered. "Which is why we should leave now."

Aurora tried to help Phaedra to her feet without success.

"I can... I can get up on my own," Phaedra moaned.

Silvanus scooped her up and carried her off, much to Phaedra's chagrin.

"You've lost a lot of blood, Your Highness. You'll need to ride with one of the paladins."

"I thought you healed me," she grouched.

"The wounds caused by the monstrosities, nothing more."

"Incompetent ass," she muttered.

"Allow me, Your Highness." The tallest paladin offered her hand to Phaedra.

With barely more than a moment of silence for the slain, they were back on the road, the wind whipping up as the early morning sky began to dim.

"No one else needs to die for our conflict, little mouse. Come to me, and let us be done with this game of ours."

Aurora gripped Silvanus' wrist.

"Drakon is close."

Silvanus cursed, wrapping her in his divine magic.

It should have silenced the Beast of Old.

But its chuckle rattled inside her skull.

"Not even your attack dog can prevent us from speaking when you're this close, my sweet."

"It's not working. It's too close to us," Aurora replied, her panic rising.

*"**He**, little mouse. Don't tell me you've forgotten all the lifetimes we've shared."*

"What do you mean, *too close?*" Silvanus asked.

"No matter. We'll have plenty of time to get reacquainted..."

"Great goddesses, the sky!" Phaedra cried.

As if ripped straight from her nightmares, the sky above darkened, winds howling past her, swirling up and up. The gentle pinks and purples of sunrise bled into crimson, black clouds forming a vortex. Thunder reverberated in her bones and lightning arced across the sky. As if rending the very air, a great crack resounded across the whole of the desert and an ugly, jagged line formed in the sky. Ripping his way through the tear, Drakon emerged.

Blood-red scales and a crown of twisted black horns adorned his head, his gold eyes like macabre beacons in the darkness he spawned. Transfixed in horror, Aurora watched as he wriggled his long, serpentine body free, keeping his gaze locked on Aurora the whole while.

"What now?!" Phaedra screamed.

"We run! Follow me!" Silvanus shouted, his voice quickly swallowed up by the rising gale.

Silvanus turned their loper around and sped towards the Dragon's Spine Mountains. As their party fled, ash began raining down, corrupting the very ground and birthing monstrosities where it piled up. With one last earth-shaking crack, Drakon freed himself from wherever he'd been sealed.

He dove.

"You grow more beautiful with every rebirth. I can't wait to sink my teeth into you."

CHAPTER 6
SILVANUS

Silvanus cursed his wretched luck. They were woefully unprepared to meet Drakon head-on. Caught between the Beast of Old and the Dragon's Spine Mountains, there was only one place to go. Doing so might save their lives, if they made it, but it would ensure his own execution twice over.

"Where are we going? We'll be trapped against the foot of the mountains!" Aurora called back to him.

"We won't!"

Sunrise became twilight as the air was choked with oily ash. Silvanus unsheathed his sword, willing it to become a spear. He raised it high, dispelling the monstrosities as far as its blinding light reached. The divine magic flowing through his veins answered his every instinct, a weapon as familiar to him as a limb, no matter that he'd only been in possession of it a mere few weeks. But without Aurora's help, the best he could do was hold off the monstrosities. He would need to call upon his wild magic if they were to survive now. He closed his eyes, trusting his loper, Neptune. Neptune knew the way and was more than capable of dealing with monstrosities.

When Silvanus opened his eyes, the world was no longer composed of light and shadow, of mass and movement. Instead, he saw what the deities did—the Tapestry. Using this forbidden wild magic, all things were but threads in the great expanse laid out around him. Divorced from the raging tempest of emotions inside him and all but the barest hint of his physical body, Silvanus was free to make the most strategic of choices. But he had to be careful in this state, for he could not only see the threads that made up the Tapestry—he could alter them, if in a limited fashion. Behind him, Drakon made his descent, a mass of angry, warped, red threads encasing something that glittered so brightly even a glimmer hurt his senses. A thin strand of fate connected him to the beast. A thicker one, as if made of a hundred bleeding cords, connected Drakon to Aurora. It allowed the beast to find her, to locate her in the gloom enshrouding the physical world. Though impossible to sever, it could be redirected.

May the goddesses forgive him for what he was about to do.

Four paladins, an imperial guardsman and the princess followed on their mounts.

Six targets on five lopers. Five chances to deceive Drakon until Silvanus and Aurora were the only ones left to attack.

He found the imperial guardsman in the rear, his thread and that of his loper paler than those touched by divine magic. Silvanus plucked the man's thread and merged it with the one linking Aurora to Drakon. When those who hated him spoke of his magic, this was it—tricking Fate, if only for a moment in time. The magic wouldn't hold for long, but it should redirect Drakon's attack away from Aurora.

Drakon closed in, almost on top of them now, and let loose a streamer of magic made of the deepest red. It engulfed the guardsman and his steed, shaking the ground like an earthquake, the trembles reaching him even in this plane. Their threads snapped and frayed, lives extinguished. The beast's magic dissipated, and the lives it had snuffed out, now translucent threads, were subsumed into the Tapestry.

A wave of anger surged down the cord between Aurora and the beast. She flinched against him in the physical world.

"That blast was meant for me!" Aurora yelped.

"Not if I have any say in the matter."

Strands of deepest crimson gathered around Drakon. The next attack. Silvanus grabbed the thread of the slowest paladin and tied it to Aurora's. Another blast. Another bone-jarring quake. Another dead when they should be alive, their goddess-blessed strand winking out of existence, cut short and woven back into the Tapestry. Another rush of anger from the beast to Aurora.

"Oh goddess, the skies!"

Silvanus looked up. All around Drakon, dark strands gathered, several becoming dozens, dozens multiplying into hundreds.

"There's no escape! He's going to rain fire down on us!"

Two of the paladins were riding side-by-side. A tinge of panic hurried his next action. Silvanus tied both their threads to Aurora's before he turned his attention to the meteoric assault of Drakon's magic. He did everything he could, working quickly and precisely, clearing the path around them, redirecting the foul magic onto objects in the distance, onto threads of the landscape, onto small creatures hiding in burrows, onto Drakon himself. His head felt like it was splitting in two, dividing his focus between the physical plane and the Tapestry.

Drakon fired another crimson bolt, annihilating the two paladins in an instant, and nearly unseating both Silvanus and Aurora from Neptune's saddle. Too close.

Ahead, Silvanus spied salvation.

"We're going to run ourselves into solid rock!" Aurora shouted.

Aurora attempted to redirect Neptune. Silvanus held the course, fighting Aurora's panic for control of the reins.

"Trust me!" Silvanus replied.

Where his physical eyes would see only rock, his wild magic saw the opening to a cave—one shrouded in protection both wild and divine. A hidden sanctuary. He reached out, parting the threads that held its gates closed.

"There's an entrance!"

And they would make it.

Except Drakon had already gathered the crimson threads of his magic, a mere moment away from incinerating them.

There was one paladin left to sacrifice—the one riding with Princess Phaedra. He'd rushed into the fray to save her in the last attack because he'd known what she meant to Aurora—that without her, Aurora would lose the strength to fight. He'd trusted Aurora's safety to Neptune and recklessly rushed in to cleanse the camp just to spare Aurora the emotional blow. Now, it would be unavoidable. Between the princess and Aurora, the princess mattered not at all. As he reached for the paladin's goddess-blessed thread, his blood ran cold.

Shock nearly dragged him back to the physical plane.

There, thick and unmistakable, a red line of fate connected him to Phaedra, the same kind that connected Drakon and Aurora. She could be destined to become his greatest enemy, hunting him down throughout all of time. Or she could become a lover whose passion would chase him across the Tapestry, inexorably drawn to his thread in every lifetime.

He hesitated, weighing the value of his own heart against the fate of Trisia. He smiled bitterly, grateful he was in the Tapestry, unmoored from the anchor of his feeling heart. Fate was a cruel mistress.

"I'm sorry," he whispered.

He tied the paladin's thread to Aurora's just as Drakon aimed his blast. But Silvanus wouldn't be a coward—he would watch in full what he'd done. He returned to the physical plane, assaulted by every emotion and sensation that traversing the Tapestry had suppressed.

He snapped back into his physical body, recoiling from the sheer weight of existence. His throat was raw, every breath that sawed in and out more difficult from the last, the very air choked by Drakon's evil, his tongue fouled by the oily ash raining down from above. Ear-splitting cracks rent the air and shook the earth beneath Neptune's pounding hooves. Dust and rock were thrown up with every crimson meteor that streaked down from the sky.

The apocalypse was upon them.

Silvanus pitched his spear forward, his muscles screaming as he pushed against the thick, bubbling black of emerging monstrosities. The whole world had been swallowed by the gloom, the holy weapon the only source of light, save for the flashes of lightning above. He turned his head, glimpsing the riders behind him.

Panic and horror dealt the next blow. Great goddesses, what had he done? He'd put a target on the backs of men and women given grace by Justice Herself. Sacrificed the lives of others with barely a thought. Nausea threatened as his heart dropped to his knees. Now he could do nothing but watch as Drakon obliterated a woman fated to find him in every lifetime, for good or ill.

Drakon's magic pierced the gloom, a streak of purple fire aimed directly at Phaedra and the paladin. Aurora turned her head, a sharp intake of breath preceding a tortured scream.

Her magic whipped out like a tongue of invisible flames, searing his senses.

But it was not enough.

Between one blink and the next, both riders and loper were reduced to ashes. The impact threw Aurora, Silvanus and Neptune into the air. Neptune landed with a bone-jarring thud, his pace unbroken, riders still mercifully seated.

They barrelled through the magical entrance into the mountain, Aurora's desperate, hopeless shrieks echoing in the dark.

As he pulled back the last of his wild magic, sealing the entrance behind them, something flew through the air and knocked them both off Neptune's back. Silvanus collided head-first with the wall, pain stealing his consciousness in an instant.

Wakefulness came to Silvanus in waves of ever-increasing pain. When at last he could open his eyes, it was to Neptune ruffling his hair with worried huffs. His head throbbed, and his next sharp intake of breath only added to the agony. With a shaking hand, he sought for purchase, cataloguing his injuries. Bruised, broken bones, most notably a few ribs, sticky blood trailing down his back from a wound on his head, but alive. It could be worse.

With a great deal more effort than he would have liked to admit, Silvanus got to his feet, leaning heavily on Neptune's saddle.

In the darkness of the cave, blue lights winked from the walls. Like sparkling sapphires that were still half-buried in the rock, they were relics of a time long past. The remains of pre-sundering technology. Without them, he wouldn't have been able to spot Aurora.

He knelt down, groaning against the pain, and pressed his fingers to her neck. A pulse. She was alive. His relief nearly drained the last dregs of his energy.

But what had knocked them off Neptune? He searched the dark cavern. Not a monstrosity, clearly. Otherwise, he wouldn't have woken—he'd be dead. And in any case, neither Drakon nor a monstrosity could ever breach the mountain's magical defences. He tried to think back to what it had felt like. Not a boulder or some other rocky bit of debris. It had been softer. A body? But everyone else had been obliterated. Perhaps part of a body.

Silvanus released a shaky breath, hollowed out by his guilt. He'd been warned a hundred times that using his wild magic in that way came with a cost. He was barely a person inside the Tapestry. Cold logic reigned supreme there, leaving his heart, his conscience, his soul, but a distant, vague tether he could easily ignore. Right and wrong were tossed aside in favour of utility and strategy. But no one could remain inside the

Tapestry forever. Silvanus tried to swallow down his unease. He'd killed them all, used them like pawns on a chessboard. Every single one of them had loved ones. Families. Friends.

He couldn't bear looking at Aurora, knowing he'd sacrificed her closest friend. She could never know what he'd done, or she would never forgive him, and any chance they had at ending Drakon would die along with her trust. Just one more secret he would be forced to keep, more lies he would need to speak in order to obey the will of the Triad.

He clenched his hands, nails biting into his palms hard enough to draw blood. He should have been kinder to Phaedra. It wasn't her fault she'd been born into the imperial family with its cruel legacy, but every time he'd looked into her fierce, dark eyes, he could only see his people's persecutor, their boogeyman. It was just as likely she would have become his executioner as his greatest ally. He wished he could see it again, the string that had connected them.

What happened to a red string of fate when the person you were destined for died? Did it become translucent, woven back into the Tapestry? He had to know. Silvanus dared to use his magic once more.

Surrounded by the magical threads of the Dragon's Spine mountain, he instead focused on the threads that spread out from him. Every connection he'd made, past or present, unravelled from his core, stretching across the whole of Trisia. Friends, family, lovers, acquaintances, rivals, enemies—all were there, a web that, if he delved too deeply, connected him to every living person in existence. It might have taken days to sort through them all, but the one he sought was unmistakable—thick and red and attached directly to where his heart should be. He touched it, exploring the connection, more curious than mournful, courtesy of the Tapestry. Pain shuddered along it, foreign and strange to his senses.

This was not his hurt.

He tracked the string with his senses, his body following, walking in the physical plane. His boot hit an obstacle the same moment he found the other end of the string. Elation dragged him back to his body before he could ascertain how close she was to death. Silvanus doubled over as agony roared through him, dulled only by adrenaline. Phaedra was here, inside the mountain!

Shakily, he pressed his fingers to her neck, praying to all the gods, both tangible and intangible, that she yet lived.

CHAPTER 7
PHAEDRA

Phaedra woke to a body made of shattered glass. Every breath was a cruel punishment. Pale, shimmering blue lights lit up the dark, and the echo of hooves on stone accompanied a sense of slow, steady movement. Tears clouded her vision as she dared move her head to the side. Aurora's bruised, unconscious face met her own. She was breathing. Phaedra's relieved sob ripped through her broken body. They were here together at the end of the world. She'd made it after all.

Phaedra sought Aurora's hand, threading their fingers together.

How the actual fuck was anyone supposed to be a match for Drakon? The beast had unleashed a cataclysm of divine proportions. It had turned the desert into a volcanic explosion, replete with ash-choked air, molten rock raining down from the sky and fire so hot it melted everything it touched. How was anyone meant to stop that? How was anyone meant to survive? Phaedra couldn't even dream of a power great enough to stop Drakon, except perhaps the Triad themselves. Trisia was doomed.

"Your Highness?" Silvanus asked.

"I'm awake," Phaedra answered through gritted teeth.

"Try not to move. You broke numerous bones."

"No shit."

"We're safe now. I'll get us to a healer."

"How? We're inside a thrice-damned mountain."

"There is a... settlement here."

That didn't sound suspicious *at all*. But beggars couldn't be choosers.

"Can you... put me into a deep sleep?" she asked. She would give anything to escape back into blissful unconsciousness.

"I... no. But I can help."

Silvanus limped to her side. Merciful Triad, he looked a fright. Bloody and bruised over every inch of visible skin. She supposed she looked worse. At least he could move. The look he gave her was inscrutable in the dim light.

"Try to keep an open mind, Your Highness."

His crystal-clear blue eyes flashed and Phaedra's blood ran cold. Gone were the eyes of a man. In their place—irises like faceted, glowing gems. Divine eyes. A power borne by the greatest villains in history. Meddlers in fate, trespassers in the sacred Tapestry.

"Monster," she cursed.

He frowned, placing his hand on her forehead.

"Don't fucking touch me! I'd rather choke on blood than get help from you." Phaedra tried to shrug off his touch, but she was held immobile by the wreckage of her body. In this state, she couldn't protect herself, never mind her best friend. She clutched Aurora's hand tighter.

Her mother had warned of people with this brand of forbidden wild magic. They had toppled kings and queens, reworked fate decided by divine mandate, cut short the lives of entire bloodlines in an instant. The Viridian crown had been especially keen to rid Trisia of people who manifested this magic. Wherever they spawned, the crown ensured they perished. And now he was going to kill her.

"I would like to say that you're wrong, that I'm not a monster. But I am. Though you of all people should know that even monsters are capable of compassion on occasion."

The worst of the jagged edges of her pain were sanded down. Finally, she could take in a full breath. Silvanus winced, removing his hand. His eyes returned to normal. It must be a trick.

"What did you do?"

"I took some of your pain."

"Why? Why not just kill me? My family has hunted down your ilk since ancient times. And here you have me, helpless. Do you think this will prevent your death? That I'll show mercy once I can walk again?"

Silvanus sighed. He left her side, limping more heavily than before. He whispered something hushed as a loper whickered softly. They were on the move once more.

"I live in hope."

"Delusion, more like."

"Believe what you wish. Ignorance is the speciality of the imperial family, after all."

"I knew about your kind, did I not?" Phaedra hissed, testing the limits of her body. She was still trapped, unable to move without causing greater pain. He'd only dulled the worst pangs, not healed her. Damn.

"But not about the mountain."

She wouldn't dignify that jab with a response. If she survived, the whole Dragon's Spine Mountain range was going to be properly mapped. There would be no hideouts left for monsters like him. She tried to pay attention to her surroundings, but there were no landmarks in the dark. As far as she could tell, she had been laid down in a small cart. Did this hideout keep such things just lying about? Maybe they had some other trappings of civilisation—like communication crystals. If she could get a message to her mother, then perhaps they could plan a counter-offensive against Drakon and Silvanus.

"Where did you get this cart?"

"It's not a cart."

"I'm in it right now. If you're going to lie, at least try to be believable."

"Is that what the imperial tutors teach princesses?"

"Fine, don't answer."

"…The cart is the holy sword."

"Excuse me?"

"The sword changes shape according to my will."

She'd noticed in the fight against the monstrosities that he'd wielded several different weapons, each glowing with divine light. She could wrap her head around that. It had been mentioned in old histories about the hero. But a *cart?* Didn't the sword have a will of its own? Or was she misremembering her lessons?

Phaedra snickered, an action she immediately regretted. Goddess, how many ribs had she broken?

"You turned a holy sword into a cart? Isn't that blasphemous?"

"The sword wasn't too pleased about it, but needs must. What, don't you think 'the holy horse cart of Justice' has a nice ring to it?"

She felt a belly laugh coming on. A tide of pain rose up, washing over her battered body.

"Fuck. Don't make me laugh."

"Doom and gloom only. Duly noted, Your Highness."

Phaedra controlled her breathing as best she could. She focused on slow, shallow breaths. No gasps. What a bloody mess.

"Just call me Phaedra. If you're going to brutally murder me after stealing my fate, the least you can do is say my actual name, preferably with less venom than you say, 'your highness.'"

"As you wish...Phaedra," he replied, his voice deepening as he said her name. It sent a shiver down her spine.

What the fuck was that? Best to ignore it.

"Don't think I didn't notice your distinct lack of promises not to kill me, *Silvanus.*"

"Hmm, I didn't think you knew my name." She could swear she heard a smile in his tone.

"I knew your name. I chose not to use it."

"How very genteel of you, *Phaedra.*"

"That's me. Genteel. A true paragon." Phaedra breathed through the next wave of pain. Damn it. She'd told him not to make her laugh.

They were quiet for a time. She tried to focus on something other than the horror of her physical reality.

"Distract me. That's an order," she whispered.

"What do you want to discuss?"

"Anything."

He was quiet, considering. Sweat trickled down her forehead and into her cuts. She hissed.

"I could tell you about how I keep Neptune's coat glossy."

"If you're going to kill me, at least make it fast and painless."

Silvanus chuckled.

"Why don't you tell me how you made it into the mountain? I was sure you'd..."

"Gotten melted?"

"Mmm."

Phaedra sighed, closing her eyes.

"You were there. It was hopeless. Drakon was toying with us, killing us one by one. I saw the paladins behind me die in that cursed purple fire. I knew we were next. And then...I don't know. Everything around me stopped."

"Everything?"

"Everything. I saw that blast of fire above me. Could feel the heat of it, but it was stuck. The monstrosities were still as statues. I tried to make our loper move, tried to tell that paladin woman to ride while we could, but they were both suspended. I didn't know how long my reprieve would be, so I fought my way off the saddle and ran for Aurora. Too soon, everything started moving again. The blast threw me up into the air and I saw the two of you disappear into that entrance. I used the last of my strength to blast myself inside while I could. What happened after I don't recall. Clearly, I made it inside."

Her heart hammered against her chest. She shouldn't have tried to speak so much. Deeper breaths only meant greater pain. *He* was supposed to distract *her*, not the other way around. Silvanus returned to her side, his eyes like eerie jewels. Instinctively, she recoiled. He placed his hand on her forehead again, dulling the pain. Why?

"I felt Aurora's magic, like a flash, gone in a moment. I had no idea she had such potential," Silvanus said.

Phaedra squeezed Aurora's hand. Guess she was a proper hero after all. There would be no protecting her now. *Don't think about it.*

"What, your divine eyes didn't tell you everything about her?"

When his eyes returned to normal, he groaned, gritting his teeth as he gripped the side of the cart.

"Contrary to your fairy tales, I don't use my wild magic so recklessly. In any case, this changes things. She *does* have the power to defeat Drakon, I just need to help her control it. If she can freeze time long enough…"

"Even if she could stop time again, how would you defeat Drakon? It can literally throw flaming boulders from the sky, melt anything its breath touches, oh, *and* it's a great flying serpent. How would you even get to it?"

Silvanus sighed, limping back to the loper's side.

"I'll figure that out when I've had more than a few hours of sleep."

Goddess, a soft bed, and something to dull the pain enough to sleep, sounded absolutely sublime. Not that she was likely to get that in this thrice-damned mountain hideout. He was probably lying about the healer. That would be appropriate for a monster, letting her hope until the pain was too much to bear, then throwing her into a pit of despair. It was a technique her less savoury imperial tutors had discussed at length.

"Will we actually be safe in here?"

"Yes."

"How?"

"Maybe, if you prove worthy of that information, I'll tell you."

She snorted with derision. There was no one more worthy of the information than she.

"Triad's titties, you sure you're not one of Orithyia's henchmen? You sound just like her."

He grunted angrily.

"I could leave you here."

Why did that make him so angry? Wasn't an avatar supposed to be devoted to the high priestesses? Though maybe not. The temples hunted down those with divine eyes almost as zealously as the Viridian crown did. After all, high priestesses could have their fates stolen and altered just as easily as princesses by people like him. She shouldn't forget what he was, even if his smooth voice was the only thing that helped keep her mind off the pain.

"You don't strike me as a coward."

"Just a monster?"

Phaedra kept her counsel, turning her head. He was a monster by anyone's estimates. But perhaps he could be useful too. Aurora slept on. Lucky, that. Less lucky was her fate. Could a fate such as hers even be altered by someone with divine eyes? Could Phaedra take this terrible burden from Aurora's shoulders?

"Can you change someone's fate?" Phaedra asked softly.

He was quiet for so long, she didn't think he would answer.

"After a fashion."

"Make me a promise, Silvanus."

"No, Phaedra."

"You haven't heard what I was going to say."

"I don't use my magic to benefit the Viridian crown."

"I wasn't going to ask for myself."

"Still no."

She ignored him.

"Promise me that if Aurora's fate is to die and mine is to live, that you'll switch our fates."

The cart stopped.

"Don't ask that of me."

Fuck him. How dare he? If Phaedra wanted to keep her best friend alive by all means at her disposal, who was he to stop her? Viridis had six princesses. It only had one Aurora.

"Why not? You hate me, don't you?"

He hobbled over to the cart and glared down at her, his eyes glittering like faceted sapphires.

"Do you want to know what I see when I stand in the Tapestry?"

"What? What do you see?" she hissed. His eyes terrified her. They were the eyes of monsters who tore empresses to pieces, who ensured innocents died like dogs. They saw all a person's hidden things. All their ugliness. All the horrors that had touched them. Yet she refused to show him her fear. Phaedra glared back.

"I see Fate's thread connecting us, one steeped in the colours of Passion and Death. I see someone destined to find me across lifetimes, for good or ill. You are my fate, Phaedra. And I am yours. Always and forever."

"No," she whispered, horrified. She couldn't be tied to a monster for all eternity. Why would her fate be so cruel?

"My sentiments exactly," he snarled, his eyes returning to normal.

Anger replaced her despair. If she were in any shape to do more than fume, she'd have snatched his breath for such an insult.

"How dare you!"

"You think I wanted this?"

"You should be so lucky. I'm a *princess*. *I'm* the one who got the raw deal here, not you!"

"Lucky?! You're as much my boogeyman as I am yours, *princess*."

"So we're fated to be enemies then, chasing each other across the cycles, like Aurora and Drakon? Then why won't you promise to save Aurora? Do you hate me so much that you would let her die just to spite me?"

"Damn it, Phaedra!" He pounded his fist on the side of the cart, sending a painful jolt through her broken bones. "We don't *have to* be enemies!"

"What else is there?!" she shouted, heedless of the agony it brought her.

His face was a kaleidoscope of emotions. Fury. Resentment. Mortification. Vulnerability. Hope.

"Oh no. No, no, no. No!"

If their bond was not one of mortal enemies, destined to slay each other, that left only one other possibility. Death's gemstone was garnet. A deep, nearly brown-red, like blood just beginning to dry. Passion's was a ruby, a deep crimson, like blood that had just been spilt. To the untrained eye, the colours were too close to distinguish. If they were not meant to kill each other, then their bond was one ruled by Passion.

"I...forget it." He scowled, turning away.

"Forget it?! *Forget it?!* Why the fuck would you tell me that? Why wouldn't you just keep your thrice-damned mouth shut?!" Goddess, she wanted to rage properly instead of being paralysed and weak. It was too much to bear sitting still. She should be screaming at him, pummelling him with fists and blade, tossing him around like a ragdoll with her magic.

He rounded on her then, his face barely a handspan from hers.

"Because maybe I hoped there might be *one person* in my whole fucking life who knew who and what I am and *didn't* want to use me or kill me! You of all people should be able to understand that much!"

He held her gaze, anger bleeding into hopeless sorrow.

She understood it all too well. As close as she was to her family, duty always came first. A disposable princess, she'd been her mother's pawn, or her eldest sister's, ferreting out disloyal courtiers, her rebellious nature and unserious mask used to lure in the unwary. Every noble house wanted to befriend her or behead her, be betrothed to her or mire her in scandal—not because she was Phaedra, but because she was a princess. Phaedra had her one true person in all the world—Aurora. She didn't need him, even if she understood that loneliness. It only made her hate him all the more. How dare he make himself pitiable—make his sorrow hurt her heart? Why did that monster's sorrow affect her at all? Was this some trick of his foul magic? Some ugly twist in the thread that bound them? Could she trust her feelings at all, now that she knew her fate? She'd hated him from the moment she'd seen him. He'd come into her life to steal the best part of it away. Now he refused to take care of the person she treasured the most.

"If you want me to be anything but your enemy, then swear you'll save Aurora. Swear you'll choose her life over mine."

"I can't—"

"You will. Because if she dies and I survive? There's no power in Trisia that'll save you from me."

"Then you'll make your own promises. To me."

"Name it."

"If we survive, you swear to keep my secrets."

Phaedra all but growled. Damn him. How was she supposed to get rid of him all by herself? He'd held back before in his tent. He could have easily killed her had he used his wild magic. And he was the avatar, a goddess' wrath waiting for any who spilled his blood. She pursed her lips. Phaedra supposed risking *one* person with divine eyes running around unchecked was worth Aurora's life.

"You have my word."

"And—"

"And? You want more?"

Greedy bootlicker.

"And in the meantime, you'll swear to explore this bond with me. Non-violently."

She curled her lip.

"You want to hold hands and make eyes at each other? Are you so desperate for a woman that you'll take your potential nemesis to bed?"

"I want to know if this pit of snakes inside my heart that seethes whenever I look at you can be tamed. I want to know if there's any hope for me, or people like me, to live freely in Trisia, if the imperial family is in any way redeemable. And the more I know about how it works, the more likely I am to be able to alter Aurora's fate."

Damn it. She had to think of Aurora. Her friend had one of these ugly bonds tying her to the greatest monster to ever live. Aurora would've put up with Silvanus' demands in a heartbeat. Phaedra could do no less.

"You think if I trip over my good sense and fall on your cock, that will undo millennia of hostility?" she goaded him.

"It would be a start. And you could do worse."

Oh, she very much doubted that. A monster for a lover? The bar was low indeed if he thought there were a great many men who couldn't clear that. She wanted to call him every kind of fool. How could a grown man be so naïve? But he was a determined fool, his gaze unwavering. She refused to be the first to flinch.

"So be it."

The polite clearing of a throat made them both flinch. Someone had snuck up on them.

"I hesitate to interrupt a lovers quarrel, but is that you, Silvanus?"

CHAPTER 8

AURORA

Aurora left the realm of dreams slowly. She'd never felt more comfortable. No aches or pains, just her, floating on a bed of clouds. She must have died. Was she in the Loom, waiting for her thread to be respun by the goddess, Fate, back into the Tapestry? Maybe she could ask Fate to be kinder to her in her next life. She opened her eyes and was met with distinctly corporeal surroundings. A rock overhang decorated with a profusion of colourful cloth, sapphire lights winking out between the rock and cloth. Had she made it inside the mountain after all? But that meant...

"Fae," she whispered, tears stinging her eyes.

"Pervert."

Aurora gasped, tearing out of her bed only to be hit by a wave of dizziness that landed her back on her side. She closed her eyes, breathing through it. Phaedra was here. How?

"Hag."

Silvanus? She'd never heard such venom from him before. What had happened?

"You take that back. I'm the most beautiful woman you've ever met."

"You're definitely the most *something* I've ever met, but it's not that."

"Admit it, you proposed this ridiculous exercise just to grope me."

"I'm attempting to concentrate—"

"On my tits."

"On the bond. Your constant interruptions only prolong this for both of us."

Aurora got up more slowly this time and parted the cloth partition of her strange bedroom. The room was cosily decorated and lit with orbs radiating light. Phaedra sat across from Silvanus on plush cushions, their eyes closed, his hand pressed against her heart. What in the Loom were they doing?

"Oh, it's pro*longing* something, you degenerate."

Silvanus opened his eyes, pushing Phaedra to the floor with a growl. Aurora covered her mouth with her hands, feeling like she was interrupting some intimate moment. She hid behind her curtain, peeking through the barest opening. Didn't they hate each other? Well, if Phaedra did hate Silvanus, she was more than equipped to deal with him as she saw fit. Suffocation tended to be an effective deterrent against most unwelcome advances.

"Trust that if I attempt to seduce you, there will be no question about it, *Phaedra.*"

"That's right," Phaedra purred, rubbing his groin with her thigh, "It would be just that, an *attempt.* And a pathetic one at that. As if a backwater little no one like you knows how to please a wom—"

He captured her lips, his fingers teasing her nipple. Aurora was about to intervene when Phaedra gripped Silvanus' moonstone-coloured hair in her hand and devoured him in turn, pressing herself against him. So now she wanted him? Goddess, Phaedra could be so contradictory sometimes. Why couldn't they do this somewhere else? Aurora hid in her little bed, mentally sighing as the two continued getting...well, whatever *that* was out of their systems. Hopefully, it wouldn't be long until Phaedra—

"If you don't fuck me *right* now..."

No, she was not going to listen to *that.* Not even for Phaedra. Aurora ripped open her curtain.

"Alright, that's enough! I'm not going to sit here listening to the two of you," she huffed, trailing off when she realised just what state they were in. Clothes and hair in disarray, hands down each other's pants, they were a single slip from the act itself. Aurora slapped a hand over her eyes and pointed in the direction of another curtain. "Please, just get dressed or go somewhere else," she groaned, blushing madly. It wasn't the first time she'd caught Phaedra in the middle of a tryst, it wasn't even the seventh, but it never stopped being disconcerting.

"Aurora! You're awake!" Phaedra launched herself at Aurora, wrapping her arms around her.

Aurora hugged her back, holding her as tight as she could. Phaedra was alive. Whole. Her heart ached with relief.

"At least wash your hands first." Aurora choked on her laugh.

"My filthy hands are as close as you've gotten to fucking in months. You should be grateful." Phaedra squeezed her back.

"Animal."

"Prude."

"I thought you'd died," Aurora whispered.

"You saved me."

"Nonsense."

She needn't speak lies just to make Aurora feel better. Didn't she know that her being alive was treasure enough?

"No, truly." Phaedra pulled back. "The whole world around me was suspended in time. I escaped the blast because of your magic."

She was about to deny it, but Phaedra was most definitely healthy and whole, not a scratch on her. But she'd never seen her in such garb before. The fabrics were soft only because they'd been worn hundreds of times, the colours dull and washed out. They looked like a well-to-do farmer's hand-me-downs. Aurora would know. Her family were esteemed cloth merchants, specializing in rare dyes.

"What are you doing up? You'll undo three days of hard work, young woman!" A middle-aged woman with tawny skin and black hair strode into the room, a bundle of clothes on top of a basket in her arms.

Aurora looked around for the person the woman was remonstrating. Silvanus had disappeared, only to re-enter behind the stranger.

"Aurora, this is Macris. Macris, Aurora."

"A pleasure to meet you," Aurora said, stepping out of Phaedra's embrace to shake her hand. Macris took her hand and led her to one of the cushions Phaedra and Silvanus had tossed aside. Macris sent him a dark look.

"Never mind the introductions. Sit down, Aurora. Goddesses, I can't believe you let her get out of bed. Weren't you supposed to be watching her?" Macris hissed at Silvanus.

"I came to get you as soon as she woke, did I not?" Silvanus replied, his cheeks red.

Macris waved him off.

"I don't understand what all the fuss is about. I've never felt better."

"That's because you've been under my care for three days. You broke your back. Among other things. You're all lucky to have survived, but you especially. Now sit still and let me have a look at you."

Broken her back? Three days? Merciful Triad. She didn't remember much after they'd barrelled into the mountain. Perhaps that had been a blessing. Perhaps that was also why, now that she paid attention, she smelled like she hadn't made the acquaintance of perfume in some time. How embarrassing.

Macris's gaze was distant and unfocused. Magic poured through Aurora as if she were a sieve, over and over. A sharp pain ran up her spine. Aurora gasped, fists gripping the fabric of her trousers. These too had been well-worn but cared for. She closed her eyes, trying to shift her focus, holding her breath as the pain built and built. Then, in a sudden rush, it drained from her.

Macris sighed.

"There. Now you're stitched up, stronger than ever."

Aurora released a shaky breath. She'd never been ill or injured badly enough to have needed a healer possessed of wild magic. The medics who studied at the Temple of Knowledge had always been able to tend her. It was a strange experience, to have another's magic coil through you, your physical body like an open book without the benefit of a sturdy cover. She hoped never to need it again.

"Thank you."

"You're welcome. You can put it on Silvanus' tab."

"You know Silvanus?"

Macris raised a dark brow, looking between her and the man in question.

"Have you not told her anything yet? Have you explained anything to either of them?"

"No," Phaedra answered with an indignant huff.

Macris stood, rounding on Silvanus.

"You said they were trustworthy! It's the only reason I didn't tell the others about your arrival. I sheltered you in secret, Silvanus. How dare you risk my place here like this!"

Silvanus held up his hands.

"There was no other choice. And they *can* be trusted," he punctuated his words with a killing glare at Phaedra.

"Will someone please explain what's going on?" Aurora asked, daring to interject.

Macris looked to Aurora and Phaedra with pity before turning back to Silvanus, pointing at him with a furious glare.

"You made this mess; you clean it up. I'll go prepare the bath," she said before storming out.

Phaedra placed herself in front of Aurora, shielding her from Silvanus.

"Sit down. We need to talk." He gestured at the cushions.

"I think we'll stand," Phaedra replied.

He sighed, taking a seat.

"Do you want the short version or the long version?"

"Short," Phaedra replied.

"Long," Aurora said at the same time.

"Of course *you* would want the long version," Phaedra scoffed.

"I like knowing the details," Aurora retorted.

Silvanus watched them as if they were a great, perplexing mystery.

"The short version is that you're currently standing in one of the last dualist sanctuaries in Trisia. I've implied that you're both dualists seeking safety, and I would appreciate it if you played along. And if you do anything to threaten its security or the safety of the people here, I, as your guarantor, am duty-bound to kill you."

"There are dualists still alive? And there's a sanctuary here? Can we see it?" Aurora asked, her heart leaping with excitement.

"Of course you're a dualist. Why wouldn't a monster also be at the beck and call of the people who caused the first cycle of calamity?" Phaedra scoffed.

"Actually, there's no evidence to definitively prove that. Most of the texts dating from that period are scanty at best," Aurora corrected her, bumping Phaedra's hip with her own.

"They're also infamously anti-imperial," Phaedra scowled at her.

"I imagine most people who are systematically hunted down by imperial decree are going to end up that way." Aurora shrugged. "And you seem to like at least one of them well enough."

"Well... he also has divine eyes! Did you know *that?*"

"He does?" She turned to Silvanus. "You do?"

Today was a day of discovery then. Blessed Triad, all the things he could tell her. All the things she wanted to ask him!

"I... You seem a lot less frightened by that than I expected," Silvanus said, staring at her like she was mad.

"But you can see the Tapestry! Do you know how few accounts of it exist? What does it look like? Have you ever encountered one of the deities there? Can you actually manipulate fate?"

"Aurora, stay away. He's dangerous!" Phaedra pulled her back.

"So are you," Aurora replied.

Aurora raised a brow. Phaedra could choke someone to death on a whim or shove them off a balcony without trying when she was in a foul mood.

"I can't mess around with your soul! He can!"

While that was technically true, he didn't seem so inclined.

"Do you plan to do that, Silvanus?"

"Only if I need to."

"See? There! He admitted it. He can't be trusted," Phaedra said, gesturing wildly.

Aurora folded her arms. If Phaedra truly thought him a threat, he'd already be dead, goddess' avatar or not. She wouldn't try to convince Aurora of it so much as deal with it outright. When she saw a threat, she ploughed straight through it and then turned around to stomp over whatever remained. Her complaints seemed to stem from shame, as the colour in her cheeks seemed to indicate. Aurora bit back a smirk.

"Then why did you stick your tongue down his throat?"

Silvanus choked on his next breath. Phaedra's cheeks heated further as she scowled. Aurora raised a brow.

"I was caught up in the moment. I've been cooped up here for three days. You know I make bad choices when I can't move around freely," Phaedra muttered.

"You would never be intimate with someone you genuinely thought would kill you." Aurora poked her in the side. Phaedra swatted her hand away.

"Yes, I would," Phaedra pouted, crossing her arms mulishly.

"Liar."

"Villain."

Silvanus cleared his throat.

"Can I get your solemn vows not to speak of what you see or learn here? And not to cause trouble?"

"Yes." Aurora readily agreed. She couldn't wait to start uncovering the mysteries of the dualist cultists.

"Ugh, so be it."

"Good."

There was a short pause as all three stared at each other. Aurora did her best not to tap her foot in anticipation. When was he going to begin his explanation?

"So, what's the long version?"

"Aurora!"

"What?"

A curious mind was a gift, according to her patron goddess.

"Why do you even care? He lied to gain your trust."

"I punched you to gain yours." Aurora shrugged.

"That was different."

"Well, he risked his life to save me, and it seems he broke the rules to make sure we recovered from our injuries. He also just told us the truth, at great personal risk. I think he's earned a little of our trust. And besides, studying dualism is something only high-ranking scholars are allowed to do! Why wouldn't I be interested?"

"Dualists actually worship Lies, Aurora. Half of everything they say will be laced full of shit."

Ah, she was getting desperate now. To think she could win against Aurora in a debate about theology or academics was a fool's errand. This was all just bluster. Perhaps she was especially embarrassed to have been discovered in this latest tryst? Phaedra was nothing if not prideful, and kissing your family's sworn enemy twice over was probably the first liaison she might be feeling an ounce of shame about.

"All our sources are laced with bias. Dualists wouldn't be unique in that."

"There's no winning with you when you get like this," Phaedra huffed.

"I know." Aurora smiled, triumphant. She turned back to Silvanus, "When can we see the sanctuary?"

"Why don't you bathe and eat first? I'll need to talk to Macris before we set out."

"Right. I stink. Lead the way!"

"I'm coming too," Phaedra announced.

Silvanus parted the curtain of the homey dwelling to reveal a soaring hallway lit with the same sapphire lights as inside the bedroom, in addition to sconces lit without the use of fire. Aurora wandered over, reaching up to touch it. How did it work? Such technology would make the use of candles and fire obsolete if she could understand it. Perhaps it had been constructed after studying an ancient artefact, like the hovering trays used at the dig site and many of their other modern amenities. Phaedra yanked her along. Hopefully, she would discover its secrets later.

The bath was heavenly, hot water supplied through pipes that came from goddess knew where. Once clean, they reconvened inside Macris' home for a hearty meal. Aurora fell on it like a starving beast, gratified that no one said a word about her lack of manners.

"Before we go out, we need to talk about your magic," Silvanus said.

Oh. She deflated. Aurora had been hoping not to think about it, preferring instead to bury herself in a new avenue of study. She'd been so good about not letting herself remember the calamity that had chased her into the mountain.

Sensing her shift in mood, Silvanus continued, his tone softer.

"You only seem to use your magic when you panic. That's not unusual with wild magic. Most wild magic is tied to the things that keep you grounded in your physical body. Emotions are important catalysts for harnessing it. I would like to try to coax it out for you, so you can get used to using it."

"How?" she asked, swallowing nervously.

"By stepping into the Tapestry and tugging on the thread of your magic. Will you allow it?"

"You don't have to," Phaedra interjected. "You don't know what that will do to you."

But if she never learned to control it, everyone else would suffer. Phaedra only survived by the grace of the Triad, not because of anything Aurora had consciously done. If it came down to it, she needed to know how to save her again.

"No, I need to learn this. Do what you need to, Silvanus."

"Close your eyes."

She complied. The room was quiet as Silvanus worked his magic. She thought she might feel something, but whatever he was doing left no physical trace. Should that make her concerned? Was her magic atrophied so badly he couldn't find it within her thread?

Aurora gasped, eyes snapping open as she pressed a hand to her chest. Silvanus stared through her, his eyes glittering like sapphire jewels.

"There. Do you feel that?"

"Yes," she groaned. It felt awful, like a wriggling creature trying to get free.

"Forgive me, your magic is...elusive. Close your eyes and focus on the feeling. Once you do that, I want you to picture your magic as an animal inside you. What does it feel like?"

Aurora closed her eyes, focusing on the writhing magic inside her. What did it feel like? Like a dog twisting and fighting her hold. But it was too elusive for that. Whenever she tried to grasp it, it evaded her. It was more like the long-eared desert mouse, jumping free at every turn. One of her earliest digs in the Aurean desert had been plagued by the little pests, and as a lowly acolyte, her job had been to chase them off.

"A fairy mouse. Slippery little beast trying to run away."

"Good. I'm going to loosen my hold. I want you to concentrate on that fairy mouse. When it tries to hide, hold its image in your mind. That's how you'll capture it."

The insistent tugging let up. She could breathe again. As her magic tried to escape her, she did as Silvanus instructed, holding it with the image in her mind. It settled, ceasing its attempt to flee her. She imagined it with colour, a coat of the palest pink, bright black eyes rimmed with dark lashes, little tan spots on its large, long ears and equally long feet. This wasn't so bad. The magic was definitely strange, but it felt good too, like she was finally stretching a muscle after a cramp.

"I think I'm—"

She felt a horrible tug.

Aurora was not where she'd been. This was no cosy abode of smooth rock and comfortable cushions. Wherever she was, all the edges of her vision were blurred, the sharp details quickly dissolving into a dark mist the closer she looked. Three statues towered above her, adorned in robes of red, black and white, gold garlands sitting atop their heads. The Triad? No. Each statue was double-sided, two heads, two bodies, merged at the back into one, so their glittering jewel eyes stared out from opposite sides. Obsidian and onyx for Knowledge and Lies. Ruby and garnet for Passion and Death. Diamond and quartz for Justice and Vengeance. Had she travelled to the heart of the dualist sanctuary?

"It's true! Justice selected Silvanus as Her avatar! I just came from Boreas. He was last seen heading out with High Priestess Orithyia. He's betrayed us all. He can't be trusted," a man insisted.

No matter how well she tried to see his face, he remained obscured by mist. As did the others gathered in the sanctuary, save for Macris.

"Silvanus would never betray us. He was given a mission by the elders—"

"To infiltrate the palace! Not to become a lapdog for a princess. Not to turn his back on dualism. Now he's wielding the holy sword for a heretic high priestess! What about that is his mission?" the younger man argued.

"You accuse him in absentia. Maybe we should ask Silvanus to answer your accusations himself," Macris said, raising her chin. "He arrived a few days ago. I've been taking care of him since then. Follow me."

Aurora gasped, blinking furiously.

"Aurora! Aurora!" Phaedra cried, shaking her.

"What? What happened?" Aurora winced, a splitting headache forming behind her eyes. She was back with Silvanus and Phaedra.

"You were wrapped in your magic. You were here, but we couldn't reach you," Silvanus explained.

"I... I was pulled somewhere. The sanctuary. A young man was angry that you'd become the avatar. Macris said she would lead a group of angry people here, to you."

"I thought her magic was about stopping time!" Phaedra hissed at Silvanus, as if he'd caused this strange turn of events.

Something warm and coppery dripped from her nose. Aurora wiped away the blood as her head pounded in agony.

"Wild magic is multi-faceted."

"What would you have done if she hadn't been able to come back? Did you ever think of that?" Phaedra hissed. "She's bleeding because of your methods!"

"Stop, both of you. Merciful Triad, if you're going to fight, then just kiss each other. At least that's quieter," Aurora groaned.

"Having a lover's quarrel again?" Macris asked, waltzing through the curtain into her home with another basket in hand. Her gaze shot to the blood dripping down Aurora's nose. "I just fixed you up. What happened?" Macris fussed over her, her magic washing over and through Aurora. Her headache eased a fraction. "No cure for overusing your magic, I'm afraid. What are you doing, overextending yourself after just recovering from a major injury? Go lie down."

How was Macris here, now? Aurora had just seen her in the sanctuary. What was it that she'd seen?

"Is there any chance we could walk around? They're eager to see the sanctuary," Silvanus asked calmly.

Macris eyed him with surprise.

"That's going to have to wait. The scouts are about to return and we've been called to the sanctuary to await their arrival. I'll see about bringing up your return with the elders after the meeting. Stay here until I come for you."

"Of course. Thank you for your hospitality, Macris."

She smiled.

"Don't think you can whittle down your tab just by acting gentlemanly. I'll be back in a few hours. I brought more food for dinner. And you—" She turned to Aurora. "Back to bed with you."

"Right," Aurora swallowed, dizzy with confusion.

Macris had been gone but a moment when Silvanus rushed for an alcove, pulling out his armour and the holy sword, donning them as quickly as possible.

"What are you doing?" Aurora asked.

"*Time*, Aurora. Your magic is time magic. You said you saw Macris in the sanctuary, that she was going to lead a mob back here, right?"

"That's what she said," Phaedra grumbled.

"Then it stands to reason that you glimpsed into time with your magic. You paused time to save Phaedra. Then you saw the future, I'm certain of it. And if you did, then we need to leave. Get dressed for a journey—quickly."

Aurora and Phaedra exchanged glances.

"You know what? At this point, anything is possible, and I'm not interested in facing an angry mob of dualists. Whatever they do to him they'll do to me ten times over," Phaedra grouched and hurried over to get dressed.

Aurora followed, numb. Had she actually glimpsed the future? Bile surged up her throat. This was too much. No one in their right mind wanted to know the future—to become an oracle.

Once dressed, Silvanus peeked out of their abode and led the way, their steps as soft as possible. Voices were raised in the distance, echoing down the cavernous halls. Silvanus pressed a finger to his lips and gestured at them to follow. The voices grew in volume as they crept through the passages. Then, as they turned a corner, the ceilings tripled in height. Aurora gasped.

"What the fuck, Silvanus? You brought us to the sanctuary?" Phaedra hissed as quietly as she could.

"It's the centre of the maze. Trust me and keep quiet," he whispered back.

He dragged them over to an area behind the statues. Here, now, Aurora could take in the details of the sanctuary. The scent of incense, the small statues and tokens placed at the feet of the goddesses, the divine magic dancing off every surface. She'd prayed to Knowledge in Her temple, begging for divine magic as a child. She'd felt Her presence in every marble tile, in the very waters of the clear, opalescent pool she'd knelt in for three days straight. But here? It was in the very air she breathed, and it wasn't just the presence of one goddess, but six. She felt small and irrelevant and inclined to beg for mercy. How had this remained hidden for millennia?

"It's true! Justice selected Silvanus as Her avatar! I just came from Boreas. He was last seen heading out with High Priestess Orithyia. He's betrayed us all. He can't be trusted," a man insisted.

Aurora jolted out of her thoughts and listened with dawning horror as the same scene replayed in front of her yet again. By the time the group had left, her heart was hammering inside her chest. This was bad. Very bad. People who saw the future went mad. The most famous oracles stabbed out their eyes, or slit their own throats, just to escape from the horrors they were forced to witness. If that was her fate, she never wanted to use her magic again. It could atrophy inside her until the day she died.

"Is this what you saw?" Silvanus asked.

"Yes...but blurrier around the edges." Aurora trailed off in a horrified whisper.

Phaedra grabbed her hand and squeezed, dragging Aurora back to the present.

"Stay with me, Aurora. Here, in this moment."

"But—"

The understanding. The pity. The fear. They were there in Fae's gaze and crushed by determination in an instant.

"I won't let you go mad."

"Let's move," Silvanus whispered.

Phaedra shot him a dirty look, but followed without comment, pulling Aurora with her. They slunk through empty halls, ducking into rooms when the sound of footsteps or voices threatened to reach them. It must have been for hours that they traversed the mountain labyrinth, until at last Silvanus called a halt.

"In here. We should be safe for a while." He pulled aside a curtain and ushered them inside.

Aurora ducked into the well-lit hall.

Only to be met with a scene from a fever dream.

"I... What... This place..." Words failed her as she rushed to the nearest glass case. Inside, a perfectly preserved Pre-Second Sundering artefact winked up at her. She had no idea what it was, only that it was intact, its characteristic geometric designs and blue crystal accents laid out like a feast for her eyes.

"Show off," Phaedra muttered.

"Fae! Look! It's a genuine Pre-Second Sundering artefact! Did you know the Boreas temple museum only has eight of these? I wonder what it is."

Aurora desperately looked for a plaque to answer her query. But then another beauty caught her eye.

"Ahh! Is that...? Fae! That's a statue of one of the tangible gods! I've only ever read about them in books! I think it's the god of the air! See how he's standing on a stylized gust of wind? He rules over your element!"

Phaedra smiled at her indulgently. Aurora beamed back, catching sight of Silvanus with a kind smile that didn't reach his eyes. *Oh*. He'd done this for her. To help her forget what her magic meant. And what it would do to her mind, if she lived long enough for that to matter. Her heart swelled with gratitude.

"Thank you."

"You're welcome. Enjoy. We have time."

Time was a luxury no one had, but she was appreciative all the same. She strolled through isles lined with glorious artefacts, the likes of which she could barely fathom. So much had been preserved in perfect condition. She could happily spend the rest of her days here. While she gasped and occasionally called Phaedra over to gush about one treasure or another, Phaedra and Silvanus mostly remained out of earshot, whispering to each other. Aurora began sneaking furtive glances at them. What could they be saying that they felt the need to hide it from her?

In her distracted state, she nearly walked into a hip-high case. As soon as her eyes lit on the object inside, that strange creature inside her shot out, latching onto it. Rounded like a globe, the object had several circular bands around it, each one notched, some with an undecipherable script on it. Her magic seethed inside her, her heart racing. Why did it look so familiar? Why did it feel like if she didn't get her hands on it, she would go mad?

"Aurora?"

"Aurora!"

She shook her head, and yet the spell still had her in its grip. Her hands shook as she tried to remove them from the edges of the case.

"This artefact. I want it so badly." Aurora gritted her teeth as her magic surged inside her, pulling her towards the artefact, warping her mind, screaming at her to take it. Goddess, how did she control this beast? How did anyone fight this compulsion?

"Hold her back," Silvanus said, his eyes like jewels as he looked at her and then the artefact.

Phaedra pulled her away, even though everything inside Aurora told her to fight her way back to it. She needed it like she needed air. Silvanus smashed the glass casing with the pommel of the holy sword before reaching inside and pulling the artefact out. Aurora rushed towards him to hold it. As she did, weighing it, marvelling at it, she had the strangest feeling this wasn't the first time. The beast inside settled, content, as Aurora's mind spun.

"Isn't that... the same kind of artefact you dug up in the old temple?" Phaedra asked.

Aurora reached into the pocket of her cloak and pulled out the only possession she still owned—Phaedra's stolen gift. She placed it into the broken case and pulled off the lid. Nestled inside was a globe, almost the exact size as the beautiful artefact she now held. Beneath the layer of rock and dirt, she even saw the outline of one of the bands.

"Whatever it is, it's drawing out your magic. Keep it," Silvanus said.

Aurora blinked at the artefact in wonder and then in horror at the shattered case.

"Silvanus, you ruined the display case! Won't you get in trouble?"

"The fate of Trisia is worth more than a dusty display case," he quipped, biting back a smile. "And if the artefact helps with your magic, then I'm happy to burn a bridge or two."

"My magic made me feel like I was losing control. Shouldn't I try to resist?"

"Normally, yes. But your magic has lain dormant most of your life. You need to keep using it, stretching it, and learning just how far you can push yourself. First, we'll work on power, then we'll focus on control."

"Oh, I didn't know—"

The three looked up from the artefact and shattered case to the man at the doorway. He was a kindly looking older man with greying hair and threadbare, yet clean clothes. That kindly façade melted away in an instant the moment he laid eyes on Silvanus. Hatred suffused his features.

"Silvanus!" he spat. "How dare you show your face around here? Traitor!"

"Run!" Silvanus called, pulling Phaedra and Aurora along behind him.

They raced through the museum and out into another hall, the man's hue and cry echoing in the mountain labyrinth. They ran as hard and fast as their feet could carry, always being chased by furious echoes.

"They can't be that mad about the display case, can they?" Aurora asked, panting.

"What in the Loom did you do?" Phaedra thundered.

"I refused to kill your family," Silvanus replied.

"What?!" Aurora shrieked.

"My mission was to kill the imperial family. I refused. I swore I would win tolerance for dualism through gaining your trust instead. My punishment was banishment."

"And you brought us *here?!* You fucking idiot!" Phaedra cursed.

"That seems to be the general sentiment."

"What now?" Aurora asked.

"This way."

They raced down a corridor that seemed to come to a dead end. Silvanus reached towards it as they neared. The rock opened, as if a curtain had parted. And not a moment too soon. Several mountain denizens wielding steel had showed up. They jumped through the opening as Silvanus sealed it behind them.

The sun stung Aurora's eyes, blinding her. She shielded her vision with a hand and squinted out onto the landscape that greeted them.

Only to see that they were near a narrow land bridge high above a mighty river.

"The Dragon's Tail Mountain range is across this span. If we can get to the tunnels inside the mountain there, they'll take us most of the way to Altanus Novus."

"Did you dualists hollow out every mountain in Trisia?" Phaedra asked disdainfully.

Silvanus only smiled.

"Come!"

"Wait!" Aurora grabbed his wrist.

"What's wrong, Aurora?" Phaedra asked.

They'd come out at the end of the canyon trade road, the border of the province of Aureum. Across the land bridge before them, The Colonnades Of The Colossus, lay Viridis proper. If they travelled south towards the sea, they would reach Altanus Novus. Not only that, they would pass by the most populated stretch of the province, town after town hugging the Dragon's Tongue River. There was barely an uncultivated patch from here to the port. Hundreds of thousands of people lived here. Hundreds of thousands would die if she went that way.

"We can't go to Altanus Novus! Drakon will follow me. He'll decimate the Aurean capital. I can't be responsible for that."

"We need to go to a temple, Aurora. It'll be the only place with enough divine magic to withstand Drakon's attacks," Silvanus said.

"Isn't there another dualist sanctuary we could go to? With divine statues? Somewhere no one will get hurt?" Aurora asked.

"There is…"

"But?" Phaedra asked.

"I don't know if we'll make it there before Drakon finds us. It's on the other side of Trisia, in the Giant's Jawbone."

"We can decide on a final destination later. Right now, we need to get into the next set of tunnels in the Dragon's Tail Mountains before the Beast of Old finds us. Once we have a mountain between us and the apocalypse, we can quibble on the best place to begin your training," Phaedra said, grabbing Aurora's wrist as she pulled her across the land bridge.

Aurora had crossed The Colonnades Of The Colossus on her way to the ancient temple in Aureum. Soaring high above the ancient waterway, the river below was a set of perilous rapids, the columns and bridge above had held since time immemorial, supposedly built on the bones of a mythical monster. She allowed Phaedra to pull her along. It was surely a mistake, one that would be paid for in blood, but what choice did they have? They'd crossed half the land bridge at a jog when the sky began to darken.

"*Did you miss me, little mouse?*"

"Drakon's found us!" Aurora shouted.

"Hurry!" Silvanus cried.

They ran for their lives.

But luck was not on their side.

A blast of purple fire hit the final colonnade, shattering it. It fell into the Dragon's Tongue River with a resounding crash. A moment later, another blast took out the colonnade leading back into Aureum.

Trapped.

Silvanus drew the holy sword, preparing for a fight they could no longer avoid. Drakon's glittering crimson form emerged from the clouds hanging over the Dragon's Tail Mountain. Ash began to swirl down from a sky turning black and crimson. Soon, the world would be overrun with monstrosities.

It was all her fault. If she'd pursued her wild magic, refused to accept her magic-deprived state as a child, she might've been prepared to face the greatest threat in all of Trisia as an adult. Now they would all die—everyone she knew and loved. Phaedra, Silvanus, her family, her friends. She was the greatest failure in the history of Trisia, unworthy of the trust the high priestess and her goddess had placed in her.

"I'm sorry," she whispered as she stared into the hatred-filled eyes of the beast.

"Silvanus, can you open the way into the mountain from here?" Phaedra asked.

"Yes, but we'll never make it across the chasm."

"Open it."

Silvanus raised a brow but obeyed. A doorway to a safe haven they would never be able to reach opened in the side of the Dragon's Tail Mountain range bordering the heart of the Viridian empire.

Was there some hope? Was this not the end?

"What now?" Aurora asked, her knees going weak at the sight of the beast slithering through the sky towards her.

"*You're mine now*," the beast cackled in her ear.

"You remember our deal, right?" Phaedra asked Silvanus.

"Yes."

"Then do it. And Aurora?"

Aurora's heart sank. Phaedra was much too calm. Where was her inner fire? Where was her determination?

"What deal? What are you talking about?"

"When you get to the other side, run."

"*No escape now. After so long, I have you right where I want you.*"

Drakon opened his maw, teeth gleaming, an unholy purple light building up in the back of his throat. They were dead, all of them. There was no getting to the other side of the chasm and it was too late to run.

With unexpected violence, Aurora was shoved up into the air and catapulted across the chasm. She landed with a sickening thud, bones cracking as the world spun. She looked up just in time to see Phaedra and Silvanus a world away, the holy sword taking the shape of a vast shield. He braced for the impact, his arm around Phaedra's waist.

Phaedra's eyes sought Aurora's. She relayed a simple message with gestures.

Phaedra pointed to her eye.

I.

Her heart.

Love.

Then Aurora.

You.

Then the blast hit, obliterating the pillar on which Phaedra and Silvanus stood. Obliterating Trisia's brightest, warmest light—and Aurora's heart along with it.

Aurora screamed.

She screamed until her magic was a raging tempest. She screamed until there was no breath left in her lungs. She screamed until the earth beneath her began to crumble and give way.

And when she fell, the raging river drawing close, Aurora welcomed the end.

Chapter 9
The Ancient Past

The silence in Theron's throne room was thick enough to choke a man. The king of Aureum could be forgiven for hoping the Viridian merchant currently prostrated before him would expire from the force of his displeasure. Having the temerity to arrive without the shipments of grain that his treasury had already paid for in full was an excellent way to ensure one died a painful death. The moment the merchant crossed The Colonnades Of The Colossus without it, he'd made himself an enemy of the kingdom. That the scum had travelled along the winding trade road through the canyons all the way to Altanus just to rub it in his face was an insult not to be borne.

"Repeat yourself."

The thunderous tone of his voice would leave no doubt in the mind of the merchant what the cost of displeasing him would be. It echoed in the cavernous throne room, bouncing off the sunstone mosaic floors, wrapping around thick columns carved with the painted likenesses of heroic kings and queens long past. The echo settled in the bones of his silent courtiers, all of them watching and waiting for a single misstep in order to pounce—either on him for a perceived failing, or on the merchant to curry his favour.

"The cost of the food has increased, Your Majesty. I must ask that you pay the full price before delivery."

To the man's credit, his tone was remarkably even.

And that simply wouldn't do.

Theron leaned forward on his throne, his deep blue and gold attire accentuating the crimson hue of his long hair. Gold-tooled leather boots had been polished enough to reflect the sunlight. Loose pants of the finest wool dyed dark blue with gold embroidery peeked out beneath a lengthy, shimmering gold tunic with sapphires sparkling in the swirling white patterns. All this cinched with a belt tooled with gold and inlaid with jewels. His crown today was relaxed—an oversight. A gold and sapphire headband cut across his temple, matching the earrings and thickly braided necklace he'd selected as his courtly battle attire. Gold cuffs and rings completed the look. At court, one could not afford to look weak or humble. While the nobles and courtiers in attendance were ostensibly his allies, enough misfortune had already beset his kingdom to make his position tenuous. Placing a hand on his knee and leaning forward, Theron chose his next words carefully.

"The problem before us is one of honour." Theron stood, stepping down from his dais, every movement calculated to instil fear, to mimic the movements of predators. He held out his hand to his sword bearer, his cousin, who placed the sheathed weapon in his hand. "When a person signs a contract or swears upon their name that something will be done, and then fails to follow through, they are punished and shunned for being without honour. Only a fool would agree to treat with a person who has tarnished themselves in such a way. Wouldn't you agree?"

"Your Majesty, I cannot—"

"You signed a contract. You were paid. Are you telling me that you are a man without honour?"

Theron began pulling his sword from its scabbard. The punishment for such treachery was traditionally whatever the king decided. And kings could not afford to be merciful. His word was law. For now.

"No! No, Your Majesty!"

"Then have you simply misplaced the promised goods?" he asked, the click of his blade falling back into its scabbard echoing in the silent throne room.

The merchant swallowed, weighing the worth of his life. He would die here and now if he failed to produce the shipment. But was the punishment for failure back in Viridis worse than a swift beheading? Though he was intrigued as to what the Viridians had over the man, the shipment of grain was of much greater value than the intelligence. After all, hungry people couldn't eat secrets.

"Y-yes, Your Majesty. Please forgive me. In my embarrassment, I have misspoken," the merchant said, trembling, sweat rolling down his neck and into the finely embroidered himation he wore. Perhaps it was not out of fear, but unfounded confidence that he'd come here without the goods. Had he been told that Aureum was weak, desperate? Enough for a simple merchant to harass and insult a king?

"I see. And where was it you misplaced the shipment?" Theron asked, his smile not reaching his eyes.

But his cruel smile was not for the prostrated merchant—it was for the courtiers who thought Theron was weak. Here, everything was a performance, and only the best actor was permitted to walk away with both their power and their head intact.

"On the border, at the end of the Queen's Road, Your Majesty."

"How foolish. Have no fear, you will be escorted back to your wayward goods and my people will take possession of them from there."

"You are most generous, Your Majesty."

"Yes, I am. Had I not sought clarity, I might have had to send you back in pieces. My honour would have demanded no less. See that you don't put me in such a position again."

"Of course, Your Majesty."

"General Canthus, see our guest back to the border and find the shipment. And if he proves to be without honour, then do what must be done."

His general bowed deeply, the noontime sun glinting off the bronze of his cuirass. He was a man of honour and could be trusted not to steal or tamper with the shipment. Canthus was also surprisingly content for a man who wielded as much power as he did. He made a fine ally, the same as all those in his inner circle. After all, Theron never trusted anyone whose weakness he didn't control.

"With pleasure, Your Majesty."

Canthus grabbed the merchant by his silks and dragged him from the throne room.

Court had begun with the first rays of dawn, and Theron had seen to dozens of cases brought before him for judgment. Farmers fighting over land and cattle, artisans complaining of substandard materials sold to them by merchants who fought over taxes and market stall placements, to say nothing of the nobles with their endless boundary and inheritance disputes. Now that the sun was high in the sky, he had other matters to attend to.

Theron nodded to his cousin, Batea, a woman sharing the rich, ochre brown skin and dark red hair of their royal lineage. But where her eyes were a brown bordering on black, his were gold.

"Court has concluded for the day," she announced, her voice carrying to every corner of the great hall.

As one, all those still present knelt or prostrated themselves on the sunstone mosaic floors and chanted, "Triad preserve the sun of Aureum."

"Your wishes have been heard. Go with the sun's favour," Theron replied.

As petitioners and courtiers alike filed out of the hall, Theron turned to Batea.

"Batea, with me."

"It would be my pleasure, Your Majesty."

"Polydorus," Theron said, turning to his most trusted advisor, a fastidiously dressed, lean man with a streak of silver in his black hair. "Ensure any who were expecting that grain today are given some from the royal stores."

"As you wish, Your Majesty." Polydorus bowed and went to his task.

His cousin followed him from the throne room to the balcony facing the Dragon's Spine Mountains. Once alone, she sighed, running a hand through her long, burgundy strands.

"The Viridians grow bolder by the day."

"The Viridian high priestess certainly does," Theron snorted.

Batea clicked her tongue, disgusted. Neither of them held any love for the grasping Viridians, or their High Priestess Orithyia XI, the true power behind the Viridian throne.

"Then Queen Flora is worth less than the silks she wears. That merchant wore her colours, her royal silks, and bore her official seal. She'll have neither power nor peace for much longer if that's how she conducts her affairs."

Theron grunted in approval. While the merchant had been yet another insult the fool queen had sent his way, it was just that—a petty insult from a petulant queen. The real danger lay elsewhere. Any monarch who bowed to the whims of the temples rather than balancing them was unworthy of their crown. It was a pity Flora had allowed such a detestably ambitious high priestess to take the helm of the temple of Knowledge and seat herself at the queen's right side. No doubt the wretched temple bitch had already poisoned the minds of Viridis, just as she was poisoning the other realms.

Just as she was poisoning his lands.

Orithyia would pay dearly for her sins. And part of the comeuppance would come sooner rather than later. He smiled, spotting the ugly spire atop the Dragon's Spine Mountain range, jutting out from the snow like a bone through bloodless flesh. Orithyia could lie about how the spire was in honour of Knowledge, a place to study the mountains, built without politics or scheming in mind, but he knew better.

It had been paid for with Viridian gold and built by Viridian clerics. And it was on his mountains.

The moment it had begun blighting his view, it had begun blighting his lands, drying up the rivers, polluting the waters that remained, and inducing sickness and disease amongst the animals, crops and farmers. Orithyia had angered the spirits with her spire, and had the temerity to blame him for the consequences. One would almost think she was one of the dualists she and her queen so ruthlessly persecuted, given how easily falsehoods fell from her lips.

As a result, the nobles of Aureum had begun eyeing Theron like a lamed stag, ripe for slaughter. For a king's most sacred duty was appeasing the spirits and bringing plenty and fertility to the land through the magical connections bestowed upon him by the crown. A king who failed to do so was either too weak to rule without a powerful queen at his side, or too weak to rule at all. The vultures were circling—all because of that bitch high priestess.

"Do we have confirmation that the high priestess has received our message?"

"The birds delivered word of it just this morning." Batea nodded.

"Excellent."

Theron had warned Orithyia to keep her spires in her own territory. But by the time she'd come to him with the proposal, it was already too late to stop her. Whatever she had over the monarchs of Niveum, Gilvus, and Roseum, it was enough that the pressure proved impossible to ignore. While he often employed such a tactic to keep his own people in line, he was enough of a hypocrite to despise her for doing the same. She'd won that round, but she would lose this one.

"Do you know what I told her?"

"No."

"That any structure built on lies is bound to crumble."

Batea's eyes lit up, a smile cracking her impressively severe façade.

"You didn't."

"I did." He grinned back. "And I should be made a prophet any moment now."

As if on cue, a dark fissure ran up the length of the spire. The ominous, thundering crack met their ears a moment later. Gravity, aided by the genius of some of Aureum's best engineers, finished it off. Collapsing in on itself and showering the surrounding area in rubble, a cloud of snow, dirt and debris shrouded the spire's newly anointed graveyard.

"And what of the survivors?"

"Conveniently unrecoverable. Those who refused to talk were left as bodies to be found. The rest are on their way to the dungeons. Take your most trusted soldiers and make sure everyone knows you're searching the rubble for survivors. The spire was looted in the initial assault, but if you find anything interesting, bring it back. Either way, we'll have proof of Orithyia's chicanery. Maybe we'll get lucky and find some new bit of sinister magic she's concocted to use against her."

"And if neither the prisoners, loot, nor the rubble proves fruitful?"

"Then at the very least we'll have cured the source of the blight and restored the rivers. My pleas to the spirits and tangible gods might finally be heard."

Batea hummed, pensive as the city roused to the sight of the fallen spire.

"There's always some shadowy trick with the high priestess. Schemes within schemes. Are you certain you know which games she's playing?"

Theron scoffed.

"You don't trust your cousin?"

"I trust you're as ruthless as you ought to be, but you're still a king, and you have honour. The woman we're fighting is shameless, bold, grasping, and has some sway over the monarchs of the other realms. She has Viridis at her beck and call. I wonder if it would be simpler to stick a dagger in her heart and be done with it."

"And risk the wrath of a goddess?"

The goddess, Knowledge, had chosen the vile woman to serve Her, and given her divine magic and protection. No matter her sins, only the other two high priestesses, or those chosen by the goddesses, the avatars, could safely dispose of Orithyia.

"Better to risk a few souls than to bend the knee to Viridis—to Orithyia."

"When we have our proof, either through testimonies, magical objects, or the sudden end to the blight, we'll have enough to make the High Priestesses Myrina and Nerio act. I cannot risk a war—and the wrath of a goddess—when our people have been hungry for the better part of a year."

The blight had killed enough crops that his people ate only because of the previous year's surplus, but even that was dangerously low. Orithyia's foul magic had devastated the grain-producing region south of the Dragon's Spine Mountain lake and along its rivers. Even the water in the capital, Altanus, was beginning to sicken the people here. She'd angered the spirits of the land and the tangible gods, and now Aureum suffered.

"That is why we should have declared war the moment that tower was built in our mountains!"

Theron pinched the bridge of his nose. Triad's tits, they'd had this fight often enough he could recite it from memory. But from the fire in Batea's eyes, she wouldn't let it go, even now.

"We would have walked right into her trap. Made ourselves the enemy of the realms, a common foe to unite against. She outplayed us."

"She continues to outplay us! You think that tower will be the end of it? Niveum has stalled marriage talks since the blight began. Our kingdoms were the closest they've ever been to uniting, and now it's as good as called off. Gilvus won't even reply to our messages for my marriage talks with the princess, and Roseum is content to wait and watch from behind the Giant's Jawbone. We should have marched on Viridis while our granaries were full."

The loss of the Nivean princess had been a bitter thing to swallow. That alliance would have given Aureum access to the crops it needed to feed its growing population in return for ores that Niveum sorely lacked. It would have been enough to stop Orithyia in her tracks. Fitting, then, that she'd perched her bloody spire in the mountains that separated their kingdoms, no doubt using the blight she'd cast on Aureum to frighten the Nivean king into compliance.

"My plan will work."

It had to work. The other high priestesses weren't blind. They knew Orithyia's nature, they tolerated her, but had no real love for her. They even abided by the unwritten rule that the temples were not to usurp the power of monarchs, unlike Orithyia, who was using her power to bolster the land-grabbing ambitions of Viridis' queen. If he gave Myrina and Nerio all the evidence, they would strike Orithyia down.

"And if it doesn't?" Batea pressed.

"Then, and only then, will we discuss more drastic steps."

While he couldn't touch Orithyia for fear of divine wrath, Flora was another matter. No goddess backed her. Only through her wild magic had she attained her crown, the same as the rest of the Trisian monarchs. And when it came to fearsome magic, Theron could not be defeated—not even by a queen who proclaimed her power to paralyse her foes on the battlefield.

"You had best hope your plan works—and quickly. We're reaching the point at which our reserves won't be able to sustain an army on the march."

Theron smiled. If all else failed, they had one thing neither the temples nor Viridis possessed.

"You mean your *pets*."

Batea returned the grin, all mischief and bloodthirst.

"Yes, well, every woman needs a hobby."

More than hobby, it was her magic. Batea could enter the Tapestry to weave new creatures into being from those that already existed. It was a pity she could not alter fate, or kill from a distance, as some with her brand of wild magic were capable of. It was a pity that so few of them felt safe enough to live openly—after all, Viridis and its spies assassinated any they could find. Batea had survived because she was a king's cousin and the most bloodthirsty royal relation in all of Trisia. And he let her do whatever she pleased to all those who tried to harm her. Theron shook his head.

"Go, see what you can find in the rubble."

Batea frowned. No doubt she had more to say on the subject of an all-out war. But they were wasting time. Any longer, and it might not appear that he'd rushed to send his best to save the doomed clerics in the spire.

"One of these days you'll wish you'd declared war," she harrumphed, gaze drifting to the rubble in the mountains. "If I must go, then I'm taking my *pets*."

Theron returned the frown. The more those damned creatures moved, the hungrier they became. The more they ate, the bigger they got. Soon, they would be unmanageable. Sometimes he thought Batea only desired war so her precious beasts would have more to eat. Though if they devoured that vile high priestess and her pet queen too, he would cease nagging her about them.

"If you must."

Theron spared one more look for the scene of devastation in the mountains, his heart swelling in triumph. Orithyia had not expected him to demolish her ugly spire. So it would be all the sweeter when he forced her clerics to testify against her, to admit to her schemes. He turned from the sight.

"Where are you heading? Aren't you going to watch your heroic cousin ride to the rescue?"

Theron snorted.

"No, your ego is big enough already. First, I'm going to heal my people. Then, I'm going to loosen the lips of some Viridian scum."

"I don't know why you bother. Beggars don't bestow crowns," Batea scoffed.

"No, but riots have been known to topple even the most fearsome kings," Theron retorted.

Batea's laughter chased him all the way to the outer courtyard, where the neediest of his kingdom had been brought. People lay on tarps, or in the arms of their loved ones, shaded by the fragrant orange trees. There were more who begged for succour these days, almost as many as when waves of torchlight fever coincided with another plague or earthquake. Pyres already burned through the night in the countryside due to the blight tainting the waters. He supposed he should be more worried for a time when there was no one left to light them.

Theron drew on his wild magic, cloaking the whole of the courtyard in its golden shimmer. He needn't be quite so flashy with his magic, but this was the spectacle they had been summoned to witness. Broken bones, festering wounds, and maladies of all kinds were banished. He was the most powerful healer in the land, after all. But not everyone here could be healed permanently. Not all illnesses could be conquered by coaxing the body to repair itself. For those, he healed as much as he could. Others were too far gone, his magic recoiling as Death dyed the fibres of their threads a muddy red. All he could do for them was to ease their suffering, severing the link between their pain and the sensation of it.

"Triad preserve the sun of Aureum!"

The weepy, ecstatic exclamation met every success of his healing magic. The people here could have been treated by his legion of royal healers, but his aides had selected those among them who had some measure of influence or eloquence or were simply known as talkative or well-liked. These would be the people to spread tales of his benevolence and generosity. And if some of the more ambitious nobles thought to topple him, he hoped they would also be the first to riot in his defence.

"Your wishes have been heard. Go with the sun's favour," Theron replied by rote, dismissing each in turn, until the whole of the courtyard was empty.

By the time he was finished, the afternoon was nearly over. Duty done, his public image secure, he dismissed his guards and attendants.

Now the real fun began.

The prisoners should be secure, the first round of questioning commencing. He could hardly contain his excitement. Orithyia's schemes were soon to be revealed. He hoped he would get to watch her execution. Maybe the high priestesses Myrina and Nerio would even appoint an avatar to strike the killing blow.

Humming a jaunty tune, Theron made his way through the palace, descending hidden stairwells that led to the dungeons. As he stepped further into darkness interrupted only by the odd oil lamp, the echoes of distant screams met his ears. His people were already hard at work, it seemed. But the closer he got, the more all-consuming the shrieks became. Theron hurried his steps as the cries began petering out, the stench of burnt hair and flesh reaching his nose.

Something was wrong.

When he stepped into the underground prison, the sight that greeted him was not of Viridian clerics in chains, spilling their guts both figuratively and literally. Instead, dismembered, blackened arms hung from red-hot chains. Charred corpses, piled atop one another, reached for freedom through melting prison bars. Pliers, knives, whips and more lay scattered about. The fire had burned so hot that there was no way to tell friend from foe. The smoke and the stench had Theron's eyes watering as he searched for survivors.

"Majesty…"

Theron peered through the thick gloom. One of his men still lived—barely. He raced to the man's side, lay his hands atop him, and dug deep for the magic in his blood. He coaxed it out, wrapping it around the injured man, healing him.

"How did this happen?"

"Magic…device…acolyte's pocket."

"And what of the other items secured from the spire?"

His magic dissipated, recoiling from the man's body. He was too near death to save. Theron grimaced, pulling on a different power. If he could not save him, then he could take away the pain.

"Damaged…" the man whispered, breathing his last.

Theron raced from the corpse down the hall to the deepest part of the treasury. Smoke billowed out of the room in which he'd ordered the contents of the spire placed. Only the ashes of burnt scrolls remained of the precious documents he'd stolen. Every stone object had fractured into a thousand pieces and the metal devices had melted, their arcane symbols warped beyond recognition. He slammed the door shut and roared. Whatever device the acolyte had activated, it had destroyed his proof.

The high priestess had outplayed Theron once again.

Chapter 10

Aurora

The stink of wet hay and horse crawled up Aurora's nose and expired there. Searing light from a bright, cloudless day and the rather jarring sway of the ground beneath her brought her out from a dark, dreamless place. She immediately regretted rousing. A sharp jolt of pain shot up from her leg, her sudden gasp alerting her to a new agony gripping her chest. She raised a hand to shield her eyes, only to gain another regret. Goddesses, she must be bruised from head to toe, or worse. What had happened?

She remembered the mountain, the museum, then the Colonnades, and then Drakon...

"Phaedra!" Aurora cried, sitting up, only to fall to her side when her injuries overwhelmed her.

Phaedra was gone. Obliterated. A sob ripped from her throat, and then another and another, until she hurt inside and out, body and soul. Phaedra had taken Aurora's place—her fate—in a final act of selfless love.

Aurora's magic writhed inside her, responding to her raw and wretched grief. It had exploded from her the moment Phaedra had died, feeding off her as it grew unstable. Unstable like the ground beneath her had been. She'd fallen. She should have joined Phaedra in death, their threads reunited in the Loom. But this was not the afterlife, unless her teachings had greatly misled her. Not unless the afterlife was a rickety cart filled with musty hay, lurching unpredictably on a muddy road.

A plump brunette woman in strange garb and a straw hat jogged to keep up with the cart, her tanned hand on the side railing as she looked up at Aurora with kindly brown eyes. What she could see of the woman appeared abnormally large, startling her from her grief.

"It'll be alright, little one. The temple isn't far, and the medics there will soothe your hurts."

Aurora was stunned into silence. The juxtaposition of the woman's rustic fashion and her fluent, almost melodic mastery of the ancient temple tongue took some time to process. Normally, only the priestesses and highly ranked scholars attained such a skill.

"You speak the ancient temple tongue? Are you a priestess?" Aurora asked.

If this woman was a priestess though, where in Trisia was she? She didn't think she knew of any priestess who wore such simple, low-quality clothes unless they were partaking in some manual labour that would dirty their finer fabrics. Her fashion was also woefully, purposefully archaic. She looked like she had just come from a costume party, except the fabric looked worn—lived in.

"I'm speaking common, little one. And just how hard did you hit your head for you to think me a priestess?" the woman asked, brow raised.

"Where is this? I don't recognise this place." Aurora looked at the scenery, stunned by the abundance of plant life.

Not even Viridis during the height of blooming season was so lush. Fields of wheat stretched out further than the horizon, separated by flowering trees taller than any she'd seen. Beyond the smell of musty hay and her own sweat, the fragrance of a thousand blooms drifted on the breeze. The other surprise? Just how many birds flew overhead. Had she been transported to another world? Was this the magic of the artefact?

Aurora gasped.

"My artefact! Did you see a small, round device with metal bands around it?"

The woman pulled the small globe from a satchel at her side and handed it to Aurora, her hands engulfing Aurora's own. Just how large was this stranger?

Relief coursed through her until she saw that the bands had been dented and warped. Even the glow of the blue stones had faded. It no longer called to her.

"It's an odd trinket. Best keep it safe. Something that unusual is likely to catch the attention of thieves. We're nearly to the gates of Boreas now, so find someplace to hide it."

"Boreas? Then this is Viridis?" Aurora asked.

"Just so. For someone with such a strange accent, you seem to know of our queendom."

"Queendom? Not empire?"

The woman laughed.

"An empire? Maybe one day. Queen Flora is an ambitious woman."

Queen Flora? There hadn't been a Flora on the Viridian throne in at least several hundred years. And there hadn't been a queen, rather than an empress, for at least a thousand. Had she been transported not just in space, but in time? Dread crept up her spine. She swallowed.

"Which High Priestess Orithyia currently sits under Knowledge's auspices?"

The woman's brows knit with pity, and maybe a little alarm.

"High Priestess Orithyia XI, little one."

Blood drained from Aurora's face. Every high priestess of Knowledge left behind their birth name when they ascended to the role, taking on the name of Orithyia, with only a number to differentiate between them. A long line of Orithyias stretched back to the very first high priestess of Knowledge, appointed after the Second Sundering when the intangible deities of Knowledge, Passion and Justice split from their sinister sides to be worshipped alone. The Orithyia who had been like a grandmother to Aurora was the one hundredth and sixty-first to bear her name. If what this woman said were true, then that meant Aurora was thousands of years in the past.

"Merciful Triad," Aurora whispered, horrified.

The woman put her hand on Aurora's.

"I don't know what you've been through, or for how long, but whatever happened, the temples in Boreas will welcome you. Knowledge's medics will heal you, Passion's initiates will help you find work, and Justice's paladins will right whatever wrongs you've suffered."

As the pungent odour of the city replaced that of lush fields, Aurora spotted the city gates, but not as she knew them. The designs and architecture were decidedly ancient, as was the uniform for the guards inspecting incoming travellers, labourers, merchants and farmers. Her heart pumped unease to every part of her aching, beaten body. She would have preferred to hide in a small corner of her mind, to focus on some harmless detail, like the construction of the kind woman's hat, or the exact shade of her brown eyes. But reality had other plans.

"Next!"

The cart lurched to a halt at the front of the gate, the donkeys braying. A guard in Viridian green standing tall with a short sword at his hip approached.

"Who's that? What kind of young girl wears trousers?" the guard asked. He was truly of a monstrous size. He peered into the cart with naked suspicion, lingering tellingly on her trousers and boots before his eyes widened at the state of her face. No doubt she was mottled with fresh bruises.

"We found her near the outskirts, attacked and left for dead by bandits. We're taking her to the temple of Knowledge," the woman answered.

The guard spat.

"Bloody dualist pigs. Attacking innocent travellers now? Let Justice's temple know about the incident before you leave the city."

"Thank you. Blessings of the Triad on you." The woman nodded. "And you. Next!"

The cart lurched into motion once more, the ride less unpleasant now that they had the benefit of flagstone streets and well-worn ruts for the wheels of the cart to follow. On the sides of the traffic, people walked along the raised walkways, by turns tempted and harassed by shopkeepers and stalls lining the avenue. Spices, silks, animals, jewels, perfumes, devotional objects, food and drink were plied between a mix of potential patrons both high and lowborn. Some things, mercifully, changed very little. Aurora never would have imagined the vibrancy of the ancient city. Nor the staggering height of its denizens!

Everywhere she looked, adults were half a person taller than she at a guess, only their children standing around her height. She'd read tales of the ancients and their giants' blood, their second growth phases, and how it had lessened in the millennia since the days of myth, but it was altogether another thing to see it in person. The ancient bones she'd seen and excavated simply didn't do their towering height justice. Even the tallest person she'd ever met, the ones in whom there was a drop of giant's blood and who experienced a second growth phase, were maybe only as tall as the average youth here. Their ears were oddly small, the points more rounded than sharp, whereas hers had always been a source of pride in how long and beautifully angular they were. Strangely, not one of them wore trousers, preferring gowns, long skirts or knee-length tunics. They looked like they'd stepped out from an ancient fresco.

Captivated by the sights, Aurora almost didn't notice when they stopped. The ancient temple of Knowledge shared the archaic style of the front gate. The entrance of the temple boasted sky-high fluted columns with minimal decoration, the sides and back made entirely of brick. Atop the columns laid the metope, a band of carved images depicting Knowledge's role in preserving Trisia during the Great Sundering. They were the only colourful part of the entire temple—the rest was the deepest black, with only the occasional sparkle and vein of silver. There wasn't a true arch in sight, only post and lintel construction. Except the puzzling part was that she was certain the arch was adopted during Orithyia XI's tenure.

"This is the temple, little one," the woman said, interrupting Aurora's wandering thoughts.

"What is your name?" Aurora asked, feeling sheepish for not asking earlier. She'd been so caught up in her own thoughts that she hadn't thought to ask.

"Cilla." She smiled as she helped Aurora down from the cart.

"Thank you, Cilla, for your kindness. My name is Aurora. I don't think there are many who would have helped a stranger, but I am grateful that you did," Aurora said as she accepted Cilla's help from the cart.

"I like to think there are a great many like me. It's the strangest thing though, I took a detour when I saw a bright light. I discovered you in the field not long after. Maybe it was fate that we met when we did, Aurora."

Goddesses, she hoped not. If this were fate, then that meant Phaedra was always meant to die. That Drakon was meant to bring absolute, unhindered destruction to her homeland. That she was supposed to find herself broken, bloodied and hobbling into the ancient temple of Knowledge, lost and miserable.

Cilla helped Aurora up steps that were a touch too big for her to comfortably navigate in her current state. From there, she was handed off to a kindly medic, a man with greying hair and a soft smile, wearing the deep grey robes of an initiate of Knowledge. One who was also much too large, just as everyone else she'd seen so far.

The medic sat her on a cot in a long line of them and asked about her wounds and tested her range of motion, his touch gentle and profession-al. He ordered splints, a sling, a variety of poultices, bandages, crutches and bedrest. As he did so, Aurora swallowed down her anxiety over the question she feared asking. But when he was about to leave, she caught the hem of his tunic. If she didn't figure this next part out, she might lose her mind.

"How long has Orithyia XI been the high priestess?"

He blinked in surprise.

His reaction was to be expected. Even a peasant of Trisia would know such a thing. New high priestesses had always been installed with a great deal of fanfare after a lengthy, Trisia-wide period of official mourning for the late high priestess.

"Seventeen years. Where have you been that you did not know this?" he asked, full of concern.

Seventeen years! A number of ill-omen, because it was in the seventeenth year of Orithyia XI's tenure that the very first cycle of calamity occurred. Had she escaped one apocalypse, only to endure another—the first, in fact?

"I have... come from very far away," she replied woodenly.

But maybe she hadn't been brought here to suffer. Maybe the artefact had brought her to this exact place after listening to her heart's dearest wish—to save Phaedra. If Aurora were here now, with her knowledge of the future, of Drakon, maybe she could prevent the deaths of Phaedra and Silvanus completely.

"Is there anyone in the city that I could contact for you? Anywhere you have friends who will take you in?" he asked.

The question caught her off-guard. Tears stung her eyes. She had no one here. Who would help her in her quest? Who would vouch for her? What was a lone woman without the help of the hero of the holy sword supposed to do to a monster like Drakon? What could she possibly accomplish alone?

"No."

"You're welcome to stay here while you recover, if you like."

"Thank you," she whispered.

But there should be one person Aurora could trust—High Priestess Orithyia. She might not be *her* Orithyia, but she was in the best position to help Aurora. And Aurora could give her what no one else could—a glimpse of the future and a chance to prevent it.

"Is there any chance I could speak with High Priestess Orithyia? It is very important."

Her hopes crashed the moment she saw the very specific polite look on his face that she was accustomed to giving pushy worshippers while she'd worked in the temple as an acolyte.

"The high priestess rarely sees worshippers in private, but when you recover, you are welcome to put in a request with her aide."

"I see. Thank you." Aurora returned his smile as he left her side.

Of course the high priestess wouldn't see a strange woman who was carted to the entrance of the temple for a private audience. But Aurora couldn't let that deter her. If she couldn't get in the front door, she merely needed to find a window to crawl through. Or a set of secret passages built into the library directly to the high priestess' chambers. Would they be here, in the earliest iteration of the temple?

After she was given crutches, Aurora hobbled into the library, wincing with every click of her crutches, in awe of all the books she would be the only one of her generation to be able to read. Honeycombed shelves twice as tall as herself were bursting with scrolls, their handles inscribed with the treasured knowledge held within. In the cycles of chaos and calamity between the world she walked in and the one she was born to, much had been lost. All that was left of some texts were oblique references in books that had been written hundreds of years later. But now was not the time to be led astray by the temptation of undiscovered ancient poets and orators.

It was nearly impossible to be discreet in her current state. Not only was she made of unusual proportions and wrapped up as though she were made entirely of splints and bandages, but she also carried the distinct scent of poultices and limped around in her trousers in a sea of skirts. She soldiered on, pretending to peruse books. Eventually, she lost her status as an immediately interesting curiosity, giving her time to ascertain that the secret passage did indeed exist. The switch was a metal handle holding up a small oil lamp, the telltale sign of crumbling plaster beneath it giving her hope that the temple plans had remained the same even across time.

But how to activate the switch without attracting undue attention? She supposed she could remain in the library until it emptied out, but there was no guarantee she would be able to stand for that long. It was hard enough in her current condition. Aurora waited until her section of the library was sufficiently empty to risk it, her heart hammering in her chest.

As she pulled hard on the sconce next to the large shelf, the mechanism clicked and shifted. A great rush of air blew through the section, rattling scrolls and leaving a mess of loose papers scattered on the floor. So much for stealth. Aurora ducked into the alcove, her heart sinking. Getting inside was only the first hurdle. The second? Climbing the hundred or so steps up to the high priestess' chambers. In splints.

"Who made this mess?" a librarian shouted.

The third hurdle made itself known by locking alarmed, accusatory eyes with Aurora.

"You! What do you think you're doing? What have you done to the wall? Paladins! Paladins, quickly!"

Aurora tripped the mechanism to close the passage door, but it was only a matter of time before she was stopped. Her quest, and potentially her freedom, could be ended before she even spoke to Orithyia.

Aurora propped her crutches against the edge of the door, hoping to jam it shut. From here, it was a matter of dragging herself up the dark, cramped staircase lit only by the odd peephole into the library itself.

Sweating, swearing, and with tears blurring her vision, Aurora had made it halfway up the steps when the commotion began in earnest below.

"Someone, break down this wall!"

Goddesses, if that happened, she'd be thrown in prison, potentially executed. She couldn't let it happen. Phaedra couldn't be allowed to die. She would not be catapulted to this ancient time and let it end like this. The creature inside her began to unfurl, stretching out as her panic rose. *One more step*, she chanted in her mind. Let her get one more step in before everything came crashing down again. *Only a few steps left*, she told herself. She was so close to her goal, to making all the horror she'd endured mean something.

"Stand back!"

A resounding crash came from below as a gust of wind whipped through the passage. Heavy boots echoed in the dark.

Aurora threw herself up the last steps, fumbling for the lever that would let her enter the chamber.

"Stop! Don't move!"

Aurora's heart leapt into her throat as she tumbled through the opening and into the high priestess' chamber. When she got to her knees and looked around, the high priestess, robed in the deepest black, was already surrounded by clerics armed to the teeth. Paladins of Knowledge. She'd not recognised them. There were scant few in her time. Moments later, she was tackled back to the floor, crying out in surprise and pain as she was searched.

"This was inside her cloak, High Priestess," one of the paladins said, passing Aurora's artefact to Orithyia.

"What is this, little intruder?"

"It sent me here from my homeland," Aurora answered carefully.

"Restrain her and bring her closer," Orithyia said.

Aurora was dutifully hauled before the high priestess and made to kneel, her pinned arms and splinted leg screaming in agony.

"Please, I mean you no harm, I only—"

"Snuck into a restricted area and barged into my private chambers with a strange item in your pocket," Orithyia interrupted, her voice like a whip. "Who told you about the passage?"

"I beg your forgiveness, but—"

"But nothing. You are clearly not of Trisia, yet you know of places which you should not. What am I to think but that you are some kind of malefactor and this item is a weapon? You will be taken to the temple of Justice, questioned about this item and how you came to know of the passage, then sentenced," Orithyia said, waving to the paladins holding her pinned as she passed the artefact on to one of the priestesses of Knowledge. "If you are very lucky, they will only cut out your tongue."

Ah, goddess, no. It couldn't end like this. She had to convince the high priestess not to sentence her to death.

"The cycle of chaos will be upon you this year. If you have not already seen the omens for it, you will soon. But it won't just be a cycle of chaos, it will be a cycle of calamity, the likes of which Trisia has never experienced!" Aurora shouted as she was dragged from the room.

The high priestess held up a hand, bidding the paladins to bring her closer. Aurora's heart swelled with hope. Until Orithyia gripped Aurora's jaw in a painful hold, inspecting her with a frightfully cold look.

"You really believe what you're saying. Either you're an oracle, or you're mad, as only the mad believe their delusions to be truth. Do you know when there was last a true oracle in Trisia?" Aurora shook her head as best she could. Orithyia's glare said it all. "Never. All were false. Only the omens, interpreted by a high priestess, may tell us the future, not the ravings of mad foreigners. Take this blasphemer from my sight."

No, not like this. What could she say to sway Orithyia? What could she give her that would win her the woman's trust? What did she remember from this time that would prove her word?

"The first monstrosities! I know where the first monstrosities will appear this cycle!"

"I'm sure you do, little creature," Orithyia scoffed.

"The Colonnades Of The Colossus! When they appear there, you'll know I'm speaking the truth!"

The paladins dragged her from the chamber and through the topmost level of the temple. All eyes were trained on her in morbid curiosity. Aurora's tears ran freely then. The only person who barely spared her a glance was a senior priestess carrying a haphazard array of books, scrolls and one badly balanced astrolabe, hurrying towards the high priestess' chambers. Aurora was carried almost to the door of the temple when a winded-looking priestess halted their march.

"Wait! The high priestess would like one more word with the foreigner."

Confused but obedient, the paladins dragged Aurora back up the many steps of the temple staircases. She felt like a broken ragdoll by the time she was hauled before the high priestess and shoved down onto the floor.

"Bind her arms. Give me the switch and leave. All of you."

"But, Your Holiness—"

"Do as you're told," Orithyia retorted.

When it was just the two of them, Orithyia sighed.

"I have just received word that the sinister planets have fully aligned. Any priestess worth her salt could have predicted that this would happen. That in itself doesn't always herald a cycle of chaos. But I've also been informed of omens appearing in places all over Trisia. Not only that, but the omens are especially dire." She tipped Aurora's chin up with the switch. "Explain this cycle of calamity."

"A cycle of calamity occurs when Drakon, the Beast of Old, rises. He is a great serpent with red scales and many horns who slithers through the skies on a bank of dark clouds. Monstrosities arise wherever he goes, and he has the power to rain fire and molten rock down from above."

"Are these the folktales from your realm?"

"They're not folktales! I've seen him! I've experienced his power first-hand! He brings the apocalypse with him."

"Clearly not, if there is more than one tale of this Drakon, more than one cycle of his coming. How is the beast destroyed?"

"A hero who wields the holy sword of Justice, an avatar gifted with wild magic as well as Her divine magic."

"You worship the Triad in your homeland?"

Aurora nodded.

"I'm an initiate of Knowledge."

"And what is your high priestess called? Where is your homeland?"

Aurora looked away. Goddess, how was she supposed to explain the circumstances without sounding altogether mad? Orithyia lashed out with the switch, her blow a hairsbreadth from Aurora's face. She flinched.

"I'm not asking these questions as some kind of social nicety, and I will not ask twice."

Sweat rolled down her aching back. If she didn't answer honestly, the high priestess was sure to know. But if she spoke the truth, would it set her free?

"My high priestess is Orithyia CLXI of the Viridian empire. This is my homeland, or it will be, in several thousand years. The artefact you took from me allowed me to travel back in time. That is why I know about the passage, that the cycle of calamity begins this year, and that the first monstrosities will appear at The Colonnades Of The Colossus. Because that is what is written in our history books," Aurora replied, mustering her remaining courage to look Orithyia in the eye.

Orithyia raked her with an assessing gaze, her brows furrowing.

"Either you're the maddest creature in all of Trisia, or you bear the saddest fate in the Tapestry."

She wished she were mad. At least then, Phaedra wouldn't have truly died. If only everything were just the delusions of a madwoman.

"What did you hope to accomplish by telling me these things?"

"I want to stop the calamity from ever happening. I want to kill Drakon so that he never rises again. I must. It's the only way to prevent the future I experienced from happening."

Orithyia laughed.

"You wish to change the course of time?"

"Yes."

"Are you certain? All threads on the Tapestry are connected. If you remove one, there is no telling how many will be affected. Everything you knew, all your *history*, could be altered beyond recognition."

Without the calamity occurring every few hundred years, no doubt the whole of Trisia would look very different. What could they accomplish without the need to rebuild every few centuries? How many brilliant minds would be born and flourish if they weren't lost to the cyclical annihilation or the simple need to survive? How much of this world could be saved, preserved, if it weren't wiped out or altered beyond repair? The cycles of chaos would still occur, tied to the alignment of the sinister planets, but without Drakon, maybe her time would stand a chance, even if she never returned. Even if she had no home to go back to, or it was as foreign to her as this one. As long as Phaedra had a chance to be born, to live, to love, to thrive, then it would all be worth it.

"I'll take that chance. The alternative...it cannot be allowed to happen."

"You are a determined little thing, if nothing else." Orithyia smiled. "What are you called?"

"Aurora."

"Aurora, I will take the information you've given me under advisement and rescind my order to have you arrested. On the chance that you're not simply mad, you will be treated with the respect due to a visiting member of a foreign temple's pantheon—with a caveat. I will not tolerate you running around my temple, causing trouble. Queen Flora owes me a favour and is accustomed to hosting foreign dignitaries. You will be assigned quarters in the guest palace here in the capital, and you will remain there until further proof is acquired as to your trustworthiness. Until then, you will keep what we spoke about here to yourself. Understood?"

Aurora's heart swelled with hope. She'd done it. If she could continue to gain Orithyia's trust, she could prevent Drakon from ever bringing another calamity. Phaedra would live.

"Thank you!"

"Do not thank me. If the monstrosities don't appear at the Colonnades, I shall have you blinded, your tongue removed and your feet cut off, after which you will be forced to crawl your way out of this queendom or be eaten by wild dogs, whichever comes first."

Orithyia pulled a cord near her chair. The door opened immediately. Another strange paladin of Knowledge stepped inside.

"Remove her bindings and see she is comfortably situated in the guest palace. Tell Her Majesty that I'm calling in that favour she owes me."

Aurora swallowed, praying the events at the Colonnades had been recorded faithfully and passed down the ages without embellishment. If not, Drakon would be the least of her worries.

CHAPTER 11
THERON

Theron glared up at the enormous statue of Knowledge.

In Her temple, he could feel Her presence in every breath he took. Like the lone mourner at a party, the black columns of the temple were a distinct incongruity in the colourful capital of Altanus, the dark robes marking the initiated devout, tapestries the shade of midnight billowing in the breeze, the glittering black floors like an endless abyss. But the temple and everything inside it, though sharing the same hue, had been embellished with the occasional sparkle and vein of silver, making him feel as though he'd been thrust into the night sky. It was as though he were a tiny speck in the universe.

Knowledge, She of the fathomless gaze, stared back, obsidian gemstone eyes glittering.

If She were present, why did She despise him so? He'd lavished the temples with all due respect and offerings. He'd constructed a statue of himself to be placed at Her feet, hands clasped, so that a part of him would always be here, praying for Her favour. And yet that bitch Orithyia blighted his lands in Her name.

"Some might consider a stare that hateful blasphemous, Your Majesty."

"Head Priestess Dia." Theron lifted the aged priestess' hand, touching her obsidian ring to his forehead.

"How is my naughtiest student?" she asked, a gentle smile on her wrinkled face. So deceptive, her smile. He remembered all the times she'd rapped his knuckles with her cane as a boy when he'd dared mouth off.

"Vexed. I came for your counsel," he answered.

"Follow me," she said, leading the way to an inner courtyard. It was a spot of living colour in the middle of the endless black of the temple. She lowered herself into a seat in the shade with some difficulty. Theron placed himself across from her.

"If this continues, there will be war," he began.

"There is no warring with bad luck, Your Majesty."

"This blight is her doing, Dia. It began the moment the spire was constructed," he insisted.

Dia sighed. She'd heard this argument from him many a time, refusing to place the blame where it so obviously belonged. Was it stubborn loyalty, or was he truly mistaken? Dia was a woman of tremendous intellect and wisdom. What was he missing that she saw?

"Now that the spire has fallen, I suppose you will discover the truth of your suspicions."

"And if I'm vindicated, what then?"

"Why do you ask, when you already know the answer?"

"Because I would hear it from you, the priestess who taught me as well as any could, a woman I trust."

"There are formal processes for deposing a high priestess. Processes, I hasten to add, that have only been used twice in the history of the temples."

"She should have already been taken to task for interfering in matters of state. She whispers in the ear of the Viridian Queen."

"As I whisper in yours, Your Majesty? As Myrina does?" Dia asked, a brow raised.

"That's different." He frowned.

"The temples have long provided counsel to monarchs when it is sought. There is no crime in that."

"You are the most stubborn person to ever live."

"I shall take that as a compliment, from the second most stubborn person to ever live."

He scowled, slouching in his seat.

"What am I to do then, Dia? My people sicken and starvation will soon follow. I've made every sacrifice and appeasement possible to the spirits in these lands. I have prayed to the intangible gods in the temples, I have made offerings to the tangible deities of the mountain, lakes, rivers, fields, cattle, sun, sky, winds, clouds, rain, and even those of every crop. I have pleaded with the spirits of every corner of this realm. I have done everything within my power to end this thrice-damned blight and pleaded to the divinities for that which I cannot do myself. Why am I being punished? My power is unmatched. My piety is unimpeachable!"

"Perhaps it is your humility which could use a little work?" she suggested, a devilish glint in her dark eyes.

"Do not mock me," he warned her, his anger rising.

"Your temper as well. You always were a hothead."

His wild magic writhed inside him.

"You think this is funny?" he demanded, pounding his fist on the arm of his chair.

"Maybe your humour too." She stared pointedly at his fist, unaffected by his outburst.

"You are lucky that drawing the blood of a priestess is punished by the goddess," he fumed.

"The Triad were wise in that." She nodded. "Have you considered taking a queen? If you had the magic of another monarch to help settle the spirits, perhaps many of these issues would be solved. I know the Lady Ino is eager to play the part."

Theron scowled. He didn't need anyone else's magic to help him do his sacred duty to the land of Aureum. Everything had been fine before that damned spire. And in any case, he wanted the Nivean princess and the alliance that would bring, not Lady Ino.

"I am not so weak as to need another monarch's aid, especially if it means putting a crown atop that harpy's head."

The lady in question had long set her cap at him, frightening off all her Aurean competition for his hand. It had worked in his favour during the years he spent waiting for one of the Nivean king's daughters to come of age and prove herself worthy.

"I'm sure Lady Ino would be most aggrieved to hear you call her that."

"Lady Ino is a cold, calculating, manipulative snake and she would laugh at any who thought otherwise."

"Ah, so the issue is that the two of you are alike in nature?"

"Did I come here for you to insult me, Dia? Is that all the help you offer when I sincerely ask for your advice?" He sighed. Had even Dia turned against him?

"Many innocents died when the spire fell."

She suspected the truth. Of course she would be angry with him. He'd done it knowing there had only been acolytes and initiates inside, not priestesses. They had been servants of the goddess, but none were important enough to warrant Her divine protection—or retribution.

"And I sent my cousin to save those who could be saved."

Of course, she'd returned with only corpses.

"Hmmm. Quite the gallant figure she cut, racing up the mountain on the back of her beasts."

Beasts that had probably feasted on the flesh of the fallen, given how few bodies she'd come back with. It was only a shame she hadn't returned with any evidence of Orithyia's scheming, seeing as how all of his had been utterly destroyed.

"She always did love a show," Theron said.

"She's not the only one," Dia retorted.

The stalemate dragged on as they stared at each other, neither giving an inch. But he knew from many years of experience that Dia never flinched first. He was wasting his time here.

"This has been a pleasant diversion from my duties, but it's time I get back to seeing to the needs of my people. Blessings of the Triad on you, Dia. I'll see myself out."

"Triad preserve the sun of Aureum," she replied, tone carefully neutral.

As he neared the edge of the courtyard, she spoke.

"Wait, come back here."

He paused, eyes widening in shock. Had she just blinked first? Had the Tapestry unravelled? Theron had never had such a golden opportunity to tease his former teacher. He smiled.

"A king does not take orders from a priestess, even one as venerable as you, Dia."

"He does if he recalls what happens to naughty schoolboys."

Theron took his time to return to her side and seat himself, drinking in this unprecedented victory. If only a court painter were present, so he could have the moment preserved for an eternity.

"Your smugness is unbecoming."

"What is a monarch, if not a person wrapped in smugness?"

But she didn't take the bait of his jest. In fact, her expression was neither reproachful nor placid. Her brows were knit with concern, her knuckles visible as she gripped the head of her cane.

"I received word that the sinister planets have fully aligned. There have also been omens. Very bad omens. I catalogued some of them myself. A cycle of chaos will begin soon. High Priestess Orithyia believes the first monstrosities will appear at The Colonnades Of The Colossus."

His stomach dropped to his knees.

"When?"

"Soon."

Fuck.

His shipment of grain was currently sitting on the other side of The Colonnades Of The Colossus, at the edge of the Queen's Road. The grain his people desperately needed. The very same grain Queen Flora and Orithyia had been trying to deny his people. If his enemies arrived there first with a few legions, who would stop them from taking that grain for themselves, commandeering it during a time of crisis, as was their right during a cycle of chaos?

Not only that, wherever the monstrosities first appeared during a cycle of chaos became a tainted place, one of deep superstition, the kind that drove people away from it for years to come. Monstrosities usually reappeared there many times unless the place was immediately purified by divine magic. That narrow land bridge was the only easily accessible land route for trade into Aureum. If monstrosities appeared there and were not dealt with swiftly, he could kiss that trade route goodbye for at least a decade.

His merchant fleet was woefully unprepared to pick up the slack. Already forced to sail through Viridian waters on the way to Gilvus and Roseum, stalked by pirates and bled dry by extortionate Viridian tolls at every harbour, it was not a viable option. He would be forced to drain the royal treasury just to bring in half of what the Colonnades did. He supposed he could use the mountain pass through to Niveum, but if King Enalos of Niveum had already refused to wed his daughter to Theron, what was the likelihood that he would help build a proper road through the pass so that traders were not deterred by rough terrain, bandits, and wild beasts?

No, he needed to protect the Colonnades at all costs. And his grain shipment.

"Does King Enalos know?"

"I suspect his priestesses have informed him as well."

Then there could be a total of three different royal legions marching to the end of the Queen's Road. It was one of the only places where three realms of Trisia met—Aureum, Viridis and Niveum. Three different royal legions who could lay claim to a king's ransom in grain. King Enalos of Niveum was an honourable man, but he would be a fool not to take such spoils for himself.

"Then I must make haste. Thank you, Dia."

He rose from his seat, lifting her hand in his to touch her obsidian ring to his forehead. If he wanted to beat the other monarchs and their legions there, he would have to use his cousin's beasts to do it, and she was likely to try to haggle with him for some problematic privilege or favour. That alone could take an hour he didn't have to spare.

"Be careful, Your Majesty..." She paused as if she were hesitant to say more. What had come over his teacher? Since when did she hesitate in anything? No one had walked through life more assuredly than she.

"Don't keep me in suspense."

"It would be...inconvenient if you were wounded by a monstrosity, Your Majesty."

"What have you read in the omens, Dia?"

He would take those with divine magic with him, paladins from the three temples, along with weapons and armour blessed by those with divine magic. Even if he were attacked, between his martial skill and the magic of those on hand, he should be in no danger. After all, monstrosities weren't known to be intelligent, merely ferocious. But if he were injured openly, in full view of his soldiers, they might worry it was an ill omen and demand that a high priestess should see to his wounds. A king touched by such evil was considered tainted, his judgement corrupted until a high priestess had blessed him.

Normally, he would not concern himself with fear over that. A king should lead from the front. And the High Priestess Myrina, his aunt, resided in Passion's temple here in Altanus. *She* at least had no interest in meddling in his affairs, unless they were matters of a passionate marriage alliance, which he had always shot down for the foolish fantasy it was.

"Only that you may be absent for some time."

"But I'm expected to return?"

"Knowledge has not seen fit to reveal that to me."

He clenched his teeth. Was he fated to die? But what was he supposed to do then? Let the Colonnades be tainted and his grain stolen? Unacceptable. He would not cower in his palace, dishonouring the royal blood flowing through his veins. He was the king of Aureum. If he were fated to die, then he would face his end with defiance.

It was only too bad that he'd needed to wait so long for one of King Enalos' daughters to mature and show promise. If she'd been but a few years older, they might have wed before the spire had been constructed, with an heir to the throne already born. But Fate was rarely so kind.

And if Theron died? Queen Flora would soon follow.

"Then I will meet my fate head-on. And if anything happens to me, I will give Aureum to Batea. And woe to Viridis then, for I am all that stands between them and her bloodthirst."

If Theron must drink from a poisoned chalice, then he would ensure his enemies choked on his blood.

Dia's eyes widened with alarm.

"You cannot mean that."

"Oh, I think I do. Pray for my safe return, Dia."

Theron strode from the temple in high spirits. A race and a battle lay before him. Just the thing to get his heart pumping. As much as he enjoyed court intrigues, sometimes a good fight was just the thing to let off a little steam. And if this was to be his last? Well, he would make it spectacular enough to live on in songs and legends.

But it was a melancholy thing to think he might never return to his great city. Altanus was the jewel of Trisia. Here, even the lowliest peasant had a roof over their head and food in their bellies. Its streets were lined with fragrant flowers and towering trees giving shade to all. Clean water glistened from beautifully sculpted fountains, surrounded by buildings decorated in the most saturated hues. Merchants dressed as richly as nobles from other realms, courtesy of mines overflowing with precious metals and gemstones. His nobles were fat off the abundance of their territories, and his treasuries were overflowing. Only the blight had dulled some of his city's shine, strained his coffers, and cast a pall over the countryside. Hopefully, soon, that sad chapter would come to an end. He only wished he would live long enough to see it.

Theron walked through the streets on his way to Batea's palace, a bevvy of guards and aides at his side, his people stepping aside for his entourage and bowing in his presence. As he gave Polydorus his instructions for advising Batea in his absence and sent his aides off with orders for the upcoming confrontation at the Colonnades, they rushed off to the various palace offices, barracks and temples. He arrived at Batea's palace and took the steps up to her home two at a time, his coming welcomed by every member of her staff. When he found her at last, she was in her courtyard, sharpening her swords.

Clearly, she was in a good mood and content to receive visitors. When she wasn't, she allowed her beasts to prowl the courtyard—most vicious amongst them were her chickens. Had Theron not the wild magic of healing, he would have the scars to prove just how spiteful the fowl could be. Luckily, he didn't need those particular creatures today.

"I need your beasts."

"I thought you hated my beasts," she replied, never taking her eyes off her blade.

"A cycle of chaos is beginning."

"Oh? Hopefully, the first monstrosities appear in Boreas. Preferably in Orithyia's bed. While she's in it."

"The omens say they're going to appear at The Colonnades Of The Colossus."

She looked up from her task then.

"The grain."

"The trade route," he added.

"Shit."

"Exactly."

"I'll go. I have just the beasts for the job. I can be there in a matter of hours. How fast can those temple rats be readied?" She stood, sheathing her blades and grabbing the bronze cuirass she'd finished polishing nearby.

"You're not going."

She had just secured the first strap of her cuirass when she paused.

"Then who?" she asked, furious.

"I'm going. You're staying here."

Her nostrils flared with anger.

"Then you can't have my beasts." She glared, defiant.

"What if I gave you war as your reward?"

She raised her brow, interest piqued.

"You have my attention."

"Dia's omens tell her I will be gone for some time. In my absence, you'll be in charge of Aureum. And if anything happens to me..."

She shot him a dark look.

"I want to fight a war at your side, not because you're dead."

"And I don't relish dying. So rule well in my stead, and make a vow to Justice if I fall."

"It is a pity that the dualists lost their battle against the temples. Because I would rather swear to Vengeance in that case, given the chance."

"Don't let the priestesses hear you say that." He frowned.

Though the dualists worshipped both aspects of the goddesses, Knowledge and Lies, Passion and Death, Justice and Vengeance, that very same worship gave the sinister planets the power they now wielded. Though he would prefer to live and let live when it came to the piety of his people, a cycle of chaos should never be courted. It was why he didn't interfere if the temples sent out their paladins to hunt down dualists in his realm—unless they belonged to Orithyia.

Batea's bark of laughter echoed in the courtyard.

"Let them sick their dogs on me. Now *that* would be a real fight."

He said nothing more on the matter, following when she led him to her stables, if the pits where she created, moulded and trained her pets could be called something so pedestrian. One pit in particular caught his eye. Her favourite pets were the giant serpents, beasts descended from dragons and great serpents who had lost their ability to fly. But the ones he saw were struggling to lift off the ground as they writhed, impressive horns radiating out from their scaly brows.

"Beautiful, aren't they? I'm close with them. One day, you and I will ride my serpents through the very skies, like in the legends."

The military applications alone had his heart racing with excitement. But today, it was not to be. As they passed by beasts left and right, his heart sank. They neared the cages for the flying creatures.

Not the eagles.

"These should be enough."

A shiver of revulsion raced down Theron's spine.

The eagles were faster than any in Batea's stables, smarter than the average man, and could carry several soldiers each. The problem was that the beasts had taken a strong dislike to him the moment they'd laid eyes on him, and delighted in doing aerial acrobatics whenever he was in their saddle. It was hardly the most dignified way to travel, but it was the fastest. If he died, he hoped the poets skipped over his mode of transportation... and how sick he would be the moment he landed.

Think of the grain.

It was what he chanted to himself over and over as the wicked beasts took to the skies, thirty warriors on their backs, a third of those from the temples. It was what he chanted over and over during the hours the feathered bastard he was strapped to crossed the Dragon's Spine Mountains and the trade road beyond like a drunken acrobat. And it was what he chanted when they finally set down and he nearly fell to his knees and threw up in front of his warriors. He was grateful he'd taken his spear with him, so he had something to prop himself up with.

Theron glared at the eagle. One day, he would slay that beast and make an extravagant fan of its feathers. Once plucked, he would roast the creature and serve it at a celebratory dinner.

Don't think of food.

His gorge rose. Theron breathed deeply, concentrating on standing without dizziness sending him to his knees. When at last he felt more like a man than a tumbleweed, he got the lay of the land. The merchant's supply caravan was sitting exactly where he'd said it would be, on the other side of the Colonnades. It was too bad Canthus hadn't set out earlier and secured the grain before now. They'd passed overhead of his general on their way here, plodding along at a normal pace on the backs of sensible, noble, land-dwelling lopers.

"Get the grain to this side of the Colonnades," he ordered his warriors. "The rest of you remain here while we wait for the monstrosities."

They needed to secure the supplies before any Viridian or Nivean soldiers came around their respective mountain ranges to poach his supplies. And before anyone could arrive and accuse him of marching soldiers into the territory of another monarch. Such a thing could result in a diplomatic incident.

Theron watched with great satisfaction as the errant caravan attendants were relieved of their goods or meekly marched across the Colonnades. Hopefully, this sent a message to the other Trisian merchants that if they tried to go back on their words, Aureum would give them no choice but to uphold their bargains. If Canthus was doing his job, the merchant in charge of the operation was being dragged behind the warriors on their way here, fearing for his life every step of the way.

It was a low blow for Viridis to enlist independent merchants against him. He was ashamed not to have thought of it himself first. Perhaps, in retaliation, he should make a deal with some of the pirates plying the Viridian coastline. If the Colonnades became a place tainted by monstrosities in the minds of travellers, then perhaps the pirates could raid the Viridian cargo ships to make up for the shortfall of trade goods.

Just as the last cart laden with his grain began crossing the Colonnades, a legion of Viridian soldiers and paladins rounded the edge of the Dragon's Tail Mountains. Theron's smile grew. They were too late. The end of the Queen's Road was the border of Viridis' official control. And they hadn't been present when his warriors had crossed, so it was too late to use their intrusion into Viridian territory as political provocation. Theron leaned against a nearby boulder, enjoying the cool shade and his triumph.

As they glared at each other from across the divide, the sun travelled through the sky, the shadows of the Dragon's Spine Mountains beginning to stretch across the narrow valley. The grain shipment was well on its way into the winding canyon pass when the shadows began to shift. At first, Theron thought it a mere trick of the light, but then the shadows began to shift again, moving as if made of gently lapping water.

"Monstrosities, Your Majesty!" cried one of the paladins, his blade drawn.

Theron readied his spear and shield as three of his archers took to the skies on the eagles, every one of their arrows tipped in divine magic. The old texts spoke of monstrosities that could fly, and he would not be caught flatfooted against airborne foes. As the shadows began bubbling around him, he stepped into the light, his heart hammering. Batea was going to be furious that she'd missed this fight.

The paladins spread their magic over the widest possible section of shadows, dispelling the evil rising within them, but there was simply too much ground to cover. As the first monstrosity reared its ugly head,

Theron thrust his spear into the beast. It dissolved back into the bubbling dark, destroyed by the divine machine infused into his weapon. Just as he wondered why his ancestors had been so troubled by the creatures, three more rose up where the last one had been felled. In a matter of moments, the monstrosities could not be beaten back before they'd fully emerged from the darkness.

Theron and his warriors began losing ground almost immediately, even with the paladins' divine magic dispelling beasts left and right. He kept them at bay with his spear, grateful that even the ones with prodigious reach could not match his own. Step by step, they were driving his line back towards the Dragon's Spine. If they were caught there, they would be overwhelmed from all sides. But if they retreated to the Colonnades where the natural terrain would bottleneck the enemy? They could gain the advantage without fear of being flanked.

"Retreat to the Colonnades!" Theron commanded, his voice booming across the battlefield. He signalled for his airborne archers to lay down cover as they retreated.

His warriors reformed at the narrowest chokepoint on the southern half of the Colonnades, and when the next wave came, they were ready for them. His spearmen gouged the monstrosities with every thrust, killing them with ease. Behind them, the paladins cast their magic, streamers of light like whips, dispelling individual monstrosities with a touch. The tide of battle had turned.

Theron held his position at the front, battle fervour singing through his limbs. Whenever he tired, he used his wild magic to bolster himself. As the shadows lengthened, the monstrosities thinned. In his confidence, Theron pushed forward into an empty pocket.

And immediately regretted it.

The shadows burst up underneath him like a geyser, throwing him back. He caught himself in time to see a field of massive, claw-tipped hands rising up from the shadows. One hand reached out before he could stab it with his spear, capturing him in a punishing grip. Theron healed himself as fast as the monstrosity broke him. It shrieked as its corrupted body met the divine magic in his armour, and yet unlike the others before, it remained intact long enough to throw him. Airborne, Theron sailed over the battle formation of his warriors. The landing stunned him, breaking bone after bone, his breath leaving him in a painful gush. When his head stopped spinning, he called on his magic to get him back on his feet and clear his mind.

"Keep formation!" he called before his warriors thought to do something as foolish as see to his welfare.

Spitting blood from his mouth, Theron jogged to grab his spear and shield. He would teach that especially foul beast just who it was fucking with. He'd almost made it back to his warriors when he heard the shriek of monstrosities. They were close. Too close. Blood turned to ice in his veins.

Theron was surrounded.

His foe had followed him, slithering through the shadows under the Colonnades and breaking over the edges of the pass like a wave. His soldiers were now split, half facing the advancing monstrosities from the mountains, the rest turned around to fight the ones forming at their backs. The archers above him peppered the monstrosities around him, thinning the line enough for him to retreat. But that retreat brought him closer to the Viridian side of the Colonnades, where the Viridian soldiers and paladins hadn't managed to bottleneck the beasts and were being slaughtered wholesale.

Was this where he died? Cut off from his soldiers, a lone spearman could only do so much. But not everyone could heal themselves as they were cut to ribbons. Eventually, his soldiers would work their way to him. Theron vowed to hold out until there was nothing in his veins but spite.

"Come at me, you ugly bastards!"

The monstrosities obliged, lunging at him. He managed to keep them at bay until one bubbled up from his shadow and clamped onto his leg with its jagged teeth. It shrieked as it died to the divine magic in his greaves, but the wound remained. Theron sealed his wounds as the next one closed in on him, evading his spear. Its claws dug into his thigh. He bashed it with his shield, dispelling it.

But in the split moment that he lost his braced position, the tide turned. The evil hands were back, dragging him from his feet. The beasts pounced on him then, ripping away his spear and the short sword attached to the belt at his hip. He used his shield to protect his head and chest, but the creatures savaged him. He fought against his own destruction, healing himself again and again, regrowing flayed skin, mending ripped tendons, piecing together shattered bones, replenishing blood. Beasts died moments after they came in contact with his armour, but every bite and blow dented and damaged the metal. Soon, they would tear it from him completely. Then it would be a race to see how fast he could regrow limbs.

Just as the next wave of horrors tore his greaves from his legs, a great light streaked above him, dissolving the monstrosities in an instant. Theron leapt to his feet, dizzy, and turned around. He spotted his spear and raced for it, lest the monstrosities recover. But when he got his bearings again, the monstrosities were mostly gone. In the distance, a young man with an enormous bow made of light aimed an array of arrows at his warriors. They had turned around to face the remaining hoard at the chokepoint. They wouldn't see their attacker before he skewered their back line.

"No!" Theron screamed.

On instinct, he hurled his spear at the young man, piercing him through the leg just as he let his arrows fly.

The arrows ripped through his people to the monstrosities beyond, obliterating the creatures in the blink of an eye. He expected his people to fall to the magical missiles, but they remained standing, entirely unharmed. The same could not be said for the young man. Pinned and bleeding, teeth gritted in agony, he shot Theron a killing glare. His appearance was unremarkable—brown hair just long enough to be tied back, tanned skin, grey eyes, neither handsome nor ugly.

Behind him, the Viridian general cried out.

"The king of Aureum has attacked the avatar of Justice!"

Fuck.

Theron had long stayed his hand, fearing the wrath of the goddess for striking a high priestess. How much worse would his punishment be for attacking the embodiment of a goddess Herself? He rushed over to the young man, calling up his wild magic, praying he could make this right.

"My sincerest apologies. I thought you meant to attack my men."

"I gathered that," the young man growled.

"Will you allow me to assist and heal you?"

"That depends, is your healing magic as good as your aim?"

Theron grabbed the spear's shaft.

"This won't hurt."

"I doubt that."

Theron cut the threads that carried pain from the young man's wound, pulling out the spear in one fluid motion. A heartbeat later, he healed the gaping wound, returning sensation the moment the operation was done. Goddess, he hoped he didn't have more people to heal. Once the battle fervour faded, he was going to sleep for days.

The young man stood, shocked that he could do so. He held out his hand.

"Hyllus of Niveum, Avatar of Justice."

"King Theron of Aureum."

Theron gripped the young man's forearm in greeting.

"I'd heard of your magic, but never thought to experience it myself," Hyllus said.

"Likewise. Though I am sorry it was necessary."

"As am I."

"I don't suppose you could ask your goddess not to curse the next twenty generations of my bloodline?" he asked, wondering when the divine punishment would happen.

"I'll see what I can do." Hyllus' smile faded as fast as it appeared. "Though the Viridians might prove to be a more immediate threat." He nodded at the bloodied general confidently striding across the boundary that marked Theron's territory.

Theron squinted. Damn. He recognised the man climbing over the corpses of his men with a fervent light in his eyes.

"Ah, Stentor. The ever-faithful lapdog of an unparalleled bitch," Theron said, smiling when Hyllus coughed to cover a snort of laughter. "Before he makes a nuisance of himself, I'm curious. Why has an avatar been summoned?"

"Are you ungrateful for my assistance?"

"Not at all. I prefer living, given the option. But I sincerely doubt Justice called upon you for my benefit."

Had an avatar been summoned to deal with Orithyia? If he had, Theron would pray at Justice's temple every day for the rest of his life.

"All I know is that there is a great evil in Trisia and I've been called upon to end it."

Typical divine omen drivel. Open to interpretation by any with an ounce of an agenda. Orithyia would take every opportunity to point her shrivelled finger at Theron. Which was why he needed to be the first to point the young man elsewhere.

"Be careful who you trust, Hyllus. Every ambitious cur in Trisia will happily point you at their foes."

"Present company excluded, of course?" Hyllus grinned.

Theron laughed. Hyllus was too good-natured to survive court politics for long. He hoped whoever, or whatever, he'd been called upon to destroy was blindingly obvious. Else Theron would soon find himself declared a public enemy, should Orithyia get her claws into the young man.

"No. Present company very much included. All I ask is that you keep an open mind, and pray for good judgement."

"Only a good man would give such advice, Your Majesty."

"I am a good king, not a good man. And a man can be only one, for the crown either grinds good men to dust or leads them to an early grave. Only kings who discard their hearts get to keep their heads."

"I shall keep that in mind."

Stentor strode over to them, a gleam in his bright eyes. He was certain he'd found wounded prey, and would do all in his power to ensure he retrieved his master's prize.

"Do you deny it, King Theron? Do you deny that you attacked the avatar of Justice?"

Just as Theron was about to tell the general that he had stepped into Aureum's territory and invite him to go fuck himself, the world went dark. Theron blinked. The unending darkness remained. There was no sound here, no hint of anything living. He turned around, but there was nothing in every direction. An abyss. He called out, only to find he had no voice. Panic growing, he tried to walk from his current position, but his feet were stuck fast. Was this Justice's punishment? Would he be trapped in this realm full of nothing for all eternity?

Between one ragged breath and the next, light returned. Screams rang in his ears. Pain exploded all across his body. Blood coated his hands. Hands that gripped his spear. Beneath him, the Viridian general with eyes wide stared up at him in terror, the spear tip a hairsbreadth from his face, the bloodied, broken bodies of Viridian soldiers at his sides.

"King Theron! Please, come back to your senses!"

He raised his head. Hyllus stood before him, terror in his boyish features, the tip of a sword pointed at his neck. One wrong move, and Theron would be dead.

"Don't make me kill you, Your Majesty!"

Theron raised his hands, stumbling back from the gruesome slaughter. A sense of bone-deep wrongness muddied his thoughts. Stentor scrambled to his feet, face white as a sheet. What had happened?

"King Theron!" his soldiers called from behind.

They stood on his side of the Colonnades, eyes wide with horror. But that meant...

"King Theron, you have slaughtered Viridian soldiers on Viridian soil."

Beyond the slaughter, a man in Nivean armour, with grey streaking his black hair, surveyed the scene with disappointment. Was that King Enalos riding atop a loper? What was he doing here? No, worse, he'd seen Theron cross into Viridian territory and commit a crime that could mean war.

"It seems I have," Theron replied, aghast.

Monarchs were sworn to guard their realms and not to trespass on the realms of others unless invited—or urged to by the tangible gods that bestowed their authority on them. His sense of rightness, of belonging, had been torn away the moment he'd stepped across the border in a state of cursed madness. He was without the anchor of Aureum's innate magics.

Agony radiated up from his palm. On the back of his hand, a glittering, diamond-like mark appeared. The mark of Justice's displeasure—of his divine punishment.

Had that abyss and ensuing madness been Justice's wrath? Her punishment? If so, it was fitting. For now he would have to slaughter all of the witnesses in order to return home. He looked back to his warriors. They were willing to fight to the death for him, but not court a goddess' wrath, for Hyllus would also need to be slain. Under the laws that governed Trisia, he would have to plead for peace...to Queen Flora. He would also need to be cleansed by a high priestess, and the only one where he was about to be sent was that bitch Orithyia.

"By the laws of Trisia, you must travel to the Viridian capital to make restitution, or declare that you have begun a war unprovoked," King Enalos sighed.

Only a few Viridian soldiers remained, all eyeing him like he'd become a monstrosity. Perhaps he had.

"Put the Aurean king in chains!" Stentor ordered. "We bring the monstrosity-cursed blasphemer to the capital!"

There was no fighting his way out of this. No scheming that could save him. Unless he wished to stain his own honour, to become an outlaw king, he had no choice but to submit to his most rapacious enemies. Justice had seen him punished. He would never reclaim his throne until he was purified. He wouldn't even have the chance if Flora simply killed him before that. Theron only prayed Justice's anger was satisfied.

Theron allowed the Viridian dogs to bind his arms.

"I'm sorry, old friend," Enalos said.

Theron shook his head. The fault was his. But if his fate was to be made into Queen Flora's plaything, then he would not go meekly. He stood as tall as his binding allowed and turned to his soldiers.

"Send word to my cousin that I courted Justice's wrath and paid the price, and that if I do not return, she will become Queen of Aureum. Let my will be witnessed by King Enalos of Niveum." Theron turned to Enalos, raising his chin.

Enalos smiled, stroking a salt-and-pepper beard.

"I, King Enalos of Niveum, hereby witness King Theron's will. May the Triad have mercy on you."

With that, he was dragged off to the only cart that remained intact after the attack and shoved inside. Whether his captors would kill him before he reached Boreas was anyone's guess.

CHAPTER 12
AURORA

Aurora sat in the atrium of the guest palace, her face turned up towards the sun, eyes closed against the brilliant light...and the unpleasant reality that had become her life. Her ears twitched as distant giggles echoed behind her. She gripped the artefact in her hands and froze, waiting to find out if she would go unmolested. The next laugh came from further away. Aurora released a pent-up breath, her head leaning against the marble column at her back. The last few weeks had been their own kind of torture.

The guest palace was a prison and she was its newest curiosity.

The doors remained unlocked, the windows open and airy, but no one who entered this place of beautiful marble columns, mosaic floors, sumptuous décor, sparkling fish ponds and lush gardens ever left. This was where Queen Flora housed the sons and daughters of vassals whose loyalty was in question. It was where the last heirs of fallen territories mouldered away, forgotten. It was where, she knew, the kings and queens who fought against the future Viridian empire would spend their final days. In the future, it would become Phaedra's palace. It was now Aurora's cage.

She felt like nothing so much as an exotic animal on display for her fellow prisoners and the curious nobles of the Viridian court. The vivarium, the people here called it. It was not far off the mark. Here was where Flora displayed her trophies of flesh and blood. That the people here lived at all was a testament to their monarch's supposed magnanimity.

Most had thought her a damaged child when she'd arrived, covered in bandages and splints, and so had left her alone with her pain. But as the swelling went down and some of the bandages came off, they'd realised she was a woman grown, despite her short stature. They heaped their humiliations on her day and night, from forcing her into children's clothes to tossing her about despite her injuries, to making it nearly impossible to bathe in the shared baths without constant, unrelenting scrutiny. It could have been worse. The guards and attendants regularly withheld necessities unless sexually gratified—a fate she'd managed to avoid thus far.

She'd foolishly hoped that her stay would be a temporary one, until she'd been woken on her second night in this prison by a priestess of Knowledge. Robed in deep black, the woman had tossed the artefact at Aurora and told her that it was but an ancient calendar, not a magical device for time travel. After that, the medic stopped coming to tend to her wounds. A letter arrived a few days later informing her that if her information proved to be false, she would suffer appropriate punishment for lying twice to the high priestess.

Aurora had lived in a constant state of fear since.

Initially, she'd been elated to find herself somewhere familiar even if it made her heart ache with memories of her friend. She'd thought she'd understood what this place was in the ancient past and had been enchanted by the sumptuous décor, excited to think she would be the first of her age to glimpse it. But that feeling of coming home and the thrill of discovery soon soured when the true nature of this wretched place became clear. Terrified that the history books had been wrong, she'd walked every inch of the guest palace, looking for a way out. Knowing it was Phaedra's palace had given her the clues she needed to plan an escape. Even though much had changed over the millennia, just as it was at the temple of Knowledge, some hidden paths had survived unchanged. But she couldn't leave until she was fully healed. And so she endured as best she could.

Aurora turned the artefact—calendar—over in her hands. The rings no longer moved around it, having been too badly damaged, and were quite immune to her attempts to fix them. But as she'd had nothing else to distract her, she'd begun deciphering the symbols along the rings. Now that she knew what it was, she could see the numbers for hours, days, months, and years. On the outermost rings, she was certain the symbols represented constellations. They'd called it naught but a calendar, but her magic had drawn her to it. It no longer held whatever internal force had compelled her, but it couldn't just be a simple calendar. If she could fix it, maybe she could travel in time again.

Where would she even go?

A stampede of footsteps jolted her out of her thoughts. She stuffed the artefact into her small shoulder satchel and ducked between the column and greenery, manoeuvring her splinted leg with some difficulty. She curled up as best she could, making herself as small as possible under the foliage. Her hiding place had proved itself many times now. She got as comfortable as she could and listened.

"There's a new arrival!"

"The guards said it was a king. And that he'd been cursed by monstrosities."

Monstrosities? Then the first had appeared! Aurora's heart sank. Orithyia would have known, and if so, then she'd allowed Aurora to rot in this prison in spite of the information she'd provided.

"Would Flora actually keep him alive?"

"She'd better, unless she wants a war."

"Move over, I can't see him!"

"Shove off, I got here first!"

"Oh! Look! He's quite tall."

"Do you think he'd make good bed sport?"

"A king? Darling, kings don't have to be good bed sport with all the people throwing themselves at their feet. You'd be lucky if he even knew where your clit was."

Aurora blushed as the nobles burst into laughter.

"We'll have plenty of time to find out either way. If he's here, Flora is going to take her sweet time playing with him."

"Unless Orithyia wants him dead."

"Now *that* would be a perfectly good waste of all those muscles. Trust if he hasn't learned to suck cock and tease clit before now, he'll be learning to do so quickly."

Their vicious laughter burned Aurora's ears. A king was reduced to future whore here in this prison. Though at least there would be a new target for their curiosity. Unless the king proved to be the worst of the lot. Given her luck, it was almost a certainty. She shivered.

"Great Goddess, he's filthy. I can smell him from here."

"What in the Loom has he been rolling in? Monstrosity-cursed indeed! My eyes are watering."

"No, I don't think I'm going to greet this one. Not until after he's been bathed."

"Agreed. Oh, that stench is turning my stomach."

"I think I might faint."

"Disgusting."

"I heard there are cakes being served on the terrace. Shall we?"

"As long as it's on the terrace on the opposite side of the palace."

Another chorus of laughter, the stampede of footsteps following. Aurora waited until she was certain they were gone before she tried to exit her hiding place. She was lucky no one could see her grunting and sweating as she struggled to get to her feet, covered in soil. She was making adequate progress when the stench of animal dung hit her full-on.

In an instant, she dropped back into her hiding spot, freezing.

The doors to the palace opened, creaking slowly. The metal click of soldier's boots echoed on the mosaic floors.

"Welcome to your new home."

"If you want to keep your tongue, you had best unlock my shackles and quickly," the king snarled.

The guard snorted. The delicate clinking of metal on metal signalled the keys. Aurora jumped when those same keys hit the ground just by her hiding place, sliding to a halt a mere two paces from her leg, hidden beneath foliage.

Merciful Triad, no.

"Fetch."

"You're a man without honour," the king said.

The soldier's laugh was uglier than even the prisoners of the guest palace.

"You're the newest addition to the vivarium, Your Majesty. You'll be sucking my cock for gossip within the year, if you live that long."

Now the king laughed, a sound so full of malice it sent a shiver down Aurora's spine.

"Do you know what I do to men without honour?"

"Get inside!"

A scuffle ensued. Metal smashed into metal. Then metal into stone. Swearing ensued as the soldier called for help. Grunts and groans of pain ended with a shrill scream. As other soldiers arrived, the king laughed through the beating they delivered.

"He bit off my ear!" the guard shrieked in the distance.

"Be glad I only took your ear!" the king called out as the door to the palace was closed.

The lock of the outer door clicked into place with finality.

"Viridian scum," the king swore as he groaned, struggling to his feet.

Aurora prayed he wouldn't find her in her hiding place. A man who so quickly turned to gory violence would no doubt delight in the screams of a small woman.

As the king shuffled close, sweat rolled down her back. Gripping her skirt with clammy hands, she held her breath as he stood before her. Only his feet were visible from her position but they were filthy, caked in mud and other unmentionable substances, and only one had a soldier's sandal on it. He leaned down to grab the keys and sat himself on her bench, unlocking the shackles that had circled his ankles. But she knew from experience that the shackles on his wrists wouldn't be so easy.

He muttered curses under his breath as he fumbled. When the keys dropped from his hands and hit the floor, Aurora jumped.

The king parted the foliage in an instant and grabbed her dress, hauling her up from her hiding spot with a snarl.

He was going to kill her, smash her head to pieces against the floor, tear her limb from bleeding limb. She'd been hauled around like a ragdoll by the others here, treated like an object instead of a person for weeks now. It was too much. She'd not done anything to deserve this. Aurora was sick to death of people manhandling her just because they were bigger. As if moving of its own accord, her fist rammed into his nose. Her magic surged in tandem as she screamed.

"Stop!" she cried.

And he did. When she dared open her eyes, he was frozen. He wasn't even breathing, as if trapped in amber. The creature inside her chest had its jaws locked around him, holding him in place, the effort straining muscles she'd never known existed.

Move. Move. Move!

It wouldn't last forever. She had to get out of his grasp before then. But his hands were fisted in the material of her dress. Aurora writhed until her gown tore. She fell to the floor, the bodice of her gown still clutched between that monster's paws. Aurora struggled to her feet, clutching the tattered remains of her gown to her chest and limped away as far as she could. But the further she got, the more difficult holding him with her magic became, as if it were a leather strap pulled too tight. With a force that nearly sent her to her knees, her magic snapped back.

The king was moving again.

And she was but a few paces away from his wrath.

He reeled, clutching his nose and swearing, torn fabric falling from his fists. He spotted her immediately, took half a step toward her and stopped, eyes wide. He held up his hands and knelt.

"My apologies, little one. I didn't mean to frighten you," he said, his rich, deep voice unexpectedly gentling along with his expression. Then he caught sight of her figure, the breasts she could barely conceal, and that gentle expression turned to confusion.

Aurora swallowed, eyes watering from his stench the longer she stared at his dishevelled face. His beard was a mess, full of blood both old and new, and his long hair was a matted nest. She couldn't even tell exactly what colour it was, only that it was dark. His clothes had fared about as well as his sandals, torn, stained, and filthy. Her insides crawled just looking at it.

Had the guard at the door not called him 'Your Majesty,' Aurora would not have believed him to be more than an unlucky beggar. An especially tall, broad-shouldered beggar with more muscles than any man ought to have. Goddess, he must be a true giant. Everyone here was enormous, but he would easily tower over everyone she'd seen thus far. The top of her head probably only met his elbows. And now he was staring at her with a piercing golden gaze that turned her insides to jelly.

She raised her chin, willing her hands to still, her back to straighten.

"I mean you no harm, madam fairy. I deserved that right hook for manhandling you in that way." He picked up the fallen keys and held them out to her, careful not to move any closer to her. "But if you would be so kind as to free me, I will repay that kindness."

Aurora waited, considering her options. She could use an ally here, and he was as big and scary as they came. But what she needed from him was a vow. One upon his honour. For the histories made mention that even the most terrifying of monarchs were bound by their honour.

"Are you truly a king?"

"I am."

"Then vow upon your honour that you will not harm me."

He smiled gently.

"I vow upon my honour as king that I will not harm you."

Aurora tentatively took the keys from his hands and shuffled forward to unlock the shackles that bound his wrists.

"Thank you. If you'll allow it, I will heal your wounds to repay you."

This filthy mountain of a man could heal? She must have looked incredulous because he frowned.

"Do your injuries trouble you so little?"

No, they troubled her a great deal, in fact. They were the only thing holding her back from escaping this prison. Though whether she could evade the high priestess' reach was another thing altogether.

Aurora chewed her lip. She supposed he'd been good enough not to attack her the moment he'd been freed. And he'd mistaken her for a full-blooded fairy, one of the founding races of Trisia, as cruel as they were whimsical and not to be taken lightly. An error she did not plan on rectifying. Whatever stayed his hand, whether fear or honour, she should not let this chance go by, even if it meant tolerating his prodigious odour.

"You may heal me, Your Majesty."

His wild magic crashed over her like a wave. Every hurt was magnified. Searing heat replaced every dull ache in her body. She gasped, biting her lip as she tensed against the next wave of his magic. By the time he was through with her, she stumbled back, leaning heavily on the nearest column for support, her breath sawing in and out. Goddess, that was unpleasant. But as the last of his magic faded, so too did the pain. She gingerly slid her arm out of its sling, tested her weight on her splinted leg, and took a deep, full breath for the first time in weeks.

"Thank you," she said. "And I'm sorry for hitting you."

"Think nothing of it."

"If you...if you wish to bathe, the baths here are extensive and they're down that hallway." She pointed to them.

"If you'll excuse me, then."

Aurora nodded, watching him slowly get to his feet and give her a wide, respectful berth. She wondered how he would fare with the others here. They were a miserable lot—bored, purposeless and angry. It made them unspeakably cruel at times, hungry for new entertainments and escapes from their lives.

"Be wary of the others here. They play cruel tricks, and already see you as their newest toy."

"Thank you for the warning, madam fairy."

"Good luck, Your Majesty."

Aurora raced off after that, eager to get to her room and remove all the bandages and splints that hindered her. If she were lucky, she could be quit of this place in a few days, on her way to Gilvus or Niveum. If Orithyia had no use for her warnings, perhaps Nerio, the high priestess of Justice, or Myrina, the high priestess of Passion, would.

Once inside her small, spare room, Aurora changed out of her ruined gown and eagerly tore off her splints and bandages. She slipped on another gown and went through her mental list. She grabbed the large travel bag she'd put together with sections of her bed linens cut using pilfered silverware and sewn using a stolen needle. Inside, she'd tucked a few of the jewels the other prisoners had left lying on their vanities, as well as the silverware, a few half-eaten loaves of stale bread, and a container she hoped would hold water. Aurora stuffed her trousers, tunic and cloak, as well as another gown and a few unmentionables inside for good measure.

On her vanity, a precious scroll with her drawings—of Phaedra, Silvanus, the holy sword...and Drakon. She'd hoped to show these to Orithyia, but Aurora had no stomach to potentially face off with the woman again. She'd tried asking the other captives here if they recognised the Beast of Old, but none had, and in doing so, she'd only given away that she was not, in fact, a child to be left alone. Placing it inside her satchel, Aurora paused.

Would the king know anything helpful? He was the most recent prisoner here, and he'd been a free man his whole life. If nothing else, he could tell her where the high priestesses of Justice and Passion currently resided. Knowing that would help her set her course once she escaped. Mind made up, she snuck out of her room and made her way to the baths.

A bath attendant was leaving in a huff, a furious scowl on her face. That boded ill.

Aurora peeked inside, only to be greeted by fragrant steam.

"Your Majesty?" she called.

"Madam fairy?" he asked back, more amused than angry.

"May I come in?"

"As long as you don't intend to extort sexual services from me in exchange for soap."

Yes, that had been a lesson Aurora had learned on her first night. She'd opted for being a bit smelly and stolen the first bar she'd found unattended, guarding it jealously. It seemed the king had managed to fight the attendant for his.

"I see you've met another of our jailors," Aurora said, slipping inside.

"Will I be dancing naked for dinner?"

"No, naked dancing is reserved for when you want new bed linens," Aurora quipped, following the sound of his voice to the far corner.

"Ah, of course, how foolish of me."

"This is a dreadful place, to be sure, but at least you're not—" She rounded the next corner only to come face first with the king. Nude. "Small..." she trailed off, eyes as wide as saucers when they lit on a rather large part of his anatomy. And what a gloriously nude body he had. She turned around, face flaming and heart skipping several beats. "I'm so sorry. I didn't come to pester you, I swear."

"Oh? Then what did you come for?" he asked, his voice deepening.

"I... I was hoping you might answer some questions I had."

"Regarding?"

"Trisia."

"Hmmm, I thought you had a strange accent. Are you a foreigner, then?"

"I...yes. My home is very far," she answered, her heart aching.

"Then it is a pity you arrived in Viridis first. Had you landed anywhere else, you would have been treated with dignity."

Doubtful, given how desperate and foolish she'd been when she'd woken up in the ancient past. She'd have just as likely made a mess of things wherever and whenever she'd landed.

"I want to ask where the high priestesses of Passion and Justice currently reside."

"High Priestess Myrina of Passion resides in Altanus, the capital of Aureum. As for Justice's Nerio, I cannot say. With no interest in marriage or romance, she is often on the move, travelling the length and breadth of Trisia. She last visited Niveum."

So it was Aureum she needed to travel to. It was a shame. That was a two-week journey if the weather held and the roads were safe. Now that the cycle of calamity had begun, travelling would be extremely dangerous. As a lone woman with no family, friends or even acquaintances, she had no one she could rely on but herself. Suddenly, her sad travel bag full of pilfered little nothings seemed wholly inadequate. She supposed she could try sneaking into *that* place, but it wouldn't be without risk.

"I'm sorry to say, madam fairy, but I doubt you will be able to meet them. Royal hostages rarely get audiences with such influential women."

No, she couldn't let herself be dissuaded. She wouldn't know unless she tried. Phaedra would move mountains for her and Aurora could do no less.

"Were you actually attacked by monstrosities?"

"Yes," he replied.

His tone suggested he didn't wish to speak more on that matter, but Aurora was aching with curiosity.

"Where?"

"At a place called the Colonnades Of The Colossus. Why do you ask?"

Bitterness nearly stole her breath. Damn Orithyia. The high priestess had known for a while now that Aurora had spoken true, yet left her here in this nightmarish place. It only strengthened her resolve to leave, monstrosities or not.

"I promise to leave you alone after this but... would you be able to take a look at a drawing? If you've seen this creature before, please tell me where and when." She unfurled her scroll to the right section. "I promise not to look," she said, turning around, dutifully closing her eyes as she held up the scroll for his perusal.

He padded over, his wet feet slapping the tiles of the bathhouse. She could feel the heat of him this close, and was grateful he'd managed to wrest the soap from the attendant. Gone was the stench of refuse, replaced by sandalwood and musk.

"I'm afraid I must disappoint you. But what reason do you have to be looking for such a beast?"

Aurora swallowed down her disappointment and turned away, rolling up her scroll and placing it in her satchel.

"It is Drakon, and it killed the person I love the most."

"And you intend to slay it?"

"I must, or it will never stop. Thank you for your help, Your Majesty. I will leave you to your bath."

Theron sat in the hot, clean waters of his bath, rubbing his newly shaven jaw with oil as he chewed on what had just transpired. Whoever the little fairy was, she knew of Batea's secret beasts. Was she a spy? If so, she was an odd choice. She would stand out no matter where she went. Green eyes were a rarity, her long, pointed ears even more so, and her stature was downright unnatural for a Trisian adult. And whatever magic she possessed allowed her to escape his grasp so quickly he'd not even seen her do it. He was lucky she was not as capricious as her mythical ancestors were rumoured to be, else she could have slit his throat.

The other possibility was that one of Batea's monsters had escaped, causing devastation abroad. After all, unlike the people of Trisia, beasts didn't depend on the protection of the Divine Triad. Outside the borders of Trisia, any Trisian would be at the mercy of foreign deities and the whims of fate, cut off from the beneficial influence of the Triad. If the little fairy had been driven here by a need for vengeance, then she had forsaken the protection of her own deities to do it. That made her either incredibly brave or incredibly foolish.

Foolish, most like. He'd seen her injuries with his magic, both current and past. She'd been subjected to horrific violence, and yet was ready to face more.

In either case, his curiosity was piqued. Not only did she present an entertaining mystery, she was the first halfway civilised person he'd met since he'd stepped onto cursed Viridian soil. No surprise, since she was not of this queendom. And if her reaction to his body was any indication, she might be persuaded to entertain him in other ways.

He washed the last bit of grime from his hair and made his way towards the entrance, determined to find his little fairy and uncover her secrets.

Only to be stopped by a veritable hoard of nobles.

Leering nobles.

Theron wrapped himself in a towel and gave them his best scowl. Usually, that was enough to cow even the most impertinent of pests, but this lot were either immune to it or simply enjoyed courting death.

"I told you he was going to be a handsome one."

"Look at those muscles."

"I never thought I'd be jealous of a water droplet, but the world is a strange, beautiful place."

"Do you know how to pleasure a woman, Your Majesty?"

"Or a man?"

"We've all been betting on whether you're a show pony or a proper stallion."

These people had no fear, no dignity, no honour. It was a shame he had more important things to be doing, because it might have helped let off a little steam had he the time to thoroughly teach them proper respect.

He unleashed a wave of his magic, pouring through the wretched lot before him, letting it trickle through their sinew and bone, ferreting out their painful pasts. And with a great and terrible pull, he fractured them along their weakest points, their mended wounds reopened, their healed bones rebroken, their greatest physical pains retold in a symphony of agonized screams.

"I am Theron, king of Aureum, and it would do you well to engrave that on your withered hearts. I will not tolerate such disrespect a second time. Now, point me to my quarters," he demanded as he strode towards the moaning, sobbing heap. One of the women pointed a trembling finger in the direction his fairy had gone. She'd mentioned they were a cruel lot. Best nip that in the bud. "And another thing. The little fairy woman? She's mine now, and I don't share."

He marched down the hall with more confidence than he felt in naught but a towel. Unease slithered through him. Losing his mind to a goddess' wrath had shaken him, her mark a dark reminder of how easily he could be snuffed out, how powerless he was. His long, humiliating ride here had only compounded the fear, every time the Viridian's eyes lit with glee forcing him to master his emotions to give them as little satisfaction as possible. He'd drowned himself in anger, in promises of vengeance, in dreams of their destruction. Theron might never be able to touch a goddess, but mortals were different. Yet as he stormed through the halls all but nude, his defences slipped.

Weak.

If the soldiers guarding this gilded cage took it upon themselves to get revenge for their recently one-eared friend, the beating would be deeply unpleasant. And he was under no illusions—Queen Flora had likely given the order to make his stay as unpleasant as possible. Every action he took to defend his honour would only compound the compensation she would demand. And that was before that bitch Orithyia had her chance to play with him. He needed proper allies, and so far, the only one in the running was a powerless foreign fairy whose name he didn't know.

Just as pressing, he needed to get his seal ring back from that bastard Stentor. The general had stolen it on the way to Boreas. If she were cunning, Flora would draw up some ridiculous treaty promising Aureum's enslavement to Viridis, sign it with his seal ring and present it to Batea as a fait accompli. Batea was much too stubborn to countenance such a thing, but it would all but guarantee a disastrous war.

An attendant walking the hallway eyed him warily and ushered him to his room. Good. A little fear would help keep these dogs in line. He was pleased to find that new clothes were laid out for him. Less pleasing was the low-quality fabric and the lack of trousers. He'd forgotten that the Viridians eschewed the practicality of trousers, preferring skirts and tunics.

Donning his new outfit, Theron walked to his terrace and scoped out the surrounding gardens below. It appeared, if not heavily guarded, then well maintained. Queen Flora was counting on political pressures to keep her prisoners in their plush cells. That, and the fact that the only obvious way out was through the front gate, one that was guarded day and night. Perhaps he should have been more concerned being the vivarium's newest curiosity, but unlike the other wretches here, he was no mere lordling's heir.

A knock on his door interrupted his perusal.

"Your lunch is prepared, Your Majesty."

"You may enter."

A servant entered, placed a platter of food on his minuscule dining table, bowed deeply and left. Theron looked over the offerings of lamb on the bone and smiled. This was why he wasn't overly concerned. He scraped the meat off to read the message scrawled on the bone by another talented healer and Aurean spy.

Friends wear red.

He defaced the message as best he could with the silverware available to him and partook of the only decent meal he'd had since he'd been taken from Aureum. The succulent juices dripped down his chin. Merciful Triad, he hadn't realised just how much he'd missed freshly cooked food. When he was finished shovelling it into his mouth and wiping it off his face, he sat back in his seat. He would be sure to keep an eye out for guards, servants and attendants wearing something red. He needed that ring back as soon as possible.

Theron looked out at the view, sighing. When was the last time he'd had so little to do? No wonder the nobles here had gone mad. At least he had the fairy woman to entertain him until Flora set a date to drag him to her court and make outrageous demands.

As he watched the breeze rustle the petals of the neatly planted flowers, a flash of colour caught his eye in the bushes. The very top of a blonde head bobbed in and out of view.

"Madam fairy?"

Theron got up from his seat and leapt from the terrace. He landed painfully, using his magic to heal himself in a rush of heat. Following the start of the treeline, he spied the small woman sneaking rather adeptly through the undergrowth. She made it to the wall encircling the palace and looked around, only to squeak in terror when she noticed him behind her.

"Merciful Triad! What... what are you doing here, Your Majesty?" She stood abruptly, dusting the hem of her skirt.

"Oh, I wasn't aware this area was off-limits." He smiled the more uncomfortable she appeared. Either she was the greatest actress in Trisia, or she was simply very bad at keeping her thoughts from showing on her face.

"It's not, it's just... well, would you mind coming further off the main path? Out of sight of the patrol about to come around the corner?"

Theron entered the underbrush. She cringed at every snapped twig and rustle of greenery. When he was about halfway, she grabbed his hand and pulled him forward, gesturing wildly for him to duck. He dutifully obeyed, but not as well as she'd wanted if her frantic look was anything to go by.

"Apologies, Your Majesty but..." She pushed him down onto the ground, covering him with her body just as the patrol passed by, gossiping about some high society scandal or another.

He blinked in surprise as she crouched over him, all her attention focused on the soldiers above. Theron had never been so thoroughly ignored by a woman who had essentially pinned him. Her long, pointed ears twitched as she listened, her slender neck straining as she kept them in her sights. It took a great effort of will to keep his eyes from following her graceful collarbones down to her cleavage. Was this her attempt at seduction?

The woman sighed when they were alone once more. Her sparkling peridot gaze searched his. A blush followed shortly.

"I—"

"Theron."

"I—what?"

"My name is Theron."

The strangest expression passed over her face before she swallowed, her gaze turning from his.

"...Aurora."

"Was there a reason you were skulking about back here, Aurora?" he asked, tucking an errant blonde strand behind her ear. He was gratified to feel it twitch, to see a faint blush on her cheeks.

"Do you vow to keep it secret?" she asked, chewing her bottom lip.

"That depends. What do I get in return?" he asked, deepening the tone of his voice suggestively.

But his little fairy didn't take the bait. She pushed off of him and offered him her hand.

"If I'm right about something, then would treasure suffice?"

He raised his brows, declining her aid and getting to his feet on his own.

"Yes, that would suffice. You have my vow."

"I'm going to escape. But first, I need something to protect myself with."

Far be it for him to tell her that people like her never escaped the vivarium. She seemed so certain of herself. Whatever the outcome, he was happy to be entertained for the afternoon.

"Then lead the way, Aurora."

She frowned at him.

"You don't think I can escape from here."

"I said nothing of the sort."

"You don't have to. The pity is written into your gaze," she said, turning away from him.

"I meant no offence. But a cycle of chaos has begun. And you must know that—"

She pulled off her gown in one fluid movement and tossed it at him.

"Hold that."

He pulled her gown from his face only to nearly choke on his gasp. Underneath her gown, she wore trousers that fitted her like a second skin and a sheer, lacey nightgown that ended at her waist. Triad's tits, how did the men of her homeland not walk around gawking every moment of the day? Her attire left nothing to the imagination.

And yet, he imagined.

She dropped to her knees and grunted as she moved a rock from the wall. Theron swallowed, feeling the faintest blush cross his cheeks.

"Hand that to me once I'm on the other side," she instructed him.

"Right."

She crawled through a hole in the wall, testing his honour with every wriggle. Once she was through, she put her hand back under and wiggled her fingers.

"Your Majesty?"

He handed her the gown and considered his options. There was no one present to enforce his captivity inside the guest palace, though it would be best to return before his absence was noted. He had no intention of running from his duties as a king, but surely a trip into the Viridian capital would be an interesting diversion.

Theron gazed at the tiny hole in the wall. Shoddy workmanship. Typical Viridian laziness. There wasn't a chance he could fit through the same tiny crack she had. But going over? He would land in the servant's laneways on the other side. He backed up and raced down the incline as fast as he could, using his momentum to climb the wall, grab the top and vault over. Aurora squeaked as he landed next to her, her gown covering the scandalous clothes beneath. She frowned, adjusting her hair to cover her elongated ears and her gown to make her appear as flat-chested as a child. Disguise complete, she took his hand in hers and led the way, escaping through the narrow servant's lanes snaking around the perimeter of the guest palace and melting into the bustle of the capital.

It wasn't nearly as splendid as Altanus, nor were its citizens as well fed or clothed. Sickness and despair lingered in the dark alleys, and children ran barefoot through dirty streets. Did the queen have no pride? No shame? How could she think herself better than him when the people in her capital suffered despite her good harvests and overflowing treasury? Was she even making proper sacrifices to the spirits and tangible gods?

"Look! A market stall!" Aurora said, pulling him closer to inspect the goods.

"Is this your first time in a city?"

"No, of course not but—oh! Is that how that's supposed to look? That makes so much more sense now," she said, her eyes alighting on another stall.

Before he could chide her, she was distracted once more, oohing and aahing over the strangest things. From the way people walked on the raised sidewalks, to the flow of traffic, to the height of the apartment buildings, to the paintings on the walls of businesses, to the explicit graffiti scrawled across every surface. All the while, she peppered him with questions. He answered her queries about everything from children's toys to how concrete was made. What in the Loom had this woman's homeland looked like for these things to fascinate her?

After a while, he gave up trying to keep her on track. Maybe the rumours of fairies and their flighty, whimsical natures were not so far off the mark. She flitted from stall to stall, from one bit of everyday paraphernalia to another, never seeming to tire. But as the sun signalled the end of the afternoon, he began to worry they would be discovered outside their cells. No need to ruin her potential future escape just because she couldn't stay focused. Though if this was how she normally acted, her freedom would be short-lived. He was fairly certain the gates of Boreas closed at last light.

"If you wish to make good on your escape, you'll need to be more mindful of the time."

"Hmmm? Oh, no, we have time yet. And I'm not leaving today. But you're right, we should probably go there now."

"And where is 'there' exactly?"

"You'll see," she said, a smile on her face.

Tugging him along to the temple district, she slipped into the alley behind the temple of Knowledge with utter confidence. She looked both ways to ensure there was no one else around and pushed in one of the bricks near the ground.

"Lead me to the fathomless depths of Knowledge," she whispered.

The bricks dropped down and moved aside, revealing a hidden door.

"How did you..."

Who exactly was this woman? How did she know about this? Not even his spies knew about a secret chamber underneath the temple of Knowledge. Did she know that some people would pay a king's ransom for such information?

"It's a secret. Now, hurry up, before someone sees us."

He followed her down into the cool passageway as she closed the entrance behind them, leaving them in utter darkness. She took his hand in hers as his eyes failed to adjust.

"How can you see?"

"You can't?"

"No."

"Don't worry, Your Majesty, I won't let you fall into any pit traps."

"You had best be joking."

"Hmmm, who knows?"

"If you're doing this to prove a point about your capabilities, consider the message received loud and clear."

Her laughter echoed in the chamber.

"It's not far now."

She stopped, releasing his hand. The sound of grinding metal against metal presaged a flash of light. He squinted against the suddenness of it before his eyes properly adjusted. And then widened as shock rooted him to the spot.

"Oh, good. I was worried the stories about this were just myths," Aurora sighed. "Come on. I need to find some kind of weapon to defend myself on the road."

"Yes, of course…" he replied, dumbstruck.

He stumbled into the glittering hoard of ancient artefacts, his jaw slack. Even one of these was often enough to suffice for a princess' dowry. Several were displayed in places of honour in Altanus' royal palace, the dowries of several royal spouses over the generations. Every single one could mean discovering an ancient technology that would change the fate of a kingdom. The last one that his father had collected contained instructions on how to treat torchlight fever. It had come too late to save Theron's elder brother, but that knowledge had been used to treat tens of thousands of children, and even spared some of the adults for whom the fever was a death sentence.

How in the world had Orithyia kept such a hoard to herself all this time? More importantly, why would the high priestess of Knowledge refuse to disburse the gifts her goddess had bestowed on the world? Even if the hoard's existence wasn't enough to take down the high priestess, the secrecy of it would tarnish her reputation.

An irrepressible grin spread on his face. Blackmail of this calibre was usually impossible to attain without a great deal of bloodshed and gold. But his little fairy had gifted it to him for nothing.

It was almost too good to be true. Was this the beginning of some labyrinthine plot by Orithyia? Or had the Triad finally answered his prayers?

What could not be denied was that if someone meant to entrap him, they'd laid the perfect bait. As Aurora picked through the hoard, ignoring him entirely, he wondered whether she'd been put in his path to destroy him...or save him.

Theron couldn't wait to find out.

CHAPTER 13
AURORA

There was a saying that one should never meet one's heroes. Perhaps they should also say that one should never meet infamous historical figures. Especially the tragic ones.

King Theron of Aureum. For millennia, very little had been known about the first calamity, until a cache of documents had been uncovered in the parched desert of Altanus. Documents that, though badly fragmented, detailed the tragic fate of the last king of Aureum, and the first monarch to die during the first calamity. Cursed by Justice for harming the first hero of the holy sword, his story was often retold in fiction as a morality play on the perils of hubris.

Aurora had been able to shove that to a dark corner of her mind for most of the day, instead delighting in properly seeing and experiencing the ancient city of Boreas. Of experiencing it with *the* Theron himself. If she ever returned home, she would have such stories to tell. So many misconceptions about the past that she would be able to resolve. And when the myths of the basement treasure hoard of the temple of Knowledge had been confirmed, her heart had soared.

The basement existed in her time, but it had long been used as storage. The treasure had been a marvellous find, made even more so by the number and variety of Pre-Sundering artefacts. Marvellous, and heartbreaking, because all those treasures would be lost in the intervening millennia. She fervently wished she could take them with her, protect them in some way, preserve them from what was to come.

It was a sentiment she was feeling towards her companion as both she and Theron left the basement to find that the sun was about to disappear beneath the horizon. She'd found something that would protect her, an ancient shield made of pure energy in the guise of a pendant. But how was she supposed to protect the man beside her? As he took her hand in his, shared a conspiratorial smile, and led the way back to the palace, she couldn't escape the dawning horror that he was no longer just a story to her. Theron was here, a real flesh and blood man.

One whose fate was as grim as her own.

One who was ultimately meant for another. And a princess no less.

Aurora had not missed his subtle flirting, nor the unmistakable close-ness of his person. She had not been immune to the pleasing scent of his perfume, nor his lingering glances. Neither was she immune to the rugged appeal of his face, nor his overwhelming size and the gentleness of his touch. The only things about him that were not overly pleasing were his barely-pointed ears, small and mostly-rounded that they were. A pity that they were so ugly, given the rest of him. But despite her fascination with his physical appeal, she was no fool. Today had been a test.

Could Theron be trusted as her new ally? If she provided him with secrets and useful information, would he reciprocate with assistance when she needed it in slaying Drakon? Would he betray her to win favour within Viridis? Or would he attempt to seduce her for more information, and then discard her when he assumed she had no more use? Aurora had met and spurned enough of those types as Phaedra's only true friend to be wary of all flattery and temptations sent her way.

As he pulled her close, out of the way of a pool of standing water, she wondered if she had what it took to play along with such a seduction while keeping her heart locked away. It had been easy to turn down the advances of those who'd hoped to reach Phaedra through her. She'd had an imperial princess to shield her from any and all consequences, and no true incentive to keep around such noxious parasites. But could she afford to turn her nose up at these games when she had no other allies, no protection, and Phaedra's future hanging in the balance?

Aurora needed someone with power and influence to reach Drakon before he became the calamity. If Orithyia wouldn't or couldn't be that person, then maybe this doomed king, whose fate she might be able to change, would be more interested in her knowledge. He would leave the vivarium soon enough, and when he met her outside the queendom of Viridis, she hoped he would be inclined to assist her.

But could she live with the person she would become by stepping into the fetid swamp of court intrigues and calculated seductions?

Could she afford not to?

"We should have left earlier," Theron grumbled.

"You were the one who wouldn't leave until you'd found the perfect weapons."

Indeed, he'd found a spear and shield that miniaturized at will, his eyes lighting up like a child's as he'd excitedly theorized about using such technology to benefit long-distance trade. That his mind had turned immediately to matters of scholarship and discovery only made him all the more attractive.

"You took just as long to find a treasure of your own," he accused her playfully before that smile vanished. "But this is a dangerous time to be about. The spirits are most active at dusk and dawn. And if this is the state in which Flora keeps her shining jewel of a capital, then I doubt she has been at pains to placate the spirits of this land."

"What do you believe these spirits will actually do?"

He frowned down at her.

"You speak as though you don't believe they exist. Perhaps they don't, in your homeland, but in Trisia, they are very real. When they're angered or abused, they bring plague, blight, drought, and more besides. Entire mountain ranges and forests become bloodthirsty and impassible." Theron looked like there was more he wished to say but swallowed his tongue. "In any case, the city gates will be closed now. You'll have to wait to enact your daring escape."

"Will you miss me?" she teased.

"The only civilised company in the entire queendom? Desperately."

"Civilised? I punched you."

"And I richly deserved it."

Aurora smiled sadly, recalling the first time she'd punched a member of a royal family.

"What has stolen your joy, madam fairy?"

"Old memories."

"Good or bad?"

"Good. Treasured, but painful now."

"The love you lost to that beast of yours?"

"Yes, my dearest friend. A princess, loyal and loving...and the most infuriating person you could ever meet."

"Am I to believe I'm not the first royal you've punched?"

"Are you offended you're not my first?"

"I may never recover. I thought our meeting was singular—unique."

"I have every hope that you'll survive this terrible blow to your ego."

As she flirted shamelessly, her heart hurting the whole while, a little girl darted around the corner of the alleyway, colliding with her. Theron saved her from falling onto her backside. Before she could ascertain the child's state, the little girl dashed off, nearly losing her balance for a few steps before she turned another corner, gone without so much as a backward glance. A pickpocket? Runaway? Or simply trying to get home before curfew?

"Are you alright?"

"Yes," Aurora answered, touching the treasure in her satchel with a sigh of relief.

They managed to get back to the hole in the wall without incident, and onto the palace grounds without getting caught. For now, her escape route was a safely guarded secret. But if this one was found, Aurora had others. After all, in the future, this place would be Phaedra's palace—and they had managed to sneak out countless times together. Aurora replaced the rocks in front of her hole in the wall and readjusted her gown as Theron kept a watch.

"I hope you'll keep my secrets, Your Majesty."

"You have my vow. Will you be leaving this place soon?"

"Yes, at first light."

The only thing more alluring than a willing woman was a woman who knew when to leave a man wanting more. Or so she'd been told. He wanted more of her secrets and he seemed intent on seduction as his method. How could he not? Aurora had seen the look in his eyes when she'd exposed her modern fashions. She'd also led him to breathtaking treasure today. Any sane man would be wondering what more she might reveal to him tomorrow.

"Must you go so soon?"

"I must find Drakon, Your Majesty."

"Your beast."

"Yes."

Aurora stepped from the undergrowth and onto the main path, hoping he would take her bait. Theron followed.

"And what if I offered to help?"

"What can you do, locked in the guest palace?"

"I'm not without my resources. And I won't be here forever. Flora and Orithyia will take their pound of flesh, but they can't keep me here for long."

"Then I will accept your help... once you're freed."

"But how will I know where to find you? Where will you go? And will you get there safely?"

"Oh my, it sounds as if you really will miss me," she chided him as they entered the palace proper.

"Keep me company until I leave, and I will take you with me to Aureum in safety and comfort. I will also ensure you get an audience with Myrina."

"And is my company all you would ask for in return? Surely you would want something more."

"You underestimate your charms."

They stood in the atrium of the palace, the sun now fully set, and the halls lit only with lamps. This man was loved by both the sun and the flickering flames of firelight. His dark crimson hair, tied back from his handsome face, complimented his ochre brown skin and fierce gold eyes. The ancient robes he wore did nothing to detract from his burly physique. She was the moth and he the flame. If she were anyone else, maybe she could enjoy his seduction without reserve. But she was a woman whose fate was tied with Drakon, and ending the beast mattered more than anything else.

"I'll think on it, Your Majesty. Tomorrow, you'll know my answer."

"Theron. Call me Theron, Aurora."

"Goodnight, Theron."

She left him there, his gaze a palpable heat on her back that chased her all the way to her room. It wasn't until she closed the door that she dared to groan miserably. Had she played her part well enough? Though she'd watched the nobles at court dance around each other, even been subjected to it on occasion, she'd never properly played this game before.

Now she needed to decide if Theron's help was worth risking another run-in with Orithyia. The monstrosities had appeared at the Colonnades if Theron's comments were to be believed, but the high priestess wasn't yet interested in anything else Aurora had to say, if the lack of an audience was anything to go by. And what if her scant remaining knowledge of this age was inaccurate? Aurora shivered. She recalled the threat of Orithyia's switch, and had no desire to find out what would happen if the high priestess remembered where she'd left Aurora to rot. She couldn't risk Orithyia's wrath with everything at stake.

Aurora changed out of her gown and into a slip more appropriate for sleeping. She pulled the new artefact from her satchel, a pretty bauble that could easily be strung as a necklace, and examined it in the moonlight. With this, she could get to Aureum on her own. She didn't need to play these games. With luck, she could get everything she needed by convincing the other high priestesses to aid her. And this time, she would approach the high priestess with her wits instead of her desperation.

Then again, Aurora knew just how valuable the help of a monarch could be in getting things done. Phaedra had smoothed every path Aurora had tread on.

She also knew how impossible it could be when one was against you, as all of Phaedra's enemies had discovered.

Aurora collapsed on her bed and threw her arm over her eyes, sighing deeply. Tomorrow. She could decide this at first light tomorrow.

She didn't remember falling asleep. Only waking up to a roaring heat, her joints aching and her head throbbing. Aurora got to her feet to find the world was spinning.

Something was wrong.

Aurora lurched to her door and into the hallway, the flickering light of oil lamps blending into the walls, giving them all the impression of melting. She stumbled onwards. Usually, there was at least a single guard patrolling the halls at night, but would they help her? Or would they leave her to be consumed by this unnatural heat? She passed no one on their rounds. Her only hope before she collapsed was the dreadful guard by the palace entrance. Sweat dripping down her neck and back, her knees aching, she made it to the front atrium of the palace.

"Trouble sleeping, madam fairy?"

Theron was there in the atrium, seated on her bench, soaking in the moonlight and surrounded by lush foliage.

"Something's...wrong," Aurora slurred as darkness swallowed her vision.

Theron squeezed through the window of his childhood bedroom in the early hours of the morning. A night of carousing with the local sons of the nobility had kept him out late. It would probably be the last time he would ever manage to get through such a tight space. At sixteen, he was finally about to experience his second growth spurt. After he'd shot up half a head over the last few months, the nobles had decided to take him out for a taste of adulthood. He'd drunk more than was perhaps advisable and had been introduced to the most beautiful woman in Trisia, to whom he had given his first kiss. Riding high, he tumbled into his room, smashing a vase full of flowers on his way to his bed.

Who put vases in front of beds?

"Your Highness!"

One of the servants ripped open his door, their face pale and drawn.

"How insolent. Where are your manners? This is my room."

"Your Highness, please, you must come. Your brother is ill!"

Tisander, his older brother the crown prince, was always ill. He'd been sick Theron's whole life. Ever since he'd awakened healing magic, Theron had been working tirelessly to keep his brother's chronic illnesses at bay. A man fully grown with the dark red hair and deep brown skin of the royal family, he was lithe where everyone else was solid, never able to put on muscle due to his frailty. But his brother was never one to fuss, nor trouble others unduly. No, Tisander was a stoic man a decade his senior full of wisdom and compassion. Someone Theron looked up to and admired. Convinced this was just his mother being especially cautious, Theron sighed and followed the servant to Tisander's room.

Only to be met with a scene from a nightmare.

Servants wept. His mother, a statuesque beauty with black hair, was crumpled on the bed wailing, her arms around Tisander. His father, a true giant who was as stocky and fierce as a bull, who'd never so much as smiled as long as Theron had been alive, was slumped at Tisander's bedside, devastation written plain as day across his face.

Theron stumbled to his brother's bedside and reached out a shaking hand. Tisander was still, his face unnaturally pale, his neck and jaw slack, dark red hair limp and slick with sweat, an angry red rash climbing up from his chest. Numb, Theron reached out with his magic, only to feel it recoil in the face of death.

Tisander's death.

"Where were you?!" his mother screamed, her amber eyes filled with hatred. "Where were you when your brother needed you?! He died of fever! You killed your brother! He would be alive if you'd been here!" she raged, her face crumpling as her heartbroken sobs echoed in the room. She buried her face in Tisander's bony chest. "Where were you?"

"Worthless," his father hissed, his face transforming from devastation to wrath in an instant. "You're no son of mine!"

Overcome, Theron ran. He ran until he was swallowed by an endless abyss. He ran across a plain of utter darkness until he couldn't run, until he was drowned by unending nothing. As he was swallowed whole, he opened his eyes to carnage, his brother wearing Viridian armour and staring up at him in terror, Theron's spear lodged in his heart.

"Save me," Tisander whispered, blood pooling at the corners of his mouth.

Theron woke with a gasp, sweating and disoriented. His magic seethed inside him, responding to the horrors of memories blended with nightmares. Closing his eyes, he focused on his breathing, willing his magic and heartbeat to settle, but there was nothing for it. Theron was awake. If experience were anything to go by, he would not sleep again tonight.

Frustrated, he ripped the covers off and dressed in the first tunic he found.

There was precious little to do in the guest palace at night, but the view of the sky from the atrium was nice enough. He sat on the bench and watched the stars wink in the night sky.

As a cloud passed over the moon above, Aurora entered the atrium. Had she come to see him at this hour? It was a welcome distraction. And if she'd come to him at this hour, there could be no mistaking her intentions. His blood heated.

Yet as his greeting left his lips, he could tell that something was deeply wrong. Theron rushed to Aurora's side, his magic wrapping around her, seeking the cause of her collapse. But the moment he touched her burning hot skin and turned her over to see an angry red rash climbing up her neck, he knew. Dread galvanised him to action. He cradled her in arms, marched to the entrance and kicked open the door to the palace, startling the guard on duty.

"Get me a tub full of cold water and ice! And bring me more ice every hour. Now!"

"What? I'm not your damn servant," the guard growled. "Get back inside the palace!"

"What's the problem here?" another guard asked, this one with a red scarf around his neck. Good, one of the Aurean spies planted in Boreas.

"This woman has torchlight fever. Get me what I need to save her and tell your queen she has an outbreak in her capital."

"I'll get what he needs. You tell the palace guard," his inside man said, racing off to do Theron's bidding, the other guard following shortly after.

Shit. Shit. Shit.

This wasn't supposed to happen.

It would take everything he had to save her. Normally, he healed people by using his magic to guide their body's natural healing process whenever possible. But this was torchlight fever. He would need to flood her with his magic, using his own energy to prevent her fever from cooking her internal organs. The worst of the fever came and went in the time it took for a torch to burn to ashes, often carrying its victims with it in that short span of time. If he could keep her alive during the worst of the fever, she had better odds of surviving.

Theron took her to his room and flooded her with his magic, healing her organs as her body fought to boil them. He kept a hand on her forehead, using the better portion of his magic to prevent the destruction of her mind.

But he was going to lose the battle if someone didn't arrive with the tub full of cold water. There was only so much he could do to heal her body if he didn't have some way to cool it down. He was about to take her to the baths and contaminate every drop inside when a group of servants came hauling a large copper tub and pails of water.

"Place it there! Fill it halfway and put in as much ice as it'll hold."

The servants rushed to obey. That done, he placed Aurora inside, his hand cupping the back of her head, submerging all but her face. She gasped, her eyes fluttering open. Her gaze was unfocused, drifting across the room until she lit on him. Tears welled in her eyes, and whatever she said next, it was in a language he'd never heard.

"You won't die, Aurora."

Her frantic, unintelligible pleading hurt a part of him he rarely allowed anyone entry to. Had Tisander's final moments been like this? His mind ripped apart by fever, reducing him to animalistic fear? Damn it. She was not Tisander. And he was no longer that sixteen-year-old child. He was the fucking king of Aureum, whose wild magic was as powerful as they came!

"You will *not* die. I won't allow it, you understand?"

He recognised one of the next words she spoke. Drakon. Her beast. Her eyes glazed over with terror.

"You're safe here, Aurora," he assured her, speaking like he would to a frightened animal. If she was too far gone to understand his words, hopefully he could convey the meaning with his tone.

She gasped again, her eyes going wide, her hand to her chest. Between one blink and the next, her fever was an inferno. His magic flared inside him. A death knell. The ice had almost completely melted and his hand burned as if it had been submerged in frigid water for a full hour. Aurora was limp in his grasp, her eyes shut, her breathing barely perceptible. He panicked, flooding her with his magic again. The fever had wreaked havoc with her body, taking her to the very brink, but how? He'd been by her side the whole time, keeping her safe.

Had he gone into that dark abyss again without realising it? Was Justice punishing him anew? The diamond-like mark still lingered on the back of his hand—proof of Her wrath.

Theron shook his head. He couldn't afford to divide his attention.

"Get me more ice!" he commanded, switching the hand that held her head above water.

As more ice arrived, he healed organ after organ on the brink of collapse.

"Goddesses help me, if I have to force your heart to keep beating, I will!" he threatened her.

For the next hour, he was forced to do just that.

But as the night wore on, the worst of her fever abated. And he would thank the Triad for it once he had the strength. Theron had never drained himself like this before, pouring every drop of his magic into her and then finding reserves he'd never known existed. He pulled her from the tub, confident that what lay ahead was a simple illness. She was still feverish, but her life and her health were no longer in jeopardy. If people could catch this wretched plague more than once in their lives, he'd have thought himself in the throes of it, for he was delirious with fatigue.

"Dry her off, change her clothes and bring her back here," he told the attendant at his door.

The attendant took her gingerly from his arms. Theron watched them take her to her room and then collapsed on his bed. He woke to the attendant entering with Aurora in their arms.

"Where would you like me to put her?"

"On the bed, at my side."

He wanted to keep an eye on her as best he could. How the fever affected the average Trisian was well known, but not how it would affect a foreigner like her. If she neared death, his magic would alert him, even in sleep. Hopefully, it would be enough to keep her alive.

As he adjusted himself to her presence at his side, she opened her eyes once more.

"Theron?"

"Sleep, Aurora. I'll keep you safe."

Aurora was asleep again in moments.

She trusted him.

It should have been gratifying, but it only unsettled him. She shouldn't have trusted him so easily. He hadn't lied to Hyllus when he'd said he was not a good man. Good men were ruled by the best parts of their hearts, after all. Theron had every intention of discovering her secrets. Of using every scrap of knowledge she possessed for his benefit. And if seduction proved the quickest path, as he suspected it did, he would pluck her heartstrings without remorse, use her body for his pleasure and discard her the moment she had nothing left to give. Anything and everything she had of value he would shamelessly take from her, so long as it benefitted Aureum or his throne. It was nothing less than the duty he'd been given the moment his brother had died. A good king ruled with his head and abandoned his heart.

That had never bothered him before.

So why did it trouble him now?

CHAPTER 14
AURORA

"Aurora. Wake up."

Aurora groaned, pulling the covers over her aching head. Merciful Triad, she felt like she'd been hit by a runaway carriage. Then had her head filled with angry bees for good measure. Then run over a second time. The sun was barely more than a hint on the horizon. No one who didn't have to be awake at this hour bothered to leave the comfort of their beds. Even soaked with sweat and feeling miserable, the bed was far preferable to surrendering to an early start.

"Aurora."

"Fae, it's too early," Aurora moaned.

"*Aurora.*"

Aurora shot up with a gasp.

"Fae!"

There, at the foot of the bed. Phaedra smiled, waving at her, wearing a gown in the ancient fashion, her hair partially done up in intricate braids. She twirled, showing it off.

"What do you think?"

She was alive. Unharmed. Whole. Tears blurred her vision, emotion choking her.

"Phaedra," Aurora sobbed, crawling out of bed. "How?"

The moment Aurora stood, her legs buckled under her like a fawn's. She reached towards Phaedra, but her friend danced out of reach with a giggle.

"Come on. I want to show you something."

"Wait! Come back, Fae," Aurora pleaded.

Phaedra skipped to the terrace, her long red hair bouncing with every step. As Aurora struggled to her feet, Phaedra sat on the railing of the terrace, her arms stretched wide. Her smile was dazzling, her cheeks rosy with health. Behind her, a thin orange line bled into the deep blues of the night sky. Outlined by the first rays of dawn, Phaedra was a vision of beauty. Of home. Aurora wanted nothing so much as to fall into her arms and weep, to know that all was right with the world once more. If she could just touch her, she could convince herself everything up until now, all the pain, all the horror, had been a nightmare, forgotten with the rising of the sun.

"I'm right here, Aurora."

Aurora lurched towards her on unsteady feet, reaching towards Phaedra. As she lost her balance, Phaedra was there to steady her, their fingers intertwined.

"I thought you'd died! I thought you were gone forever. Why did you do that? Why did you take my place? It should have been me, not you! You were supposed to live, Fae! I never wanted—"

"Shhhh. It's alright now," Phaedra said, leaning her forehead on Aurora's. As Aurora wept, Phaedra wrapped her arms around her. "Come with me."

Then Phaedra pulled.

"Aurora!" Theron shouted, grabbing Aurora around the waist and dragging her from Phaedra's grasp.

"No!" Aurora cried as Phaedra fell from the terrace into the gardens far below. She struggled in Theron's hold, fighting for freedom. "Fae! Fae!"

"It wasn't her," he said, his voice calm.

"No! She fell! She might be hurt! Let me go!"

"It wasn't her, Aurora. Look." Theron walked towards the edge with her secure in his arms. Aurora frantically searched the ground below but there was no one.

"No, she was right there. She was here," Aurora sobbed. Despair ripped through her fragile heart, all the more vicious now that she'd been given a ray of hope.

"It was a spirit. An angry one. They see into your heart and present you with what you want most in order to bring you harm," he explained, his tone gentle.

Theron carried her back to the bed and sat her on the edge. Aurora curled up, hugging her knees to her chest, and wept. She didn't want him to see her like this. She didn't want anyone to see her as her heart shattered anew. She wanted to be back home with Phaedra and her favourite book, in a world without spirits, or Drakon, or the fate that tied her thread to all the worst things in the Tapestry.

Theron whispered to the attendant at the door before returning to her side. He sat beside her without a word, his warm hand on the back of her neck, keeping vigil as she grieved. She'd kept herself together this whole time, never once coming apart. How could she have? Surrounded by predators, in constant pain, she'd merely survived. Grief had been a luxury for a prisoner in this gilded cage. But now it poured out of her, her walls irreparably fractured. And like a fool trying to clean up shattered glass with her bare hands, Aurora cut herself on every memory.

Phaedra's last message, her death, played in her mind over and over. The moments before the device took her back in time, her fall, repeated over and over. Why hadn't she been allowed to die? Was Fate really so cruel? She wished she could scream it aloud, but she knew the answer.

If her fever-addled memories could be believed, her wild magic had exploded from her last night, leaving her trapped and suffering without Theron's magic to ease her. It wasn't until she'd drained her magic dry and passed out that she'd had any relief from the pain. Fate truly was the cruellest of the goddesses. What was the point of a magic that would drive her mad with visions, or trap her in time, or cruellest of all, give her enough hope to want to survive through the suffering ahead? Magic was an untameable beast in her chest, and she never wanted to be at its mercy again.

Through all her dark thoughts, Theron sat at her side, his warmth seeping into her. She cried until the tears had leeched the worst of the poison from her system, until the raw, aching wound in her heart had been numbed. For now.

"Drink this." Theron offered her a lukewarm cup.

"What is it?" she asked, wrinkling her nose.

"It'll help with the fever and pain."

If only she could have swiped a bottle of wine and drowned her sorrows, but in her current state, the hangover might do her in for good. Aurora sipped at the bitter brew.

As the sun rose, bells rang throughout the city.

"What do they mean?"

"They're plague bells, warning travellers not to enter the city, and for its inhabitants not to leave their homes if they can help it. There's an outbreak of torchlight fever."

All the more reason she should escape while she had the chance. If there were a plague, then the temple of Knowledge would be overrun with the sick. Orithyia would no doubt be too busy to send anyone after her, even if she did realise Aurora was gone. Aurora sipped the bitter drink. Wait, Theron had called it a fever. Then...

"Is that..."

Had she been infected with this plague? The fever she'd experienced last night was unlike any other. She'd been certain it would kill her.

"Yes."

"Why did you help me?"

She'd given him the location of the ancient artefacts. It was one of her most precious pieces of information, and he could easily use it to bargain his way out of the guest palace and back to his kingdom. If he'd let her die, then he could have that information all to himself, with no chance of it being leaked to someone else, and no one left to repay.

"I had it as a child, so I can't be reinfected."

Aurora frowned. He was being obtuse.

"That isn't what I meant."

He raised a brow at her, a twinkle in his gold eyes.

"Do I need a reason to save your life?"

Aurora sighed. She waited until the attendant left their post. Some things shouldn't be said while others were around to overhear them.

"I should leave the city while I can."

"You won't be able to. The city will be locked tight against people who might flee and spread the fever."

"For how long?"

"A week, if we're lucky."

Another week? Locked up with this man who she knew she shouldn't trust but whose actions were honourable? She prayed for the strength to resist his kindness and attentions. But maybe she didn't have to... Maybe she could outright ask for an alliance, instead of playing games she wasn't certain she could properly win. Aurora didn't want to have to become someone she didn't recognise.

"Would you be honest with me, if I asked it of you?"

"That depends on what you ask."

Frustrating man.

"Why save me when you know about the artefacts? You're intelligent enough to use them to get out of here and back home."

"You're the only civilised person in the whole of Viridis. Is it so strange that I desire your company?"

"Enough to run yourself ragged keeping me alive? Yes. You're a king, and while you might not have Viridis at your beck and call, you more than likely have some of your people even here."

He slapped a hand over her mouth.

"Watch what you say. Even the walls have ears here, Aurora."

She pulled his hand away, rolling her eyes.

"Your ears aren't as sensitive as mine. I wouldn't have begun this conversation if I weren't certain no one else could hear us."

He frowned, puzzled by her.

"What is it you want from me?" he asked.

"I want an ally I can trust enough not to turn on me before I've done what I need to."

"To slay your beast?"

"Yes. I thought Orithyia would be that ally, but I was mistaken."

"So you betrayed her in the hopes of purchasing my loyalty the other day?" he asked, brows raised as a smile turning up the corners of his lips.

Why did that make him happy? Shouldn't he be angry that she'd tried to manipulate him? Shouldn't he be wary of her for giving away temple secrets?

"To prove that you would get as much benefit from a partnership as I would," Aurora replied, her heart racing. Would he be satisfied with just her knowledge, or would he demand more?

"What do you propose?"

"My knowledge in return for your help defeating Drakon."

"This beast seems troublesome. Are you certain your knowledge will be enough recompense for my efforts?"

If the veritable hoard of artefacts wasn't enough, she doubted anything else she could tell him would suffice. There was no guarantee that he would believe she could see glimpses of the future, or that she'd come from his future and knew his fate. Orithyia had kept her alive because it cost her nothing to do so. But would Theron act with such cold cunning, and not just toss her to the wolves?

What a mess. If only the hero of the holy sword were here, then she would have a true ally. Whoever, or wherever, they were in Trisia, she hoped she could meet them. No records existed of their name, nor had any statues depicting them survived the millennia. Aurora had to hope she would be able to spot the holy weapon to identify the wielder. Only together could they deal with Drakon. She had to remind herself that Theron was merely a stepping stone to that outcome, and while his resources could be invaluable, she also couldn't afford to slip and fall.

"Never mind. I'm not sure I could afford your loyalty anyway. I'll return to my room. Whatever your motives, thank you for saving me, Your Majesty." As she got up to leave, he caught her wrist.

"You asked why I saved you. My brother caught torchlight fever as an adult—a death sentence. Just like you. Except this was a time before we had any inkling of how to treat it. He didn't survive. I didn't want to watch someone worth saving die like that in front of me if I could help it."

She put a hand over his.

"I'm sorry for your loss."

Worth saving. She blinked in surprise.

"You asked for honesty, and I would count myself lucky to be your ally. But I have my own conditions."

Aurora swallowed nervously. Could she really be so fortunate as to count a king, doomed though he may be, as an ally? All without the need to make herself his plaything?

"What conditions?"

"That you help me get back to Aureum. And that you remain with me until then. I vow to protect you in the meantime."

She gripped the fabric of her nightgown. All the stories said he was meant to return to his kingdom soon enough, so it wouldn't even cost her anything, except a delay to her travels, which, given the sound of the bells, was unavoidable anyway. And the protection of a king was worth its weight in gold. Would it really be so simple? Had something finally gone right for her? It was almost too good to trust, and yet, she couldn't find a reason to deny him, except if his demands kept her here until it was too late.

"As long as it doesn't interfere with what I need to do, then I agree."

And not a moment too soon. The next attendant had come to wait outside the door. Aurora leaned in to whisper in his ear.

"The walls have sprouted ears again."

"Then let's put them to good use." Theron stood and marched towards the door. "Bring us a warm bath, new clothes, new sheets, and breakfast."

She was about to tell him that it didn't work like that here in the vivarium, where the baths were shared, new clothes a rarity, new sheets earned and all meals served in the dining hall under a watchful eye. But to her shock, the attendant not only rushed off to do just that, but did so without any rudeness. He chuckled at her open-mouthed stare.

"If you think my being a king warrants better treatment, save your shock. This is because I warned them of the plague last night, and took it upon myself to care for you in their stead while keeping you sequestered here to prevent any spread. Had I not, many of their friends and family would not have been able to flee the city before the gates were shut this morning."

"Am I still a danger to others?"

"No, the red mark is gone, but leaving this room would make them feel uneasy."

"Still, I should go back."

"Why? So you can sit alone in your room? Is my company so odious?" He grinned.

"It's not that..." she said. But she always kept her artefact close at hand. The idea of being parted from it, potentially allowing someone to steal her only link back to her own time, was too much to bear. "I have very little left in the world, but it's all in that room."

"I see," he said, going to the door once more. "Clear the hallways. We're gathering her things and bringing them here."

A call went through the guest palace to clear the way. Theron held out his hand for her.

"Madam fairy."

Aurora took it, leaning on him for support. Her fever was worse than she thought, for by the time she arrived at her room, a new layer of sweat had her nightgown clinging to her. She grabbed her hidden pack, stuffed her new artefact inside, grateful it had remained hidden, and then added in the few other odds and ends she'd been provided. Theron carried her pack as she all but hung off him for the return journey. By the time they were back, a tub with a folding screen, a change of clothes and food had been placed inside his room.

"I'll sit on the terrace to give you a chance to bathe, Your Majesty."

"You look like you'd get carried away by a stuff breeze. No, you're going to bathe first so you don't fall asleep and drown in the tub while I'm not looking."

She had no energy to fight him on it. If he preferred chivalry, she wouldn't protest. The bath did feel nice, as did scrubbing herself clean without worrying about a leering audience. It was getting out of the tub that proved troublesome. The warm waters were intrinsically soothing for her aching joints.

"You haven't fallen asleep, have you?"

Aurora was jolted out of her dozing by Theron's voice.

"Almost," she admitted, hauling herself from the tub and drying off as best she could.

She ran a comb through her hair, slipped into a gown and left her hair to dry as she approached the small table seated near the window. The food didn't appear particularly appetizing in her current state.

"Eat," Theron warned her as he left to bathe himself.

She picked at the platter before her, not really tasting much of anything, before she gave up and laid down on the bed.

The bed.

That they'd shared last night.

Aurora covered her face as a heat wholly unrelated to her fever crept up her neck. It hadn't been like that, she reminded herself. She'd been severely ill and he'd been taking care of her, and they'd both been far too exhausted to do anything but sleep. Now that they'd established themselves as allies, there would be no more questions about potentially illicit goings-on between them. Besides, he couldn't possibly want her to remain in his room overnight again. There was simply no good reason to get worked up over this.

Theron walked out from behind the privacy screen, his long, wet hair a veritable bird's nest. She'd noticed the other day that he'd tied it up, but that it had been messy then as well. He scowled at the comb before abandoning it.

"Are you not going to brush your hair?"

"It's a tangled mess. I'll have one of the attendants do it later," he muttered.

Aurora giggled. He really was a king.

"I'm surprised you managed to bathe yourself, Your Majesty," she teased.

"My hair is a mess because I spent two weeks living as a Viridian general's captive," he growled.

Aurora smiled and held out her hand, not at all intimidated. He was only sulking, after all.

"Give me the comb and some oil, and sit there." She pointed to a place at the foot of the bed.

"One night in my bed and already you order me around." He smirked, handing her the items and seating himself. Aurora sat behind him and began working the comb through the ends of his hair. Though it was of the deepest crimson, brushing it reminded her of her time with Phaedra and her friend's red hair. Goddesses knew how many times she'd been roped into making her presentable mere moments before some important function, and all after they'd just come from some ill-advised adventure or another.

"We're allies now. You don't have to flirt with me anymore," she reminded him as she worked out the first big knot. Or was she reminding herself?

"I flirt with you because you're attractive."

Aurora gritted her teeth as another blush crept up her neck. She did *not* need him saying such things in his deep voice. Especially when he was either being flippant or manipulative.

"I doubt that."

"You asked for my honesty." He shrugged.

"I honestly look like I'm half dead. If that's what you find attractive, then I have grave concerns for your taste," she retorted.

He laughed.

"I'm also not the only one flirting."

Did he consider insults flirting? Goddesses help her. In any case, it was best to be direct and clear with such misunderstandings, especially as they had a tendency to get more complicated the longer things were left unsaid.

"Only yesterday. I thought I had to, in order to gain your help. It's different now."

"And what about before that?"

Before yesterday? They'd only known each other a day now. It seemed like so much longer, given all that happened.

"Before?"

"When you came into the baths and got an eyeful. Given your reaction then, I had assumed the attraction was mutual. Was I mistaken?"

It had not been her intent. She'd had other things on her mind then. Admittedly, she hadn't fully thought through her actions, desperate as she'd been for answers. The people of this time were singularly unconcerned with nudity, unlike herself, so she'd not thought he would mind. And when he'd been standing there, fully nude instead of submerged, it had come as a great shock. Try as she might, the image of him had been branded into her mind. *Some* things could never be unseen.

"I—"

"And do try to be honest."

She supposed that was only fair but...she didn't want to think about that. If the histories were to be trusted, he was meant for another. What she knew of his fate was that he had attacked the avatar of Justice, that he was sent to Boreas for a time, and that he had married a princess—two of which had already occurred. Even if she did have an attraction to him in a purely physical sense, which was, when she thought on it, a base, instinctual thing and not something she had any control of, she had no intention of acting on it. There would be nothing to gain but heartache. Aurora had enough of that already. That, and he was a distraction she could ill afford. Pleasant though it might have been in other circumstances, she had something she needed to accomplish.

But, if she were being honest...

"You're not...unattractive."

"Be still my heart, such high praise!"

And even that felt like she'd given him too much. He struck her as someone who, once they were given any ground, pushed until one was overwhelmed completely.

"I would very much like to discuss something else." She squirmed as she made short work of his knots.

"Hmmm, I'm sure you would," he teased.

They needed to find another topic to discuss. Something less fraught. And preferably something he could expound on at length so she would be free to rebuild her walls as she focused on the methodical task before her.

"Tell me about Aureum. I've only ever read stories about it."

He was a window into a world that had been utterly lost. What remained in her time was a backwater province that had mostly become arid plains and desert, with only a sliver of green closest the border to Viridis.

"Such a blatant change of topic. And catered exactly to my interests."

"Please?"

He chuckled.

"What would you like to know?"

"When we go there, what will I see?"

"Hmm, well, first—no, give me a moment. I have an idea," he said, rising from his position and walking to the door, his hair only half combed. "Bring me a minds-eye stone," he ordered the attendant.

"Your Majesty, that might be a little—"

"Are you saying that the Viridian capital is so impoverished, it can't even afford one minds-eye stone?"

"Of course not, Your Majesty." The attendant bristled. "It will take but a moment."

He settled back into his spot and leaned his head back. Aurora continued brushing, working out the worst of the tangles with the help of a little oil.

"What's the stone?"

"You'll see."

She worked in companionable quiet. When she was done, she combed the full, silky length of it. As it dried, his thick hair developed a beautiful, loose wave. Most women would kill for hair such as his. Theron sighed contentedly.

"What do you suppose it would cost me to have an attendant comb my hair like this every day?"

"Given the cost for a bar of soap? Probably your firstborn."

"And what would you charge, madam fairy?"

She concentrated her hearing. No one had taken the absent attendant's position at the door. Orithyia had threatened her not to divulge this information, but what she didn't know wouldn't hurt her, Aurora hoped.

"Information and favours."

"Oh? What kind of favours?" Theron asked, his voice deepening.

Aurora snorted. It seemed Theron was still angling for something she planned on guarding.

"Military aid, to start."

Theron laughed.

"Planning to conquer Trisia while you're here?"

"Hardly. Drakon is an enormous flying serpent who can summon molten boulders and rain them down from the skies. He breathes a fire so hot it turns people to ash in an instant. It will take considerable force to subdue him."

If it could even be done. She could only hope that here, during the first cycle of calamity, his powers were not as devastating as they'd been in her time. After all, the great serpents of myth and legend grew in strength and potency as they aged, and the Drakon of her time had been thousands of years old.

"And aside from my military, what else would you demand for your hair-combing services?"

"Help with finding someone."

"Oh? I had no notion you knew anyone in Trisia. Should I be jealous?"

"I don't know them, precisely. But I will need their help to slay Drakon."

"And my military won't be enough?" he asked, slightly affronted.

"No. I wish it were that simple."

He turned around, his gold eyes taking her measure, trying to puzzle her out. But no matter how penetrating his gaze, he would not uncover her secrets so easily. Aurora could ill afford it. For what kind of sane man would believe her full story? Orithyia hadn't, and she had knowledge no one else in Trisia possessed. No, she needed his aid more than she needed to unburden her soul, more than she wished she could be fully honest.

"What aren't you telling me?" he asked.

Her ears twitched as the attendant marched through the hallways. Aurora had never been more grateful for their presence.

"It'll have to wait. We have company."

He cupped the back of her neck, drawing her close.

"You *will* tell me."

Aurora said nothing, returning his stare, refusing to be the first to flinch. The longer she held out, the more wicked his smile, and the more his gaze dipped to her lips.

Theron only released her when the attendant knocked on the door to deliver the stone, an opaque blue crystal the size of her fist with a copper colour band around it inscribed with ancient symbols. She'd never heard of such a device, though it bore some similarities with her artefact. Theron took the stone and sent the attendant out.

"I fear my words won't do my kingdom justice, but I can picture it clearly in my mind. This device will allow me to share it with you."

Theron closed his eyes, holding the stone in both hands. Images flashed before him, a magic wholly unknown to her, lost in time and never recovered. Her eyes widened, taking in the unexpected sight.

"We would cross The Colonnades Of The Colossus, a land bridge that soars over the Dragon's Tongue River, and enter my eastern-most province, the Dragon's Flank. The land is hilly, bordered by the Dragon's Tail and Dragon's Spine Mountain ranges, and gradually meets the sea in the south. In spring, the whole landscape is covered in colourful wild-flowers. Small towns hug the rivers, and the largest city is the harbour."

He was showing her what remained of Aureum's habitable land in her time. She recognised the Colonnades, but the water was higher, faster, a series of rapids beneath. The landscape was shocking in its beauty and abundance, green and dotted with flowers in reds, pinks, yellows and whites, vast forests where she only knew arid wine country. The towns were of particular interest. So little remained of old towns, where the original buildings were buried under thousands of years of occupation. Their plans were strikingly orderly, the buildings taller than she would have thought possible. But if her day out in Boreas were any measure, just seeing more than the ankle-high walls was still surprising to her.

"But we wouldn't stay there long, or travel south far enough to see it. We would travel the winding trade road through the canyons to Aureum proper, where Altanus lies. This time of year, it should be carpeted in grazing lands and fields of wheat..." He trailed off, a scowl on his face.

High, green cliffs soared overhead of a well-tended road that abutted a river along the same path, occasionally widening in places where water-falls rained down from above to create small ponds of striking depths. It was a feast for her eyes, all the more so because of what she remembered. The old trade road had been as dry as a bone, the waterfalls as extinct as the river, the small, deep ponds turned into wells that had long gone dry. But when he brought her out of the mouth of the canyon and into the old Aureum-proper, she could barely stifle her gasp.

Gone were the arid plains and seemingly endless desert beyond. In their place, a land of vibrant green, sparkling rivers, an enormous lake at the foot of mountains capped with dazzling snow. The city itself was no less spectacular. Painted buildings, colourful roofs, a bustling market, tree-lined streets, tranquil parks and rising above it all, a palace more resplendent than even her wildest imaginings. She'd always thought the ancient Aureans lived less splendidly than the Viridians, their cities poorer, their architecture less advanced. Perhaps what she'd learned had been more fairy tale than truth, if what Theron was showing her was to be believed.

"But the cursed blight has devastated much. The once-mighty rivers are polluted streams and the fields have become arid and patchy. The lake at the foot of the Dragon's Spine just north of the capital used to be crystal clear, but ever since Orithyia's tower went up, angering the spirits, that picturesque place is now a shadow of itself."

"A tower?"

He showed it to her then, an alien construction shooting out of the mountains, a white spire, darkening the snow that surrounded it. The rivers trickled through the land, the farmland suffered, the lake waters turned murky, and everywhere in his mind, there were people who were hungry, sick, their eyes hollow and hopeless.

"She constructed it in my kingdom without permission and angered the spirits. Ever since, my lands have been blighted. It fell not long ago, and I hope that will be the end of it."

He dispelled the images, setting the stone aside.

Was it truly a blight brought on by angry spirits, or merely a drought? She'd gathered he had a contentious relationship with the Orithyia of this time. She sympathised, but was he putting the blame in the right place or merely placing it where it was most emotionally satisfying? She put a hand on his.

"Your kingdom is beautiful, Theron. I don't think I've ever seen anything so full of life."

"Did you miss the part about the blight?"

"Even so, it was stunning. You're right to be proud of it."

"Hmmm, I can't tell if you're being sincere, or if you're buttering me up for something else."

Aurora laughed. It felt good, cleansing after everything that had happened.

"Will you tell me about your kingdom's myths and legends?"

"If you insist," he grumbled. "I shall tell you of the dragon whose body became Aureum and Niveum."

Aurora curled up against the pillows on the bed and listened, rapt by the stories Theron told of ancient heroes, the tales of giants and faeries, of the dragon who fell in love with a unicorn and gave her wings, and of the First Great Sundering. But as the sun rose in a cloudy sky, Aurora's eyelids drooped, until sleep took her in its gentle embrace. Her last recollection was of Theron tucking her in and wishing her sweet dreams.

A crack of thunder woke her moments before the door to the bedroom was swung open. Lightning flashed in the darkened room, painting two paladins of Knowledge in vivid detail. They marched inside and dragged her from the bed without so much as an explanation.

"Theron!" Aurora cried.

But as she searched the room for him, it was apparent he was gone. She was alone in whatever was to come.

Arms pinned and tied behind her back, Aurora was roughly ushered from the guest palace and into the rain, across empty, muddy streets and towards the temple of Knowledge. Outside, men and women wailed, waiting on the steps as acolytes kept them from entering.

Had Theron betrayed her after all? Traded her disloyalty to Orithyia and the secret hoard of artefacts for his release? Her magic uncoiled inside her, a beast scenting her rising panic. Orithyia had threatened to have her tongue pulled out, her eyes blinded, and her feet cut off. Aurora instantly regretted not sleeping with the protective artefact around her neck. She'd been such a fool to trust he would be an ally.

As she was dragged into the temple, everywhere was packed full of the sick and dying, temple medics rushing between patients, desperate to keep them from death. The children outnumbered the adults five to one. This was the plague of torchlight fever. Children lay on threadbare blankets as acolytes pressed wet compresses to their heads, others urging them to drink a bitter brew. Adults who had succumbed were removed from their places on the floor, only for it to be filled moments later. And everywhere, the moaning of the patients mingled with the harried commands of the medics.

Aurora was pushed through the narrow, wending path between the victims and up stairs where even here, patients lay. The second floor was nearly as crowded as the first. It was only the third that was devoid of patients but instead crammed with clerics either passed out in corners, their clothes dirty and their hair dishevelled, or staring blankly at walls with dark circles under their eyes, unable to rest amidst the clamour. It was through all this suffering that Aurora was ushered until at last she was made to kneel at Orithyia's feet in a private chamber.

"Leave us."

The priestesses left, closing the door on their way out, and the din instantly silenced. Here, Aurora could hear her own ragged breaths, the rush of blood roaring in her ears as her heart tried to escape the cage of her ribs. She tried to marshal her magic to her bidding but it remained elusive, like grabbing hold of rushing water. Orithyia touched the tip of her switch to Aurora's cheek, just below her eye.

"Tell me all you know about this hero you mentioned. The avatar of Justice."

It took a moment to register that the high priestess had not dragged her here to dispense with gruesome punishment. Or confront her with the theft of the artefacts. Theron hadn't betrayed her then. But why was she asking about this now, when the plague should be taking up all her resources? Where had Theron gone?

Orithyia scowled.

"I have a city beset by plague, and no spare time for your dawdling. Do I need to use the switch, girl?"

"No! No," Aurora assured her. "I don't know what more I could tell you. The hero of the holy sword possesses both wild and divine magic, as I said, and as far as I know, that has always been the case. He's made an avatar of Justice before Drakon comes to Trisia. His mission has always been to seal the beast away."

"And after the beast is sealed, what then?"

"I...I don't know. His life after that is never really mentioned."

Aurora didn't even know the first hero's name—no one did. So much history had been lost throughout the cycles of chaos and calamity that some periods had no more than a few distinct potsherds to define them by.

Her scowl deepened.

"You said Drakon brings a veritable apocalypse with it. This hero, he seals the beast away alone? How?"

Aurora swallowed, her magic twisting inside her chest. She didn't trust this Orithyia, not with her secrets or her safety.

"I can only surmise it has to do with the weapon he wields."

The first lash came without warning. Fire raced down from her cheek to her chest. Aurora screamed, curling in on herself. The high priestess had struck like a viper.

"You think I don't know by now when someone is lying to me? The next time I use this," she tipped Aurora's head up with the end of her switch so that their eyes met, "I will not be so generous as to avoid your eyes."

"I-I'm supposed to help," Aurora replied, her eyes swimming with tears.

"*You?*" she asked, incredulous.

"Yes."

"How?"

"My wild magic."

"What is someone with wild magic doing serving in a temple?"

She'd forgotten. In the past, those with wild magic never served in the temples, instead being pressed into service with the royal houses. That had only begun to change recently in Aurora's time.

"I didn't know. I thought it had abandoned me."

Orithyia rolled her eyes.

"Goddess preserve me. They must have taken you in out of sheer pity. So? What is so special about your wild magic?"

"I..."

She didn't want to tell her. Maybe it would be better to suffer the beating, knowing Theron could piece her back together. But she didn't think she would be able to hold out for very long. She was no warrior, accustomed to taking blows with stoicism.

The second lash raked across her face, ripping through her scalp, her right eye, her cheek, her nose, her lips. Fire gave way to a rush of blood. Aurora's scream only further split open the bloody wounds. She couldn't see! *She couldn't see!* Her magic surged, but nothing happened. It was too late. The damage had been done. Half her world had gone dark.

"You waste my time at the expense of people's lives. You were warned. Answer."

"I can p-pause time," Aurora sobbed.

"Hmmm," Orithyia hummed, mulling her words. "Clearly not very well, or you could have avoided my switch."

She hated it then, this creature in her chest. All it did was writhe inside her, never obeying her will, doing whatever it liked. It had nearly killed her last night. Today, it couldn't even protect her from having her face split open. She was no better than a mouse facing off against a lion, and she didn't even have the protection of tooth and claw.

"I h-have no training. I only l-learned about it a few days before I was s-sent back to your time."

The high priestess studied her for some time as Aurora wept, her blood and tears mingling on her ruined cheek and raining down on the floor beneath her. She wished she could remove it, this magic that felt more like a curse than a gift. But there was no tearing it out. It was embedded in her soul.

"I can see now why you failed in your time. You're a brainless twit." Orithyia grabbed her face, her finger pressing on Aurora's open wound. Aurora shrieked. "A condition you have yet to overcome, if your choice of company is any indication. Don't think that I'm unaware of your seduction of the Aurean king. If you have any good sense in you, then heed my words—Queen Flora has plans for him, and when he is gone, *you* will still reside in the guest palace. I suggest you do your best to prove your worth to me." She released Aurora with the flick of her wrist and pulled the bell-pull, wiping her bloodied hand with a pristine scrap of silk. The paladins entered, awaiting instruction. "Take her back. Give her parchment and ink." She speared Aurora with an uncompromising stare. "You will draw this holy sword, as well as the beast, so that my people will know what it is they're to look for. Now go, I have a city to care for."

Aurora was pushed through the temple, bloody and beaten, until she was back out on the streets, the rain adding insult to injury. Every drop felt like acid against her wounds. By the time she was deposited back in the atrium of the guest palace, she was a mess, soaked to the bone. She stumbled back to her room and collapsed on her bed, hoping desperately that Theron would return.

CHAPTER 15
THERON

So, his little fairy was flustered by even the mildest flirting? Theron smiled as he tucked her in and wished her sweet dreams. He sat by the terrace, intending to enjoy the view of the gardens, but found his gaze drawn to her again and again. She had so many weaknesses, he had a veritable buffet to choose from to wrap her around his finger. Her heart was an open book.

Provided, of course, she was not the most talented spy in Viridis. In that case, he'd kept everything important from her, showing her scenic glimpses instead of areas of vital importance. But what kind of spy asked to hear epic stories of times long gone instead of stories that might give her actionable intelligence?

It wasn't impossible, but it was beginning to look less and less likely that she was anyone's spy. Unless she was being threatened. The spirit had taken on the form of the one she desired most to see, a small woman with pointed ears and red hair, another fairy. But the words Aurora had sobbed as it had lured her into its embrace had been genuine. The woman she most wished to see had died in Aurora's place. Her guilt and longing had prevented her from seeing the truth, even as the spirit had tried to end her life.

Yes, his little fairy was so full of openings she would be easy to control. She was vulnerable, physically and emotionally. She was lonely, easily seduced, far too trusting, and not at all accustomed to participating in intrigues. Her honesty alone would have seen her eaten alive at even the most backwater of courts. Openly asking for an alliance, his military aid, and admitting the need to find someone? She might as well have rolled over and showed him her belly.

While Aurora had been able to hold onto some of her secrets, with the right pressure, she would crack and satisfy his curiosity. If her knowledge could free him from Viridis before that, all the better. It might not be honourable as a man to use her thus, but as a king, his honour was bound up with the fate of his kingdom. Anything and everything was acceptable for the sake of Aureum.

Yet it left a bitter taste in his mouth.

Theron hated this feeling. It was a weight around his legs, sure to drag him to his death. He could admit he felt a certain spark with her—to deny it would be foolish. Her unexpected fits of boldness and familiarity held a certain charm. But to allow lust to cloud his judgement and wriggle its way past his defences was intolerable. The sooner he bedded her, the sooner he could rid himself of its hold on him. And the sooner he could control her.

A knock on the door interrupted his thoughts.

Goddess, he hated that this place had reduced him to answering his own chamber door. He supposed he should be grateful that at least they hadn't taken to barging in unannounced.

He opened it to find a new guard, this one wearing finer armour, Viridian green and a small red earring.

"Yes?"

"You're to be presented to Queen Flora."

"When?"

"Now."

Theron sighed. He was wearing clothes better suited to a merchant of modest means. Not even linen, his garments were made of plain, undyed wool without a single decorative stitch in sight. No doubt she meant to humiliate him in these rags.

"And there have been...developments."

"Come in then, but keep your voice down."

As Theron rummaged hopelessly in the wardrobe for something of finer quality, the spy gave his report.

"Bandits attacked the grain shipment. Most of it was recovered, but the nobles are using it to suggest it was the Viridians' doing."

Of course, the ones slavering for war would take anything as a provocation. They had sons and daughters hungry for the kind of honour only a battlefield could bequeath, and mines rich in the metals needed for weapons. War could be profitable for the nobles whose lands were furthest from the Viridian borders.

"Was it?" he asked, giving up on his fruitless search for better garments. At least his hair was no longer a mess, courtesy of his sleeping fairy.

"There is some evidence of it."

"Definitive?"

"No."

Thrice-damned fools. Couldn't they see what they would risk with war? Did they think nothing of the people and livelihoods that would be erased by open conflict? One where they didn't have the moral high ground? Who would come to their aid if they didn't have a good enough reason for their attack? Not Niveum or Gilvus. And who would be able to spare the soldiers or supplies? Their losses would only be compounded during a cycle of chaos. Every kingdom that had risked war during a cycle of chaos had been reduced to ashes and dust. Much as he loved Aureum, Theron was not fool enough to think it would be different for his realm.

"Is there anything else?"

"Dualists tried to breach the palace. Batea's beasts devoured them."

And a good thing too. The cultists believed the monarchs were heavily responsible for their plight. They were as fanatical as they were organised.

But the attack would only give Orithyia more reason to encroach on his territory.

"Let's get this charade over with."

"I apologise, but you're required to wear these."

The spy produced a pair of gold handcuffs.

Theron barely repressed a snarl. Maybe war wasn't such a bad idea after all. He held out his wrists and allowed himself to be bound. As he was led from the guest palace to the main palace, it became clear that today was meant to be a public humiliation. Even the servants of the main palace were dressed better than he in dyed and patterned linen garb.

No doubt Queen Flora meant to have him reenact her own humiliation before Aureum's court when she was but a young, hotheaded princess who thought she could claim the Colonnades for Viridis. His parents had let her off lightly, forcing a public apology and for her to pay the lifetime wages of all the Aurean soldiers she'd killed to the bereaved families her attack had created. Flora had been obsessed with retaliating to sate her damaged pride ever since.

She'd envisioned herself as a conquering hero, trying to recapture territory her great-grandmother had lost long ago. The moment she'd been crowned queen, Flora had been a thorn in his side, along with her high priestess.

His parents could have declared war all those years ago.

They *should* have beheaded her as their price for peace.

But they'd had no appetite to fight Viridis then. And only a few years later, they'd been carried off by disease, leaving Theron to shoulder Aureum himself. It had taken a decade to whip the unruly, ambitious nobles of Aureum into line. Had they fallen in line more quickly, he might have defeated her all those years ago. More's the pity.

Theron stepped into the royal receiving hall, a nightmare in vivid green, as if the whole palace had suddenly been swallowed by a carnivorous plant. A nightmare made all the more grotesque as the sky outside darkened, thunder rolling ominously in the distance. The sneering crowds he might have expected under normal circumstances were absent. Theron smirked. With a plague, they'd likely fled the city to hide out in their rural mansions. Only the most sycophantic loyalists remained to pad out the queen's meagre retinue. Not even Orithyia was present.

Flora sat on her emerald throne wearing a jewel-encrusted gown of the same, a triumphant sneer twisting her tanned features, now showing her advancing age. Grey threaded through the deep brown of her elaborately coiffed and bejewelled hair, her crown like a spray of green and silver snakes on her head. Her dark eyes sparkled as her gaze lingered on the handcuffs.

"On your knees, Theron. This is Viridis."

As a guard approached him to shove him to his knees, Theron glared the man into submission.

"A pair of gaudy handcuffs won't stop me from rebreaking every bone in your body."

The guard was frozen, caught between his queen's implicit order and Theron's explicit threat. Theron turned his glare on Flora. He should keep his head, truly, but she was just so fucking prideful. So much so, he knew exactly how he wanted to humiliate her in turn. She expected him to be beaten and disgraced, to be fighting in vain to preserve his honour. There was only one remedy—shamelessness.

"I seem to remember that when last you visited Aureum, you were treated with the respect due to your station. Has Viridis fallen into barbarism since, or has it always been thus?"

That wiped the sneer from her face.

"It was not I who slaughtered Viridian soldiers on Viridian soil!"

"No, you simply tried to start a war on Aurean soil...and failed miserably."

Heat crept up her neck as her knuckles whitened on the arms of her throne. It was a beautiful sight.

"And yet, only one of us has the ignominious reputation as a blasphemer. I may have warred against Aurean soldiers, but you attacked an avatar."

Theron stood straighter.

"The avatar has forgiven me my transgression, and the goddess has punished me. Interesting though, that the horrible fate the goddess bestowed on me was to send me to Viridis. To Boreas."

A few of the courtiers blanched. He smiled. If being sent to Viridis was divine punishment meant for him, then it tarnished both him *and* Viridis.

"Is it not obvious that Justice is favouring me? Placing my enemy in the palm of my hand seems like a fitting reward."

"I wasn't aware we were enemies, Flora," he said, examining his nails.

Rage had her flushing anew. Yes, that's it. Let her lose her head. Let her come out from this insulting audience the loser. Let her know she wasn't even worth the title of enemy.

"One cannot expect all kings to know basic history, it seems. But the fertile valley belonged to Viridis. Aureum transgressed first."

The fertile valley, known as the Dragon's Flank, had been contested between Viridis and Aureum back as far as the times of myth and legend. But Aureum had ruled it for generations now. No one still living remembered a time of Viridian rule.

"Perhaps the Viridian royal tutors forgot to teach you the last two hundred years of history where the Dragon's Flank is concerned, but I must inform you that it has been Aurean for some time now."

"Then that changes today."

She snapped her fingers, and a servant bearing a tray with a document in parchment approached her.

"Read it," she commanded.

One of her toadies dutifully picked the document up and read it aloud.

"For the undisputed crime of murdering fifty Viridian soldiers on Viridian soil, the blasphemer King Theron of Aureum will cede the entirety of the Dragon's Flank from The Colonnades of The Colossus to Dragon's Talon port to Viridis as compensation. By signing this document, both Queen Flora and King Theron agree to these facts as true and these terms as just and fair."

His magic rose like a tempest inside him. That filthy, godless whore. The entirety of the Dragon's Flank?! Did she actually believe he would let her have it? Lightning flashed in the distance, thunder echoing in the humid hall. No. Calm. If she wanted him to sign it, that meant she hadn't used his stolen seal ring to falsify his agreement. More fool her. She really was useless without Orithyia.

"I will never sign that," Theron said.

"You will if you ever want to leave the guest palace."

"I'm not one of your helpless prisoners, Flora. I remain in your guest palace as a courtesy, not out of necessity."

"If you're so powerful, where are your servants? Why is it you wear the clothes of a commoner, without even a single ring on your finger? At least accept your loss with a shred of dignity."

"As you did, all those years ago? Teach me your ways, Queen Flora."

"You will learn respect, or you will never wear a crown again."

"My respect is reserved for those who earn it, and my crown was bestowed by the ancient magics at the heart of Aureum. It cannot be taken by the grasping hands of a mortal queen."

"Your dominion ended the moment you stepped into Viridis. I could have your head for your atrocities."

"You could," he conceded. "But then Aureum will be ruled by Batea, and you'll face both a cycle of chaos and possible war. Do you think you alone, contrary to every other overly ambitious monarch throughout history, will survive both?"

"Is that a threat?"

"Merely some well-meaning advice."

"Given your current state, perhaps you shouldn't be so quick to give advice. Perhaps you should be open to receiving some instead. Sign the declaration, or I'll ensure Orithyia remains too busy to purify your blasphemer's mark. Without that, you'll never wear the crown again."

If that were to happen, it would be because Orithyia had already planned it as such. It was true that no one would accept a man tainted by a goddess' wrath on a throne, not unless he'd been purified by a high priestess. The threat was all too real, and yet, she'd just left herself vulnerable.

"You would dare interfere with the duties of a high priestess? How would you propose to stop her? Or does Orithyia do your bidding?"

That stopped Flora. If she could command Orithyia so easily, then was it Flora who had ordered a tower built in his lands, interfering with his guardianship of Aureum? That was as good as a declaration of war. Anyone with sense knew that without the proper rituals, building in such a location would anger the mountain spirits. Rituals that had most definitely not been conducted, seeing as those were the purview of monarchs and nobility.

"Orithyia is like a mother to Viridis, and every mother worth her salt can identify a threat to her child when she sees it." Flora glared at him.

"Regardless, I will have to decline your offer of advice. I'll never sign that document. First and foremost, it's full of lies."

"The only liar here stands before me in commoner's rags."

"I murdered, at most, ten soldiers. The rest fell to the monstrosities. A mere fraction of the soldiers you killed during your failed conquest, for which your punishment was an apology and monetary compensations to the victims of your unprovoked hostilities," Theron continued as if she hadn't spoken.

"And as to these commoner's rags, as you so eloquently put it, am I to believe that the queendom of Viridis is so impoverished that even the royal palace cannot provide suitable garments for a king? A pity indeed, if so. For I recall that you were given everything befitting a princess when you stayed in Aureum." When she tried to speak, he held up his hand.

"As for my lack of any adornment, when I crossed into Viridis, I wore only my armour and my seal ring, which was stolen by none other than your General Stentor. I would appreciate its return, lest it fall into the hands of someone who might consider using it to sign that spurious document without my consent. I hope you will see fit to have it returned to me. Lastly, I would rather give up my crown than cede the Dragon's Flank to Viridis. It's worth far more than the lives of ten Viridian soldiers, and pretending otherwise is an insult to the intelligence of everyone gathered here. I will pay reasonable monetary compensation for my transgressions, but you will not have my kingdom."

Flora pointed at him, her ire flashing in her eyes.

"You dare to stand there, a blasphemer and a murderer, and dictate terms in my court? You falsely accuse an honourable man of theft, and a queen of valuing the lives of her soldiers too highly? Your shamelessness knows no bounds, Theron!"

"The only shameless thing in this room is that document. I have told no lies, nor made false accusations. As for your soldiers, what is the price a Viridian noble pays to the crown if he kills a soldier? According to your own law codes, he pays the man's weight in coppers. Silvers if he is of a middling rank. Am I mistaken?"

"Those laws apply to the citizens of Viridis. Not to foreigners."

He had her on the retreat now.

"Then allow me to offer to pay the weight of each slain soldier in gold as compensation. That is fair by any measure."

"And what of the servants of the guest palace? What will you pay for terrorising them?" She raised her brows.

Flora really was making misstep after misstep. Her vivarium was a gross insult to the sacred concept of hospitality. After all, a host was judged based on the welcome they gave their guests. That she was too blinded by her own arrogance to see it spoke poorly for her ability to remain on her throne.

"Nothing. They gave the first insult. Unless it was you who ordered them make indecent demands in return for basic necessities? I was incredibly lenient, given the magnitude of their insults against me. In Aureum, such disrespect would be met with a whipping, at least. But perhaps making vulgar demands of royalty is merely your custom in Viridis."

"Oh, then perhaps you would like to follow the Aurean custom for captured royalty? I believe it is to be paraded through the streets of the capital in chains."

"Which your general Stentor already did. And that is the custom for captured war leaders, yes. But I neither declared nor initiated war."

"Your actions at the Queen's Road were as good as a declaration. That I have not marched on Aureum is due to my magnanimity."

And her wariness of starting a war during a cycle of chaos. If she'd really wanted a war, she would have had him beheaded the moment he'd arrived. It could still happen, but she wanted the Dragon's Flank instead. If she got it, she would cut him off from Aureum's only profitable port and its most accessible trade route. Flora was, as ever, a bundle of contradictions. She wanted revenge for her failed war, but needed to humiliate him and Aureum before she could be satisfied. Her weakness was her sadism. Rather than deal with the threat he posed in the most expedient of ways, she needed to toy with him.

Had Queen Flora been brought to Aureum for the same crimes, he would not have let her lead him by the nose in his own court. He would have forced a public audience only once he'd beaten her down in private. But she was so needy for his humiliation that she'd not considered he would turn it against her. Flora expected him to be fearful and humbled by his circumstances, as she had been. That she could not conceive of a worldview different than her own was an astounding oversight. It made it all the clearer that the one who truly ruled Viridis was not this petulant creature, but the cunning high priestess. Without her mistress keeping a firm hand on her leash, Flora was a dog chasing her own tail.

Just as he'd long suspected.

"My actions at the border were a result of divine madness. Surely your general relayed this to you."

"Princess Epicasta, Your Majesty," the guard at the door announced.

The queen's sycophants looked grim as the princess swept into the room. She didn't spare him a glance as she approached her mother wearing a gown in the deep red of mourning along with a silver and green tiara atop her dark, veiled hair.

"I heard you were entertaining a guest, Your Majesty," Epicasta said, her gaze flicking over him.

"Hardly. This is King Theron, a shameless blasphemer who dares dictate what his punishment should be for killing Viridian soldiers in my queendom."

"I would be delighted to teach him proper respect if you would allow it, Your Majesty."

Flora's eyes lit at that.

"Be my guest."

Epicasta's dispassionate grey gaze swept him from head to toe. This was the infamous glass princess. One who had murdered her last three husbands for daring to bruise her delicate skin. A crime against the royal family, the queen had pronounced. That those same husbands had been highly influential and opposed to Flora on matters of state had not escaped anyone's notice. That Epicasta had also bankrupted her husbands before their executions only fueled her infamy.

With a twist of her wrist, Epicasta wrenched the air from his lungs.

"Kneeling before the queen of Viridis is custom," she said.

He did his best to resist, to fight for even a hint of a breath, but his suffocation brought him to his knees. As she'd intended. Thus brought low, he was freed from her magic. He gulped in air to Flora's obvious delight. Rage burned in his breast. How dare she assault him?

"Your Majesty, I believe I can handle things from here. Allow me to escort this barbarian back to the guest palace and explain his circumstances to him. He has stolen so much of your precious time already. I will ensure he is made properly grateful that you have provided him an audience in these trying times."

Was this the true ruler of Viridis? This cunning bitch who so easily managed her hot-headed mother? But then why put up with Flora's antics at all?

"Is it already time for Council to meet?"

"Yes, Your Majesty," Epicasta replied.

"Very well. See this blasphemer back to the guest palace. I'll deal with him another day."

The moment Theron attempted to stand, Epicasta choked him with her magic. Flora swept past with a laugh and exited the royal receiving chambers, taking her party of lickspittles with her. It was only once the grand doors closed that Epicasta released the hold she had on his lungs.

Theron gasped, sweat drenching his back. This bitch was going to pay for her actions.

"You may stand," Epicasta said, never once flinching as he stood to his full height and loomed over her.

"Do that again and I won't hold back, Princess," Theron growled.

"Learn some humility, and I won't have to. Come along, we have much to discuss." Epicasta headed towards the door where the guards were already opening it with a respectful bow.

By the time he caught up with her, the storm was beginning in earnest. Servants rushed to get under the covered walkways and out of the heavy rain, or duck back into the maze of buildings. She led him in silence back to the guest palace, never once bothering to check he was still following after her, the crack and rumble of thunder and lightning taking the place of any pleasantries between them. She was about to turn towards his room when he stopped her. His little fairy was inside, and he didn't want this venomous creature anywhere near her.

"The gardens will do," he said.

In this deluge, it would be as private as a room, and at least there he could see any potential eves-droppers.

The princess raised a brow at his hand on her. Only when he let her go did she detour. When at last they came to their destination, a small pavilion overlooking the fishponds and greenery of the guest palace, she sat down and motioned for him to follow. When he did, she produced the key to his handcuffs and freed him.

"As I said, we have much to discuss," she began.

"If you plan to persuade me to sign that toe rag your mother calls a treaty, then think again."

She tilted her head.

"I could force you."

"Batea would depose me—with my blessing."

Epicasta produced his seal ring from her pocket, twisting it this way and that.

"Who would know it was against your will until it was too late?"

"Anyone with common sense, Princess."

She placed his seal ring on the table and pushed it towards him.

"You're welcome, by the way. The plan was to present the treaty to you as an open and shut matter, with your seal used to ratify it."

"Oh? So why didn't you allow it?" he asked, securing his seal ring back on his finger. Perhaps he should destroy it, so that it couldn't be stolen again.

"Because it wouldn't have satisfied Her Majesty. She wants you to sign the document yourself, however unwillingly, and she wants the signing to be public."

Ah. In that case, he would most definitely use such an occasion to destroy his seal ring.

"That's not going to happen."

"I suggest you get comfortable with the idea that it will, in some way or another. I also suggest you find some way to give Her Majesty what she desires before she decides to get...creative."

Theron regarded this Viridian bitch with some amusement. As far as courtiers went, she seemed to be most effective. Every emotion had been drained out of her, her grey eyes as unmoving as stone. Time to see if he could provoke her.

"I can't understand why you haven't already deposed your mother."

She didn't even flinch at his words.

"That would be pointless."

"Because you agree with her aims? Am I to look forward to dealing with another rabid dog barking at my borders once you ascend to the throne?"

"I would not expect to live quite so long, were I you, Your Majesty."

"We'll see." Theron leaned back in his seat.

"You're rather obtuse, aren't you?" Epicasta sighed.

The rain picked up, coming down in torrents now. Lightning flashed over the city, the crash of thunder resounding moments later.

"I pride myself on standing in the way of Viridian entitlement to my lands."

Epicasta shook her head.

"Who am I, Your Majesty?"

Theron raised a brow.

"And what game is this, Princess?"

She squeezed the air from his lungs. He lunged across the table dividing them, his hand on her throat.

"Who am I, Your Majesty?" she hissed.

"A dead woman," he retorted as he fought to fill his lungs.

"Who. Am. I?"

He squeezed harder. She gripped his hands with a grimace.

"The glass princess, about to shatter."

She returned his breath to him. He let up, but not completely.

"Precisely," she replied. "And how does Her Majesty deal with especially troublesome adversaries?"

He let her go as if scalded.

No.

Not this mangy bitch.

He would never allow some Viridian whore to claim even a single slice of Aureum. He would sooner take an actual whore as his queen than allow any Viridian to bind themselves to him, or Aureum's magics—to corrupt them, to own them. He would sooner slit his own throat.

"Never."

"My sentiments exactly," she replied. "Now, if you're quite done with your barbarism, please sit."

"I don't see what there is to discuss. The moment you drag me to the altar is the moment I renounce my kingship. A wedding between us will end in one way—with a funeral. Yours, to be precise."

She rolled her eyes.

"Are you done beating your chest? I have no desire to tie myself to Aureum. Or to you." She curled her lip at him.

"Then what do you want?"

"Sign the treaty with Her Majesty. Do it publicly. Give her the triumph she so desperately craves. When I come into my throne, I'll return the Dragon's Flank to Aureum."

"As if I would believe a word out of your mouth."

"You had better start trying. Because if she can't entrap you with this, she will entrap you with me. Then it will be my duty to have your heir, dispatch you, and eventually cede all of Aureum to Viridis while placing your child on the throne of your client kingdom. Do *not* make me."

"Why are you telling me this? The only incentive I have now is to murder you outright."

"I'm telling you this so you understand what the rest of your short life will look like if you don't sign that treaty."

"I'm not some spineless Viridian noble, Princess."

"There are foul magics in Trisia capable of sapping a man's will."

"I'll not allow myself to be overcome by foul magics, nor will I be used by you."

Her brows pinched with pity.

"Do you know who else thought that way? Each of my three late husbands. Please, for both our sakes, do whatever it takes not to become my fourth."

Epicasta rose from her seat. Theron didn't bother showing her the courtesy of standing or bowing. Courtesy was reserved for those with honour. Epicasta, with her foul magic, had none. How dare she threaten to use magic to obliterate his will, to rape him, to murder him and then to enslave his kingdom. He would never allow himself to be taken alive. It was time to inform his spies in Viridis to take action. If Flora had access to such magics, he needed to wrest them from her control, and then kill anyone who had the ability to replicate them—lest she and her scourge of a daughter get their claws into him and his kingdom.

"I will give you some time to contemplate your future, Your Majesty. But do it quickly. I suspect Her Majesty will have something planned for when the plague abates."

She didn't fear him. She pitied him. Was so bloody certain of her eventual victory. That needed to change. She thought to light a fire under him. He would return the favour. His magic exploded from him. Theron turned around then, shooting out of his seat. He crowded her out from under the shelter of the covered walkway and into the mud, into the driving rain.

"You threaten to use magic to destroy my will." He flooded her with his own. Her eyes widened in alarm. "You threaten to violate me," he continued, letting his magic trickle through her muscles, her bones, seeking out her history of hurts. "To enslave my people as surely as you plan to enslave any child you get from me." He found it then, her litany of healed bones, her scars, her brutal past. And yet he felt no pity. "Know this, Princess. You will not survive long enough to do so. I have found the past written in your flesh. I will shatter you long before you choke me. It is not I who needs to accept the predations of Viridis, but you who needs to use your guile to manage your mother."

She eyed him up and down, scowling.

"You're a fool, Theron."

Her eyes caught on something above him.

"We're done here," she announced, pushing past him.

"No, we're not," he snarled, grabbing her wrist.

"We are being watched."

He flicked his gaze upward.

Aurora.

His heart seized in his chest. Her face was a mess of gore and blood. How? He'd left her sleeping peacefully.

Princess forgotten, Theron stormed into the building, all but running through the halls of the guest palace. He tore open the door to his room, but she wasn't there. Had she gone to her own? He raced back down the hall towards hers, ripping open the door. She sat there, curled up by the terrace, a hand to her ragged face.

Aurora was soaked through from the rain, her white nightgown stained red as blood poured down from her scalp, her cheeks, her nose, her lips, her neck. Theron rushed over, wrapping her in his magic. He pulled her hand away to better assess the damage—only to choke on his rage. Her eye had been nearly gouged out. Instead of using his magic to convince her body to mend itself, he poured it into her, filling her up, allowing his magic to draw on his energy instead. There would be no pain from this healing.

"Who did this to you?" he snarled.

Had it been one of the animals in the vivarium? Had it been one of Flora's guards, trying to hurt him through her? Whoever it had been would pay with their lives.

Her tears fell in earnest then. She crumpled in on herself. He swept her up in his arms and held her close.

"Orithyia," she whispered.

He tightened his embrace as every ugly thought raced through his mind. Maybe Batea had been right. Maybe the curse of a goddess was worth ridding the world of Orithyia's taint. His little fairy had already nearly died of fever and been attacked by a vengeful spirit. She didn't deserve this. Aurora wept in his arms.

"They came and you weren't there. *Why* weren't you there?" Aurora sobbed. "You were gone and they took me. Where were you?"

Lightning flashed, transporting him in an instant.

"Where were you?!" his mother screamed. "Where were you when your brother needed you?!"

He was no longer a man grown, a king, but a scared young boy with a weight crushing his heart. His mother's shriek rang in his ears in time with the thunder.

Theron shoved Aurora from his arms. She fell to the floor, her elbow taking the brunt of her weight. Her sharp intake of breath was drowned out by his racing heartbeat. Pain, as sharp as any blade, bloomed in his chest. Memories and nightmares alike assailed him, his gorge rising. He beat back his panic, but only just. He forced his memories away, pushed through the nightmares clinging to his waking mind. Fear and anger held him in their grip, and so he reached for anger, for safety.

"I am not the villain here! I am not responsible for your life!" he shouted.

Shock and fear flashed across her face as she clutched her injured arm. Then betrayal. His gut sank. Shame scalded him—he couldn't believe he'd lost control so badly as to physically hurt her. Theron reached out a hand to heal her.

"Don't," she growled, slapping his hand away.

She gritted her teeth, her tears turned to rage in a heartbeat. Aurora stood, wincing, her wet, bloody gown clinging to her lean form. She was a wicked spirit, come to haunt him for his failures.

"I trusted you! I thought we were allies! You promised to protect me but you left me to get maimed by Orithyia and now merely asking where you were makes *me* the villain?! Get out!"

Why did her accusations hurt so much? Why did it make him so angry? She was nothing to him. *Nothing.* How dare she wound him in this way? How dare she worm her way past his defences? How dare she remind him of his worst moments, when he'd been a moment away from regretting his actions towards her!

"Ungrateful swine!" he shouted.

"Worthless bastard!" She spat at him.

Another flash of lightning.

"Worthless," his father hissed, his face transforming from devastation to rage in an instant. "You're no son of mine!"

His father's voice thundered through him in time with the tempest outside. She'd reduced him to that same cowering child, the horror of his ineptitude dawning on him. One life had depended on him then, and in his carelessness, he'd let it slip through his fingers.

He fought back another tide of rising nausea, fought to remain in the present, his heart pounding in his ears. He gripped her jaw in his hand as she glared daggers at him.

"You'd be dead if not for me!"

"Death would be a blessing!" she retorted, pulling free, tears streaming down her face, her eyes flashing with hopeless fury as another bolt of lightning lit the room.

"Save me," Tisander whispered, blood pooling at the corners of his mouth.

He tried to push that nightmare away, but Tisander morphed into Aurora, blood leaking from her ruined eye. He'd failed her, and she'd paid in blood. Just as Tisander had paid with his life.

No! This isn't the same! I healed her!

Yet his heart paid no heed to his head as the thunder boomed as loud as his heart. Dread and rage ripped his last bit of sense to shreds between their teeth. How dare she talk of throwing away her life?! How dare she, when there were so many he'd lost? He rounded on her then, crowding her against the wall, pinning her. His magic swirled around them in his senseless wrath. How could he hate her so much in that moment, and yet be grateful that his magic assured him of her heartbeat?

"Don't you say that! Don't you *ever* fucking say that!"

She pushed him away with all her might.

"Get out! I never want to see your thrice-damned face again!"

"Likewise!" he retorted, storming off and slamming the door shut on his way out.

Her sobbing chased him all the way back to his quarters, where he sank to his knees, his heart and mind in tatters.

CHAPTER 16
THERON

For the next few days, Theron was no better than an injured dog, liable to lash out and bite anyone who got too close. His heart was a raw, gaping wound that refused to heal. Aurora had slipped through his walls, and with unexpected violence, she'd thrown every nightmare, every crippling memory, into stark relief. Her words had cut him to the bone and then served him his bleeding heart on a silver platter.

He hated her for it.

With only a few words, she'd stripped him of his strength, his control, his sense of equilibrium. No one had ever done that to him and lived to tell the tale.

Except her.

As much as he'd wanted to stomp down that hallway and beat down her door so that he could rail against her, give some outlet to the ugly, fetid swamp of emotions riding him, a small rational part of him knew she was not to blame for it. Not really. Those wounds had been inflicted by his parents in their darkest hour and then left to fester for a lifetime thereafter.

As Theron lounged in the courtyard, soaking in the sun, he had a sinking feeling in his gut. His anger had abated, leaving remorse in its wake. It was uncomfortable, and every time he thought he'd managed to cleanse himself of it, her angry tears invaded his mind.

The benefits of being a king meant never having to apologise to any-one beneath you. And as a king, everyone was beneath him. But if he wanted to salvage some connection with Aurora, he was going to have to. Her value had not diminished just because he'd lost his temper. She knew things no one else did. Theron was still convinced he was going to need her before his trials in Boreas were through, and his intuitions were rarely wrong.

The problem was that by the time he'd calmed down enough to know what he needed to do, he couldn't find her anywhere. She no longer slept in the room she'd been in. Like a ghost, she seemed to pass through the walls of the guest palace unseen. Only his spies had been able to detect her. According to them, Aurora moved rooms daily, snuck into the kitchens at odd hours, and slipped between guard rotations to bathe at night. He tried to catch her one evening, but she'd never showed.

His only consolation was that she hadn't managed to relieve him of her pack of ill-gotten goods. Theron was confident she wouldn't leave the capital without them, and so he'd taken to keeping them on his person at all times. Naturally, he'd sorted through them many times during the interminably dull days in the vivarium. Stolen treasures from the other prisoners, a coveted bar of soap, a few gowns, her foreign clothes, her ancient artefacts, and her scroll. He turned to it again, unrolling it to see her drawings.

He recognised the woman, the same face that the spirit had taken. Phaedra. Rendered in loving detail, this one had an air of mischief about her. The next was a man with long, pointed ears, much like her own, and a kind look in his eyes. Lover? Family? He didn't know. The next was a sword, the hilt drawn in intricate and precise detail. Something about it bothered him, scratching at the back of his mind, like a forgotten word trapped on the tip of his tongue. The last was of a fearsome beast—a great serpent, a multitude of horns curling from its head, eyes wide with madness, gaping jaw full of endless teeth. It looked exactly like something Batea would create, if she hadn't already. With a striking resemblance to her most recent giant serpents, he couldn't help his unease. Perhaps the ambition to soar through the skies on the backs of dragons was one better left to the imagination than brought to reality.

He tucked the scroll back into her sack and pulled out her small circular artefact, marvelling at his handiwork. With nothing better to fill his time, aside from thinking up all the retorts he wished to lob at both the princess and her wretch of a mother, he'd turned to repairing it. But the metal bands around it had resisted his every effort and refused to bend even when heated. It was only when, in a fit of pique, his magic had swirled around him and latched onto the artefact that he'd uncovered something truly unique.

That was when he knew Aurora would forgive him. The inquisitive little fairy would no doubt be fascinated to learn her artefact was in some strange way a living organism. He planned on trading that information, along with her fully restored artefact, for her forgiveness and continued aid.

It would be enough, surely.

As a servant came up the covered walkway, Theron slipped the artefact into the crudely stitched satchel at his side. This servant wore a red bracelet. She made to clean up his morning dishes.

"Word is the queen has something humiliating planned for a party to celebrate the end of the plague and the reopening of the city."

Perhaps this time she would force him to appear in nothing but a soiled loincloth. Though it was bold of her to risk humiliating him in front of an audience. Even one as hostile as the nobles of Boreas could be made to turn on her with the right invective. No monarch ever rested on their laurels with such bloodhounds as usually stalked the courts.

"Typical. Anything else?"

"No word of weddings, if that's what concerns you."

That was the first bit of good news he'd heard in a while. If Flora hadn't convinced herself she'd just come up with a brilliant solution for a fourth time in a row after allowing Epicasta to escort him, he should thank the Triad. He would pray that it remained so. Much as he blustered the other day, he had no desire to test his mettle against a magic foul enough to deprive three men of their will. Nor did he have any illusions that his refusal to hand over the Dragon's Flank wouldn't result in a more dire situation.

"And the magic?"

"No word on what it might be."

Theron cursed.

How was he to protect himself against a magic he knew nothing about? How was he to circumvent it so that he could assure himself that he could kill his potential black widow of a bride? It was clearly not Epicasta's magic. The bitch princess could suffocate him all she liked, he would abdicate long before he allowed such torture to sway him into ceding the territory. But her mother? From what he understood, she had the ability to paralyse her victim for a short time. While possible that she'd used it to allow Epicasta to consummate her marriages with unwilling husbands, the very thought was so repellent to him that he couldn't imagine Flora would still be queen if she'd used her magic in such a way. Surely her own nobles would have deposed her long ago.

"Have someone look into what Flora was doing while Epicasta's husbands lost their will to fight."

The servant's eyes widened as she piled up his dishes on her platter.

"Yes, Your Majesty."

He needed to know how Flora or her daughter had subdued the princess' late husbands into total submission. After all, it would've had to have been lasting in effect for Epicasta to thoroughly bankrupt them all before they'd faced execution. He'd always assumed it had been accomplished through fear alone. But if the princess hadn't been lying to force his hand, then he would have one more weapon in his arsenal for dealing with Flora. If he could uncover it.

"And have you been able to find my lit—Aurora?"

"I believe she is on the grounds somewhere at present, as all her usual hiding places within the building proper were searched today."

That didn't account for unusual places she might know of that no one else did though. How was he supposed to regain her aid if he couldn't find the slippery woman? Theron sighed. At least he had her satchel. She would never leave without it. He reached down to grab it as the servant left.

His gut sank to his knees.

The satchel was gone.

Theron scanned the surrounding garden but there was no one in sight save for the retreating servant. The little minx must have used her magic to grab it before he could blink, the same as she had the first day he'd met her. That meant her escape was imminent. He launched into action, racing towards her little hole in the wall. Theron sent his magic out in a wave before him. If there were a living body anywhere in the thick foliage, he would find it.

Luckily, he didn't have to go far.

When his magic found her scampering through the greenery in almost total silence, she gasped. No doubt she could feel it coursing through her. If he allowed it to reassure him that she was in good health, he would never breathe a word of it.

Stealth forgotten, Aurora picked up her pace.

His blood sang in his veins as he raced towards her. When he caught sight of her blonde head, his smile was irrepressible. Fast as she might be, he had the longer legs. Within a few strides, he was in front of her. Aurora skidded to a halt, winded, her cheeks flushed and her hair in disarray. And she was wearing the clothes that fit her like a second skin. It felt indecent, staring at her and feeling the strangest urge to devour her. To take her to the ground and press his teeth into her neck and make her submit. He swallowed.

Why were those trousers of hers the most erotic thing he'd ever seen a woman wear?

Her green gaze was uncertain, as if she expected him to lash out. Unease crept up his throat. An unpleasant thing, to know he'd caused that in her.

No, he wasn't supposed to think this way. He was acting like a fool. Aurora was a means to an end, one he was certain would be well worth the effort. Physical attraction was one thing, but this weakness in his heart needed to be scoured out of him. Only by ridding himself of it would be able to maintain control of her. Of himself.

"Hello, my little fairy," he purred. "I've missed you."

When her cheeks heated with more than just her exertions, he knew he'd chosen the right tactic. She was weak to him, whether she liked it or not. And a weakness like that was begging to be exploited.

She'd been so close.

But Theron had realised her theft almost the moment her magic had failed her. She shouldn't have stopped to put on her trousers and top, but she didn't want to risk losing them again. That she'd been able to use her magic at all had been a minor miracle. One she credited to the artefact that had called to her from inside her satchel. It had been calling to her for days now. She'd tried to convince herself to leave without it, to hide out in town, to find another artefact from the veritable hoard inside the temple of Knowledge.

But she couldn't.

The artefact was her only link to her own time. It was also the only thing that had managed to draw out her magic. Magic she was going to need to stop Drakon in this ancient era. Aurora had prayed Theron would leave it in his room unattended, but the clever bastard had taken to carrying it with him at all times—even to the baths.

But as he stood before her, the scent of his perfume lingering in the air between them, his seducer's grin lighting up his eyes, her heart clenched in her chest. Wariness was mixed with something more she didn't care to name. All she knew was that she'd not managed to extricate him from her thoughts in the few days she'd managed to stay away. Nor was she able to forget that while she had been maimed, he'd been busy flirting with another woman. He'd said dreadful things to her, and she in turn to him. In her fragile state, she'd trusted him without even meaning to. It was no wonder that she'd suffered the consequences for such foolishness shortly thereafter.

It was a foolishness that needed to end now before it became something...complicated.

"Please move aside," she said.

"And if I do? What then?"

"I'm leaving, Your Majesty. If I'm to survive long enough to do what I came here to do, it's clear I must be somewhere the high priestess is not."

"You think you can hide from her?"

No, not really. Not for long. The Temple of Knowledge boasted a wide network of informants, even in the ancient past. But long enough to find the avatar? She had to hope it could be possible.

Aurora glared at Theron. She didn't need this right now. If what the servants were saying was true, then the gates to the city would be opened soon. There hadn't been a new case of torchlight fever for two days now. A few more without incident, and the gates would open. Aurora intended to leave the moment they did.

In the meantime, she'd made drawings for Orithyia and prayed she would never see the woman again. Even now, the clash of banging doors and stomping through the halls set her heart racing. All the nightmares of the lashing, of Drakon, of Phaedra's last moments—they haunted her whenever she closed her eyes. There was no peace to be had in this cursed place. And there were certainly no true allies.

Theron had sat beside her as her walls had been torn down, had provided some small measure of comfort when she'd needed it most... and then abandoned her. She hated that he'd made his way into some small corner of her heart and then proven himself to be unworthy of it. She hated it even more that it hadn't diminished the effect his presence had on her. At best, he was a distraction she didn't need, and at worst, a liability.

"What I *think* is that the only person I can rely on is myself."

"Have you decided you no longer need my military? My support? My protection once I leave Boreas?"

In past cycles of calamity, the hero of the holy sword was said to have slain Drakon alone. Now she knew that the hero required her assistance, or someone like her. But would they also need an army? Had the aid of other warriors been left out of the histories in order to bolster the hero's fame? She didn't know. But the longer she remained here instead of searching for the hero, the likelier she was to face Orithyia again. Another beating like the one she'd endured could not be allowed to happen again. After all, there was no guarantee Theron would heal her.

"And if I stayed, will I get them, or will you turn on me as you did the other day?"

"That was...regrettable. As an apology, I repaired your artefact."

How had he managed that? She'd done her level best to warp the metal bands no to avail. But there was no denying that it was drawing out her magic as it had done when she'd first found it in the dualist museum. The question was on the tip of her tongue. She mentally shook herself. No, this was just another way for him to delay her.

"Apologies usually begin with the words 'I'm sorry' and continue with acknowledging one's transgressions." She frowned.

No doubt a man like him would balk at such a demand. Let him prove himself unworthy of her trust once again. Let her heart and mind be in accordance.

"There are better ways for a man to apologise to a lady," he purred.

Aurora fought a blush.

"You overestimate your dubious charms, Your Majesty."

"You've never experienced my charms, dubious or otherwise, Aurora."

"I will only be satisfied with a proper apology. If you can't give me that, I have no reason to stay."

"And if I promised I could satisfy you with an *improper* apology?"

"I would tell you to please move aside."

He stepped closer then, making it impossible to ignore him, the heat of his skin, the sheer width of him. It was getting harder to ignore what an improper apology might entail.

"*Aurora*," he said, his deep voice rumbling.

She clenched her fists at her sides, refusing to back down from his hypnotising gaze. It didn't matter that the sound of her name on his lips made her insides feel like jelly. It didn't matter that he physically appealed to her every feminine fantasy. He was a snake.

And he'd already bitten her once.

"Tell me you don't want me. Make me believe it," he said, his eyes pulling her in.

No, that way lay madness. If she kept playing this game, she would lose—and they both knew it. It was time to stop playing by his rules.

"Is this how you charmed that other lady, Your Majesty?" she said with more venom than she'd meant. A mistake. He seemed far too pleased.

"As gratifying as your jealousy is, there is no other lady." He smiled indulgently.

Aurora all but growled. It took a great effort of will not to spit at him.

"I may have been missing one eye at the time, but I clearly saw you in the gardens with a lady. The one you snuck out of the room to meet while I was busy getting maimed."

That wiped the grin from his face. Replaced with a haunted look that was gone in the blink of an eye. He settled for a scowl.

"I didn't sneak out of the room."

"Call it whatever you like. I woke to two paladins barging into the room to drag me off and you were nowhere in sight."

He furrowed his brows.

"I don't have to explain myself to you."

"Then we have nothing to discuss," she said, moving to get around him.

Theron shifted to intercept her. Goddess, if only she could properly control her magic, then she could do as she liked with ease, or at least without so many obstacles.

"Your Majesty—"

"Theron. I asked you to call me by my name." He raised his chin.

She returned his scowl.

"And *I* asked for an apology. It seems neither of us is getting what we want today."

A vein at his temple began throbbing. Good. He should share in her frustration. He tried to glare her into submission but she wouldn't bend.

"I was called to an audience by Queen Flora. Afterwards, she set her daughter on me. There was no flirting. There was barely even a discussion, merely a great number of threats. Now then, I have explained myself." He crossed his arms, clearly put out that he had been forced to do so.

Now it was her turn to feel a little sheepish. That did explain why he wasn't there when the paladins had come...but it didn't excuse how he'd treated her afterwards. In fact, it didn't explain a damn thing about how abominably he'd acted. So what if she'd been upset with him? He'd acted like she'd defaced his family mausoleum.

"I...fine. But what about after that? You treated me horribly for no reason."

There again, that haunted look, quashed in an instant, replaced by another impressive scowl. What was he hiding?

"I... You made spurious accusations! How was I supposed to react?"

It was a weak excuse. She pressed forward.

"You could have told me what you did just now!"

"And you could have been more reasonable!"

She all but shrieked with indignation. *Reasonable?!* He'd expected her to be reasonable after the trauma she'd endured? He was lucky she'd been lucid!

"After everything that had happened that day and the night before, I wasn't in my right mind! What's *your* excuse?!"

"My *excuse?!* Do you think you're entitled to an explanation for my every word and deed just because you want it?"

Merciful Triad, spare her from arrogant swine.

"And you? Do you think you're entitled to my forgiveness just because *you* want it?"

"I am a *king*," he snarled.

"And I don't give a damn," she hissed. "If you want my help, you'll treat me with respect." She punctuated her point with a finger to his chest. He brushed away her hand.

"And what of the respect I am owed? What of your apology to me?"

Aurora curled her lip.

"Fine!" She stomped her foot, glaring at him and wishing she could burn a hole through his thick skull. "I'm sorry for thinking you owed me anything at all. I'm sorry for thinking you cared about anything more than what you could get out of me. I'm sorry for thinking you could be trusted. I'm sorry for thinking you were capable of true kindness.

I'm sorry for thinking there was a man beneath your mask instead of a snake! Now get out of my way!" She pushed passed him, eyes misting with foolish, angry tears.

He grabbed her wrist, spinning her around.

"We're not done here."

"I have nothing more to say to you!" she retorted.

He searched her eyes, as if looking for a surrender. It would never come.

"You can't seriously mean to leave. Where will you sleep? How will you purchase food? Even if you get out of the city, what then? Do you know how to light a fire? Do you know where it's safe to camp and where it isn't? What if you meet bandits on the road, or worse, monstrosities?"

He didn't really care. He was just trying to keep her from leaving. As she ought to.

"Why do you care? As you said, you're a king. I'm no one. My fate should be immaterial to you. Unless you're merely asking in an attempt to shake my confidence?" she taunted.

"Why must you be so bloody stubborn?" he growled, advancing on her.

"Why won't you just let me go?" She tried to wrench her wrist from his grip.

"Because it's dangerous out there."

"It's dangerous *in here*." She finally succeeded, pulling away from him.

"You said you would stay." He narrowed his eyes.

"That was before. When I thought you could be trusted," she huffed.

"Then I demand you repay me for healing you. Or are you someone who doesn't pay their debts?" He smirked.

That rat bastard! She gritted her teeth, certain she was going to fracture them with her pique. Was it still considered regicide if he'd died thousands of years before she was born?

"Fine! But after this, I want nothing to do with you," she warned him.

Aurora grabbed a spare piece of paper from her satchel, charcoal, and marched to the wall encompassing the vivarium's garden. She held up her paper against a smooth brick and started drawing. When she was done, she shoved the drawing at Theron.

He took the drawing and stared at it, brows furrowed in bewilderment.

"What is this?"

"An aqueduct. You said Altanus is having issues with the water being tainted. If you build this on a slight angle, you can funnel the water from the mountains directly to the city. Or all over Aureum, if you prefer."

"And this semi-circle?" he pressed.

"It's an arch. It distributes the weight of the topmost section more easily. It shouldn't take too long for your engineers to figure it out. Now, are we done?"

He looked from her drawing to her, and she knew the answer. A new light dawned in his eyes, covetous and determined. Good Goddesses, she'd made another mistake. Aurora backed up, her heart racing. Those weren't the eyes of a man who was satisfied with his spoils. They were the eyes of a predator tasting blood for the first time.

"Do you know what this knowledge is worth?" he asked quietly.

"More than what I owed you for healing me." Aurora glared at him. "My debt is paid."

"And now I am indebted to you." He advanced on her again.

"Then let me leave in peace." She backed up.

"No."

"I thought you were a man of honour!"

He held up a hand.

"Allow me to secure you safe passage. I am not without resources, even here."

"This is just your attempt to slow me down," she accused him. This was all just another trick of his.

"This is my attempt to ensure your safety. A lone traveller is an easy target. Especially one who doesn't know their way."

"I can find my way just fine," she lied.

She only had to follow the Queen's Road to the Colonnades. From there, he'd shown her the way to Altanus, where High Priestess Myrina would be. But she'd never travelled those roads without assistance. Certainly not with only a few baubles and a prayer that they would be enough to pay for food along the way, to make no mention of lodging.

"Oh? With what map? I've not seen one among your possessions."

She bit her tongue, preferring instead to glare. That secret was something she had no intention of divulging.

"No doubt you'll decide that a map will cost me my freedom. I'm not interested."

That's who he was. If she accepted his aid now, she would soon find her debts impossible to repay.

"Let me help you."

"You don't want to help me, you want to control me!"

He laughed, pushing his hair from his face, his smile as beautiful as it was dangerous.

"Oh, Aurora, I have a feeling that under the right conditions, you would very much enjoy being controlled by me."

Her breath caught. Blood rushed to her face in earnest then. Her heart crashed against her ribs. No one knew those dark desires. How dare he speak them aloud? How dare he assume he was someone she would trust with that? This arrogant pig. He closed the distance between them again.

"When was the last time you truly surrendered yourself to someone who could handle you?"

Aurora swallowed thickly. Triad preserve her, this man was dangerous for her.

"Surrender requires trust. And you've proved you're unworthy of mine." She raised her chin and glared, even though all she wanted to do was run. Were her fists trembling, or was that merely her heart pumping so hard she could feel the thrum under her skin?

"You are utterly maddening," he scoffed.

"As are you," she spat back.

"You stand there with the confidence of a monarch and treat my offers of aid as tainted. Where do you fit all that pride?" He asked, smiling genuinely, as if being thwarted were his favourite pastime.

Aurora sighed, pushing down her jitters. She'd tarried long enough. If she allowed him to speak any longer with his silver tongue, she was in danger of either losing this game of wills or scratching his eyes out. Or worse—surrendering.

"Your Majesty, I neither need nor want your assistance."

"And if I apologised?"

"Then you would be doing the bare minimum of courtesy." She narrowed her eyes.

He sank down to one knee before her, surprising a gasp from her. What was a king doing, *kneeling* before her? Monarchs only knelt for two reasons—prayer and defeat. He took her hand and kissed it.

"And if I apologised on my knees?"

As bold as she'd been towards him, as familiar as she'd acted in his presence due to her long association with Viridian royalty, this felt like a step too far. Not even Phaedra dared kneel to Aurora, even in jest. If anyone saw him like this, it would tarnish his honour...and put a target on her back. After all, whoever could get a monarch to kneel was not someone to be ignored.

"Your Majesty..." she began, flailing in her panic. She didn't hear anyone on the garden paths, but that could change in an instant.

"Theron," he corrected her, as calm as could be. As if his reputation weren't a single pair of eyes and loose lips away from being tainted.

"Theron, you're taking this too far."

"You asked for my apology. I apologise for losing my temper with you. Will you forgive me?"

Her insides twisted in knots. This was a mistake. A dangerous mistake.

"I will, now please just stand, or loom, or do *something* other than this."

He pulled her close, his eyes sparkling with mischief.

"Would you like that improper apology now?" he asked, his hands skating up her legs.

"I—I—n-no," she stammered. "P-please just stop kneeling."

"It won't be kneeling if you join me," he said, hands gripping her thighs before he trailed them back down her legs. "You have a king on his knees. Why not take advantage?"

Her brows pinched. How could he suggest such a thing? They'd been at each other's throats just moments ago. Maybe she would never understand him. Once again, she was playing *his* game. He might be on his knees, but he remained in control. Goddess, he was bad for her. She couldn't forget who and what he was, even for a moment. Every time she did, he turned the tables on her. Time for a course correction.

"Then tell me why you lost your temper with me."

"That—"

His eyes shuttered. He made to stand. Aurora placed her hand on his shoulder, stilling him.

"—Or do I not actually have a king on his knees?"

His hands gripped her thighs as he glared at her mulishly. Better. This was much preferable to falling for his tricks. If he wished to ensnare her, he'd best not fall into his own traps.

He remained there for some time, hands gripping her thighs, refusing to let go. Long enough for her to recognise that he was wrestling with demons and not just stubbornness. And the moment he saw that she'd understood that, he jerked away as if burned, getting to his feet. Aurora advanced on him, refusing to give him space to rebuild his walls. If he could smash through hers without a thought, she would return the favour. Let him be on the defensive for once.

"If you can't answer me, we're done. You'll never see me again," she threatened.

"That's not—"

"What? *Fair?* When are *you* ever fair?" she interrupted, raising her brow.

He ran a hand down his face, weighing his options. It was clear he considered being vulnerable a weakness he simply didn't tolerate in himself. She had to know if he were capable of truly giving something of himself to her. It was clear he was happy to share his physical body, but not his heart. And a man who couldn't share his heart was not to be trusted.

He snarled.

"As you wish. I told you of my brother. The moment I awakened my magic, I was responsible for his health. The night he died, I'd slipped away to drink and carouse. When I'd returned, he was gone. What you said...it reminded me of that night. There, are you happy? *Satisfied?*"

Oh, merciful Triad, no wonder he'd acted the way he had. He blamed himself. Just as she'd blamed him.

"How could I be?" she asked, her brows pinched.

He lunged at her, fury in his eyes, tackling her to the ground. She braced for the impact, but even in his anger, he'd cupped the back of her head, preventing any hurt.

"You dare—"

"Theron," she said, her voice soft. "I'm sorry. No one with a heart would be happy after hearing that. You must've been young when it happened."

"I don't want your pity!"

She reached up to cup his face. Goddesses forgive her, she'd stepped on the tenderest part of his heart without knowing it. Beneath all his bluster and scheming, he was just a man. She recalled that night again, the things he'd said, the things she'd shouted back, but now she understood.

"What about my kindness?" she offered.

"I don't need your coddling."

"Then what *do* you need?"

He froze, as if he couldn't name the thing he needed—dare not name it. He swallowed, eyeing her like it was *she* who was crouched atop *him*, pinning him down in the dirt. In that moment, her heart hurt for him. For them. Two people who had no one they could rely on utterly for warmth and compassion. At least she'd had Phaedra. Would have her again if she succeeded. Had he ever had anyone like that?

"Are you proposing to give me what I need?" he asked, leaning into her touch.

"Within reason," she replied, sweeping her thumbs across his cheekbones.

She could be kind to him if he proved he could be the same without ulterior motives. It would ease some part of her to have even a sliver of that warmth in her life again.

"And if I asked..." His gaze wandered down her neck, his womaniser's grin back in place.

Aurora rolled her eyes. That didn't last long.

"Not that," she snorted.

"Shrew," he accused her playfully.

"Pervert," she retorted, a hint of a smile tugging at the corners of her lips.

He smiled. A real smile.

"Harridan."

"Tyrant."

"I suspect you would enjoy my tyranny."

"And I suspect you enjoy my scolding."

"Doesn't that mean we're perfectly matched?" he raised a brow.

"No, it means we're perfectly mismatched, Your Majesty."

He leaned in. She could feel his breath on her lips. She need only lift her head a fraction to claim his. Or shift her hips to discover how ardently he desired her in turn. Some reckless, mindless part of her wanted to. Warmth could be had in more ways than one. In different ways to the one she truly needed.

Why couldn't she have met this man in her own time, before her thread had been twisted with Drakon's? She could have revelled in carnality then, free from the death and duty that stalked her. She could have given him what he desired, indulged in what he'd offered, secure in the knowledge that such a dalliance would not come back to bite her.

But she was not in her own time, and that life was long lost to her.

And this man had very sharp teeth.

"This is usually the part where a lady closes her eyes for a kiss, Aurora," he said, his lips a whisper away from hers.

"Then I must disappoint you, Your Majesty."

Theron sighed, leaning his head on her collarbone, his breath fanning her chest. Her nipples hardened, despite the heat. This was surely her punishment for neglecting her prayers to Passion on more than one occasion. It would be fitting indeed to be struck by lust for a man so wholly wrong for her at exactly the worst time.

"One day soon, you'll look back on this and wonder why you didn't just kiss me," Theron chuckled, heaving himself off her. He got to his feet, leaned over, and offered her his hand.

Aurora took it, dusting herself off once she regained her balance.

"If I live long enough to dwell on such regrets, I'll count myself lucky indeed."

In an instant, her magic surged from her.

She was torn from the gardens, a puppet hurtling through the air, an invisible hand yanking on her strings.

Aurora stood in the atrium of the vivarium. The place was bathed in the light of the setting sun, but the details were fuzzy around the edges, as if a painter had forgotten to fill out the full canvas. Guests milled about, dressed in opulent finery as servants plied them with wine and delicacies. Her heart hammered in her chest.

"Please, you must leave!" she shouted, pleading.

Instead of heeding her, they laughed, leering at her. She bunched her fists in the gauzy fabric of what could only, with the greatest charity, be referred to as a dress. The fabric was all but transparent. The other prisoners of the vivarium were similarly attired, living trophies for Queen Flora's guests to gawk at and mock. Only prostitutes wore such garments, a fact made all the more apparent by the presence of the very same in attendance dressed in better garb than the prisoners.

She watched the area beneath the musicians, waiting for what she knew was to come. A warm hand touched her shoulder. Theron looked down at her with a calmness she couldn't fathom. He was a statue made of gold, covered from head to toe in glittering paint and an absurd number of green jewels, his dignity spared by the presence of a mere loincloth.

"You should go somewhere safe now, madam fairy."

"I can't! They won't listen! They're going to—"

"Aurora, you did everything you could."

"Please, don't stay here! Come with me!"

"I will not run from my fate."

"It *can't* be fate! I can change it!"

Screams erupted. The shadows beneath the musicians roiled like boiling water. Some managed to flee, while others were devoured whole by the monstrosities clawing their way out of the shadowy muck. Nobles, entertainers and servants fled, tripping over themselves. Chaos erupted in the atrium as monstrosities began ripping and slashing and devouring.

Everyone the beasts could snatch became a gory splatter. The green and gold of the vivarium was swiftly painted crimson.

"Aurora!"

She gasped, her eyes searching wildly for the monstrosities pouring out of the shadows. But there were no screams here. There were no floors covered in viscera and walls painted in blood.

She was drowning in Theron's magic, pouring through her like water in a sieve.

"Aurora!"

Her eyes met his and she released a shaky breath. He was terrified, searching her for some injury. If only. Merciful Triad, she'd had a vision. She covered her face in her hands and whimpered. Was this some test? Was she supposed to face it or flee? What could she do against monstrosities, without a drop of divine magic in her?

"Does anything hurt? What happened?"

"I..."

How could she explain it? No one in their right mind would believe her.

"I thought you were having a seizure. But you didn't exhibit any of the other signs and my magic couldn't find what was wrong. Is it some kind of fairy sickness? What can I do?"

It didn't matter if he didn't believe her. So what if time magic was so rare it was almost unheard of? If her vision came to pass, he may very well die before he ever got back to Aureum. That wasn't how history was supposed to happen. It wasn't how she needed to change it. What if she held back, and she made everything worse?

"Monstrosities. In the atrium."

His eyes widened. He held her closer, eyes darting towards the guest palace.

"You can hear that from here?"

"I..." She swallowed. Well, at least if he thought her mad, he was more likely to send her on her way. Some small silver lining to bolster her faltering courage. "I saw it. It's not happening now. But it...it will. In the evening. On the night of a party. The prisoners here will be dressed as prostitutes. You will be painted in gold. The monstrosities will come up from underneath the musicians."

"You...saw it."

"Yes," she whispered, eyes askance.

"And you're not hurt?"

"No, not by seeing it."

Not physically, at least. If she lived long enough, she was apt to lose her mind. The same as every other oracle. An early death or a slow slide into madness. Such lovely options.

"Wait here." He sat her down under the shade of a tree.

Aurora made to stand.

"No, stay there," he commanded.

There was something in his tone that made her heart sink. He was repelled by her. Perhaps he thought her mad, and that it was catching.

"Are you coming back?" she asked softly. "It's alright if you're not. I'll understand."

"I'm coming back," he said quietly, his expression guarded.

So this was goodbye. She squeezed her hands and nodded, trying to keep her smile from faltering.

"I'll wait," she lied.

She waited until she couldn't hear him. Then she waited a little more. But when she could no longer deny the truth, she stood shakily. Well, that had been easier than she'd imagined. Aurora could have saved herself a rather stressful afternoon if she'd just told him about her magic. Funny, how quickly things could change. There was no chance of gaining his aid now.

Aurora found her hole in the wall and removed the stones covering it up. If the stones appeared blurrier than before, it was nothing more than a combination of the summer heat and her sweat. Or a bit of dirt. She couldn't be blamed for getting a bit of dirt in her eyes. In any case, her tears would take care of it soon enough.

Another shaky breath escaped her lips. She could do this. Phaedra was counting on her. Silvanus too. What did it matter that one doomed king thought her delusional? If nothing else, he'd taught her to guard her heart more closely. She'd been reckless, letting him in so readily. That wouldn't happen again. Aurora needed to let people prove themselves before placing such trust in them. There, lesson learned. Nothing was a waste so long as she learned something from it.

Aurora placed her satchel by the entrance to the hole so that she could grab it once she'd gone through. As she got down on her hands and knees, she heard sounds in the bushes above. Sounds that became more frantic.

"Aurora?" Theron called.

She sat there, dumbfounded. What was he doing back here? Had he come to relieve her of her artefacts? What else could it be but that? They were worth a great deal. She pushed the satchel into the hole and shimmied in after it. She'd almost reached the other side when he grabbed her ankle.

Aurora shrieked as he pulled her back through.

"I told you to wait."

"Why should I? You think I'm mad. You probably only came back to take my artefacts," she accused him.

He snatched her wrist and pulled her forward, his expression severe.

"Stop!" she cried.

He placed a blue crystal orb in her palm. The same kind he'd used to show her Aureum.

"Show me."

"What?"

"Show me what you saw."

"But... You... You believe me?"

"I believe what I can see. Show me, Aurora."

"How do I...?"

"Focus on what you want to see. Hold it in your mind."

She did as he'd asked. She focused on the feeling of that inescapable tugging, on the things she'd seen. Between blinks, she was reliving the horror with Theron as her witness, the hopelessness, the screams, the fear, the blood. She was glad when it was over.

"Queen Flora is planning a party to celebrate the end of the plague and the reopening of Boreas. By the lighting, it appeared to be early evening," Theron mused.

"You really believe me?" she asked, cautious hope taking up residence in her heart.

"I don't want to. It would be easier if you were mad. But your visions explain a great deal. And dressing me like some kind of gaudy golden statue after I complained of the quality of the attire she provided is exactly Flora's style of pettiness. Now we must find some way to avert the future you saw."

Her heart felt like it would burst from her chest.

And then her magic ripped her away.

She hurtled through vast emptiness until she found herself back in the atrium.

Monsters poured out of the shadows, tearing through guards like wet paper. Severed limbs and bloody guts littered the slippery floors. More soldiers poured into the space, desperate to keep the monstrosities contained. Theron led from the front, keeping them from devouring her with his shield and spear.

Aurora tried to scrabble to her feet, to her artefact that was so tantalizingly close in the melee, but slipped again when an elongated arm shot out from the nearest shadow. It dug its taloned paw into her ankle and dragged her towards its serrated teeth as she screamed.

A group of paladins joined the fray. Aurora prayed they would make it to her in time.

Theron turned, seeing her being dragged to her death. He leapt to her defence, jabbing his spear into the beast. He looked back to assess her condition.

It was but a moment, but in that moment, everything changed.

The next monster that rose drove its talons through Theron's body, showering Aurora in his blood and guts. Red poured from a wound the size of a dinner plate. A river ran down his back and legs, covering gold with the deepest ruby.

Aurora gasped.

Then screamed.

Chapter 17
Theron

Theron knocked the orb from Aurora's hands, ending the vision of his demise. As the scream from her vision bled into the scream tearing out of her throat, Theron wrapped her in his arms. She clung to him as her scream faded into a tortured sob, desperately clawing at his back.

"I'm here. You're safe," he whispered. "You're safe. You're safe."

He said it as much for his sake as hers. If her vision proved true, his days were numbered. From her vantage point, he'd watched that monstrosity punch a hole through his torso. It was impossible to say exactly what it would destroy, but if it got his heart, or he passed out from the shock of pain and blood loss, there would be no healing himself.

Aurora swallowed her next sob. She breathed through the next.

"Are you hurt?" he asked.

"I—it had my ankle."

"Did you feel it?"

She nodded, biting her lip.

He petted her head, holding her close as she regained her equilibrium. His mind raced in time with his heart. Were her visions spun from fates decreed by the weft and weave of the Tapestry, or was there some way to use them to avoid what was coming? He'd be a fool not to try, but what were his options?

"We h-have to leave. Now. While the guards are on the other side of the vivarium. O-otherwise..."

He shook his head.

"I can't. Not until I've paid restitution to Flora and the high priestess has purified me. But *you* can. And you should. I'll arrange your safe transport to Aureum. You'll leave the moment the gates open."

If she were removed from play, then he would never be in a position to defend her when the monstrosities spawned. He'd have her sent directly to Aureum. A true oracle was an almost unheard-of advantage. Even if he perished, Batea would put her to good use...provided she could stomach beheading a few of her beasts to placate the little fairy.

If he wanted to survive, he had a great number of things to get done. Theron had to plan for every possibility—that the vision could be false, that it could prove true, that it might be avoided altogether, that it could merely be altered, and that it was written in stone. Flora's gaudy spectacle would happen in three days' time. He didn't have a moment to lose.

"You saw what happened! Please, come with me," Aurora pleaded.

"I'm staying *because* I saw what happened. I was killed protecting you. If you're safe, I can focus on my own safety until the paladins arrive."

He wondered about the man in her vision, the Theron of a few days' time. Had that man always seen her vision, knowing what was to come? He'd never been given to self-sacrificing heroics—kings couldn't afford to die so frivolously. What would change in the next few days to alter that? Or had it already happened? Had the future been determined simply by viewing it? What could not be denied was that her powers made her just as valuable a player as he, or more so, though she didn't yet understand that.

In any case, he would be better off without her here, putting herself in danger and distracting him.

"And we can change that future completely if we both leave! Don't you see?" she asked, gripping his tunic.

"Have you never considered that your visions are immutable, madam fairy?" He cupped her cheek.

Was she so desperate to change the things she saw that it had never occurred to her that she might not be able to? Had her grief truly prevented her from confronting the possibility?

"I can't accept that. I won't." She shook her head.

"Have you managed to change the outcome of one of your visions before?"

"I...no. But I didn't understand them before. Are you telling me I shouldn't try? That you're willing to accept your death without even trying to stop it?"

"I'm not. But I do know one thing—that you have no place on a battlefield, your magic notwithstanding. I've fought monstrosities before. I now know what's to come and I can protect myself accordingly."

"You stubborn ass! I'm *trying* to save you!"

He smiled.

"A shared trait."

"You—"

He held up a hand.

"Aurora, what do you suppose would happen if we run now? Do you truly believe I could escape the city, with Flora searching for me? I'm her most coveted prisoner. And you shouldn't underestimate Orithyia's network. If she's as cunning as I believe her to be, you'll have enough trouble evading her grasp without me drawing the attention of the Viridian crown. My life is my responsibility, and I intend to take that seriously. It's *your* continued safety that needs addressing."

Aurora grabbed his hand.

"We don't have to get away for good to succeed. We just have to stay away long enough not to be there when the monstrosities appear. A few days, at most, would make all the difference."

"And if we're caught before then?"

"Then I...I know at least a dozen ways out of here."

"You assume that all they'd do is slap you on the wrist once you're caught."

Given the sadistic natures of the guards here, and the high priestess' liberal nature in doling out maimings, she'd be lucky if they didn't cut off her feet just to start. He'd have anyone who touched her killed, naturally, but even he might not be able to prevent her inevitable punishment.

"Whatever they do couldn't be worse than death, right?"

"There are worse fates than death, Aurora."

Her green eyes were like chips of ice as she stared him down. Fierce little creature.

"No, there aren't. As long as you're alive, there's a chance. So are you coming with me, or do you plan to die here?"

"You'd leave without me?" he smiled.

"If I could drag you from here, I would. I want you to survive, but if you're determined to die here, I can't stop you. And what I need to do is too important. One life isn't more important than killing Drakon." She shook her head.

Theron pulled away, walked over to the orb and picked it up. It was time to see what this Drakon really was, and why she was so bound and determined to kill it. If he was to die, he wanted to at least have his curiosity sated. To know why she could so easily toss aside the only ally she had in Trisia.

"Show me your monster."

Aurora bit her lip, hesitating to touch it. No doubt she feared another vision. She released a shaky breath and took it from him, closing her eyes.

And showed him a nightmare a thousand times more horrifying than her previous vision.

An expanse of desert was shrouded in unnatural darkness. The skies were crimson, choked with black clouds, the air thick with falling ash. Lightning streaked across the skies, painting the scene in vivid detail. Monstrosities bubbled up between every grain of sand and rock, a veritable sea of diabolical ink, every flash drawing their claws closer and closer. Their shrieks rang out across the land, drowned out only by the roaring thunder. He'd never imagined so many could appear at once. In numbers like that, they would devour towns in an instant, no matter how many paladins you threw at them.

The lone, constant light was a man holding his spear high, its magic banishing the darkness and the monstrosities around him. Behind, a small party of riders, their steeds chasing hers at a frightful pace. But her eyes were drawn to the skies. In the centre of the clouds was her beast. Her picture had not done it justice—it was larger than a palace, its red scales glittering in the lightning flashes, yellow eyes full of madness trained on her. A shiver ran down Theron's spine.

"Did you think I wouldn't find you?" it asked, its voice unnaturally deep and rumbling. "Did you think I would let you live?"

Its hatred oozed from every syllable, its malice raising the hairs on the back of his neck. The beast could speak!

Flaming boulders rained down from the skies, spewing rock, dirt and molten material as the beast laughed. Every single one was large enough to flatten a home. Bile rose in the back of his throat. There was no winning against such overwhelming power.

Then it opened its maw, gathering purple fire at the back of its throat. The beam hit the rider at the back of their party, reducing him and his steed to nothing in an instant. Theron's heart raced in his chest. If this was what awaited them, they were all doomed. That beam alone, aimed over a city, could cleave it in two. The very ground shook and swayed, the loper nearly thrown from its breakneck stride. Between insults, curses, and unfathomable horror, the rest of the riders were similarly obliterated.

When it was down to just two, Aurora opened her eyes, the image disappearing shortly thereafter.

"Merciful Triad..." he swallowed. "*That's* your beast?"

"Yes," she answered calmly.

He covered his mouth and rubbed his jaw.

"And it's coming here, to Trisia?"

"If I'm correct, it's already here. I need to kill it before it regains the power to do what you just saw."

His heart dropped to his feet. Everyone he'd ever known and cared about would die. Not one person in the whole of Trisia had the power to fight something like that effectively. It was why Batea had been creating her great flying serpents, because with control of the skies, they would own the battlefield. But even if she succeeded, they'd be nothing but gnats battling an eagle.

"How did you survive? How did *anyone* survive?"

"I got lucky. Everyone else died," she answered, her voice hollow.

This was bigger than him. Bigger than Aureum and Viridis and their eternal bickering. If this Drakon had come to Trisia, then nothing else mattered more than killing it. Forget his scheming, his honour, every-thing—he needed to get Aureum's spies searching for the beast and his army prepared. He needed to force the temples to anoint as many paladins as possible, and for their priestesses to infuse divine magic into every blade and pitchfork in the whole of Trisia. Fuck Flora and her petty posturing. Fuck the vivarium. Aurora was right.

"Let's go."

"Do you mean it?"

"Yes. That thing cannot be allowed to destroy Trisia."

Though if it destroyed Boreas alone, he wouldn't mind overmuch.

Aurora smiled, relieved.

"Then come. We used this route the other day. I know a better way for someone your size."

She took his hand and led him away, back into the guest palace proper. They wended their way to the baths, expertly avoiding every guard and attendant. As they entered the empty baths, she pulled him to a far corner where the sculpture of a unicorn's head spouted water from its mouth. She pushed in its eyes, cutting off the flow of water and then pressed on the face with all her might. A gush of air cleared the area of steam as the once-seamless wall swung open as a door. Aurora motioned him inside and closed the door behind them.

"How in the Loom do you know of this?"

She tapped her temple and placed a finger on her lips.

"The walls aren't overly thick where we'll be going, so go as quietly as you can."

As she led him through a maze of dark corridors, he heard the chatter of guards, servants, cooks and nobles alike. No wonder she'd managed to elude his spies. Not only could she see the future, she knew of every secret crevice in the whole guest palace. He couldn't help wondering if she really was a spy. Maybe not one belonging to Viridis, but perhaps back in her homeland. If they survived this, he hoped to get an answer.

Before they reached the exit, Aurora donned her gown, adjusted her hair to cover her ears and grabbed his hand. She pushed down on a lever, and the wall swung open as a door, soundless as a whisper. He squinted against the harsh light of day as Aurora closed the way behind them. They had exited out from a defunct fountain whose water was but a trickle, the bottom full of refuse. The street was abandoned, as expected with the torchlight fever epidemic still burning through Boreas.

"Where now?" he asked.

There were few enough places that would admit strangers during an outbreak, and most of those were controlled by the temples. Scrutiny they couldn't afford.

She eyed him up and down.

"To the temple of Passion for our rations. They hand out food during outbreaks, do they not?"

"You want to go towards where we're most likely to be recognised?" he asked, aghast. Had he truly put his life and freedom in the hands of a simpleton?

"I won't be." She adjusted her clothes to hide her curves, to appear more like a small child. "I'd planned on getting the rations and hiding beneath the temple of Knowledge. It seems like few enough know of the hoard, and I suspect Orithyia has more pressing things to attend to than counting her treasures."

"Did you plan to use these few days until the gates open sifting through the ancient relics?"

A blush crept up her neck.

"Maybe."

He might have laughed if the fate of Trisia didn't depend on slaying her beast. He sighed, pinching the bridge of his nose. There wasn't anywhere else in Boreas he knew to hide. Perhaps his spies had a safe house or two, but that would mean potentially outing his spy network in Viridis. Damn, he shouldn't have been so shaken by the beast she'd shown him. He should have stopped to think.

Out of options and with daylight wasting, he nodded his head and gestured for her to lead the way.

"Once we get to the temple district, go to the back of the temple of Knowledge. I'll get the rations and join you there." She handed him her small pack. "For safekeeping," she added.

They trekked through the city and he was struck by the eerie quiet. Stray dogs fought over scraps from rubbish heaps while the stench of death and smoke clogged the air. Moaning and weeping could be heard coming out of the odd window or rickety door, but most of the city waited with bated breath, fearful of drawing the attention of angry spirits with even a single whimper.

They only saw the odd person, giving each other wide berths as they passed, or simply turning away to go down a different street. But soon they would come across some of the temple clerics. Passion's acolytes and initiates were responsible for finding the dead, recording their passing, and transporting their bodies to designated pyres to be consecrated and burned. Death, Passion's sinister twin, might not be openly worshipped, but Passion had taken over Her rites since dualism had gone underground.

The closer they got to the temple district, the more of Passion's people were in the streets, going into homes and apartments and bringing out the decaying dead. With the plague winding down, they'd begun clearing the city of corpses. It would take them days to sweep the city. Three days, if Aurora's vision were true. He held Aurora back as one group of acolytes entered the nearest building, waiting until they were ensconced before he ushered her to walk quickly passed. They dodged four more groups before they came into the heart of the temple district. Here, there were a great many more people, either begging at the temple of Passion, or wailing at the temple of Knowledge. Justice's people were there to keep the peace, to resolve disputes among the bereaved and starving.

"Are you certain you'll be alright alone?" he asked.

"Yes. Go slip behind the temple of Knowledge and make sure no one notices you. Do you remember how to get into the basement there?"

"I do, mostly."

He'd informed his people of the basement, but none had managed to open it yet. Finding one brick among thousands was no easy task. He remembered its general vicinity, but that was all.

"Good enough. I'll be there shortly."

She went to join the messy queue of Boreas' hungry citizens. He kept his eyes on her as long as he could, but with her short stature, she was quickly swallowed by the crowd. It seemed there were perks to being so small.

But just as he turned to find his way behind the temple of Knowledge, a contingent of royal guards spilled into the plaza. It was then that he knew their bid for freedom had been doomed by his absence from the vivarium. The guards would not have bothered with Aurora, as she'd managed to stay hidden for days without arousing their suspicion. He shouldn't have let his fear overrule his better judgment. He should have let his spies secret her away in the dead of night. If he gave himself up now, would that be the end of it? Would they consider their quarry caught? He had to hope so.

Theron marched into the centre of the plaza and was immediately surrounded. It drew the attention of the people gathered outside the temples so that most of the eyes were trained on him. He could only pray that Aurora could see it and would know to stay away. They pulled and pushed him to the ground, binding his hands behind his back. Another pulled her satchel from him and searched it.

"He has a dress in here," the guard remarked, puzzled.

Another guard pushed his way into the group surrounding him—one missing an ear. He ripped the dress from his fellow's hand, glaring at it and Theron in turn as his mind turned slowly.

"A dre—the temple's prisoner has escaped! Find her!" the earless guard shouted.

Shit.

"Couldn't leave your whore behind, could you, dog?" the guard sneered at him. "Well if she's good enough to tempt a king, perhaps we should have some fun with her when we get back to the vivarium."

"I didn't realise you were so eager to lose another ear." Theron grinned.

If she were a prisoner of the temple in truth, then there would be little he could do to protect her within the bounds of the law. If the temple saw fit to toss her into the vivarium, then they'd resigned her to a fate like those who had been left to rot there—with all the attendant predations. But if she were tied to him in some way, he could reasonably interfere on her behalf, in a legal sense, at least. But there was no priestess here to consecrate a royal concubinage. Outside of that, all he had were threats and violence, which would land him in deeper trouble with Flora and her disgusting daughter. Theron was once again left praying that Aurora would escape their search or that his threats would be enough to prevent violence against her.

Theron watched from the corner of his eye as the guards pushed through the crowds of the hungry and desperate, ruthlessly shoving aside any who were too slow to comply with their orders. Clerics of both Passion and Justice took umbrage, pushing back and defending the crowds. Perhaps Aurora could use the distraction to slip away.

"There!" shouted one of the guards.

Those who could disengage from the clerics pursued a small figure through the startled crowds.

"Got her! I have her!" one of the guards shouted.

Aurora was hauled into the circle of guards, now very much on the defensive with the riled-up clerics. The guard gripped her by her hair and her forearm, which he'd twisted behind her back as he shoved her forward.

"Let go of me! Let go!" Aurora screamed.

The guard tossed her in a heap in front of Theron. Their eyes met for a moment before the first guard was on her, dragging her back.

"You touch her at risk of your life," Theron growled.

"You heard him!" the earless guard sneered. "Any injury done to one of us will be done to her tenfold, Your Majesty. Search her for weapons!"

"Theron!" Aurora screamed as the first guard ripped her dress, revealing her foreign clothes underneath.

There was a collective gasp amongst the guards before the guard made to tear more of her dress. She grabbed his wrists but was quickly losing her hold. The guards closed in on her in a circle, egging their friend on, taunting him for failing to strip her. Her shrieks of terror turned to those of white-hot rage. Then the guard was the one screaming in agony.

Theron pushed passed the legs of guards as they stood back. When he caught sight of her again, her breathing was laboured, her green eyes wild with fury, her nails crusted with blood. In a heap before her was a wizened old man, his skin papery thin, his face a mass of wrinkles. What little hair he had was as white as a cloud. And yet the man wore the uniform of the royal guard, now much too large for his skeletal frame.

"Merciful Triad, what...what did you do to him?!" the earless guard shrieked.

"What I'll do to you if you dare touch me," she hissed.

But Theron knew it was a bluff. Sweat rolled in rivulets down her face and neck and the red that had suffused her cheeks was already draining away. She'd used her magic recklessly—exhausted it.

"He got what he deserved for angering a fairy," Theron crowed.

The guards took a collective step backwards, eyeing her with wariness. But her screams had attracted the attention of Justice's paladins. They pushed people aside in their righteous fury.

"Back to the palace! Now!"

Theron was hauled to his feet and rushed towards the palace gates. He tried to look behind at Aurora, but several guards pointed their swords at him, urging him forward. Aurora tried to call out to the paladins, only to find the blades of the royal guard trained at her throat.

"Move!"

She complied.

The rest of the guards held the paladins off as best they could until those who had him and Aurora hostage managed to enter the palace gates. Once closed, the paladins would have to ask Flora's permission to enter, which would never happen. Thus trapped, both Theron and Aurora were herded back to the guest palace. He was shoved onto the cool stone tiles as Aurora was put in chains, the collar at her neck linked to her bound wrists, and tied to the nearest column, blades trained at her throat the whole while.

"Strip her," the earless guard ordered.

"But—"

"Look at her. She's sweating, pale-faced and about to pass out. She's used up her freak magic for today. Strip her, take any weapons she's got on her, and stop whining."

"Don't touch her!" Theron roared, getting to his knees before another guard shoved him down again.

"My order still stands, Your Majesty. You hurt one of us, she gets it worse."

The earless guard shoved one of the younger ones towards Aurora. All the while she glared them down.

"Do you want to pit yourselves against me? I could kill you all before you touch a hair on her head," he threatened. His magic rolled off him in waves, pushing through each of them. He relished the shivers that stole down their spines.

"She must be quite the skilled whore to have gained your protection. But this is the vivarium. This is what your protection is worth here. Strip her, now!" the earless guard ordered.

The youngest fumbled with her top as Aurora thrashed against him.

"I'll rip away every year you have left in your miserable life if you don't stop touching me!" she screamed.

"I can't—"

The earless guard grunted with impatience, shoved the younger one out of the way and took his blade to her clothes.

"Squirm, and my blade will slip, *fairy*," he threatened.

In seconds she was stripped down to nothing, her foreign clothes in tatters. Aurora's eyes widened in panic. Theron saw red. His magic exploded in a tidal wave. He rebroke every healed bone in the guard's body in the same moment he revisited every bruise, cut, laceration, and illness back onto him. The guard crumpled in a howl of agony, bleeding out onto the floor.

"You were warned," Theron growled.

Guards rushed to drag the dead guard from the guest palace while others held shaking swords trained towards him. He let loose another blast of magic at the remaining guards.

"Who else wishes to test their luck against my magic?"

They looked to each other and lowered their blades. Some snuck glances at her. Theron snarled.

"Anyone who so much as looks at her gets their eyes gouged out! Now get out!"

They retreated from the guest palace and locked the doors behind them.

"Aurora? Are you hurt?" he asked as he struggled to his feet, his arms still bound behind him.

"A few cuts..." she replied, her voice hollow.

He let his magic wash over her, healing the hurts of her flesh. But the terror he saw in her eyes could not be so easily treated. Theron walked toward her and turned around.

"Can you untie these knots?" he asked.

"Mmm," she replied.

He could feel her hands trembling as she worked the knots loose. Soon he was free.

"I'll get something to cover you."

"Wait!" she grabbed at his tunic. "Please don't leave me. What if they come back?"

He looked over his shoulder at her, refusing to turn around completely. He could spare her that indignity at least.

"They won't come back yet. Be brave, just for a few more moments."

She released a shaky breath and let go of his tunic. He raced to his room, grabbed a thick blanket and returned, keeping his gaze on hers as he returned and fashioned as best an outfit as he could with her chains.

"Can you take this off?"

He inspected the collar and manacles.

"No. It requires a key."

"They were going to…" she trailed off.

"And the ones who tried are dead. Between the two of us, no one will ever hurt you in that way."

She crumpled into a puddle of tears. Theron held her as the sun dipped down and the moon rose, until her tears had given way to exhaustion. In the dead of night, a guard roused him from a fitful sleep with her in his arms. Theron might have resorted to violence but for the very visible red scarf tied around the man's neck.

"Your Majesty, the guards are refusing to patrol inside the guest palace, but that might change soon. I have a report. Each unlucky groom of Princess Epicasta met with Queen Flora before official engagements were announced. Once they left the meetings, they were all reported to have become resigned to their fates. Flora then went about her usual schedules and appearances. Curiously, every time one of the husbands appeared in public, Flora was present. We tracked down a former nanny of the queen's who requested asylum for her information. She was taken to a safe house and said that the queen's wild magic was that of a soul swapper."

The blood drained from his face.

Epicasta had been speaking truth. Except that the foul magic belonged to her mother. But as a soul swapper, Flora couldn't take over the bodies of others herself, merely insert another soul inside for a short time. Had his parents known of the danger back then, that she could more than paralyse with her magic, they would have surely killed her. Had this power been why she'd been able to slay so many in her campaign? After all, she needn't put another soul into a body that she'd violated with her magic. A body left empty, even for a moment, was long enough for any half-decent warrior with a blade to dispose of. A shiver ran down his spine.

Had she exhausted herself on the battlefield all those years ago? Was that why she hadn't violated the royal family? What had they done with the unwilling husbands in the times between, when her magic was spent? Who would have volunteered their soul in Flora's plan?

"Find out how long she needs to recover between uses of her magic. And the distance over which she can work it. Find out everything you can. Be especially alert to times when those husbands were either unable to use their wild magic, or used one they hadn't awakened."

Epicasta would've only been wed to some of the most powerful families, and anyone with the kind of sway to threaten Flora would have wild magic of their own. Their magic would be well-known. Whereas a new soul would possess different magic altogether if they possessed it at all.

"Yes, Your Majesty."

Aurora shifted in his arms, her chains clinking.

"Find the key to her fetters. This woman is the most important asset in the whole of Trisia. More important than me." The spy widened his eyes in shock. "She's an oracle, and in two days, the day the queen throws a party here to celebrate the end of the plague, monstrosities will appear in the vivarium. She gave me her bag, now confiscated. There were two ancient artefacts inside. Retrieve them along with the scroll. The beast she drew on it must be hunted down and eliminated at all costs. Do you understand?"

"But Your Majesty, are we to protect her over you?"

He looked down at her. Even in sleep, her brow was furrowed with anxiety. He brushed a blonde strand from her face. Was she more important? Was her life worth more than his? If he died, Batea would have a small army of capable, loyal advisors whose secrets she knew well enough to manipulate. A good king ensured his kingdom was so robust as to function in his absence. If Aurora died, the greatest power in Trisia went with her.

"Yes. Find a way to get her out of here as soon as possible. Spare no expense, use every resource. And protect her by all means necessary. I don't have to tell you how valuable a true oracle is."

"I will relay your orders...and have some of the more sympathetic attendants see to you both in the meantime."

"One more thing," he added, taking his own miniaturized ancient artefact from the lining of his tunic. He handed it to the spy. "Have this infused with divine magic. On the day of the attack, they'll paint me in gold, and force the rest of the prisoners here to wear the garb of prostitutes. Have both my gold and whatever garb is made for her similarly infused with divine magic. Any of our people here that day should do likewise."

"I'll see to it at once."

He waved him off.

Once the spy left, Theron tried to get some sleep.

He didn't like the idea that this one woman was more important than he was, that her life mattered more. Once again, he wondered at the Theron from her vision, the one who had stepped in front of the monstrosity. Since that afternoon, he'd begun to understand why he might be willing to sacrifice his own life to save hers. Aureum needed her. Trisia needed her. She understood the gravity of the situation to come and acted accordingly. It was simply his good fortune that she didn't seem to understand the leverage that afforded her.

Always, she bargained from a place of weakness. It made her so easy to control, as Orithyia seemed to know. But where Orithyia had decided to control her through fear and pain, Theron knew the better option was through softer, more insidious means. Aurora was alone and scared, so he would show her how steadfast an ally he was, how protective, how...loving. This was a woman who was wary enough not to fall for his seductions, but not guarded enough to rebuff even the most minor kindnesses. In the few days he had left in her company, he would tie her to him so thoroughly that even if he died, she would feel indebted to him—to Aureum.

Theron closed his eyes and leaned against the hard column at his back. It figured that in this wretched queendom, he'd only managed a few days of sleeping in a paltry excuse for a bed. When he woke in the morning, it was to Aurora pleading with the attendant.

"Please, you must tell the queen or the high priestess that monstrosities will appear here in only a few days. She can't hold her party here. People will die!"

"You're insane. There's no such thing as an oracle. Now, let go of me!" The attendant shoved Aurora off her and went on with her tasks.

"Please, whatever you do, just don't be here that day! Please!"

Theron reached out to her. She turned around to face him, shaking beneath his touch.

"Save your breath, Aurora."

"We can still stop it. No one has to die!"

"Very few will believe you. You know that, right?" he asked, trying his best to calm her. She really was made in a different mould, to care about the lives of people who had treated her with such disdain and cruelty.

"Then I'll save the ones who do."

But over the course of the next two days, all she'd accomplished was to earn the contempt and derision of the attendants and guards she pled with. The atrium had become a place most preferred to avoid, save for the necessary tasks of delivering food and drink or escorting Aurora in chains to relieve herself. Even then, she begged them to heed her warning. It didn't help that rumours had begun to spread about what she'd done to the guard in the temple plaza, or that the temple of Justice had begun a quarrel with the palace in the meantime. There was no one inclined to listen to her within the walls of the palace, not even when he lent his voice to hers.

Except his spies.

Unfortunately, Flora had decided to take note of Aurora and Theron's connection to her, and so the queen kept the key to Aurora's fetters on her at all times. Worse, not one of his spies possessed the magic to destroy the chains in a fashion that wouldn't rouse the guards forever stationed just outside the doors to the atrium. He was beginning to lose any semblance of hope that the future she'd witnessed could be changed at all.

When the morning bells announced the end of the plague and the reopening of Boreas, it was all he could do to tamp down his terror at his looming execution. Shortly thereafter, the attendants and guards entered the atrium en mass. His last ray of hope extinguished as he spotted the garments they held in their arms.

Pale green and see-through, the airy wisps of nothing were the garb of prostitutes. Two attendants carried a vat of gold paint, struggling with the weight of the liquid between them. Just as her vision had shown. Moments later, the other residents of the vivarium were herded into the atrium, giving him and Aurora as wide a berth as possible.

The head of the attendants, a plump older woman with tanned skin and grey streaks in her black hair stepped forward and clapped her hands to garner everyone's attention.

"Tonight, Boreas' most illustrious citizens will gather here. You are to be bathed and attired in celebration of the end of the plague. If you resist, the guards have been authorized to force your compliance. Please Her Majesty and her guests, and your accommodations may be made more comfortable. Upset Her Majesty or the guests, and you will rue the day you were born."

She motioned for her small army to march forward to their charges.

"Theron," Aurora whispered in a panic.

"I won't leave you alone with any of them. No one here will touch you," he promised.

As the guards and attendants dragged them all to the baths, the guards stood outside, facing inside, leering at their charges as they were forced to strip. Aurora began shaking once more.

Theron stepped into one of the corners where attendants waited with buckets to douse them. He glared every man into retreat.

"I'll shield you," he reassured her, pulling her close. "I'm going to unwrap this sheet, alright?"

She nodded, biting her lip.

"My brave little fairy."

"I don't feel brave," she whispered, her breath hitching as the sheet came loose.

"And yet you're standing here with me in this den of vipers. Do you wish to ready yourself, or will you allow them near you?"

She ran a hand through her messy locks, looking around at the attendants near them. Her shoulders dropped a fraction when she saw only women.

"I'll allow them to help."

"If they touch you in any way you don't want, you tell me."

She nodded.

He snapped his fingers and brought two attendants over, commanding them to hold up the sheet so that the guards at the entrance were denied a view. Theron covered her as best he could, always putting his own body in the way of any extra set of eyes that could be avoided. All the while, his gaze never strayed from hers. As the attendants moved to do their work, he watched her for any sign of distress at their touch.

In focusing himself entirely on her, he could dull the sharpest edge of his own terror. But in every sluice of water against his skin, in every slide of a comb through his hair, in every hesitant touch of a frightened attendant, that terror shredded more of his reserve. Nothing could stop what was coming. If he fled now, he'd merely be dragged back. If he used every last ounce of his power to cripple the guards, more would come, and then he'd be without even the slimmest hope of surviving the lethal blow, of healing himself.

Theron was going to die.

When they were brought back to their chambers to be dressed and ornamented, he insisted Aurora join him in his room. If he gave himself even a moment alone, he feared he would lose his nerve. He needed the reminder of why he was meant to die—of why his thread would be cut short. Aureum must have its oracle, and her beast must be destroyed.

Aurora donned the insulting attire, covering herself as best she could, shamed and scared. Given only the barest of coverings and ordered to allow himself to be painted, Theron took comfort in the fact that another of his spies was among the attendants. Aurora's attire pooled around her, and so his spy pulled out a sash of fabric to cinch the dress at her small waist. The attendant caught his eye as she slipped Aurora's pendant shield into the knot.

It was only once the same attendant stuck his own ancient artefact into the braid of his hair that he felt a surge of resentment. Why should he die? And in the home of his most hated enemy? He ground his teeth. At least he would go down fighting. There was some small measure of comfort in that. As the paint dried on his skin and he was covered in emerald jewellery, Aurora's face was painted in the thick, gaudy style of a prostitute. Then they were given a small meal. His last, he supposed. A pity it was so paltry.

"We could still flee," Aurora whispered as they were left alone in their room.

"They've strengthened security," he said, nodding to the scene beyond the terrace. Outside, royal guards patrolled every inch of the grounds. Five stood outside his door alone.

"Just before it happens, we could find some excuse not to be in the room."

"I won't be allowed to leave. But you should, just before it happens."

"We could warn them when the queen arrives, we could warn all the nobles too. There's still time."

"Aurora…" he said, placing his hand on her cheek.

She leaned into it as tears filled her eyes. She knew as well as he that no one would listen. There would be no warning them. Her vision had made it clear they'd tried everything and failed, that no one with the power to prevent the massacre had bothered to listen.

"I can't give up! We're still alive! We still have time to change the future!"

A guard barged in.

"Princess Epicasta has called you, Your Majesty."

Aurora grabbed his arm, frozen in fear. He put a hand over hers and squeezed.

"Anyone who touches you will die."

She shook her head.

"Try to warn her, please."

"I will."

As he was taken from the vivarium and paraded through the halls of the palace like a living statue, servants and guards alike gawked and stared. Here was the king of Aureum, humiliated for their amusement. He vowed bloody vengeance, anger a much more palatable substitute for fear. The palace would soon be overrun with monstrosities, and then Batea would paint the walls in blood—vengeance was assured even in the event of his death. When he was finally brought before the princess in a receiving room, she waved the guards off.

"I'll take it from here."

Once they were alone, she sighed.

"You should have signed the treaty," she began.

He shrugged.

"You're about to have bigger problems."

"Oh?"

"Monstrosities will soon appear in the vivarium."

She barked out a laugh.

"Was the paint poisoned? Have you gone mad?"

"If you have any sense left in you, allow the paladins of Justice to enter the palace and negotiate peace with them. Keep them here until the sun fully sets. If I'm mad, you'll merely solve a headache for the palace. If I'm right, you'll save your wretched guests from being devoured. Well...some of them."

She eyed him with complete bewilderment before she wiped the expression from her face.

"As I said, you should have signed the treaty. You might have saved yourself this humiliation. And there is more to come this evening, for you, and for your...paramour."

"If anyone touches her—"

She held up her hand and rolled her eyes.

"No one will. You, however, will be expected to, intimately, in front of an audience. You should have left her alone. Instead, you brought her to Her Majesty's attention. What happens now is a result of your poor choices."

The last little piece of the puzzle in his mind fell into place. No wonder he'd been so keen to accept his fate in her vision—why he was now determined to face the monstrosities rather than risk flight and eventual capture. If he tried to survive, to flee, to resist, Flora would use her magic and force someone else's soul inside him, using his body to violate Aurora for a crowd, rendering him without honour for all to see. He would rather be dead than do that to Aurora—to allow someone to do so through him. Given the choice between a noble death protecting her and living as his fairy's nightmare, he would always choose death. A strange sense of calm swept over him. There was no escaping what was to come. In fact, he had no desire to. Better an honourable warrior's death than a wretch's life.

Theron tuned out most of the rest of what Epicasta threatened, numb to it all. Soon, her scheming would be someone else's problem. He didn't know how long she went on for, only that the sun had begun dipping low.

"If you'll excuse me, I have a party to attend," he said.

"You…you haven't listened to a word I've said." She raised her brow, her expression acidic.

"No."

"Serves me right for trying to help you," she muttered.

"You should call the paladins now."

She rolled her eyes and rung a bell. The guards entered and took him back to the guest palace, where entertainers were beginning to set up in the exact spot the monstrosities would bubble up from. For some reason, it gave him hope. He would die with his honour intact. Aurora was already waiting for him, doing her best to warn whoever so much as glanced at her. But just as all the times before, no one listened to her.

Guests began arriving, leering at him and Aurora, at all the prisoners of the vivarium. Entertainers began playing music, servants circulated through the growing throngs with food and drink. Theron refused to reply to every jab and insult. What did it matter? Soon they would be dead, the same as he. Aurora continued her fruitless attempts to save them, to convince them to flee, only to be met with mockery and sneers. He did his best to shield her from their views, pulsing his magic into the eyes of any who dared allow their gazes to linger on her, a not-so-subtle warning to find their perverse pleasures elsewhere.

But as the sun dipped lower, and the scene was bathed in the exact same light as her vision, he prepared himself. His blood thrummed through his veins in anticipation.

"You should go somewhere safe now, madam fairy."

She could still escape, flee to one of her hidden paths out of the vivarium.

"I can't! They won't listen! They're going to—"

"Aurora, you did everything you could."

She truly had. Aurora had exhausted herself trying to convince them to save their worthless lives. That she'd tried at all made her a better person than any other now standing in the vivarium.

"Please, don't stay here! Come with me!"

She tugged on his arm. But he would not be moved. If he survived, Flora would force him or his body to hurt her in unspeakable ways. Epicasta had been correct. What he did now had been the result of his choices, and they had been poor. Aurora would be safer once he died. His people would free her, his cousin would protect her.

"I will not run from my fate."

"It *can't* be fate! I can change it!"

And yet, she could not.

As foreseen, screams erupted. The shadows beneath the musicians rose up like a tide. Guests began fleeing. Others were swallowed whole in an instant. Theron enlarged his artefacts, giving himself both shield and spear. As chaos erupted, Theron was the eye of the storm, his body primed for battle as blood and viscera flew in every direction. The green finery of Viridis was soaked in crimson.

He knew what to do as soldiers poured in, more warm bodies for the monstrosities to tear through. He led his own charge, widening the protective space in front of Aurora as they were backed against a wall. Fleeing nobles and entertainers nearly knocked him to his feet. He tried to take the brunt of it for Aurora, but one sent her to her knees, her protective artefact slipping from her grasp. Theron forced himself to turn away, to focus on the battle in front of him. The divine magic infused into his artefacts dispelled the creatures as they bubbled up. But he already knew from experience and her vision that any relief from the onslaught was temporary. Soon, more would come up than he could handle.

Aurora screamed just as a group of paladins joined the fray. He turned to see her being dragged into the open maw of a monstrosity. Leaping back to her side, he thrust his spear into the beast, dispelling it. He looked back at her one last time, taking in her gore-spattered dress, her wide, panicked eyes, her bleeding leg, her manacled wrists.

Theron braced for the end.

A monstrosity drove its talon through his body, its own destroyed by touching the divine magic in his gold paint. The wound was lethal, his magic unable to heal the damage even as shock prevented him from feeling the pain. He stumbled as blood gushed from the enormous wound, and then collapsed on the floor. His magic recoiled from the wound, no truer sign that his thread had been cut.

Death swept over him in Her dark and endless embrace.

CHAPTER 18
AURORA

Aurora screamed, crawling over to where Theron had collapsed in a pool of his own blood. He couldn't die! She was supposed to change this fate, to fight against it. If she couldn't even do that, then how was she supposed to change anything—how was she supposed to save anyone? Her magic swirled inside her like a storm, itching to be freed. She had no control over it, but as the monstrosities began pouring out of every shadow, her options dwindled.

Not even the paladins were making headway, though they were distracting the beasts, keeping their focus off Aurora and Theron.

Aurora fumbled for the protective artefact nearby, activating it. She was covered head to toe in the shield, like a bubble shaped just like her, protruding from her skin by only a handspan. How long it would hold was anyone's guess.

"Please, save him," she pleaded, unleashing the magic inside her, begging it to suspend him in time, to keep him from death.

But it was stuck, trapped between her skin and the shield. She could feel it raking its claws against the shield, trying to get out. If she wanted to save him, she would have to risk her own life. Hand trembling, she turned off her shield.

Her magic latched onto Theron like prey, sinking into every bone and sinew and vein. The pool of blood around him stopped growing. Had she done it this time, as she had when they first met? She reached forward to try to move his hand but couldn't, just like before. But just as she dared to hope, a monstrosity rose from the shadow of a dismembered torso, its eyes fixed on her.

As it clawed its way into her world, her heart crashed against her ribs. Was this the end for both of them? Was her fate to die not in her own time, but in the distant past, the future doomed?

"I'm sorry," she sobbed.

Sorry for getting Phaedra and Silvanus killed. Sorry for dooming Trisia. Sorry to the deities who had entrusted her with this fate. Sorry for proving unworthy of her Orithyia's faith. Sorry for meeting Theron and driving him to this end. He wasn't supposed to die here, not like this. For all she knew, her presence in the ancient past was why the monstrosities had shown themselves in the guest palace. The only thing she'd changed was shortening his thread even further. The only thing she'd accomplished was becoming the most miserable disappointment in the history of Trisia. Every other Trisian given this task had succeeded. She'd been the first to fail, and given what Drakon would do in her absence, likely the last.

Aurora grabbed for Theron's spear, swinging it wildly at the monstrosity. A task made all the harder by the fetters that kept her arms shackled. It easily dodged her fumbling attempt at self-defence, her arms shaking with the dual effort of keeping Theron suspended in time and holding up the massive weapon. She swung again. The beast dipped under the arc of the spear and lunged at her.

Just as its claws raked her face, a flash of light blinded her, and the shrieks of the monstrosities rang in her ears. She squeezed her eyes shut as tears streamed down her face at the sting of that light. The screeches of beasts were replaced by the groans and cries of men and women. Had they been saved? Who had wielded such power?

When at last the spots had cleared from her vision, she looked around. Paladins were busy healing the wounded, while palace guards bowed in reverence to a young man with a bow.

A bow with a very familiar symbol on it.

The holy sword...and the hero who wielded it.

Her head spun as her magic drained from her. She wouldn't be able to suspend Theron much longer.

"Avatar! Please, help me!" she shouted.

The avatar duly obliged and stuttered to a halt.

"King Theron!" he gasped.

The avatar's eyes widened as he looked over the king's attire and then her own, rage darkening his features. He went to his knees and tried to move Theron without success.

"Please, I'm holding his death at bay, but I can't hold on for much longer. You can heal any wound caused by a monstrosity. Heal him, before I exhaust my magic."

The avatar nodded, pouring his divine magic over Theron. Slowly, slowly, the wound healed, closing up as both sinew and bone were restored. Sharp pain shot through her head and blood dripped from her nose yet still she held onto the magic. Her vision was swimming and her lungs crushed in a vise by the time the avatar was done. Aurora collapsed on her side the moment she released her magic, spent. The avatar came over to her side and used his divine magic to heal the wounds on her leg and face.

"Is he...?"

Aurora was terrified of the answer. What if she'd been too late? Her magic inadequate?

"He's breathing. You did well."

Relief crashed through her. She held back her tears. Though she hadn't been able to prevent the events of the vision from taking place, at least he was alive. But questions lingered. Had she truly changed the future, or merely ensured it would happen as she'd always known?

The avatar picked her up, searched the halls for the nearest room with an intact bed, and placed her down gently.

"What's your name?" she asked, her voice thready and weak.

"Hyllus, my lady."

"Aurora."

"You're a good woman, Aurora, to put yourself at risk to save another," he said, covering her with a sheet.

She almost laughed. She was a bloody mess—literally. Whosever sheets she was currently soiling would be livid when they discovered it, given how stingy the vivarium's attendants were. If they'd survived, that is. The thought sobered her. Before exhaustion took her entirely, she needed to tell Hyllus what was to come, and their parts in it.

"I need to tell you something." She grabbed hold of his tunic before he could leave.

"It can wait until you've rested, my lady."

"No. It can't. There's a monster we must slay, Drakon. And we must do it before he has the power to destroy the whole of Trisia."

"We?" he asked, a doting look on his tanned face as he searched her head for bumps and bruises, glaring down at the metal binding her wrists, following the chain to the collar at her neck.

What could she say that would convince him she wasn't mad? That she didn't in some way deserve her fetters? Nothing she'd said since she'd arrived had been believed, save by Theron, and even he had needed to see her visions. She wracked her foggy brain.

There was a theory that in every lifetime, a person had the same magic, tied as it was to the soul. If Hyllus was the first incarnation of the hero, and the hero was the same in every cycle, then he would share the same magic as Silvanus. It seemed she'd be putting her theology teachings to the test.

"I met another hero of the holy sword. Silvanus. During a cycle of calamity, he was given divine magic and made the avatar, his purpose to seal away a great evil—Drakon."

"There can be only one avatar of Justice at a time, my lady." He frowned, still looking for a wound on her head.

"I know. Silvanus had wild magic, as expected of an avatar. The magic of divine eyes. Just as you do."

"My lady, I fear you've hurt yourself in ways I cannot heal." While his tone was full of concern, she didn't miss the fear in his grey eyes.

"I kept his secret because he was a good man."

"And yet you told me."

"Hyllus, I suspended Theron, kept him from the moment of death. But I couldn't heal him. What do you suppose my wild magic is?" she asked. The hero in her time had been the first to realise her magic for what it was. Hopefully, Hyllus was the same.

His eyes widened.

"Time."

"Yes. And I never betrayed Silvanus' trust. Use your eyes, you'll know I'm telling the truth when you step into the Tapestry."

Hyllus searched her eyes, looking for traps and lies he wouldn't find.

"My lady, if you're simply mad, I'll have to silence you."

To protect himself and his secret. Those with his magic had been hunted since the earliest times by all and sundry. She understood his caution.

"I know."

He paced the room a few times. His wavy brown hair was held back by a tie, some of his more unruly locks escaping confinement as he shook his head.

"So be it."

When he gazed at her again, it was with eyes glittering like grey jewels. His face contorted in bewilderment, his brows furrowing with strain before he came back to the material world. He blinked in shock.

"Your thread is...I cannot describe it. It is here and not of here, displaced but not by distance. I cannot see where it came from. I saw the thread that bound us, one of fate and friendship, our paths converging. And there is another thread attached to yours. I've never seen one so thick and malevolent. What did you bring with you?"

"My fate is tied to Drakon, the monster we must seal. If we don't stop him here and now, the cycles of calamity will repeat."

"Repeat?" he asked, before light dawned in his eyes. "Then you... travelled through time... How? Why did you come here?"

"I didn't mean to. I expected to die."

Hyllus paced the room.

"This is...a lot." He sighed, pinching the bridge of his nose. "Though at least now I know what my true mission is—the great evil Justice wants me to deal with."

"I'm just glad I don't have to search the whole of Trisia looking for you," she laughed. "But why did you come here?"

"Truthfully, I was coming to see if I could help King Theron. He attacked me, and Justice punished him, even though I hold him no ill will. He struck me as an honourable man, and I want to ensure he's back on his throne...before his cousin does something rash. May I ask why you risked your life to save his?"

"Because he was the only one who believed me and was willing to help. And he has been kind...sometimes."

Hyllus laughed.

"That sounds like him."

"Hyllus, we're both prisoners here. His jailor is Flora, and mine is Orithyia. I went to her for help first and...let's just say that I offended her, and though she let me live, I...I don't want to meet with her alone again. I saw a vision of Theron's death, of the monstrosities here. We were trying to escape the city when we were caught and forced back here. I tried to warn as many as I could but no one believed me."

"You see visions as well?"

She nodded.

"I would rather not," she answered glumly.

He gripped her hand in his. Hyllus must know what it meant—that eventually, the visions would drive her mad—provided she lived long enough.

"I'll protect you, Aurora, and I *will* free you. The title of avatar should be enough for that. And then together, we'll slay this beast."

Tears sprung to her eyes. She sobbed. His brow creased with concern and he pulled her close. Aurora would have flung her arms around him if her wrists weren't still bound by manacles attached to the collar at her throat. She settled for pressing herself into the cuirass of his bronze armour, not caring about the hardness of it against her skin.

It had been so long since she felt so hopeful and safe. She'd found the one person in this time that she could fully trust. There was no need to bargain with Hyllus, no need to give away what she would rather guard. Indeed, there was no need to guard herself at all. And certainly no need for scheming or playing games.

As she wept in his arms, the weight crushing her heart and forcing her to harden herself lifted. Shared with a partner she could trust, the burden of the future didn't feel so heavy.

"Thank you for finding me," she whispered.

"I only wish I'd found you sooner," he replied.

"It has been...difficult."

Hyllus chuckled.

"And why do I suspect that to be a monumental understatement?"

Aurora choked out a bitter laugh. He had the right of it. Pain and fear had been her constant companions since she'd learned of her fate.

"Do you know what this place is called?" she asked.

"The guest palace?"

"The vivarium. A display case for the queen's living trophies. A place where you either steal your daily necessities or bargain sexual favours for them. You see how I'm dressed, how Theron is dressed. The queen is cruel, Hyllus. She delights in using humiliation to break people. If you mean to free us from this place, you must be very careful."

"I am well acquainted with Flora's...personality. I'll let the other paladins of Justice here know what's been going on. They've been intent on entering the palace since the royal guards attacked someone in the temple plaza. You wouldn't happen to know anything about that, would you?"

"They attacked me. I...I defended myself, and then they dragged us back to the palace. The guard who stripped and chained me, he...Theron killed him."

His hold on her tightened. Hyllus held his tongue, but when he loosened his arms, she could see the rage swimming in his eyes.

"That won't happen again. Never again," he swore. "I'll see if you can be made a guest of Justice's temple instead."

"Thank you."

"You don't need to thank me. Any honourable person would do the same."

"I'm still grateful," she sighed. Her head felt light and her body heavy.

"Rest. I'll take care of everything else."

He tucked her in as her lids began to feel heavy. But there was something else he needed to know, some other advantage she could give them in the fight to come. She gasped.

The artefacts.

She strained her hearing, but outside the door, people were in pain, paladins called back and forth and healers had just arrived. She hoped no one would hear what she needed to say.

"Hyllus, wait! One more thing."

"What is it?"

She crooked her finger for him to come closer.

"There's a hoard of ancient artefacts hidden in the basement of the temple of Knowledge that might be able to help us," she whispered. "Press on the brick on the third row up from the ground, exactly halfway across the length of the back wall of the temple. Then speak the words, 'Lead me to the fathomless depths of Knowledge.' It's dark inside, too dark for your eyes to see, but at the end of the hall is the door to the vault."

His eyes widened. Hyllus smiled then, an impish glint in his eye.

"You're unexpectedly full of mischief, my lady."

Aurora laughed.

"And don't you forget it." She winked, returning his smile.

Hyllus laughed.

"I won't, I promise."

Theron woke with a gasp as his lungs filled with air he shouldn't be breathing. This wasn't the Loom, where all the threads of the world were collected to be respun by Fate back into the Tapestry once more. His surroundings were...physical. A pool of blood cooled beneath him. His blood. And yet he was whole, unharmed, as if the attack had never happened. Theron fumbled to his feet and was immediately sent crashing to his knees. His head swam. Triad's tits, there it was, the proof of the attack, the blood loss. He leaned against the nearest wall and waited out the dizziness, calling on his magic to replenish his blood.

Theron opened his eyes to find the world had mostly righted itself...for him at least. The atrium of the vivarium was still splashed in blood, guts and gore. Bits and pieces of people were strewn about, with no way to discern the noble from the entertainers and whores. Paladins sifted through the mess, looking for any lingering survivors. It was simply too bad Flora hadn't been here in time to be devoured. He dragged a hand down his face and sighed, exhausted. How had he survived? And why? He'd died for a reason—a purpose.

"Aurora," he whispered.

Where was she? Had she managed to flee? Had she died? He got to his feet, ready to search for her when Princess Epicasta inserted her very unwelcome self in front of him.

"How did you know?"

He grinned, enjoying the advantage of knowing something she didn't. Apparently, the rumours of his little fairy's predictions and supposed madness hadn't made it to this one's ears. That was all for the better. Once her true power became known, it would make it harder to secure her for Aureum.

"Why did you believe me?" he asked.

"I didn't."

"And yet..." he chuckled, looking around her.

Aurora was nowhere to be seen. Was that because she'd survived...or because she hadn't?

"Who are you looking for?"

"Your mother. Perhaps I got lucky and she was eaten."

"Her Majesty is safe in the inner palace."

"What a shame."

"Watch your tongue."

"Watch your tone. I'm still a king."

"Clearly." Epicasta looked him up and down before raising a brow.

He didn't have the energy to be embarrassed. But he did have it in him to be crafty still. He caught the eye of a nearby paladin and waved him over.

"You're a paladin of Justice, are you not?"

"I am, your..." The paladin looked him up and down, unsure exactly what Theron was. Though he spoke like a high-born, he was dressed like an ornament.

"Majesty. I am King Theron of Aureum. Thank you for your heroic efforts. If you had not been here at the right moment, everyone would have perished. How did you know when the monstrosities would appear?"

"We didn't, Your Majesty. We'd been invited to come to the palace by Princess Epicasta to investigate a matter which occurred in the temple plaza a few days ago."

Epicasta's eyes widened a fraction as she caught on to his ploy.

"Which I will be happy to rectify with you. If you would please come with me?" Epicasta smiled, trying to pull the paladin away.

But no one who had become a paladin of Justice had done so without being hardheaded and stubborn in the extreme. Like a bloodhound on the scent, once they caught a whiff of injustice, they were as unmovable as a mountain. He might have just found his way out of the vivarium.

"I believe I know of what you speak. The woman attacked by the royal guard is a friend of mine. When we were dragged back here, the royal guard stripped and chained her to that column for days leading up to this...party. Have you found her yet?"

"No, not yet. But when we do, she'll be taken to the temple of Justice for protection. You, too, will be welcome to take refuge there until the matter has been seen to. Given your status, you may wish to remain there until High Priestess Nerio arrives to oversee your case."

Theron smiled and bowed to the paladin.

"Blessings of the Triad on you, paladin. I'm grateful for your assistance."

He gave the paladin Aurora's description, being sure to make clear that she wore manacles and a collar as well as the garb of a prostitute. Every detail only seemed to enrage the paladin more.

After all, attacking someone in the temple plaza was an affront against the Triad. The royal palace might as well have spit on the statues of the goddesses themselves. By law, the moment Aurora had been assaulted in the plaza, she was a ward of Justice's temple, and her treatment after that moment was a serious insult. But Flora had never worried herself over taboos and consequences, not when Orithyia and her daughter always cleaned up after her. He would save the details of what Flora intended to force him to do for the right moment. Perhaps at the trial?

When the paladin gave Theron instructions to return to the temple with a paladin once he'd collected his things, Epicasta stood like a statue beside him.

"Fool."

"You lost this round, Princess."

"The temple can't save you. You still need to be purified and pay restitution. Rest your head under the temple's roof if you like, but you can't escape what's to come."

Maybe not, but at least Aurora could. It might have been better to find a way to allow her to slip away in the middle of the night, but now that she'd come to Flora's attention, only the attention of those with some power in Viridis would protect her from Flora's worst caprices.

"Nerio will purify me. And with her arrival, any restitution I'm forced to pay will be fair and *just*."

"And where is the wandering high priestess? How long will it take to find her, bid her to come, and wait for her arrival? Much can happen, even in the span of a week." She looked around at the gory scene before them pointedly. "Besides, even if you hide behind the temple walls, Her Majesty is within her rights to demand your attendance at court. After all, it wasn't she who attacked your paramour or chained her here. All you've done is given yourself a paladin babysitter whose sense of justice rarely sits well with the machinations of court."

She had a point, but it was a challenge he believed himself capable of overcoming. Besides, his paladin babysitter, as she called it, would be there to observe Flora's behaviour as well.

"That's a great many words to say 'I lost.'"

"You're an ingrate and a fool, Your Majesty."

Theron snorted. What need did he have to thank her for doing as she was told? Once the dust settled, she was going to be hailed and fêted. She'd brought the paladins in the nick of time, saving all who could be saved.

"I'm sure you can spin this to appear like a prescient hero."

"It would have been better had you died."

When he'd stood in front of that monstrosity, knowing what would happen and knowing the consequences if he'd lived and been forced to do as Flora was going to command, he'd agreed. But now that he was alive, given a second chance, he would never wish for it again.

"Run along then and sulk in your room, Princess. I have more important matters to attend to."

"Goddess save me from arrogant swine," Epicasta muttered. "The avatar took your paramour to the room down the hall, and has yet to emerge."

"Was she...? No, move out of my way."

Theron pushed passed the princess, flinging open the doors to rooms where furniture had been trashed and guests hid. Finally, he came to one where he could hear Aurora's voice coming through the thin door. He was about to fling open the door when he heard her laugh. It caught him up short, his hand hovering over the handle.

He'd never heard her laugh like that before.

Theron opened the door just a crack. Aurora was tucked in bed, Hyllus seated at her side. The way they were looking at each other, the genuine light in their eyes and smiles, it was like they shared some amusing secret no one else was privy to. It made him feel ugly inside. She'd never smiled for him like that. Never looked at him like he meant the world to her.

Theron wanted it with a ferocity that shocked him.

He clenched his fists at his sides and tamped down on his magic as it seethed inside him. Of course she looked at Hyllus like that. The avatar was a 'good man.' He exuded boyish charm. In his naivety, he believed in the good inside others, and found it reflected back to him in those with similar, naïve dispositions. And it helped that he'd probably been responsible for saving everyone still living in the vivarium. He need not be jealous of the—jealous? Jealous?! No, that's not what this was. It was preposterous. He was not some dog growling at any who approached his new toy. He was the King of Aureum. If he wanted Aurora, he would find a way to make her come to him pleading for the pleasure he could give her. Against a young man with no experience in matters of seduction, he had nothing to fear.

So why did he hesitate to intrude on them? Why did he still feel like there was a pit of snakes in his heart?

There was nothing for it. Any longer out here and he was going to become the fool Epicasta accused him of being. Theron pushed open the door.

"Theron!" Aurora sat up, her face pale and drawn.

"Your Majesty!" Hyllus jumped from his seat on the bed and clasped forearms with him.

"Do I have you to thank for my life?" Theron asked Hyllus as he gripped the avatar's arm in turn.

"Not entirely. Aurora risked life and limb to keep you alive until I got here. She's incredibly brave."

"Yes, I know," he said, taking in the sight of her.

His fairy had stayed to save him, even knowing what would happen. Even though she'd had no guarantee of her own safety. Hyllus could only hope for such devotion. Everything Theron had done had been worthwhile. She was his.

Hyllus waited for a moment, assessing Aurora for any sign of discomfort. As if he might need to protect her from Theron. She was not Hyllus' to protect, to care for. That was Theron's self-appointed charge.

"Aurora, I'm going to speak with the paladins here. They'll take you to the temple of Justice and safeguard you until you're ready to leave the city. Your Majesty, I'll do the same for you, though you may need to wait a little longer to leave, since Nerio is usually the one to see to cases amongst royalty."

"No need, Hyllus. I've already done so by speaking to the paladins here."

Hyllus smiled.

"Good. See, Aurora? Everything will work out."

"Are we...are we really getting out of here?" Aurora asked, her eyes full of cautious hope.

"Yes, we are," Theron answered.

"Thank the Triad."

She should be thanking him. But he would let it slide, just this once. His little fairy looked like she was going to collapse at any second.

"Sleep, Aurora. I'll wake you when I retrieve our belongings," Theron said.

"Mmm," she replied, her eyes closing the moment her head hit the pillow.

Within a few heartbeats, she was asleep.

"Your Majesty." Hyllus waved him out of the room and into the corridor. Once the door was closed, he kept his voice low. "I won't be staying in Boreas long, but I intend to take her with me when I leave. I thought I should tell you in case the two of you..."

At least the young man had the sense to know there was something, however tenuous, between them.

"And do you truly believe you're capable of protecting her? Do you even know who her enemies are?"

"I know she fears both Orithyia and Flora. I'm confident my status as the avatar will shield her from any future meddling."

"Hyllus, the only person protected by your status is you. Do you know what she is? What she's capable of? What she seeks? The risks involved?"

Hyllus furrowed his brows.

"Yes, of course. She told me as much."

She'd told him?! A man she'd known less than an hour? He'd had to wheedle and cajole even the barest hint of that information from her. What made Hyllus so much more trustworthy? So deserving of her secrets?

"You seem upset by this. I assure you, her secrets are safe with me."

Secrets. Plural. What did Hyllus know that Theron didn't? Theron tamped down on his anger. That even the avatar could sense it was a slip he never should have made.

"Then you know that if Orithyia or Flora wish to harm her, there will be little you can do to stop them. You are one man against armies of soldiers, spies, and assassins. Avatar or not, you will need the resources of a kingdom to guard her."

"Do you love her?"

"I—"

Of course he didn't. What kind of king could afford to love? Love was a weakness for those with real power and more enemies than they could count. Love was for good men like Hyllus, not good kings like Theron. But that wasn't what a good man wanted to hear about a woman he'd sworn to protect. So Theron told the avatar exactly what he wished to hear.

"I do. I have not...admitted as much to her." That would hopefully forestall Hyllus from telling such outrageous lies to Aurora in the meantime. Good men respected the secrets of others. "And I cannot, in good conscience, allow you to take her from my side. Once this business with Flora is sorted, I'll escort her back to Aureum in comfort and safety. When it comes time to slay this beast, she'll have the might of an army behind her."

And once the business with her beast was done, and this cycle of chaos over, she would remain at his side, her visions used to ensure the peace, safety and power of Aureum. But Hyllus didn't need to know that.

Hyllus clapped him on the back with a smile.

"You see? I knew you were a good man."

And as long as the avatar believed it, he was a fool.

CHAPTER 19
THERON

In the temple of Justice, everything was blinding white. Pure white limestone columns held aloft a ceiling of the same, while white tapestries with the barest hints of silver threading flapped in the breeze. The floors were immaculate and sparkling, washed every few hours by acolytes whose initiation was a series of brutal menial tasks designed to weed out any whose convictions were lacking. All Her clerics hurried about their tasks, never stopping to engage in chitchat or distraction, and all dressed in varying shades of white and grey. The lowliest had robes more like a storm cloud, and the higher they rose in the temple's hierarchy, the brighter their robes shone. The alabaster statue of Justice herself dominated the main hall, her diamond eyes catching the sun and throwing rainbows across the hall, the only hint of colour allowed within her temple. Her robe was the brightest white of all, accentuated by an almost opalescent sparkle, the same sparkle that had been applied throughout the temple for maximum blinding effect.

Theron felt ill at ease. It was little wonder that he did. Good kings rarely had clean consciences, and the mark of Her displeasure burned on his hand. In Her temple, it was an ever-present distraction. He tried to put it from his mind as he sat in the temple's courtyard under the shade of a fruit tree on one of the few benches in the temple. Idleness was not to be borne in Her clerics, and so places of rest and relaxation were few and far between. It was here that he held court in miniature, healing any of Her people who came before him with an injury or illness. It ingratiated him to the people here, but only just. The mark tainted him, no matter that the avatar had vouched for him.

He would be glad to be purified and rid of this place. The only real upside was that he was no longer directly under Flora's thumb in her twisted little display case of a palace. He might have counted Aurora's presence here as another, especially since she'd been smiling and laughing more, but she'd almost exclusively reserved that joviality for Hyllus.

Worse still, in the few days they'd been guests of the temple, he'd not been alone with her for even a moment. Every time he tried, she managed to slip his grasp.

Even now, she was walking the halls in the company of the avatar, smiling and talking, her laugh carrying across the courtyard. He caught a glimpse of her in her deep grey robe, her ears and curves exposed. Unlike him, she was treated with all due respect. Priestesses and paladins alike allowed her to question them about their lives and routines, sneaking in objects of one kind or another to show her how they worked or were constructed. What valuable knowledge was she giving away for free? No doubt she was undoing all his plans to keep her insights entirely to himself.

Indulged like a child but respected as an adult, she was a beacon of light and life in this staid, serious place. It chaffed that he was not able to hoard it for his own, or even afforded the luxury of standing near that light.

As he finished his healing duties for the day, a messenger in royal green approached him, flanked by priestesses in white who eyed the messenger with even more suspicion than they did Theron.

"Your Majesty, Her Majesty Queen Flora has invited you to the palace to discuss restitution," the guard said as he bowed and handed the sealed scroll to Theron.

It seemed the royal personnel were on their best behaviour today. The paladins' investigation must really be irritating Flora. All of the witnesses to her malicious behavior were being protected, away from her influence. He'd noticed a fair few of the vivarium's other political prisoners taking up residence in Justice's temple, likely with years of horrors and gripes to unload on the shoulders of the paladins. Perhaps Flora would manage to worm her way out of the consequences, but this scandal could also spell the end of her reign.

A man could dream.

Then again, given her magic, she was just as likely to find a scapegoat to blame it all on. The head maid or the highest ranked guard, most like.

Theron tore open the Viridian royal seal and scanned the paper. It was exactly as the guard described. Had Flora mustered her wits? Or would Orithyia and Epicasta be holding her reins today? He tapped the letter to his lips in thought. There was no good reason to refuse.

"Very well. I'll accept Her Majesty's invitation. Provided, of course, the priestesses and paladins here can spare one of their number to accompany me. Given their investigation is ongoing, I wouldn't want to taint it by fraternising."

"A paladin is waiting for you by the door, Your Majesty," one of the priestesses tipped her head in the direction of the entrance.

So bloody punctual, these servants of Justice. The idea of fashionable lateness was entirely foreign. Theron stifled a sigh as he stood and adjusted his dark grey acolyte's robes. At least the quality was superior to the rags provided by the palace. It even had silver embroidery on it. Unfortunately, grey was most definitely not his colour. Yet again, he wondered when his own entourage would arrive. He should have received a letter from a runner the day Boreas opened its gates, and an entourage of servants, soldiers and more by now.

Theron tried to put his worries from his mind. He had bigger problems to deal with. Though he was confident he could corner Flora into making some gaffe or other in front of the paladin escort, his divine madness at the border was just as likely to be thrown in his face multiple times. On the other hand, if Orithyia planned to attend, he could reasonably demand she purify him. It would be nigh impossible for her to refuse in front of witnesses like the paladin.

Alas, by the time he was brought before Flora, the high priestess was nowhere in sight. Not even the princess was present. A boon. That sharp-tongued harpy was quickly becoming one of his least favourite people in Boreas, and given the company, that was saying something.

Instead, the obnoxiously green and silver hall was filled with scum as the sun retreated behind the clouds. He could smell the promise of rain. A feat, given the stench of those present. Viridian nobles of every standing jostled for space with wealthy merchants and other influential allies. Her most loyal and sycophantic toadies stood closest to her emerald throne. Her eyes sparkled with wicked glee. He almost smiled. It seemed he would be dealing with the mad dog today.

Theron made a decision then to grate on her every nerve while remaining perfectly compliant with every bit of noble courtesy. Let all her people see her for the maniac she was.

He tipped his head, refusing to bow and scrape and make himself lesser in her court.

"King Theron, the sun of Aureum greets the bounty of Viridis, Queen Flora."

"The bounty of Viridis acknowledges your arrival. Though it looks like, yet again, your wardrobe is lacking for a royal audience. Have none of your countrymen come to serve you?" she asked in mock pity.

Goddesses, how had this woman managed a stranglehold on Viridis for so long?

"I'm honoured to wear the robes given me by the temple of Justice, where I'm residing while Her paladins investigate your guest palace," he said, emphasizing her scandal.

Her face darkened with rage, her jaw clenching before she took a calming breath.

"It is a wonder they tolerate you, given you wear the mark of Justice's displeasure. Tell me, blasphemer, does it trouble you while in Her temple?"

"It only troubles me that High Priestess Orithyia might purify me, as the avatar wishes, and yet Her Holiness remains busy elsewhere."

"Boreas needs their high priestess. A blasphemer king cannot take precedence over the needs of the people."

"Yes, I agree. A pity the people of Boreas are in such dire straits. Why, just the other day, during the height of the plague, my room, nestled safely within your guest palace, was visited by an angry spirit."

He could have heard a pin drop in the silence that followed. He'd all but accused her of shirking her sacred duties as a monarch to pacify the spirits of the land. He'd all but pointed his finger at her for causing the plague through negligence. Except that he'd only relayed a simple truth.

In her stunned silence, he pressed his advantage.

"Such a thing has never occurred in the Aurean royal palace. If you like, I would be more than happy to share some basic rituals for the protection of your domicile."

There were a few gasps at his offer. Not only had he called her incompetent, he'd suggested she was incapable of performing her duties better than even a child. Flora's face reddened with embarrassment and rage.

"And yet none of it protected your brother, Tisander, when a plague took *him*," she retorted.

Theron's magic exploded from him as he advanced on her throne, overtaken by unparalleled rage.

"Keep his name off your tongue. You're not worthy to speak it."

Her eyes flashed with glee as her guards barred his way with spears. He'd fallen into this imbecile's trap and it took all his willpower to keep himself from murdering the bitch where she sat.

"Such a temper. One wonders if you really were overcome with divine madness when you slaughtered Viridian soldiers on Viridian soil."

"The avatar can vouch for me," he ground out.

"And where is he? I don't believe he's here to corroborate your claims."

"I suspect he is busy purifying the city so that the monstrosities that appeared in the guest palace don't return. After all, Boreas has suffered so much recently," he retorted, regaining his composure.

Stupid fool. He never should have let her goad him.

"The bounty of Viridis thanks you for your concern," she replied with venom. "But enough of pleasantries. I have summoned you to make restitution for your crimes." She snapped her fingers and one of her closest toadies took out a large piece of parchment. "Read the treaty."

Theron waited impatiently to find out just how outrageous she'd become in the interim. Would she demand Aureum's royal palace this time?

"For the undisputed crimes of murdering a dozen Viridian soldiers on Viridian soil, and conspiring with a worshipper of the sinister goddesses to attack the Viridian royal palace, the blasphemer King Theron of Aureum will cede the entirety of the Dragon's Flank from The Colonnades Of The Colossus to the Dragon's Talon port, as well as Aureum's territory in the Dragon's Spine Mountains, to Viridis as compensation. By signing this document, both Queen Flora and King Theron agree to these facts as true and these terms as just and fair."

Gasps filled the gathered crowd as Flora eyed him with a smirk.

It seemed she'd learned to count since last they met, but she'd slipped further into madness. What fresh nonsense was this about conspiring with sinister goddesses? What game was she playing at? Before he could ask, his paladin escort stepped forward.

"Greetings to the bounty of Viridis. I am Itonus, paladin of Justice," he announced, bowing deeply.

"The bounty of Viridis acknowledges you."

"Your Majesty, you claim the King of Aureum is conspiring with a worshipper of the sinister goddesses. If you believed this, why have you waited until now to announce it? According to the law, such crimes must be reported the moment they are suspected."

"I am reporting it now, young paladin. Did you think you were the only ones launching an investigation into the appearance of monstrosities in my guest palace? In the days leading up to the attack, a woman was threatening that the monstrosities would appear, and even indicated the day and time. Naturally, my attendants thought she was mad. Preferring to be compassionate rather than suspicious, my attendants cared for her all the same. Many who heard her claims are either dead or recovering, and one of the survivors informed me of her threats this very day. I could only conclude that King Theron had conspired with her, an agent of chaos, to bring the monstrosities here, as she is his paramour, and he was overheard threatening the arrival of monstrosities, the same as she. Given the magnitude of His Majesty's crimes, I thought the compensation I've requested to be eminently reasonable. What the temples wish to do with him and his agent of chaos affiliate once he's faced the political consequences of his actions is entirely up to the judgement of the goddesses."

This was bad. Very bad. The best he could do was to stall for time. The paladins would now be split between investigating Flora's house of horrors and his supposed turn to evil. It might mean dragging out both for longer than he'd like, but he was confident that the truth would come out. Though if it did, that would present further problems. To prove her innocence, Aurora would have to demonstrate her ability to foresee the future. And once she did, it would take a minor miracle to get her out of Flora's clutches. As much as he hated it, he needed to involve a woman he hated to ensure Aurora's safety in the meantime.

"I proclaim my innocence, and demand an investigation into your baseless, slanderous claims," Theron announced. "And I would also like to proclaim the innocence of High Priestess Orithyia."

That caught the bitch off guard.

"High Priestess Orithyia has done no wrong. It is you who have conspired with agents of chaos."

"I agree that High Priestess Orithyia has done no wrong here. After all, the woman you accuse of being an agent of chaos was an honoured guest of the high priestess. And it was the high priestess, vouching for her identity, which allowed the woman in question to enter the royal palace as a guest here. I fully believe in High Priestess Orithyia's judgement of the woman's good character."

Flora was clearly vexed by his maneuvering. That boded well. It made it much more likely that Orithyia had been unaware of Flora's newest machination to devour his kingdom. Now that he'd tied Aurora's character to Orithyia's judgement, the old crone would either have to defend Aurora or admit to ignorance. And ignorance in the high priestess of Knowledge was shameful at best.

But Flora regained her composure and smiled in a way that had Theron doubting his advantage.

"Very well. You may retire until after the court has consulted with High Priestess Orithyia. In the meantime, my daughter, Princess Epicasta, will keep you company while I speak more with paladin Itonus."

"Your Majesty, respectfully, I must escort His Majesty while he's outside the temple."

"Is your highest duty to watch him, or to uncover heresy, young paladin? I should think the latter more deserving of your attention. If you fear he will flee, I understand. I shall keep my most capable guards on his person at all times."

The paladin seemed torn between his two duties. But if Theron wished to appear confident in his innocence before the court, he had to cede this minor victory to Flora.

"You have my oath as King of Aureum that I will not flee these accusations. I swear it on my honour."

The paladin nodded, and was ushered towards the queen while Theron was taken away by the palace guard for what he could only surmise was another round of threats. Once seated before the woman in question, dressed as always in Passion's deep red mourning robes, the guards swiftly abandoned the room. Lit with flickering candles, the first droplets of rain percussing the gardens below her open window, the room was otherwise quiet.

She was silent for some time, and Theron refused to be the first to break the impasse. Silence was preferable to speaking with the vile creature. She sipped tea, her gaze drawn to the window. After what felt like a lifetime, she spoke.

"Tea?" Epicasta asked as she sipped from her cup.

Knowing her, his cup was probably poisoned.

"No."

As if seeing through his thoughts, she rolled her eyes and leaned back in her seat.

"I take it you were surprised by the new accusations."

"Offended, actually."

"Naturally."

"Naturally."

"You realise this is only the beginning, don't you?"

"This ludicrous farce will be over soon enough. Your mother will be lucky if it doesn't strip her of whatever credibility she still clings to."

"You erred when you made that poor girl your paramour. Her Majesty will use her to come after you. And it won't stop until either the girl breaks and betrays you, or you break and give Her Majesty what she desires."

"As I've said before, she will never have Aureum."

Epicasta shook her head.

"You should have ceded the flank when I gave you the chance. Here." She reached into a pocket of her gown and tossed the letter at him. "Be grateful my people intercepted it before Her Majesty's."

"And have your little spies already read the contents?" he asked, bored.

"I don't need to. My 'little spies' have already given me a good guess as to its contents without the need for such discourtesies."

It was Canthus' seal, his trusted general. Theron opened it and prepared to school his face.

Greetings to the sun of Aureum.

Please forgive my impertinence, Your Majesty, but you must return home with all due haste. Bandits continue to harass all shipments of grain, and dualists are attacking outlying settlements, forcing your esteemed cousin Batea to chase after them. Given the circumstances, the war faction is questioning her suitability as acting queen. I fear they may goad her into imprudent action, or seat one of their own on your throne.

Triad preserve the sun of Aureum.

Your loyal servant,

General Canthus

Theron stood and walked to the nearest candle, holding the letter above it until it caught fire. He watched it burn, refusing to let it go until it was ash, allowing the pain of the fire to ground him while giving an outlet to his restless magic.

If his capable, level-headed general was sending him a pleading missive, the situation must be dire indeed. But he'd just schemed his way into spending more time in this wretched city. Had this been Epicasta's ploy? To light a fire under him? Then he couldn't allow it.

"You should follow your calling, princess. Clearly you were destined for greatness as a delivery woman. First my ring, and now my mail."

"And not a word of thanks for either, I notice."

"My gratitude is reserved for those who deserve it."

A knock on the door interrupted their posturing.

"Your Highness, a letter has arrived for you from your cousin, Thisbe."

The princess' face paled in an instant. She noticed his keen interest and tried to regain her composure.

"The guards will see you back to the temple, Your Majesty."

Whoever this Thisbe was, Theron wished to make her acquaintance if she affected the princess so. Perhaps he should spare a spy to look into the matter. At this point, he would use any blackmail he could get his hands on.

"Far be it for me to keep a princess from her correspondence," he chuckled, allowing the guards to escort him.

They dragged him through the rain, now a driving force that soaked him through his robes. Once the guards deposited him before the temple of Justice, they turned and left. Theron wrung out his clothes as he stalked the halls of the temple, the brand of Her displeasure burning on the back of his hand. He needed to find Aurora as quickly as possible. Hopefully, he still had time to warn her of what was coming.

Aurora heard Hyllus' swift steps coming up behind her long before she saw him. An impish grin curled her lips as he caught up to her.

"You little sneak-thief! How did you escape the kitchens without being seen?"

"That's a trade secret," Aurora gloated as she pulled out an extra biscuit from the fold of her himation.

"I see how it is. Leave me to face the cook's wrath while you get away with the goods. Cruel."

He pouted. A look that reminded her of her younger brother, the little beastie. It made her homesick and happy all at once. Though the two looked nothing alike, she felt a kinship with Hyllus, a bond somewhere between brother and close friend. He was easy to talk to, to relax around, to share her secrets with.

And to tease mercilessly.

"It's not my fault you're bigger, louder, *and* slower."

He snatched the next biscuit right from her hand and shoved the whole of it in his mouth. He grinned at her open-mouthed stare.

"Avatar tax," he said as he swallowed his ill-gotten gains.

"Cheeky bastard."

"Always."

"Is the avatar allowed to be so underhanded?"

"I've yet to be punished for my audacity, so I'm taking it as a good sign."

Aurora laughed as they walked along the hall bordering the courtyard. Her gaze was invariably drawn to the man in the centre, a line of the ill and injured waiting their turn for his healing magic. Her heart was an acrobat in her chest—racing, leaping, and then sinking to her knees.

"You can't avoid him forever," Hyllus teased.

"I can certainly try."

"Look at him. He's pining for you. When are you going to put the poor bastard out of his misery?"

Aurora dared sneak another glance at the man in question. Theron sat in the courtyard, back ramrod straight as he perched on the austere bench as if it were a throne. The sun loved him, burnishing his brown skin in a golden light, making his hair shine like liquid rubies. His every move was graceful, powerful, sensual. She dared not stare too long, or risk losing herself, wondering how far away she could stand while still admiring the golden hue of his eyes.

"He's meant for another."

And a princess at that, if her ancient sources were to be believed.

"So you keep saying. And yet your histories neglected to mention a name. Who's to say they got it right? Who's to say that woman can't be you?"

"I was never meant to be here, Hyllus."

"Exactly. You're already changing the fate of Trisia by your travels. Why not change his as well?"

Goddesses, how she wanted that. He'd chosen death to save her. How could she not be fundamentally moved by his brave sacrifice? For all his faults, all his obvious scheming, at heart he was a good man. Hyllus had been privy to some of the findings of the investigation. In addition to uncovering more everyday horrors visited on the denizens of the vivarium, he'd discovered what Flora had planned for the evening's entertainment that fateful day. Aurora suppressed a surge of nausea at the thought. Now she understood why Theron had been so adamant about facing the monstrosities, about why he'd chosen death.

She would never be able to repay that selfless sacrifice. Nor would she, it seemed, be able to quash the rising tide inside her whenever she thought of him. Not the jolt of pleasure whenever she saw him stride through the temple. Not the fluttering in her chest whenever their gazes met. Not tightening in her throat whenever she contemplated losing him. Not the ache in her heart whenever she reminded herself that he was not for her.

Now that her magic had replenished itself, whenever she had a strong upwelling of emotion, she would get a sense of déjà vu. The few days she'd spent in the temple had been peppered with the uncanny sensation. She was lucky she'd not had another vision, given the tempestuous beast inside her.

"I hope to go home when all of this is done. I have people I need to save."

"When we succeed, they'll already be saved, Aurora. Would the people who love you begrudge you a lifetime of happiness in the here and now?"

She liked his optimism. It gave her hope that maybe he was right, that their task was not insurmountable. She'd not showed him what Drakon was capable of, not in the way she had for Theron, but she'd spoken in detail about his abilities. Given how dragons of legend were said to have grown, the Drakon of this time wouldn't be quite so large. At least, she hoped as much.

If Drakon could be slain, would that save Phaedra and Silvanus in her time? Aurora wanted to hope so. It's what Hyllus believed. In truth, she tried not to think about it too much. If she saved the future from the horrors of the cycle of calamity, her world might be as foreign to her as this one. Maybe Phaedra wouldn't even know her. It was impossible to say. But would Phaedra begrudge her happiness, even if it meant they were separated? She didn't know. She'd never seriously contemplated a life without Phaedra in it, and she suspected the same went for her friend. But if their roles were reversed, would Aurora want Phaedra to find happiness, even if it meant their separation? Yes.

But was there happiness to be found at Theron's side? That was an altogether different question. Passion, to be sure. Happiness seemed a wild impossibility.

"No, but...he's a king. He'll need to find his queen and have heirs eventually. And he'll be marrying soon, if the flow of history hasn't already been altered. I don't...I don't think I could handle it if I acted on my...my feelings for him, and then had to watch him marry another. It already hurts so much."

Hyllus took her hand in his and squeezed, his eyes tightening in sympathy.

"I know that pain well. But Aurora? Loving is never a waste. Never."

He'd hinted at his loss but never spoken openly about it. Not in specific details, at least. She wondered at the woman he'd loved, who had loved him in return, and what had driven her to choose another.

"I wish I had your conviction. And your bravery."

"Bravery isn't fearlessness. You're extremely brave, Aurora. Don't ever forget it."

She squeezed his hand back.

When she heard the ominous clack of boots marching through the temple, she turned around. Royal guards were streaming into the temple to the anger of Justice's servants. The biscuits turned to rocks in her belly as the guards locked their eyes on hers and advanced. Hyllus took a step forward to shield her as the guards came to a stop before her.

"Aurora, you have been summoned to the royal court to face charges of being an agent of chaos and summoning monstrosities to attack the Viridian throne. Please come with me and face the charges."

Aurora was stunned into silence by the accusation. Her? An agent of chaos? She'd spent days trying to warn people away from the monstrosities, and now she was accused of controlling them.

"Has your queen gone mad? Aurora is innocent!" Hyllus pronounced.

"Then she can defend herself in court."

"This is an outrage! Is this your attempt to intimidate a victim of the royal guard and the indignities of the guest palace?" Hyllus protested, moving to fully stand before her.

"I am merely a messenger from the royal court, Avatar. And I must insist the accused answer the summons."

"Then I'll go as her escort."

"I was under the impression only a paladin of Justice may accompany her to the palace."

"You think the avatar of Justice unworthy to stand in place of a paladin?"

"Not at all. I am merely trying to follow the law so that there is no question as to the integrity of the investigations."

The guard had the right of it. Only a paladin of Justice, famous for their clear-eyed impartiality, was allowed to escort witnesses out of the temple. Any break in custody could call into question the outcome of the investigation. In truth, the paladins protected witnesses from intimidation as much as they watched them for signs of deceit.

As much as she appreciated Hyllus' protection, she couldn't ignore the charges against her. If it escalated, she would not only lose the temple's protection, but her association with Hyllus would taint him in the eyes of Trisia.

"I'll go, provided there is a paladin who can escort me."

"Aurora, there's no need to dignify these accusations with a response."

It was in moments like this that she was reminded that Hyllus was younger than she and not versed in courtly machinations. He was all about boldness and righteous action. She had no doubt that on the battlefield, he would be unmatched. But in the halls of the palace, he was as likely to compound the issue as to get himself caught up in it.

"I'm confident that this matter will be cleared up shortly."

"Then I'll go with you."

"I regret to inform you, Avatar, that only those with invitations may enter the palace. Even someone of your status."

His brows pinched with worry. He knew as well as she that in order to prove her innocence, she would be forced to have another vision. In her current state, it might not even require much prodding on her part. But given all she'd seen thus far were threats and horrors, she was not at all keen to glimpse into the future. Once they knew what she could do, it wouldn't be long before everyone was demanding she use her magic for their benefit. Aurora had never been overly fond of the spotlight. She suspected what was to come would be deeply unpleasant.

"I won't let anyone hurt you," Hyllus assured her.

How she wished he would be able to keep his promise. She gave him as reassuring a smile as she could and allowed the guards to lead her away. A paladin was waiting by the door of the temple and accompanied the guard to the royal court. Once again, she was an animal caught in the palace's snare.

Aurora felt the hostile stares of the packed court on her like an icy breeze. Despite the darkening sky, the throne room was splendid, done in emerald and silver. But she couldn't stop to admire the intricate mosaics or the rich tapestries. Waiting for her by the queen's side was the high priestess Orithyia. Aurora nearly tripped at the sight. A crack of thunder in the distance made her flinch, remembering the crack of the switch carving ruin into her face.

"Greetings to the bounty of Viridis." Aurora knelt with her head bowed.

"The bounty of Viridis acknowledges you."

Aurora stood, awaiting the accusation.

"You have been accused of being an agent of chaos and conspiring with the sinister goddesses to bring a hoard of monstrosities to attack the guest palace. Witnesses have come forward to tell that in the days leading up to the attack, you and your lover, the king of Aureum, threatened the attendants of the guest palace with talk of the monstrosities you planned to unleash on them. How do you answer these charges?" Queen Flora asked, though she seemed almost bored with the proceedings.

"I am innocent, Your Majesty. In the days leading up to the attack, I begged the people of the guest palace to heed my warnings that the monstrosities would appear and to absent themselves. Even as the party commenced, I tried to warn the guests and attendants to run," Aurora said, doing her best to conceal her shaking hands in the fabric of her acolyte's robes.

"Are you claiming your innocence by asserting that you're an oracle?" Flora raised a brow.

Snickers whispered through the crowd.

"Yes, Your Majesty."

Flora sighed.

"How tedious. Now I must determine whether you're an agent of chaos or simply mad."

"I'm not mad, Your Majesty. My wild magic allows me to see into the future."

"Then why not avoid this trial altogether, hmm?"

Onlookers laughed again. Hot embarrassment crept up her neck.

"I'm not omniscient, Your Majesty."

"Clearly." The queen chuckled, giving her a lazy smile. "What are you, girl? Surely, you're not Trisian-born with that height and those ears."

Aurora swallowed.

"The blood of fairies runs strongly in my veins," she answered.

Technically it was a truth. One of the founding races of Trisia, fairies were here before the First Great Sundering but in small numbers. More would come as refugees to the lands she called home. They probably wouldn't arrive for another several hundred years though, sometime between the second and third cycle of calamity.

"As a naïve foreigner, perhaps you were unaware of the company you've been keeping. King Theron is a blasphemer and a criminal. Initially, I was convinced you were behind the monstrosities in my palace, but perhaps he merely led you astray. If you speak the truth about your lover, you may yet save yourself the humiliation of being proven mad before the court. Did King Theron summon the monstrosities, or did you?"

So this was her ploy—to turn them against each other. The queen was giving her a way out, an olive branch, however rotted. If she did as Flora wished her to do, Theron would take the blame, and she would be freed from scrutiny, never needing to prove her magic before the court and become hunted for it. As the crowd leaned forward in anticipation and Orithyia stared at her with chips of ice in her gaze, Aurora wished she could disappear.

Bravery isn't fearlessness. You're extremely brave, Aurora. Don't ever forget it.

Hyllus was right. She would never be able to live with herself for taking the easy way out, no matter what it cost her. She could be brave for Theron, who had sacrificed himself for her.

"Neither of us summoned the monstrosities, Your Majesty. We're innocent." Aurora raised her chin in defiance.

Flora's glare made her blood freeze. Courtiers conversed in angry whispers.

"Your Majesty, if I may," Orithyia began, silencing the din with a single tap of her cane on the mosaic floor. "I have brought the tools to prove Aurora's innocence."

"Please proceed, Your Holiness."

Orithyia nodded at Flora and approached Aurora. Two paladins of Knowledge carried an item each on golden pillows in her wake. One she recognised—the minds-eye stone. The other she didn't. It was a wicked-looking wrist cuff with spikes pointed inward. Aurora swallowed down bile.

"I have brought with me two objects. The first is an ancient artefact used to draw the magic out of a person, no matter if they try to resist. The second is a minds-eye stone, so that we may see what visions her magic conjures. With your permission, I will force a vision from her to prove her innocence and her status as an oracle."

"I give you my leave, Your Holiness." Flora waved her on.

Aurora had to will herself not to retreat as Orithyia advanced on her.

"Whatever happens next, remember that you brought it upon yourself," the high priestess whispered so that only she could hear.

Orithyia took the cuff from her paladin and attached it to Aurora's wrist. She clenched her fist as the spikes broke the skin with the weight of the cuff. She took Aurora's palm, prying open her fingers and placed the minds-eye crystal in it, closing it once more. Then she activated the device.

Aurora screamed as the spikes sank into her wrist, piercing deep. Blood flowed from the wounds as she fell to her knees. Her magic rose up like a vicious beast inside her, wholly outside of her control. She tried to resist the pull. She didn't want to glimpse the future again. Trying to prevent it last time had proved impossible. What if what she saw was another horror she couldn't prevent? What if it only proved that fate was immutable and Phaedra was gone forever?

But in the end, her resistance did no good.

She was dragged through a void, only to open her eyes in the streets of Boreas. The people were dressed for a celebration. The streets were awash in colour, decorated gaily in the bright afternoon light. Well-wishers sang songs and shouted joyfully, raining flower petals down from the tops of buildings.

Despite the gaiety, her heart was broken. She could feel its ache, a pain that rose like a tide inside her and never relented. Aurora squinted. This vision was less clear than the ones before. As before, the edges were blurred. Even the colours and details in the centre of her vision were dulled by a slight red haze. She looked to her side to find she was carrying a large walking stick with feathers and beads embellishing a slightly bulbous top. Other women were walking at her side, all dressed in red with long veils atop their heads. In the centre of the group, a green and gold palanquin fit for a princess was carried by eight women. Seated inside with the sides open to the crowds, sat another dressed as Aurora seemed to be. Atop her head was a veil, but beneath that gauzy red fabric was the unmistakable glitter of a crown. Beneath the veil, the woman on the palanquin was a princess.

This was an ancient bride-kidnapping ceremony and Aurora had been invited to participate in it.

"Protect the bride!"

The hue and cry went up, and the crowd cheered as bare-chested men in pleated kilts of red advanced on the palanquin. Every man that converged on them was covered in an ugly mask, each one more hideous and intimidating than the last. Here were their mock-captors. The groom meant to run off with the bride while the others were to capture her protectors. A ritual that would end when the princess' intended carried her over the threshold of a temple for the wedding ceremony.

Amidst the masked men, Aurora recognised Theron. His powerful physique and crimson hair were unmistakable. He wore gold jewellery while the other participants in this hunt wore none, and his staff was made of the same shining metal. While the other women fought off the approaching masked men, Aurora was transfixed. With his every step, her heart broke anew. Theron was the princess' intended. This was their wedding ceremony. Tears blurred her vision further until she could no longer make out any details. She did her part, fought off the masked men, and allowed one to capture her, as per the ritual. She closed her eyes, wishing herself somewhere—anywhere—else.

Aurora gasped with pain as her mind was brought back to the Viridian court. Blood pooled beneath her and tears clouded her vision. Orithyia took the minds-eye stone from her grasp and removed the cuff, its spikes retreating from her flesh, forcing another scream from her lips.

"Your proof, Your Majesty. It seems congratulations will soon be in order. Princess Epicasta is to wed King Theron."

And now Aurora knew the name of the woman who would take Theron from her. She wished she could curse the princess for her part in breaking Aurora's heart.

"This is an auspicious day indeed, High Priestess." Flora snapped her fingers and a healer rushed to Aurora's side to close her wounds.

She ground her teeth against the agony of her flesh knitting back together.

"Aurora, you have proven your innocence and your magic. In light of your trials and honesty, I will award you a noble title and a position in my court."

Approving murmurs raced through the crowd as Aurora's gut sank. So it had already begun. Once hostile faces now smiled, their greed barely repressed.

"The bounty of Viridis is overly generous. I must decline your offer."

"Nonsense. It is what you deserve. You are welcome to stay in the royal palace," she said, nodding to the slack-jawed paladin who was only just recovering from his shock, "once the investigation concludes."

So that she could be Flora's pet oracle. She'd be lucky not to be wearing Orithyia's torture device every day for the rest of her short life.

"I cannot accept your offer, Your Majesty. I have come here with a greater purpose. If the High Priestess will allow me to hold the mind's eye stone, I will show you what it is I seek."

Let them see Drakon and tremble. Let them know what was coming so that they would put aside their machinations for a single hour. Long enough for her to get back to the temple of Justice while they wallowed in their dread. Long enough so she could find a place to hide and lick her wounds.

Theron would be wed to the princess. Seeing it really had been as gutting as she'd feared. And she'd be expected to participate, to watch him carry the princess over the temple's threshold and swear a vow of marriage in front of the whole city.

"High Priestess, if you would be so good as to allow Aurora a chance to explain why she rebuffs my generosity?" Flora said, her smile tight.

"Of course, Your Majesty," Orithyia replied, a censorious look in her gaze.

Aurora ignored it. Orithyia had forgone her chance to help. It was time to take matters into her own hands. Aurora took the stone from Orithyia and closed her eyes, forcing herself to relive the horrors of

Drakon's pursuit once more. The crimson skies, the choking ash, the lightning streaking across the sky to show a great serpent riding on a bank of dark clouds, raining molten boulders and purple fire down from above while monstrosities blanketed the ground below. She relived his taunts, his curses, the madness in his glowing yellow eyes as he promised pain and destruction. She relived it as Drakon obliterated every paladin and guard, until only Phaedra and her paladin remained.

Aurora opened her eyes. The apocalyptic scene ended. Silence held the courtroom in thrall.

"I hunt Drakon, bringer of the cycle of calamity. Together with the avatar of Justice, I will slay him. This is why I must refuse your offers, Queen Flora. If you'll excuse me, I would be grateful to retire to the temple of Justice in the meantime."

Perhaps it had been unwise to reveal her part, her fate. The Orithyia from her time had warned that dualists and heretics devoted solely to the sinister goddesses would see her as a grave threat. But she didn't care. Not right now, when her heart was shattered and bleeding.

"You are excused," Flora replied, her voice hollow.

"Triad bless the bounty of Viridis." Aurora bowed, turned on her heel, and walked as swiftly as decorum allowed, the paladin trailing after her.

She was grateful her minder had left her in the mire of her own thoughts. It wouldn't last long. There would be questions about Drakon. Some would be easy to answer. Others would require her listeners to take a leap of faith. It was one thing to be an oracle, another to have come from a far-flung future.

Hyllus greeted her at the doors of the temple. She hadn't even realised she was wet and shivering until he wrapped her in a warm, dry towel, his eyes roving over her, looking for injury.

"What happened?"

"I wish to be alone."

She wanted a chance to cry without a witness. To be angry without judgment. To wallow in sorrow without someone else's pity.

"When you're ready, I will listen," Hyllus said, squeezing her shoulder in sympathy.

Even that was too much to bear. Aurora stormed off. The people of the temple gave her a wide berth, their gazes averted. With the driving rain, the only place she could be truly alone was in the courtyard, where even the connected halls were to be avoided. Aurora turned her face towards the sky and bit her lip as hot tears cascaded down her face.

She'd been the greatest fool, to have let him into her heart. Aurora hated him. And she hated the princess even more. Why should she be the one to have him when Aurora could not? She took the drenched towel from around her shoulders and threw it to the ground in rage. It wasn't fair. None of it. She'd lost everyone she'd ever loved, lost everything she'd ever known, sent to this miserable time in history. Now she would have a front-row seat, forced to watch as the man she'd wanted most in her life married another.

Aurora screamed, howling in rage. It hurt. It hurt too much to bear. She was the greatest fool in Trisia. She'd known all along he wasn't for her. Thunder cracked and rumbled overhead. She flinched. Unable to put Orithyia's switch from her mind, she shivered. She closed her eyes, sobbing as she fell to her knees. It was a mess—her heart, her mind, her future—everything.

Weak. Stupid. Failure.

"Aurora!"

She opened her eyes.

Theron.

Not him. Not now.

Would Fate never cease torturing her?

"Aurora, you'll make yourself sick standing out here." He helped her to her feet, her acolyte's robe plastered to her form. "Triad's tits, you're cold as ice. Come. There's something I must warn you about."

He pulled on her. Aurora stood her ground.

"No."

"Aurora, don't be stubborn about this. I don't know what I've done to earn your displeasure these past few days, but we have important matters to discuss."

"I saw you get married to Princess Epicasta."

He stilled, horror and rage sweeping over his features.

"I won't let that happen."

"I had a vision. Orithyia forced it out of me in front of the whole royal court."

What did it matter if either of them strived against it now? Flora had seen a future she wanted. Aurora suspected all who opposed it would pay in blood, and she was tired of hurting.

"No," he said, his vehemence palpable. His magic washed over her, coiling around her in threat.

"I suppose congratulations are in order," she hissed. How dare he be angry with her—threaten her—when he was the one in the wrong?

"Walk away now, Aurora. While I still have some self-control," he growled.

"No, *you* walk away! All your fucking attempts to seduce me, all your bluster about how much you hate her, and you're still going to marry her!" Aurora shouted back. It didn't matter that it wasn't a fair accusation. She wanted to scour him from her heart, rid thoughts of him from her mind—she wanted to be free of him and all the pain. And if he was going to hurt her, she would show him her fangs.

He rounded on her, gripping her upper arms in an unbreakable hold.

"I would rather be dead than marry that vile bitch!"

"Liar! I hate you! I hope you're miserable for the rest of your fucking life!"

Just like she would be.

"Unfeeling vermin!" he hissed.

"Loathsome snake!"

"You are the most ungrateful wench in the whole of Trisia! How many times have I saved your life?!" he yelled.

"All so you could use and trap me! You have no honour!"

"I sacrificed my life to save you from humiliation!" he shook her.

"And then you broke my heart, you monster! I should have let the monstrosities eat you!" she stomped on his foot.

He swore, crushing her to him and lifting her off her feet. She pushed at him, beating her fists against his chest as he laughed at her pitiful attempts to hurt him. Her magic roared to life.

"I hate you! I hate you! I hate you!"

"That's right, you vicious little beast. Let me see you angry!"

"Disgusting pervert!"

His grin was feral.

Theron pulled her head towards his, lips a hairsbreadth from hers. His hot breath made little clouds in the cold rain, warming her lips. She gasped. His golden eyes sparkled with lust, capturing her gaze and holding her captive.

"I'll take every last year from you," she threatened, her heart hammering in her chest.

His hand slid up her thighs, a warm brand on her backside as he squeezed. She fought a groan. His thumb swept lazily against her, pressing against her hip.

Theron smiled—a look promising passion and torment in equal measure.

"Then I'll die a happy man."

He captured her bottom lip between his and nibbled, his eyes never leaving hers.

Aurora shuddered as a thrill of pleasure shot through her.

Her resistance crumbled in the face of her need. She broke, her arms circling his neck, her fingers digging into his scalp. Aurora slanted her mouth over his, welcoming his thick, hot tongue. Mindless and needy, she pressed herself fully against him. He took his hand from the back of her head and hitched up the sopping skirt of her gown. Pushing aside her underclothes, he slid his fingers along her molten core.

"So wet for me," he rumbled against her skin as he kissed her neck and nibbled on her sensitive ear.

She moaned, regretting the loss of his mouth on hers. Aurora gripped him by his hair, taking pleasure in his groan of pain, and forced him back to her lips.

"I'm not done kissing you yet."

His eyes flashed with approval. Theron's next kiss was rougher than the last, his fingers pressing harder against her wet heat. Cold and rain forgotten, she burned for him, for his touch, for his tongue on hers, for the press of their bodies. Her head swam as the world around her faded to nothing. All that remained was Theron, his wicked mouth and his teasing fingers. It was bliss. In that moment he was hers alone, and she was his.

His finger breached her, stroking her inner walls. She broke from their kiss as her breath left her in a rush. His lips were on her neck again, unerringly finding the spots that made her shiver.

"My little fairy is so tight. I can't wait to ruin you," he growled in her ear.

Yes, she wanted him inside her, wanted to follow this bliss into oblivion and never surface. She would make him hers, brand him with her body and never let him go. And she would turn any who stood in her way to bones and dust.

He sank his teeth into her neck as he slipped another finger inside her. She cried out, stretched tight and aching for more.

"Everyone will know who you belong to when I'm done with you," he growled, easing the sting of his teeth with kisses.

As she leaned in to give him a matching mark she froze. Dark red hair plastered his neck. Red, like the princess' wedding veil.

Theron wasn't hers. He never had been, and he never would be. This was pure folly. The dreamy haze of passion was torn away in an instant.

"Put me down. We're done here," she said, her voice flat.

He blinked in surprise, withdrawing his fingers as if burned.

"Did I hurt you? Did I do something you didn't like?" he asked, setting her on her unsteady feet as he searched her face for the answer.

"Soon, you'll be married to someone who isn't me. I think it would be best if we stopped here."

His eyes darkened with anger.

"Where is your fire? Your determination? Do you plan on rolling over and accepting your vision without a fight?"

"I wasn't able to stop the last one! Why would I be able to stop this one?!" she shouted back.

Especially when this one was more than just foreseen, it was the history she knew, recorded in ancient times by the king's own biographers. There was no escaping the fact that he would wed another. And she didn't think she had it in her to fight against the full weight of both prophecy and history only to fail.

He gripped her chin in his hand and glared daggers at her.

"And yet I survived. You don't see everything," he hissed.

"I see enough," she whispered, her voice cracking.

Theron released her in a huff and stormed off, leaving her to her misery and the pouring rain.

CHAPTER 20
THERON

Theron was in a foul mood. More letters had arrived from home, all from his most loyal advisors begging him to conclude his business in Viridis as quickly as possible. As if his imprisonment in Boreas were some holiday he'd irresponsibly taken without tying up loose ends first. As if he wished to bear a blasphemer's mark and had been negligent in getting it purified. As if he had a bloody choice in anything that had happened to him since he'd stepped foot in this cursed queendom.

He burned the latest missive, informing him that Batea was being led by the nose by bandits and dualists alike, pulling her focus in all directions and leaving Altanus, the capital, undefended on more than one occasion. No doubt some of his more scheming courtiers were demanding she prove her worth by seeing to every skirmish personally, hoping that if the capital were attacked, they could unseat her. Clearly, a number of his courtiers didn't believe he would return from Viridis—or hoped he would not.

Aurora vexed him almost as much. He'd finally had her in his arms, her lips hot and demanding on his, and she'd spurned him. They'd been a breath away from rutting like animals in the open, and then the greatest passion he'd ever felt had been snatched from him in an instant. How dare she show him her fire and then leave him cold. It was maddening. Now, he burned for her, yearning like a witless fool. Perhaps it had been her plan all along. If so, she was a more skilled seductress than he'd given her credit for. Because whenever he caught sight of her in the temple, his blood heated.

He wanted to run her down and tackle her to the floors of the temple and desecrate it with her cries of pleasure.

He despised the look of defeat and melancholy he sometimes caught on her face when she looked at him and didn't think he noticed. It was impossible not to notice her eyes on him. Like a caress against senses he'd not known he possessed, she tormented him with her nearness. Near enough to be reminded of her body crushed to his, the feel of her silken heat, the taste of her tongue, her skin, and yet not near enough to reach out and pull her close to relive the experience, to know if his recollection had done her justice.

The pain in his hand, his divine mark, flared again as prayers rang out through the temple. Theron swore. He kept a curse for the goddess off his tongue, but only just. When his next piece of mail was delivered to his room, he braced himself for yet more pleading. But it was from the temple of Knowledge.

Theron's mood darkened further.

A summons from the high priestess of Knowledge. One written in neat, precise letters telling him where and when to present himself to Her Holiness, the wizened bitch of Boreas. Maybe she meant to taunt him about his mark. No doubt she would use her ability to purify him as leverage to gain some concession for her mad dog of a queen. It's what Theron would do in her place.

It seemed escaping irritation would be impossible today. Theron sighed and headed for the temple entrance where a paladin was already waiting. They crossed the plaza to the temple of Knowledge where the paladins of Knowledge led him and his escort into Orithyia's private office.

"You may stand outside the door, paladin of Justice." Orithyia gestured to the door.

"Your Holiness—"

"I understand your sacred duty, but the King of Aureum will come to no harm in this room, you have my word."

The paladin hesitated for a moment, looking to Theron for consent. He had to give the young man credit where it was due. Being such a stickler for the rules that he was willing to stand up to a high priestess took more conviction than most would ever possess. Theron nodded, sparing the young man the conflict. After all, this confrontation had been a long time in coming. Perhaps, if he were doomed anyway, he might as well kill her and spare Aureum from her constant meddling.

"Welcome to the temple of Knowledge, Your Majesty."

"It is your great honour to host me, I'm certain," Theron replied.

"If that is what you'd like to believe." Orithyia smiled.

How quickly could he break her? As the high priestess, she'd never been involved in combat. The rituals of initiation for Knowledge's temple were meant to test the intellect, not the body, unless one wished to become Her paladin. As far as he knew, she'd lived a peaceful existence. If he wished to kill her, it would be best to rely on his physical strength and speed to do it. He was confident he could silence her before she managed to call for help.

"My, what dangerous thoughts swirl behind your eyes, Your Majesty. Aren't you curious as to why I summoned you?"

"You have caused a great deal of harm to my kingdom, Your Holiness. For your sake, I hope it's because you wish to make restitution."

"Ah, yes, Dia has told me of the drought and plagues of Aureum. Troubling indeed. But is it not the monarch's sacred duty to calm the angry spirits of the land?"

"Yes, just as it is the duty of the high priestesses not to interfere in matters of state."

"And yet you seemed perfectly happy to involve me in your dispute with Queen Flora."

"When a dog snarls and snaps, is it not the animal's owner who is responsible for reining it in?"

"Is that what your cousin does, Your Majesty? Reins in her beasts?"

"When it is appropriate to do so."

"Because I have heard troubling reports that when the research outpost collapsed and Batea raced to the rescue, her beasts devoured the bodies of many acolytes and initiates," Orithyia replied, her tone darkening.

Then whoever was reporting to Orithyia had been part of the rescue. When next he met with his spies, he would inform them of the traitor.

"Did your reports also inform you that your spire contaminated the mountain streams and lakes?"

"I believe it was good fortune that we set up the spire when we did. My people were investigating a cure for Aureum's ills. But with all my researchers dead, who knows what knowledge was lost?"

His magic swirled around him as he clenched his fists.

"Your spire poisoned my lands, and you dare call it good fortune?"

"Your cousin's beasts devoured my people, and you dared call it appropriate," she retorted.

"You built that spire without my consent and without appeasing the spirits. You meddled with magic and forces that were outside your purview and brought incalculable harm to my people and yours. The tragedy of your people's deaths would have been entirely preventable had you kept your claws out of Aureum," he growled.

"Just as the tragedy of this 'cycle of calamity' might have been prevented, had you made a concerted effort to defeat the dualists in your lands."

Yes, the dualists, always the scapegoats for the failings of the temples. The temples blamed them for the cycle of chaos, the dualists pointed the finger back at the temples, and the small cult of the elder gods, those who solely worshipped the tangible gods, blamed the temples and dualists both. He allowed dualists to be hunted in his lands for the greater good, but could hardly be expected to believe they were the root of all ills. What would Orithyia say once they were all slain and yet cycles of chaos continued to be visited upon Trisia? Would she then blame the tangible gods and those, like him, who were blessed with their wild magic?

"Or perhaps it might have been prevented altogether, had you not locked up the only person who knew what was coming in the vivarium and then proceeded to maim her."

"I took responsibility for my failings by trusting her when I had little reason to and protecting her at court by proving her innocence. What did you do, aside from setting a target on her back?"

Theron snorted with derision.

"I wasn't aware that 'taking responsibility' meant doing the bare minimum to satisfy common decency. Thank you for enlightening me, Your Holiness."

"I can see why you exasperate Dia so. But your clever rhetoric will not help you here. There are more important matters at stake, and I simply do not have the time or patience to play your games. So I come to you with an offer—I will purify you here and now, provided you make a sacred vow to wed, as Queen Flora is so determined to see happen now that she has glimpsed her daughter's future."

He would rather be flayed than marry Epicasta, knowing what he did about Flora's vile magic. It was altogether possible that Orithyia purifying him was merely the first step in Flora's scheme to put another soul in his body. But if he refused Orithyia's offer, there was no guarantee that he would escape Boreas in time to set Aureum to rights. Nerio could be anywhere in Trisia, and even if he begged Myrina to come to Boreas for him and she agreed to help, it would be weeks before she arrived.

"You would deny me purification, simply because I do not wish to take that snake as my wife?"

"I am under no obligation to purify you. Neither are Nerio or Myrina, for that matter. Purification is reserved for those who have repented for their blasphemy, and who have shown a willingness to change. Can you really tell me that your experience has left you humbled and wiser, rather than infuriated? That you have changed your ways?"

"If the avatar of Justice himself has forgiven me, I fail to see why you should withhold purification. I would rather wait patiently for a high priestess to come to my rescue than cede my kingdom to Viridis. As a good king, my own comfort and desires must come second to what is best for my kingdom. If you had hoped I would break so easily, then you were sorely mistaken."

Her face darkened with rage. She slammed her bony fist against the arm of her chair.

"What does it matter who sits at your side on Aureum's throne when the end is upon us? Did you not see what comes for Trisia? What destruction it will bring? Every moment you waste sitting here rather than allying with Viridis and preparing Aureum for what is to come, will be repaid in the blood of innocents! Your people, my people, none of it will matter when we're all reduced to ashes and bones!"

He almost smiled. What she said was true, but also a masterful deflection. He wouldn't fall for her bait.

"High Priestesses have no right to play games with the thrones of Trisia. If you truly wish for my kingdom to be stabilized and ready to fight what's to come, then there could be no worse choice of queen than Epicasta. Unless you've decided to turn a blind eye to the fate of every husband she has condemned to death. If you truly wish to save as many as possible, then do not deny me purification and delay my return to Aureum any more than Queen Flora already has with her ludicrous demands!"

"You speak of being a good king, and yet I would not need to meddle in your affairs if you had left a competent person in charge of Aureum. Your own kingdom is on the brink of tearing itself apart with your cousin on its throne, in spite of knowing that a cycle of chaos is already here!

Marriage to Epicasta is the fastest way for you to return. And of all the daughters she could have tried to force upon you, Epicasta is the wisest, most restrained woman of the lot. As a princess, her fate is controlled by her mother. As a queen, she would be free to act according to her conscience."

Theron almost laughed. Epicasta had made certain to tell him what his fate would be if they were forced to wed—violated and then murdered. He would not be so foolish as to believe that had miraculously changed.

"Or you could end all this now by purifying me and ordering your mad dog to accept reasonable terms for restitution. As you should have done from the start."

Orithyia laughed, cackling as if he were a simpleton.

"And when would I have accomplished this? Before you arrived, or while a plague ripped through the city?" she scoffed. Orithyia leaned back in her seat, sighing bitterly. "There might have been a small window of opportunity for that, before Flora saw Aurora's vision, but that ship has long since sailed. Fate has decreed that you shall wed Epicasta. Accept it, and save us both some time and aggravation."

Rage tore through Theron.

"Your delay nearly cost me my life! It nearly cost Aurora's as well! Had you acted when you had the chance, had you done anything to rein in Flora's abject cruelty, none of this would be an issue!"

"How dare you speak to me of delays! You have already delayed Aurora's freedom with the investigation of the vivarium! And do not pretend that she does not remain here for you. You seduced her for sport and made her a target for your enemies! She should be quit from here in Hyllus' company, not trapped in Boreas while the wolves at court conspire ways to use her power and slow her down! If you believe, as I do, that she's instrumental in what's to come, then break her heart and send her away now, or agree to my offer and take her with you as soon as the marriage can be arranged."

Theron laughed bitterly.

"The High Priestess of Knowledge is advising me to keep a mistress as she forces a marriage upon me? Will wonders never cease?"

"I'm advising you to do whatever is necessary for the good of Trisia, and by extension, Aureum. As you say, a good king puts his kingdom first, and his own comfort and desires second. Delaying the inevitable may well cost more lives."

As much as he despised her, as much as he knew this was a trap either of her making or Flora's, he could not deny she spoke sense. It was clear from the letters he'd been receiving that the situation in Aureum was politically dire. If he tarried here, waiting for Nerio, would he even have a throne to go back to, or would he be forced to fight whoever had managed to place themselves on it in the meantime?

Yes, Orithyia spoke sense, but wasn't that the best kind of trap, where the bait was an undeniable truth? Except he too was well-versed in chicanery. As long as he remained in control of his own body, he could have Epicasta executed and blame it on monstrosities the moment he crossed into Aureum, or imprison her for Flora's good behaviour. After that, securing the line of succession was a simple matter of appointing official concubines and letting Epicasta rot. Whether that was in the belly of a beast or somewhere as comfortable as her mother's vivarium would be something her behaviour would determine.

As for Aurora, she was heartbroken now, but he had a feeling he could sway her to his side. There was an undeniable spark of lust between them, one she was weak to. Once she realised the marriage was political, with nothing between the bride and groom but a power-sharing agreement he planned to undermine at the first opportunity, she would understand it had just been a ploy to return home sooner.

But what to do about Orithyia? If this was part of Flora's scheming, he needed insurance. The kind the high priestess couldn't deny giving him without tipping her hand or Flora's. Perhaps agreeing to Orithyia's scheme was the best option to save himself from the mad dog's magic. Who better to force conditions on than the mad dog's owner?

"If I agree to this, you will make your own sacred vows. I know Queen Flora is a soul swapper, and I know she used her magic on Epicasta's victims. You will vow to prevent her from ever using her magic on me, and you will swear it on your goddess so that if you fail, you will lose your place as high priestess. Second, you will vow to force Flora to accept my terms for restitution. I'm not shackling myself in marriage just to see that greedy bitch take my territory. Third, you will make a vow to purify me the moment I speak my vow. You will not trick me into this vile state of affairs and then renege on your promise."

If she were surprised by his knowledge of Flora's magic, she made not a single twitch to indicate it. Her wizened face was a mask of bemused tolerance.

"You would force three vows from me for one of yours, two of which depend on the actions of another?"

"I would demand protection from the mad dog whose leash you hold the same as I demand your integrity. I would ask that you swear on your honour, but I don't believe you have any. Be glad I did not demand restitution for your part in Aureum's blight."

Orithyia laughed until she had to dab tears from her eyes.

"Perhaps I should. Pay restitution, that is. Admit to these fanciful crimes you've accused me of. Though it would relieve me of the office of high priestess, unable to purify you. Then again, I could finally catch up on some sleep and leave the care of unruly royal houses to my successor, Triad spare her." Orithyia shook her head, the joviality wiped from her mien. "I agree to make those vows before the goddess' statue, if you agree to make yours."

He hadn't expected her to be so reasonable. Then again, he hadn't expected to agree to the damned wedding either. His gut churned. Wed to a viper, daughter to a reviled enemy. But so long as he didn't vow to love, respect, cherish, or even keep his intended alive, all he needed was to complete the ceremony and wash his hands of her. In light of that...

"I will not agree to be wed in the temple of Passion," he added.

As a king, he could be wed in any temple he pleased. For political marriages, Justice was common. For most other kinds, Knowledge and Justice were the normal choices. Passion's temple was only sought out by lovers, often by those whose love was forbidden, and usually chosen by the short-sighted. A wedding conducted at Passion's feet could only be performed if there was true passion between the couple, had to be consummated in her temple, and could only be ended by death. A true nightmare for most with a modicum of sensibility. People changed, betrayed each other, and realised that passions always cooled. Marriages ended for a myriad of reasons, political ones all the more so, and the freedom to leave saved lives. A lifetime commitment was as good as a lifelong prison sentence, willingly chosen.

"Myrina will be crushed, of course," Orithyia replied dryly. "But I agree. It would be an insult to Passion, and you've angered one of the Triad already. Best not to court the wrath of She of the fiery gaze."

He swallowed, his throat parched, his mind spinning. Theron could not renege on this vow. Sacred vows could so easily be broken if the wording was too vague or too specific. If he vowed to wed Epicasta specifically, Flora might decide one daughter's life was worth sacrificing in order to kill him. Flora was unfeeling enough to wed her daughter to three men just to kill them. He couldn't take any chances.

"And I refuse to make my vow using Epicasta's name."

Orithyia raised her brow at him.

"If anything untoward happens to Epicasta in the coming days, the goddess would strike me down for being unable to fulfil my vow. This, at least, prevents Flora from killing her daughter in order to kill me. The queen will get her wedding, but I won't let her take my life."

Orithyia nodded her head, though her scowl was impressive. Angry that he'd slipped her trap, or that he insulted Flora's character?

"Then we are agreed? Your vows first, then mine, then the purification."

"We are agreed," Orithyia said.

Orithyia stood and led the way out of her office and down the staircases, the paladins following close behind. They descended into the temple proper where the statue of Knowledge, carved in black, glittering rock and clothed in shimmering midnight robes stood, her obsidian eyes winking in the low light. They arrived at the foot of her statue, amongst the offerings and statues of notable, wealthy people bent in supplication so that a part of them would always be praying.

Sweat beaded along his spine. Was this really the wisest course of action? Had he accounted for all her tricks?

"I, High Priestess Orithyia XI, make a sacred vow to Knowledge that I will prevent Queen Flora of Viridis from using her magic on King Theron of Aureum. I make a sacred vow to convince Queen Flora of Viridis to accept his terms for reparations. And I make a sacred vow to purify King Theron of Aureum once he has made his sacred vow to wed," Orithyia finished, raising her brow at Theron.

"I, King Theron of Aureum, make a sacred vow to Knowledge to be wed before I leave the city of Boreas."

Orithyia raised her brow at him, mocking his caution no doubt.

"That's as specific as I'm willing to get, given Flora's nature."

Orithyia laughed, grinning wickedly. Ice crept down his spine.

"To fulfil my sacred vow, I hereby purify you of the blasphemer's mark," she said, holding her hand high as divine magic gathered at her fingers.

He'd not expected the pain.

Fire shot through his veins, the source of the blaze the diamond-like mark on the back of his hand. Theron crumpled to the floor in agony as the process stole his breath. When it was done, he felt light-headed and weak, his heart racing as the last of the pain ebbed away. He staggered to his feet.

"You did that on purpose," he ground out.

Orithyia smiled.

"Because you wasted my time and insulted me. Now, if you'll excuse me, I have a monarch to speak with and a royal wedding to prepare for. You may return to the temple of Justice. I believe there are people waiting for you. Oh, and you'd best hope Flora doesn't delay the wedding to keep you here indefinitely. You did vow to remain until wed. Rest assured, if you cause trouble for me, I will tell her the exact wording of your vow."

Fuck.

Aurora collapsed in her bed, groaning as her face hit the pillow. The paladins had concluded their investigation and brought their case against Queen Flora to the royal court, whereupon a veritable army of guards and attendants admitted their guilt. To no one's surprise, all testified that Flora had been unaware of their conduct. Their penance was to serve one day in seven praying at the temple of Justice for the next fifteen years. Flora agreed to pay a hefty fine for each person who had come forward with tales of mistreatment, and to allow her political prisoners to remain in the temple, but not leave the city. Aurora, of course, had been exempt from that rule, given she was not a political prisoner...yet.

Every day, the palace inundated her with gifts as Flora's nobles sought her favour. It made her skin crawl. She'd repurposed nearly every gift to benefit the temples and sold the rest for coin. She'd just returned from her latest outing, the coin for an unwelcome gift of an emerald bracelet sitting on her unadorned bedside table. At least the jewellery could be sold. The flowers simply rotted, the clothes were impractical at best and suggestive at worst, and the delicacies were better used filling the bellies of those who sought succour at the temple of Passion.

She reached out and looked over the bust of Flora on the gold coin. Aurora and Hyllus would need it when they set out. Strange, to think that a year ago, finding a perfectly preserved gold coin from the first calamity period would have been the discovery of a lifetime. Now, it was simply weight in the bag she was packing. Aurora curled up into herself.

Since her display at court, she'd spent her days reliving her worst memories to prepare the paladins of the temples for what was coming, and cried herself to sleep. She had so many painful things to choose from, after all—Phaedra, Silvanus, her fate, and Theron. As if she'd needed more heartache.

Foolish as she'd been, she'd hoped to journey in Theron's company. But now, he would be marrying Princess Epicasta, and the thought of having to watch him be her husband made her ill. And if her vision was anything to go by, she was about to have a front-row seat for the ceremony. Hopefully, Hyllus would get her good and drunk and whisk her away as soon as possible.

A knock sounded at her door.

"You have a visitor," the paladin outside her door said.

"If they're here with bribes, tell them to go away," Aurora replied.

"I've come only as myself. Will that do?" a woman's voice asked.

Were they sending women now that she'd rejected all the men? Merciful Triad, would they never relent? How many times did she have to tell them that she wasn't going to agree to a marriage, a concubinage, a fling, a tryst or even one bloody kiss? Aurora grumbled as she got out of her bed and opened the door.

The woman before her stood in a gown the dark red colour of mourning, lifting her veil to reveal her face. A sliver of dread stole down her spine and ignited a spark of bitter anger in her heart. The woman from her vision—Princess Epicasta.

"You're a difficult woman to speak to."

"Maybe I prefer it that way."

Epicasta tilted her head.

"Will you make an exception for me?"

"Will you give up trying if I don't?"

"No."

Aurora sighed and waved her in. Epicasta glanced inside the small room and seated herself on the only stool. The paladin looked to Aurora for guidance.

"It's alright. You can close the door."

The moment it was shut, Epicasta turned her grey eyes to Aurora.

"You'll hear about it soon enough, but I wanted to inform you that Theron swore a sacred vow to wed in return for purification and the resolution of this most recent dispute between Aureum and Viridis."

Her breath left her in a rush. She sat down on her bed as her legs gave out on her.

"Why did you come to tell me this?" she asked, voice hollow.

Had she come to taunt her? Assert her dominance? Warn her off?

"Because I want this marriage as much as I want my legs broken, that's why. And because I need to know if your visions always come true."

Aurora blinked at Epicasta in shock. But Theron was a handsome king whose kiss was as intoxicating as wine. True, their realms weren't on the best of terms, but he was protective, worldly and shrewd. What more could a princess ask for?

"I...I don't know. The last few have come true exactly as I envisioned them."

Epicasta stood, pacing from one end of the room to the other.

"Well, how hard did you try to change them?"

"I did everything I could," Aurora replied darkly. "No one believed me."

"But things are different now."

"How?"

"Because I refuse to let it happen."

"Why?"

Epicasta stopped pacing.

"I thought you'd be pleased. He's your paramour, is he not? Rumour has it that you two have been in foul moods since your vision at court."

Aurora groaned. Of course there were rumours. It made sense now why Flora had sent every halfway handsome man to the temple in an attempt to woo her. She thought she saw an opening to lure Aurora in with seduction.

"Why should I trust you? Theron is a better match than you could ever hope to make, a guarantee of being a queen. How do I know this isn't some plot concocted by your mother?"

If Flora wanted Aurora to stay, what better way than to accuse her of trying to sabotage a royal wedding? Once she had grounds for a complaint against her, all Flora had to do was demand compensation in the form of another vision. It was hardly a leap of imagination. After all, Flora had accused Aurora of summoning the monstrosities, all in an attempt to discredit Theron. How much worse would it be when she turned her full attention to Aurora instead?

"Do you know what I'm called, Aurora?"

Aurora shrugged. As if she wanted to know about the woman who would take Theron from her.

"The glass princess. The moment I came of age to wed, Her Majesty married me off to one political opponent after the other. Each time, I am ordered to bankrupt my groom. Each time, my groom is accused of harming me. And each time, Her Majesty decides that is reason enough to execute them. I have been the death of three men, and the moment Her Majesty saw your vision, she has been salivating at the chance to make it four. If Theron succeeds and does me no harm, I would not put it past Her Majesty to plot my demise to get what she truly wants—the

Dragon's Flank. This marriage will end but one way—death—mine, or his."

Aurora eyes widened in horror.

"Then…Then why would you ever agree to marry? Why didn't you run away?"

"Because she found my weakness. And if I don't do as Her Majesty commands, the only person I've ever loved will die."

Oh. Guilt washed over her. Epicasta wasn't her enemy. Of course she didn't want to marry all those men. Of course she didn't want to be a villain for her mother. Why else would she put up with such abuse if not for love?

"I'm sorry."

"So am I." She shook her head sadly. "I received a letter with proof that he still lives, trapped in one of her many dungeons. Her Majesty swears that once the Dragon's Flank is hers, that he will be freed."

"And you believe her?"

Epicasta laughed bitterly.

"No. She always promises that this time will be the last. And I don't want to believe he still lives. I pray he died the day he was captured. That way, only I had to suffer, and he will never know what I've done for love of him."

And yet she'd done as she'd been told, because a part of her still believed he was alive, still hoped he could be saved. Aurora felt ill. Merciful Triad, she'd hated this woman whenever she thought of what the princess' marriage would steal from her. She'd never known what burdens the princess had been forced to carry alone. Never considered that the marriage would only be the start of another nightmare for her.

Aurora reached across the space between them and placed her hand on Epicasta's.

"I didn't know."

"No one does, aside from Her Majesty and Her Holiness."

And now Aurora.

"I'm so sorry."

They were the only words she had, and yet they felt wholly inadequate. Aurora could only imagine what pain she'd suffered.

Epicasta seized her hands, a desperate light in her solemn grey eyes.

"If you have pity for me, then help me. If there's some way to circumvent this marriage, if you've had any visions that might show a different future, please tell me."

She hadn't had any more visions, just more of the same strange feelings of déjà vu whenever her emotions overwhelmed her, which was most of the time. But if a different future was what the princess needed, there were other ways. For the first time in weeks, hope sparked anew in her chest that maybe this time, the future she'd seen could be averted. After all, Aurora knew the palace like the back of her hand.

"I haven't had any visions, but I can tell you at least ten ways to sneak out of the palace unseen."

CHAPTER 21
THERON

Theron sat in the courtyard of the temple of Justice with his eyes closed and his face raised towards the sun. At midday, the temple was at rest for meal time, but every cleric was seated in the dining hall, conforming mindlessly lest their convictions be questioned. Theron couldn't stomach the thought of food. In just a few days, he would be married. Not in Aureum, amongst his court with the streets lined by well-wishers. Not to a woman he liked or could even tolerate. Not because it would benefit Aureum or him politically.

Theron cursed his choices.

Trading his safety for purification had been the coward's choice. He should have had the resolve to be patient, no matter the consequences. But no, he'd let his panicked courtiers lead him by the nose. He knew he should have just trusted Batea to handle it, knew he should have told his people to get Aurora out of Boreas immediately. Theron had panicked—erred, and now he reaped the consequences.

What did it matter if he returned home in a timely fashion if his wife managed to murder him before he could set his court to rights, or found a way to steal the Dragon's Flank for her foul mother? What did it matter if he managed to keep Aurora close at hand if her stubborn refusal to yield to their passion kept her heart out of his reach and thus his control?

Flora might have agreed to his reasonable terms of restitution, Orithyia might have purified him, but he'd still fallen into another trap. The queen was already making noises about sending an entire legion of Viridian soldiers along with her daughter 'for safety.' Orithyia had insinuated that she would also be making plans to visit Aureum in the near future—now that he'd allied himself to Viridis through marriage. Theron had managed to keep Viridis at bay his whole life, and now the most pernicious women in this cursed queendom would finally get their claws into his kingdom.

He'd failed Aureum. Chosen to act selfishly out of fear, and now his kingdom would pay. Unless he could find a way to convince Epicasta to deny the need for soldiers and rebuff Orithyia's intrusion without her telling Flora the exact wording of his sacred vow, he was going to lose ground. Already, he was on unstable footing, and Viridis was pushing him into a corner.

When he sighed and opened his eyes, he caught sight of Aurora. She was across the courtyard. Her eyes widened a fraction. He'd caught her staring. Theron smiled and stood. She turned to dart away. His heart raced.

Not again. Not today. He was sick of her running from him, from the connection between them. Theron gave chase, his longer legs closing the distance in moments. Aurora squeaked when he grabbed her around the waist and tackled her to the floor with him, landing on his shoulder to spare her any pain.

"What do you think you're doing?" she accused him.

She writhed in his arms. He chuckled, turning to flip and pin her to the temple floor, her arms above her head. The moment he flipped her, Aurora stopped struggling, her gaze flitting between his eyes and lips. Did she know the way she was looking at him, full of lust and longing? Did she know that even as she rebuked him with words, she shifted, rising to meet him as he closed the space between them?

"I could ask the same. Have you become a shameless voyeur in our time apart?"

"I—"

"I could punish you if you like," he purred, rubbing his nose along her slender neck, taking pleasure in her hitched breath. "I would use my teeth to make you confess," he whispered, nibbling on her long, pointed ear as she gasped. "I would use my lips to make you repent," he said, kissing a trail down her neck. "I would use my tongue to teach you a lesson," he said, pressing his tongue and teasing her nipple as it pebbled against the fabric of her gown. Aurora groaned, arching her back for more. "And only when I use my fingers would you know that you were forgiven," he whispered, trailing his hand up the side of her gown. "Tell me you want to be punished."

Did she realise that he'd stopped pinning her wrists, that she held them above her head exactly where he'd first grabbed them? Colour rose up her neck, her breath coming hard and fast, her gaze full of desire. She was beautiful like this, his fairy. He could see she wanted to surrender as much as he wanted to conquer.

Slowly, she raised her hands to his face, as if a sudden move might make him bolt. Didn't she know he'd captured her, and not the other way around? Her soft hands memorized the planes of his face, her fingers threading into his hair as she urged his lips to hers. Theron let her lead the kiss, let her tell him how she wished to be savoured in that moment.

Her lips were soft as she caressed his in a series of light kisses. She kissed his upper lip, the bottom, the side of his mouth, unexpectedly tender. When her tongue bid him to open his mouth for hers, he obliged, drinking her in slowly, reverently. Her leisurely exploration made the world around them fade away, until all he could taste was her, until his every breath was filled with her, until he imagined himself falling into her and never emerging.

Aurora pulled away, her gaze as tender as her kisses had been.

"I want you to be mine. Only mine," Aurora whispered.

"You already have me, Aurora," he said.

She shook her head.

"I want everything. All of you."

He sighed, his thumb caressing her lip. Theron finally had her wrapped around his finger, and now he would have to convince her to stay. Her possessiveness pleased him, but now that same trait posed a problem.

"I would give you everything if I could."

"Don't marry her, please. She doesn't even want it."

His heart warmed at the sound of her pleading. Her jealousy.

"Then the feeling is mutual. But if it's not her, it'll be another of Flora's daughters. I made a vow I can't escape."

And if he balked at marrying Epicasta, Orithyia would tell Flora exactly what he'd said and he'd be a prisoner in Boreas for the rest of his days.

"She'll be forced by the queen to kill you."

He chuckled.

"I know, and I have countermeasures ready. Is that what you fear, that she'll take me from you?"

Aurora blushed, nodding. Theron pressed a kiss to her forehead.

"The marriage will be in name only, a political necessity so that I can return to Aureum. She'll have no power to harm me, to vex you, to rule—nothing. What we have together won't change. My attention, affection, respect, devotion, all of it is already yours. And if you want an official place at my side, then the very moment I'm finished that farce of a ceremony, I'll make you my one and only concubine. When we return to Aureum, our binding ceremony will be a hundred times more lavish than any wedding ever held. You will be my wife in every way that matters."

He could see that she wanted what he offered, that she craved to own a piece of him no one else could touch. But her brows pinched and tears gathered in her eyes.

"I can't," she whispered.

"Yes, you can," he replied.

She covered her face with her hands as her breath hitched with sorrow.

"No, I can't. I can't do that to her. I can't be another reason she's forced to suffer. It's not right."

Another reason? Had Epicasta spoken with Aurora? What had she poisoned his little fairy's mind with? Theron pried her hands from her face.

"What did she tell you?"

"That she loves another. That if she doesn't do as she's told, he'll die, and the only way he'll be free is if Flora gains control of the Dragon's Flank. I can't let that happen to her."

So she had a lethal weakness and Flora had decided to ruthlessly exploit it? Normally, he would put all his resources into acquiring that weakness for his own purpose. But the look in Aurora's eye, determination mixed with something else, made his blood run cold.

"What have you done?"

Aurora sympathised with Epicasta, and was cunning in her own way. She knew of dozens of ways to sneak out of the vivarium. Who's to say she hadn't ferreted out countless more snaking through the main palace? If she'd helped Epicasta flee the capital, Orithyia would blame him, accuse him of causing trouble. He would never return to Aureum.

Aurora pressed her lips in a mulish line, defiant.

His gut sank.

"If I've succeeded? Changed her fate."

An explosion shook the ground. Theron grabbed Aurora and lunged into the relative safety of the courtyard as the columns swayed and cracks raced up the walls. His eyes widened in shock.

"Did you just...was that your doing?"

But her eyes were as wide as his. She shook her head.

Theron got to his feet and hauled her up as the people of the temple rushed outside to see what had happened. When the doors of the temple were flung open, the plaza was shrouded in a cloud of dust. Screams rang out as paladins and priestesses rushed in. Amidst the clamour, one voice, a man's, rose above it all.

"Justice and Vengeance, Knowledge and Lies, Passion and Death! They are two sides of the same goddesses! One cannot exist without the other! The Second Sundering was heresy, and your temples are an insult! Now the trove of ancient treasures hoarded by the heretic Orithyia belongs to the true believers! Cower and atone! Embrace the truth of dualism!"

"The hoard," Aurora gasped.

Theron tightened his grip on her hand.

The dualists had gone and stolen the lot, no doubt. He cursed his horrid luck. If they'd waited just a few more days, it might have all been his—Aureum's.

As the dust settled, palace soldiers rushed into the plaza, headed by General Stentor, adding more bodies to the confused mess. If Theron and Aurora went into the plaza, they risked getting caught between the furious paladins and soldiers. But if they stayed within the temple, there was a good chance it would come crumbling down on their heads. Who knew what other attacks the dualists had planned? Anyone not associated with either the temples or the palace was quickly fleeing the scene, ordinary citizens and likely some of the dualists mixed in.

"There, on the roof!" a paladin cried.

On top of the splintered entrance lintel of Knowledge's temple stood a lone figure. With a blast of wind, he sailed from the wreckage of one temple onto the roof of another. Passion's paladins raised a war cry as he touched down on their temple, scrambling to climb the temple or shoot him full of arrows. Just before he was overrun, another blast of air allowed him to land on Justice's temple roof.

"Shit," Theron cursed, dragging Aurora away from the temple entrance, covering her with his body as soldiers and paladins streamed back into the temple.

The dualist played with the enraged paladins and soldiers a few more times, leading them by their noses, expertly dodging every missile sent his way. This was a distraction, plain and simple, but the paladins and soldiers were too angry to realise. It still wasn't safe to flee the temple, and so he shielded Aurora against one of the entrance pillars of the temple of Justice. When at last the dualist began blasting himself away from the temple plaza and across the roofs of nearby homes, Stentor seemed to regain the barest hint of sense.

"Secure the gates! Archers to the walls! Don't let him escape!"

Anyone with a modicum of strategic thinking could see the dualist was the bait. No doubt his comrades were headed in the opposite direction, fleeing the city from one of the lesser gates, where soldiers were less likely to care about thorough inspections. If they hadn't already left, treasure in tow, hours prior.

But like an angry bee's nest, the paladins and soldiers followed the dualist, never considering that the real thieves might have been less brash than the man pirouetting across the roofs of the city towards the main gate. He had another sinking feeling in his gut.

"Aurora?"

"Yes?"

"Which gate is the princess escaping through?"

Her eyes widened with alarm as she realised the path the mob had taken. She swallowed nervously and looked away. He gripped her jaw in his hand and forced her to face him, his temper barely repressed. If Epicasta died in the brawl to come, he might be saddled with an even worse bride who wasn't wise enough to know she should stay quiet and out of sight. One who might foolishly demand he lay with her, one who would be inclined to meddle in his affairs more than strictly necessary—one whose weakness he didn't know. Or worse, Orithyia would take out her fury on him. It was her temple that had been attacked, after all.

"Which. Gate."

"The main gate."

"Stay here," he ordered her, about to race after the mob.

"Theron, wait!"

She grabbed for his robe. He snatched it from her grip, levelling her with an accusatory glare.

"Pray your foolish pity hasn't gotten the woman killed!"

She glared in return.

"Follow the West wall. It's faster. Help her escape if you can."

Theron took off at a sprint. He made it to the West wall and followed it without hindrance to the main gate. The mob had chased the dualist through the busiest thoroughfare, trampling carts and stalls and citizens alike. They were finally closing in as the dualist landed from the nearest roof onto the ground just inside the city gate, landing on top of a group of travellers. Stentor was screaming for the guards to close the gate, to no avail. Panicked citizens raced to and fro, desperate to escape being caught between the half-closed gate and the weapons wielded by the paladins and soldiers alike. Inside the gate, travellers dispersed as the dualist was surrounded by the guards and a familiar group—soldiers wearing the colours of Aureum and paladins wearing the reds of Passion.

His people were cut in half, some trapped outside, some inside. In the din, they wouldn't hear his orders, wouldn't know Epicasta's face even if he ordered them to protect her. No one but him knew she was likely to be here.

In every frightened face, he sought the princess' but she was nowhere to be seen in the melee. Theron pushed passed the fleeing people and the soldier manning the staircase to the top of the defensive wall. Racing to the top in spite of the shouts, he surveyed the scene from above. Then, as his eyes met those of his people inside and outside the gate, he caught sight of the princess, crawling away from the dualist who had used her as a cushion to break his fall. If he didn't move quickly, she was likely to be trampled in the fighting. His people would follow him wherever he went, hopefully providing the protection they would need from the mob.

From his position on the top of the wall, he jumped, bracing for an impact that would break his bones. Severing his sensation of pain just before he hit the ground, his landing pushed fractured bones through skin and burst organs. He willed his magic to make him whole and was on his feet, blood soaking his clothes as he rushed into the tightening knot of soldiers and paladins. As the mob closed in, the dualist kept them at bay with powerful blasts and whips of air made into razor-sharp blades. Blood, limbs and soldiers went flying, but more and more rushed into the fray, replacing the fallen.

"Your Majesty!"

"His Majesty is injured!"

"Kill the dualist!"

"Tear him to pieces!"

Theron ignored their cries and dove into the middle of the melee, landing atop the princess. He grabbed her around her middle and rolled to his feet as she shrieked in pain. Theron shouldered through the on-slaught of frenzied soldiers and paladins, letting their weapons cut him to ribbons, shielding the princess as best he could. When at last he'd made it outside the vicious huddle, a bloodcurdling, triumphant cry went up. Someone raised the dualist's head high.

"Your Majesty!" one of his people cried.

"Get them back! The princess is injured!" Theron ordered.

He wrapped her in his magic, healing broken bones and deep gashes, a punctured lung and a fractured face. When he was done, he turned his magic to healing his own wounds. Only when he was surrounded by the armed soldiers of Aureum, their backs to him as they kept the surging crowd at bay, did he relax a fraction.

"Should have let me die," Epicasta spat at him, tears running down her blood-stained face.

"Maybe, if you're very well-behaved, I'll indulge you—after our wedding," he hissed quietly so that only she could hear.

"I shouldn't have hoped. I've only sealed my fate," she sobbed.

And he his. Theron closed his eyes and sighed.

"If you tell me where your mother is holding your lover, I'll free him for you. You may even keep him by your side, if you swear to stay out of my way and keep your mother on a leash."

Epicasta laughed bitterly.

"It's too late for that now."

"The princess is here! The dualist attacked Princess Epicasta! Guards, to me! Get the princess back to the palace safely!" Stentor cried, riling up the crowd.

Epicasta closed her eyes and sighed, wiping the tears from her face, resignation and resentment turning her grey eyes flinty. Theron held out his hand to help her stand but she slapped it away. She struggled to her feet, glaring at any who dared meet her gaze or offer assistance.

When Stentor's ragtag band of bloodthirsty soldiers saw Epicasta emerge from the huddle of Theron's people, their eyes widened at the state of her—hair in disarray, her clothes torn and gory, her skin marred by dirt and blood, the evidence of horrific wounds painted in crimson across her gown. It ignited a frenzy. They turned from her to the body of the dualist and screamed, falling on it as they tore it apart. Only a few kept their heads and surrounded the princess, keeping the people at bay with sharp bronze and barked orders.

As the soldiers turned to wolves, hungry for the flesh of their enemy, Theron's people retreated from the carnage.

"Report," Theron ordered.

The nearest Aurean soldier got to his knee and bent his head.

"Greetings to the sun of Aureum. We travelled from Altanus in the company of High Priestess Myrina and a contingent of her paladins the moment word of your predicament reached us. We were attacked twice on the road, once by bandits, once by monstrosities, leading to our unpardonable delay. Her Holiness is just behind us, outside the city, and has come to purify you as well as chastise Queen Flora for keeping you, Your Majesty."

If people could explode from a combination of self-hatred and rage, Theron would have decorated the cobbled streets of Boreas in a grisly splatter.

He'd been a matter of days from his complete freedom. If he'd had the patience and resolve, he'd have avoided this detestable marriage, Orithyia's meddling—everything. He could have fucked Aurora to within an inch of her sanity and finally—finally—wrapped her around his finger for good. He'd have had an oracle begging for his touch, his to control, no complications in sight.

Now, because his fairy had a bloody conscience and deep-rooted need for total monogamy, his odds of controlling her were slim at best. Instead, he'd made deals with the two women he despised most in Trisia and was marrying the third on that ignominious list. Theron released a hissed breath through clenched teeth as his magic burst from him.

No, not because of Aurora, because he'd been afraid. He cursed himself. Cursed his cowardice.

And vowed to make Orithyia and Flora pay.

Because he should have received numerous letters announcing that his people would soon arrive, Myrina in tow. They would have had runners delivering the mail a week in advance of their coming, at the least. He should have received word the moment the gates opened, but the letters had no doubt been intercepted. And those two conniving snakes had known—they must have. All her bluster about the fate of Trisia and still Orithyia was Flora's creature through and through.

He'd been played for a fool.

Theron laughed, a bitter sound with an edge of hysteria. His soldier looked at him with concern.

"Your orders, Your Majesty?"

"To the temple of Passion for an audience with High Priestess Myrina."

By the time they arrived in the temple plaza once more, his people had helped him change out of his soiled temple robes and into something finally befitting his station. Boots polished to a high shine and decorated with gold fittings, loose linen pants in a deep blue, a belt encrusted with gold and jewels, an open robe that sparkled as if spun from pure gold, sapphires glinting in the swirling decorations. He donned a thickly braided gold and sapphire necklace accented with pearls. They tamed his long hair and adorned him with a matching set of gold and sapphire earrings and a headband of the same that cut across his forehead. The look was completed with golden cuffs and rings. Theron felt more himself than he had in weeks. It would have to do for now.

Myrina had taken charge of the chaos, ordering priestesses and paladins alike to recover the people buried in the rubble, treat the wounded, and ensure order throughout the city. She was in her element amongst the chaos. It suited her.

When she caught sight of his approach, her amber eyes glittered with pleasure. She barked out a few more orders, getting the whole relief effort organised in a matter of moments before she approached him.

Myrina wrapped thick, welcoming arms around him and kissed his cheeks.

"My little lion, I've missed you!"

"And I you, Aunty," Theron returned the hug, enveloped in her warmth and softness. A part of him came home for the first time in weeks.

"That's High Priestess Aunty to you, young man!" she giggled, wrapping him on the forehead. But his smile must have shown his troubles, because her amber eyes softened and she pressed a hand the same rich, ochre brown as his to his cheek as her dark brows pinched in sympathy. "Oh, my poor boy, what did they do to you?"

He pressed a kiss to her forehead, on hair so deep a shade of red that it was nearly black, just showing streaks of grey threading through. She was the only one he'd ever dared unburden himself to, the only one he fully trusted with his sorrows, his joys, his weakness. It was Myrina who had kept him whole when his world had shattered as a young man, forced to take the crown long before he was ready.

"Nothing that your presence can't make better."

"Come, my little lion. Anything can be solved when we put our heads together over a cup of tea."

How he wished that were the case.

Inside the temple of Passion, everything was dipped in red, like being swallowed whole. Here, Her energy felt like a lover's sigh, like a current of fervour shivering and shimmering everywhere he stepped. It was here he felt most at home, wrapped in the embrace of Passion's ruby-red columns, tapestries and mosaic floors. When they reached the foot of Passion, Her statue adorned in gold and sparkling crimson, Theron and Myrina knelt, paying their respects. The incense settled his mind at the same time as it energized him.

When they stood, clerics in ruby uniforms ushered them to Myrina's quarters, returning once they were settled with tea and biscuits, both of the highest quality. Passion was a goddess who advocated for the patronage of those most passionately dedicated to their crafts, after all, and many repaid the patronage given by the temple by serving it in whatever way they could. Walls were decorated with paintings and sculptures made by the most talented artists while the temple was, at most times, filled with the sweet sounds of musicians mastering their skills.

Myrina settled her plump, beautifully adorned self into her seat and sipped at the aromatic blend in her cup. Theron relaxed into his seat across from her, staring into his cup.

"I've fucked up, Aunty."

"Why don't you start at the beginning?"

He pinched the bridge of his nose and sighed, telling her everything he'd experienced since he'd landed at The Colonnades Of The Colossus. From his divine punishment to meeting Aurora, her magic, the plague, Flora and Orithyia's meddling, the queen's magic, her daughter's threats, the vivarium, the attack by monstrosities, his brush with death, the paladins' investigation, and finally, his deal with Orithyia. Myrina listened without judgment.

"You didn't receive my letters?" she asked, pained.

"No." He shook his head.

"Why didn't you wait? You've always been so cautious."

"I didn't think you'd come, Aunty. I thought I was alone."

"Oh, my little lion." Myrina got up from her seat and held him in her arms once more. "I will always come for you. I'm sorry I didn't get here sooner."

"As am I. Now, my wedding takes place in a matter of days, and it'll be a miracle if we manage to get back to Aureum without Flora trying to start a war using her daughter as the catalyst." He put his head in his hands.

Myrina sat back, pondering the situation, sipping her tea as she gazed out the window at the palace beyond.

"I'd always wanted you to marry for love."

"You knew that was never going to happen," he chided her gently.

"I just wanted you to have what I had." She smiled sadly.

Though uncommon, high priestesses could marry. Myrina had run away from the palace as a young woman to wed her lover and join the temple. What she and his uncle had shared had inspired plays and songs dedicated to their romance. But he'd died young, and Myrina had dedicated herself fully to the goddess who had given her the greatest love of her life.

"Not everyone is fated for a great and passionate love, Aunty."

"And yet, the way you speak of Aurora gives me hope." She smiled conspiratorially. "Don't think you can convince me otherwise with all your talk of using her magic for Aureum. She can be both your greatest asset and your greatest love." She poked him in the arm to emphasize her point.

He snorted. Always the incurable romantic, his Aunty.

"It's lust, not love." Theron waved her off.

"Passion approves of and encourages both." Myrina nodded sagely.

"How is it, that after I tell you of all the horrors I've endured, you only wish to discuss romance?"

"Bad habits." She shrugged, unrepentant. "You should cultivate some."

"Incorrigible."

"Guilty as charged." Myrina grinned briefly, before her expression turned pensive. "I'm quite cross with Orithyia. Leave her to me. That hoard of treasures alone will be enough to push her off her snooty pedestal."

Triad willing, it might mean the bitch's retirement altogether.

"Also, I wish to meet your intended, Princess Epicasta. It sounds like she might be convinced to side with you, or join my temple, if for no other reason than the protection I can offer."

Theron groaned.

"Aunty, if not her, then I will simply be forced to wed another of Flora's spawn."

"Yes, that sacred vow of yours. We'll have to be careful of that, but I have some ideas. First though, I need to meet the princess."

Theron wasn't entirely sure he wished for his Aunty to put herself in the thick of things like this, but if anyone could handle herself, it was Myrina. At the very least, it was worth considering whatever schemes she had in mind.

"Then shall we depart for the palace?" He put his cup down and offered her his arm.

"Yes, I think so."

They left the temple, whereupon Myrina was forced to see to the lingering issues of the attack. Theron took the opportunity to look for Aurora. She was no longer at the entrance to the temple of Justice. His heart constricted with worry. She was safe at least, wasn't she?

"Who are you looking for?" Myrina asked, finished with her tasks.

"No one."

"That's an awful lot of concern for *no one*."

"Aunty..." he warned.

"What? I'm a busybody. It's my goddess-given talent and I hone it to perfection to honour Her."

"And maybe if you say it often enough, you'll make it true."

"One can only hope." She patted his arm with an irreverent smile.

With Myrina on his arm and both her paladins and his soldiers at his back, he felt more confident than ever marching into the Viridian palace. For the first time since his arrival, he was treated like royalty instead of Flora's plaything. It was probably for Myrina's benefit, and only because he was to be their princess' groom, but it was a refreshing change nonetheless.

With Flora busy dealing with the attack, both he and Myrina were greeted by another of Flora's daughters, who was quickly cowed into letting them into Epicasta's private quarters. Outside the set of interconnected suites, a heavy guard had been placed. No doubt Flora had realised she'd been mid-escape when she'd been embroiled in the melee and had taken precautions against a second attempt. But as they were ushered into the inner sanctum of Epicasta's rooms, two voices were raised in a dispute. Before the attendant could intervene, Theron grabbed her wrist and shook his head.

"Go, and speak of this to no one."

"My goddess will be most displeased with you if you breathe a word," Myrina threatened with a smile.

The attendant left them on their own.

Theron held a finger to his lips and pressed his ear to the door. Myrina did likewise. Theron recognised Epicasta's shrieking, but the other voice was baffling.

"Hyllus?" he whispered, bewildered.

"The avatar?" Myrina asked in hushed tones.

Theron nodded.

"You told me he was dead!" Epicasta screamed, followed by the crashing of a vase.

"I said he was no longer under Flora's power!" Hyllus explained.

Another crash, another shriek.

"Which is the same damn thing!"

"Please, calm down, Cassy."

"Don't you dare! You have *no right!* I don't care if you were his best friend and that you shared the same name, don't you dare call me what he did! You could have saved him when he was first taken and you ran like a coward! You don't deserve to share his name!"

Something heavy hit the door, followed by Epicasta's sobbing.

"Is he dead? Is he alive? Where is he? Tell me!"

"He's here, Cassy. I'm right here."

"What are you saying?! He's in Boreas?! Where?!"

Theron looked to Myrina. It was time to interrupt. They opened the door as quietly as possible. Just in time to witness Hyllus kneeling before Epicasta as she wept on her knees on the floor. The avatar took a pendant from beneath his tunic collar, an ancient artefact by the looks of it. He pressed it, and in an instant, he was transformed. His hair lengthened and lightened to the colour of ripe wheat, his eyes transforming from grey to bright blue, his freckles melting off his bronzed skin.

Theron's eyes widened in shock. He'd been hiding behind an ancient enchantment this whole time? How had he managed to get his hands on it?

"I'm here, Cassy. I escaped that first week from your mother's prison, and I hid at the Nivean court under my friend's identity, working to become the ambassador's bodyguard so I could save you from your mother. But then I was named the avatar and I knew I had to get you out of here while I still had the chance."

So the avatar was Epicasta's weakness? That made things significantly more complicated. Not only had the man freed himself from Flora's clutches, there was little Theron could do to threaten the man into keeping Epicasta on her best behaviour. Nor was he likely to take too kindly to Theron's plans for the princess. Merciful Triad, what a mess.

"You...you're really *my* Hyllus? You're really alive?" Epicasta's hand trembled as she reached for his face.

"Yes. And I finally have the power to save you. Please, let me."

Myrina gasped, her eyes filled with tears. Epicasta and the transformed Hyllus turned towards her, their eyes wide with shock and terror. Hyllus reached for his bow. Theron stepped in front of Myrina, a snarl building in the back of his throat. He'd rather be twice punished by Justice than allow anything to happen to his Aunty.

"Bound by the thread of fate and dyed in the deepest red. My goddess blesses you with Her passion," Myrina said, her voice breathy and reverent.

Triad preserve him, he'd seen that look on her face only a few times but it always spelled trouble. The kind where she did all in her power to wed whoever it was who caused it. She'd not spoken too often about the powers Passion had bestowed on her as high priestess, but she always knew who was deeply in love with whom, who was having an affair, whose love was unrequited, and who her goddess had tied by fate.

"High Priestess Myrina?" Hyllus asked, bewildered, lowering his bow.

"It is I, Avatar, and what a pleasure it is," Myrina replied, scurrying over to the two lovers and pulling them up off the floor. "And you must be Princess Epicasta. The last time I saw you, you were no taller than my knees! Oh, I'm so thrilled to meet you again."

This boded ill for their former plans. Theron groaned and closed the door behind him as his Aunty fluttered and fussed over the couple. How was he to salvage this? It was clear to him at least that Aurora's visions couldn't be changed. But how was he to go through with a wedding ceremony with Epicasta while not marrying her and managing not to incur Knowledge's wrath? A headache bloomed behind his eyes.

"You simply must be married in Passion's temple. No one will be able to legally challenge your union then."

Theron cleared his throat.

"That's my intended you're speaking to, Aunty."

Myrina laughed.

"Oh no she's not, my little lion. She's his." She pointed to Hyllus, who hugged Epicasta closer, a look of warning for Theron in his bright blue eyes.

Theron cursed. Epicasta sighed, defeated.

"No, he's right, Your Holiness. I don't think we can circumvent Aurora's vision. I tried by running away, but as you can see, all that got me was caught in the middle of a mob and now placed under heavy guard."

"But she only saw you in the middle of the abduction ritual, right?" Myrina asked.

"That's right," Hyllus said, his eyes sparkling with hope.

"What about after that? She didn't see you both completing the ceremony, did she?"

No, she hadn't. Just like she hadn't seen Theron being saved by the avatar after the monstrosity had punched a hole through him. As he'd already told her, she didn't see everything.

"If we're to believe her visions are of what is fated, then we needn't circumvent them to alter the future. A rock in the middle of a stream forces the water around it. We can't change that the rock is there, but we can make choices that allow us to bend our path."

Maybe they couldn't change what Aurora saw, but Myrina was right. Now that they knew what was to happen, they could alter the flow of events before and after, as they were doing now.

Theron grinned.

"I have an idea."

CHAPTER 22
AURORA

The day dawned with a blood-red sky. Such a sign was considered the best of omens on a wedding, indicating Passion's pleasure in the match to be made. The palace had been buzzing since before the sun had risen, when daylight had only been a suggestion in the pre-dawn sky. Aurora would know, as she'd been all but ordered to participate in the wedding as one of Epicasta's bridal warriors. She sat in the bridal chambers allowing herself to be washed and oiled, perfumed and painted, dressed and ornamented.

The day had come, light spilling into the airy room decorated in pinks and greens and golds, tranquil pastoral scenes painted along the walls with animal mosaics running in circles on the floors. Silks and the softest cottons were paired with rich, lacquered woods, and a mirror that must have cost a small fortune rested in a gilt frame along one wall. This was the princess' chamber, and yet there wasn't a single personal touch in the room, nothing to mark the owner's presence or personality.

Aurora focused her mind on the most minute of details to keep her eyes clear of tears—the heat of the water, the fragrant steam. She let her mind wander as combs glided through her hair, wondering on the exact recipe of the oils they used. The notes of the perfume they'd dabbed on her neck and wrists were next, trying to identify the warm notes below the top notes of florals. Aurora sat as paint was applied to her face, concentrating on the ingredients of the make-up they'd used, what they chose to emphasize and how it differed from her era. When it was time to don the gowns and veils, she kept the pit in her stomach at bay by latching onto the quality and cut of the red gown she wore, pondering where they might have sourced the material, how long the fine silk would have taken to ship from Gilvus, where so much of its production had been centred in the ancient past. She kept her eyes dry as she weighed the heft of the jewels she wore, finer than any of the other bridal warriors. Another bribe, no doubt.

But when the preparations were done, and then the serving of small appetizers and drinks was complete, Aurora had nothing left to distract her from what was coming. Epicasta sent the other bridal warriors to wait in the room outside the bridal chamber while ordering Aurora to remain.

"Have you ever participated in this ritual before?" Epicasta asked, her tone stripped of all emotion.

"No," Aurora whispered, her voice cracking.

The wedding rituals of her time were quite restrained in comparison, especially for the untitled. Usually, a bride was walked through the streets with her family, soliciting the well-wishes of her neighbours as they made their way to her intended's house, whereupon she was welcomed, feasted to, and the couple encouraged to retire to the bridal suite to consummate the marriage. Only after that did the new couple go hand-in-hand to the temple of their choosing—usually Knowledge or Justice—to have their names and union recorded.

The rituals for nobles and royalty were much more extravagant, and the wealthier the couple, the more elaborate and taxing the ceremony. Some lasted days, with multiple feasts, games, tournaments, and all manner of public spectacle before the couple was registered in the temples. Only after the party were the couple allowed to retire to consummate their union. Phaedra's eldest sister's wedding celebrations had gone on for a straight month as she toured each of the provinces and brought the party with her. Aurora and Phaedra hadn't wanted to so much as look at a bottle of wine for the next three months afterwards.

Thinking of Phaedra threatened her resolve, her eyes stinging for the first time all morning. What would her friend have done? Probably kidnapped her lover and given the middle finger to her mother as she ran off into the sunset. But Phaedra wasn't here, and there would be no keeping Theron for herself. Today he married another.

Epicasta gave her a sad smile as she sipped a cup of tea.

"You're to guard my palanquin as we walk through all the districts in Boreas. The people will be rowdy and drunk, as the festivities began with the dawn. Soldiers will be taking care of the real security, so you needn't worry about that. When we near the palace, the groom and his warriors will attack the palanquin. The fights are purely for spectacle, so there's no need to fear."

"Once I'm taken from the palanquin, your job is to be captured by one of the warriors, who will bring you to the temple of Justice with the rest of mine and Theron's warriors. The groom will profess his right to wed through right of capture, and I will consent in front of the priestesses, whereupon we will sign our names in their ledgers. Afterwards, Theron and his warriors will carry us to the gates of the palace where the real celebration will begin."

"Be ready to have your outfit changed at least six times over the course of the day and into the night, and pace yourself with the wine, lest you wish to be seduced by one of the groom's warriors. While the couplings aren't frowned upon, the groom's warriors will be fellow nobles, and Her Majesty hasn't given up hope on marrying you to one of her allies. If you wish to partake free of consequences, drink this." Epicasta poured another cup of tea and slid the dubiously scented beverage towards her as she sipped her own. "It's an effective contraceptive."

Bile rose in her throat. How could she offer that? How could she think Aurora would be in the mood to tryst on today of all days? Why would she sip it in front of her, as good as telling her what she planned to do later that day?

But as Aurora held back tears, she stared into the murky liquid and a hot coal of anger sparkled to life inside her. If Theron was going to make her watch him marry another, she was going to seduce one of the Aurean soldiers or retainers who would inevitably celebrate. She would find out whomever he found most objectionable and torture Theron as he was set to torture her. Let his heart be set aflame by jealousy, let his gut roil with anger, let his throat constrict with sorrow. Aurora hoped she would make him as miserable as she was.

Aurora took the cup, braced herself and swallowed it down in a single gulp.

She wished she could hate Epicasta, truly hate her. In her heart, Epicasta was the villain, taunting her as she married the man Aurora burned for, but as her eyes saw the truth, her mind recognised she was just another victim. The tea was a sensible precaution to protect some small part of her as she was forced into a marriage she'd never wanted.

"How are you holding up?" Aurora asked.

"As well as could be expected, given the circumstances," Epicasta replied.

"I'm sorry."

"It's not your fault. None of it."

"If I hadn't had that vision—"

"Then you would have been accused of being an agent of chaos. Or worse. Her Majesty had planned to use your suffering to hurt King Theron. In truth, I knew the moment he was captured that this was a likely outcome. I tried to warn him, but well…he's stubborn and proud. What exactly do you see in him?"

Aurora bit her lip, giving herself a physical pain so she could pretend her heart wasn't shattering as she swallowed passed the emotion choking her. Did she know how cruel it was, to ask her that? To want a defence of the qualities she admired in him? But cruelty wasn't her intent, and if they were to wed, Epicasta should know that there was goodness in him that deserved her acknowledgement.

"He can be kind in a way few are capable. Protective. Selfless when it counts. He chose his own death over my suffering. If that doesn't prove he's a man of honour, then nothing else will."

Epicasta's brows rose in bewilderment.

"Merciful Triad, the sex must be transcendent," she said, sipping her tea. Aurora choked on her next breath, heat creeping up her neck. Epicasta's eyes widened in shock. "Wait, don't tell me you've never...that you feel all this and he hasn't even..." Aurora felt her face sizzling the more wide-eyed the princess became. Goddesses, why couldn't she just crawl under a rock and perish? "Triad's tits, I think we need something stronger," Epicasta muttered.

Epicasta left to rummage around in the vanity by the window. She opened a drawer and took out a bottle. The princess returned, downed her tea in an unladylike fashion and then filled their cups with a brew whose bouquet was certain to reach the guards posted outside the door.

It smelled like something that could strip paint and melt metal. Even a single sip had Aurora wheezing as it set fire to her tongue and burned down her throat.

"What is...oh goddesses..." Aurora coughed, fanning her face to beat back the tears the brew had brought to her eyes.

Epicasta sipped it as if it were no more offensive than a rich, smooth wine.

"A princess' best friend. I've been saving this bottle for a special occasion worthy of being completely obliterated from my memory. I think today merits it."

Aurora had barely managed a few more sips when the guards opened the doors of the bridal chamber and Queen Flora strode inside in a gown of dazzling green and silver.

"What is that stench?" The queen strode over and confiscated the bottle. "Really, Epicasta? Drinking? This is your fourth marriage. What's there to be nervous about?"

Aurora wished she could blend into the friezes as Epicasta wiped every emotion from her face and set her teacup aside.

"Nothing, Your Majesty. But the oracle was nervous about the proceedings. She's never been a part of this kind of marriage ritual before."

Aurora only had a split second to glare at Epicasta. The last thing she wanted was the queen's attention focused on her.

"Oh? Well, it's quite invigorating. Drink up and be merry, Aurora. Who knows, you might even find yourself swept off your feet. Passion has blessed this day, after all."

Aurora pretended to choke down as much of the liquid as she could while under the calculating gaze of the queen. When she set it aside, the queen nodded. If Flora wanted her drunk, then it would be unwise to let her guard down. It seemed she would have to spend the rest of this miserable day distressingly sober.

"The ritual will begin momentarily. It's time for you two to join the bridal warriors."

The queen ushered them from the room and down the maze of corridors leading to the front entrance of the palace. Epicasta was helped into a palanquin of emerald and gold, the gauzy green drapes pulled to the side so that all could witness her coming. She pulled the veil down over her crowned head as Aurora was instructed to do the same. The world took on a red haze.

As they walked through the city, jubilant cries met them from all corners. The citizens were dressed in their finest clothes, wearing crowns made of flowers. The cobbles under their feet were made precarious by the thick layer of petals as the people showered them with fragrant, colourful blooms wherever they went.

It was a mockery—every last smile, every last hearty congratulation. Aurora looked up to where Epicasta was seated, a tight, unfeeling smile on the princess' face as she waved at her people. Aurora couldn't even muster a mask, preferring to hide her face behind the walking stick she carried, the tinkling of its beads and feathers drowned out by the gaiety of the crowd. As they paraded around the city districts, the sun beat down mercilessly on her back, the veil trapping the heat of her breath close to her sweat-slicked skin.

Unpleasant as it was, Aurora wished it would never end. Because the moment it did, she would be forced to watch Theron abduct Epicasta from her palanquin. Every breath she took as they neared the palace district once more brought an insistent ache in her chest. Every step she took was one where she was forced to crush her own shattered heart beneath her feet. She wanted to scream, to weep, to tear at her hair. This wasn't a bridal party, it was a funeral procession, and her heart had been laid out for the pyre.

"Protect the bride!"

The words pumped dread through her veins.

The crowd rejoiced, a deafening cacophony. The groom's warriors with their staffs, in their red pleated kilts, bare chests and ugly masks, converged on the bridal party. The other bridal warriors faced off against them, putting on a show as the crowd ebbed and flowed around them.

Aurora recognised Theron despite his fearsome, horned mask. His golden staff glinted in the noontime sun, its rays catching the gold necklace, earrings, cuffs and belt he wore, making them blaze as if imbued with arcane power. He was glorious as he stood above the crowd, scanning the ritualized melee. Skin of glowing brown ochre, his crimson hair blowing in the breeze, his muscles oiled, he was everything she wanted and the only thing she couldn't have. As he approached the melee, his steps like those of a predator, her heart broke over and over. She wanted to double over and curl in on herself. Yet she was forced to stand and partake in this farce. Tears blurred her vision as she played her miserable part. She didn't see the man who absconded with her and didn't resist either.

As she was picked up and carried off, she closed her eyes, her heart racing. Faster and faster it beat. She would have to watch him stand at another woman's side and abandon her hope. She couldn't do this. She couldn't. Heart racing, Aurora couldn't catch her breath, her chest caught in a vise. She gripped the material of her gown, struggling to take a deep breath, her body shaking. Her captor increased his pace, seeming to sense her distress. He lifted her veil but Aurora refused to open her eyes. If she did, she would break and break until she was nothing but splinters.

"Aurora, breathe. Just breathe."

She opened her eyes with a gasp.

Theron.

He'd removed his mask, his golden eyes swimming with concern as he held her. His magic washed over her, a comforting cocoon.

"I have you, my fairy. Just breathe. That's right."

"No. You." She couldn't form the words. Couldn't speak her thoughts without gasping. Tears slid from her eyes.

"It's alright. You're safe. Everything is alright."

But it wasn't alright. He was supposed to marry Epicasta. He was supposed to abduct the princess. What was he doing with her in his arms?

"What's wrong?"

Epicasta? That was her voice. Were they already at the temple, making a spectacle of themselves in front of all?

"Is she hurt?"

Hyllus? But what was he doing at the ceremony? He'd said he had no wish to be there.

Aurora shivered from her attack of nerves. As the princess and avatar came to her side, they looked on her with concern. Except one of them wasn't Hyllus. The man sounded exactly like the avatar, but looked nothing like him. With his bright blue eyes and wheat-coloured hair, he looked more like Silvanus than the avatar of the first calamity. What in the Loom was going on?

"She's just catching her breath," Theron said, more assuring her than answering them.

"I knew we should have told her," Hyllus grouched.

"The woman is incapable of keeping a straight face. It would have been suicide," Epicasta snorted. "And on that note, we need to hurry. We'll meet you in Aureum. You'll catch her up to speed, Your Majesty?"

"I will. Congratulations, Epicasta, Hyllus."

"Don't congratulate us until the deed is done. There's still time for this to go tits up," Epicasta hissed.

Aurora took stock of her surroundings as her breaths slowed. Red. Everywhere was red. Not white. Not the temple of Justice, but the temple of Passion? Why?

"You're doing well, Aurora. Not long now," he cooed, carrying her deeper into the temple, the sounds of the crowds growing dimmer.

"What's h-happening?" she asked, gasping.

"Just breathe. I'll explain," he said, his voice gentle.

Aurora pressed her cheek into his chest, savouring the feel of his skin on hers, of the steady thump of his heartbeat. She let herself believe, even if only in that moment, that she was safe, that all was right with the world, that he would continue to hold her like this every day forever.

"We're changing fate, Aurora. Your vision has come to pass, but we're not bound by the expected conclusion of that event."

Breaths finally steady, she gazed up at him, his smile a brilliant beacon of hope.

"What do you mean?"

"I made a sacred vow to wed before I left Boreas, fearing that Queen Flora would use any vow more specific to kill my intended and blame me. But there's still time to thwart her, to take the fate we want and make it ours." He nodded at the statue of Passion.

Theron set her down, her legs shaky. He steadied her. At Passion's feet, Epicasta knelt with the blonde man, and a woman who could only be High Priestess Myrina stood over them, reciting a prayer. The high priestess' ruby-red chiton dress hugged her ample curves, the pink and gold embroidery decorating the hem, her veil secured atop her head by her ruby-encrusted gold diadem. But as beautiful as her attire was, it was the young man who aroused her curiosity.

"Who is…?"

"Hyllus. That's his true face, one he hid with an ancient artefact. He's the man Epicasta loves, and so to escape Flora, they're choosing to be wed in the temple of Passion. Their plan is to escape the city before Flora discovers the ruse."

A marriage that could only be dissolved by his death or hers, one unassailable by the courts. Not even Flora could undo it. Epicasta would have her freedom after all.

"But then you…?" Aurora looked up at Theron.

If Epicasta married Hyllus, then Theron would be forced to wed another of Flora's daughters, per his vow. Just as the histories stated.

But where she expected resignation in his eyes, instead they sparkled with mischief. He knelt before her, taking her hand in his and kissing her knuckles with reverent care.

"Aurora, will you do me the honour of becoming my wife?"

She stilled, frozen, her heart hammering against her ribs. He must have mistaken her shock for reticence. He pulled her closer.

"You will be the only woman in my life, adored, protected, respected. I will belong to you alone, everything I am, everything I have—yours."

"But don't you need a queen?" she blurted out.

He laughed.

"*You* will be my queen, Aurora. With an entire army at your back to hunt down Drakon, and a whole kingdom's worth of resources to do it."

"But I…"

"Will be a great and compassionate queen, a role you will come into a little more each day. Say you'll marry me, Aurora. Whenever I look at you, a fire rages in my chest. One I thought could be quenched by your lips on mine, but every touch, every sigh, only makes it burn brighter, hotter, until you're the whole of my world. Become mine, and make me yours. Irrevocably."

Aurora wrapped trembling arms around him, their noses touching. Did she want to be bound to this man for the rest of her life? She already knew she couldn't live with the idea of him belonging to another, that she wanted him fiercely. As she stared into his golden eyes pleading with hers, a part of her felt like it had the hope of a home, a feeling she thought lost to her forever. Theron could be hers. With only a single word, the man who set her heart ablaze would dedicate himself to her for the rest of her days. Was this a dream? If so, she never wished to wake.

"Yes."

He swept her up against him with a triumphant cry and pressed his lips to hers. She threaded her fingers through his hair and pressed herself as closely as she was able, drinking him in like he was the first rain after a drought.

"Ahem." A woman clearing her throat interrupted the moment.

It was the high priestess. Now that Aurora had a good look at her, she had the same ochre brown skin as Theron, her hair so dark a shade of red that it appeared almost black, save for a few silver strands. Her amber eyes were kind and full of mischief.

"You're welcome to consummate the marriage anywhere within the temple, but first you need to be wed for it to count."

Aurora fought a blush and lost.

Theron laughed.

"Aunty, may I present my soon-to-be wife, Aurora."

"Aunty?"

"I was once a princess of Aureum, and half-sister to the late king, but that's a story for another day. If you hope to be married before the palace realises what's happened, we shouldn't delay." Myrina winked before her brows knit with concern. "Goddess, but you're tiny. Hmmmm." Myrina clucked over Aurora, sizing her up and then Theron.

Theron set her back down on the pink and ruby mosaic floor as Myrina whispered to one of her acolytes, who rushed off. Then the high priestess ushered them to kneel at the feet of Passion's statue.

"Now, let's get a good look at the two of you," Myrina said, her eyes seeming to look right through them. "Oh," she said, tears gathering in her eyes. "It's a blessed day after all."

"Aunty?" Theron asked, his brow raised in question.

"Bound by the thread of fate and dyed in the deepest red. My goddess blesses you with Her passion," Myrina said, her breath catching. "I'm so happy for you, my little lion."

Theron gazed down at Aurora, blinking owlishly, more shocked than she'd ever seen him.

Her mind raced with the implications. They were fated? But what did it mean that the person Passion had chosen for her had been born thousands of years before her? Was she always meant to come here, to this time, this man? If they wed here and now, she would alter the history she knew—for he would marry a commoner, not a princess. Was she meant to change history—fate—after all? Could she be meant for more than just suffering? Tied to more than just the worst things in the Tapestry?

"I thought...I thought the only fate I was bound to was Drakon's," she said, her voice hitching. Was it possible her fate was not entirely soaked in the garnet tones of Death, her life not wholly one marked by loss and despair? Was Theron her hope? The light to balance the bitter darkness of her path?

"In all things, balance. Chaos and peace. Tragedy and love. This Drakon might have stained your path with Death, but Passion has blessed you as well."

Aurora bit her lip and wiped the tears from her eyes. It seemed she was fated to be a mess today. She must look atrocious. Aurora laughed.

"Are you ready?" Myrina asked.

"Yes," Aurora replied.

"Yes," Theron said, clearly still recovering from his shock.

"Then make your offerings to Passion," Myrina said, her eyes glowing with divine power. Suddenly Aurora could feel the goddess' gaze on her, a hot, nearly choking heat that wound its way around her.

Theron took off one of his golden cuffs. Aurora took off one of the bracelets she'd been given. They laid them amongst the other offerings. She recognised Epicasta's necklace and one of the staffs wielded by the groom's warriors. It must have been Hyllus'.

"Bind your chosen, your fated, from this breath until their last, to be reunited in the Loom and spun anew with your blessings."

The fiery heat sank into her sinew and bones. Aurora crumpled to the floor, melting as she was prepared to be reforged anew. Theron was there beside her, struggling against the weight of the goddess' brand. He reached out to her and gripped her hand in his. Something within her unfurled and then tangled, anchoring her with a weight she didn't recognise. She kept her gaze on Theron's. His eyes flashed with red flames before the pressure suddenly eased. Catching their breaths, Aurora and Theron simply stared into each other's eyes. Deep inside, something settled into place. They stood up on shaky legs as Myrina smiled.

"You are wed by Passion. Please complete your prayers anywhere within the temple. If you prefer privacy, my acolyte here will lead you to a room."

Aurora flushed again, looking up at Theron as her heart raced. The marriage wasn't binding until they consummated it. She remembered the sight of him nude on the first day she met him, wide and solid and strong. But she also recalled just how large he was. Everywhere. Trepidation bloomed in her chest.

"Please take these as a gift from my temple," Myrina said as another acolyte approached with a small case decorated in suggestive imagery. "And not to spoil the mood, but you'd best hurry. I'll keep them off your scent as long as possible, but it won't be long now." She urged them to follow the acolytes. "If you run into any, erm, *difficulty*, remember that an orgasm each will suffice for the purposes of the binding!"

Theron shot Myrina a killing glare. And if Aurora wasn't mistaken, the tips of his slightly pointed ears heated. For some strange reason, it made her less nervous about what was to come. In record time, they were taken to a cosy room on the third floor with a view of the crowded plaza below. The attendants set the case inside the room, wished them well, and closed the door behind them.

Aurora and Theron stared at each other as the silence dragged on. Fated. She'd never given the idea of a fated match much thought. Such things were rare. Precious. And her life had held enough precious things in it—her family, her scholarship, Phaedra—that she'd never wished to tempt bad luck by wishing for more. She swallowed, her throat suddenly parched. Aurora spied a pitcher of water and poured herself a glass.

Theron was frozen to the spot, staring at her with the same disbelief she felt. No doubt it was doubly jarring for a king. Royalty never married for anything but politics. She glanced away from him, looking around the room but seeing nothing. And always her eyes were drawn back to him. A man whose thread was intertwined with hers. Triad, this was awkward. She tried to speak, but the moment she opened her mouth he did the same. Aurora shut hers, just as he covered his own and coughed.

She'd thought she would simply feel the urge to leap into his arms and lose herself in him, but this was different. They were different. Something important weighed heavily between them—a lifetime commitment, the blessing of a goddess, two lives made one. Fate was not to be taken lightly. It made her nervous. Perhaps she should have drunk the whole of Epicasta's paint-peeling alcohol.

"I'm—" He pointed at his clothes.

"Right—" Aurora gripped the fabric of hers, palms sweaty.

They had to see things through, to pray—to consummate.

"Perhaps we should—" He tipped his head towards the bed.

Fear galvanized her steps.

"I'll go see what's in the box." Aurora rushed over to it, swallowing a groan.

Stupid. Stupid. Stupid.

When she opened it, the contents did nothing to quell her anxiety. Her mind reeled as it processed what was laid out before her in a custom, velvet-lined case. She choked on her next breath, slamming the lid shut.

Theron padded over, his hand on the lid.

"No!" Aurora fought him to keep it closed.

Merciful Triad, please let a hole swallow her up and take her shame with it.

"It can't be that bad," he argued as they wrestled for the case.

She covered it with her body, clinging to it with all her might. But Theron was a trained warrior and he quickly pried it free, one limb at a time. When he finally won it from her, holding it above where she could reach, he peeked inside.

"Hmmm. She's nothing if not practical."

"P-practical?! T-there are d-dildos in there! *Glass dildos! EIGHT* of them! What are we meant to do with *eight dildos?!*"

"And in a range of sizes," he said, a slow smirk lighting on his face. He plucked one from inside and tested it in his palm. "Catch," he said, tossing it to her.

She caught it before it shattered on the floor. Like a fool. Her face blazed. Her fingers didn't even meet when she held it the damn thing was so enormous. He set the case aside.

"Why would you—"

"That's my size," he said, his eyes raking her with heat.

"But this is the biggest one!" she accused him, shaking the thing at him.

"So it is."

"Oh goddess..."

He advanced on her. She backed away, holding the dildo out as if it were a sword. It might as well be. She could probably kill someone with it. Given the size, it might do her in.

"Will it fit?" he asked, backing her into a corner, looming over her until she was holding the dildo less like a sword and more like it was a lifeline. She averted her eyes as her mind spun. He tipped her chin up so she was forced to drown in his golden gaze.

Just the heat in his look made her ache. Her grip on the glass tightened.

"I don't...uh...maybe? Its...the...well, um... it's really big," she spluttered out, her words ending in a whimper.

He wrested the dildo from her grip and set it aside.

"Then we'll complete our prayers another way. Once we're fully bound, I'll go slowly, ruining you one toy at a time until you can take me. Would you like that, Aurora?" he purred.

Heat crept up her neck again as she envisioned just what he might do to her. Things she'd only dreamt of.

She nodded.

"Then say it."

"Yes," she whispered.

"Yes, what?"

Her breath came fast. Was this how it was to be between them? Him speaking her fantasies into being, making her say words that had spent a lifetime trapped in the back of her throat? She swallowed.

"Yes, I would like that."

"And if at any time you don't like something, what will you say?"

Merciful Triad, she was required to think during this ordeal? They were both quite doomed.

"Stop?"

He smiled.

"Good enough. Clothes on or off?"

"Off. On! Wait…oh, I don't know," she groaned.

Theron chuckled and scooped her up, his eyes glittering gold. He sat down on the edge of the bed and arranged her in his lap, the skirt of her gown hiked up around her thighs as she straddled him, her knees on either side of his hips. He divested her of her veil and began pulling the pins from her hair, massaging her scalp. She leaned into his expert touch, the tension leaving her shoulders as he freed the last of her hair from its confines. Aurora helped him out of his headband, necklace and earrings. He ran his finger along the edge of her ear, sending a shiver down her spine when he freed her from the weight of her earrings. Her eyes were on his lips. She remembered how soft they were, how sweet his kisses could be, and how demanding, how consuming. He leaned in for a kiss and she placed a finger on his lips.

"You're really alright with this? There's no going back. No undoing it."

The question took him aback. A flash of something, maybe vulnerability, crossed his face. He looked away, threading his fingers through hers.

"In a perfect world, I would have preferred more time to know you. I know you're courageous, infuriatingly soft-hearted, that you're intelligent, devious when it suits you, but I might have preferred to wait until I knew if you could smile for me the way you do for Hyllus, if you could laugh with me as you do him. In a perfect world, I would have liked to give you the choice of temple, the choice to leave if you so chose. But this world is flawed, as are we all. I'm a jealous man, a bad man who has chosen to be a good king, honourable when it suits me and wicked when it doesn't. In this world, you're the only one I would choose to bind myself to. But maybe the more salient question is this—are *you* alright with this, knowing there's no going back?"

Aurora swallowed. He wasn't looking at her, giving her time to sort through her thoughts without the pressure of his desires. But the answer was yes. She'd wanted him from the start, much as she'd tried to resist. She knew he was flawed, calculating, possessive, but he'd also, time and again, seen her through the worst both she and the ancient past had to offer and still chose to remain by her side. That didn't mean she wasn't afraid of what the bond would mean, how it would alter her life, her future. But courage was not borne out of fearlessness.

With her fingertips on his jaw, she turned his head to hers, their lips meeting in a tender kiss. She chose to be brave—to take a leap of faith and trust that this man who was meant for her would stand by her side for all that was to come. That what they had together now would blossom and grow.

He deepened their kiss, one hand on the back of her head, the other slipping under her skirt. Nerves assailed her as she placed her hands on his chest. His heart hammered against her touch, and a part of her anxiety quieted. Theron was as nervous as she—of course he was. Warmth bloomed in her chest. They could be brave together.

He rubbed her through the fabric of her underclothes, swallowing her cries. She fought his belt off in increasingly jerky movements as he played with her. When Aurora finally freed him, she took his silken length in her hands and explored him as much as she could while he teased her to distraction. She wasn't certain how something that large would ever fit inside her, but as he brought her to the edge of the precipice, she found herself more and more eager to discover the means.

Theron's kiss became rougher, more demanding, his hips rising to meet her strokes. And yet his touch on her remained feather-light and maddeningly close to the ecstasy she needed. Aurora returned his kiss as punishingly as she was able. She needed and he was denying her. As she crested the peak of desire, she squeezed him harder. Bucking in her hold, he growled as he spent in her hands. He pressed hard on her soaked underclothes and she broke off their kiss to cry out as she joined him. Breathing ragged, she rode his palm until the pleasurable shocks faded.

It was unfortunate their first time had needed to be rushed like this. Their eyes met as they caught their breaths.

Aurora gasped.

Fire raced down her spine, her nerves set alight with unexpected pleasure, as strong as the orgasm she'd just experienced. Her mind felt foggy with lust and need, the world taking on a haze of red. A need so overwhelming, so voracious, crept up and over her, until she was shaking. Theron stiffened, his eyes wide as the gold was replaced by fiery red.

What was happening? Fear and arousal rode her in equal measure.

"Theron?"

"It's alright. It's alright," he groaned, a shiver racing down his spine.

The heat concentrated on her core, building and building until Aurora was a panting, shaky mess. She'd never felt such need before. It trampled every other thought in her mind, every other sensation, until she was nothing but overwhelming lust trapped inside the flesh of a woman. Seeking the pressure of his hand, her body demanded another release.

Theron wrapped his hand around hers, pumping it along his hard length as he gave her what she sought with the heel of his other hand. Without finesse or control, they used each other for pleasure, overcome.

Their lips met, each fighting for dominance. Everywhere he touched, her skin felt scorched, and she yearned for the burn more than her next breath. Aurora sank the nails of her free hand into the flesh of his chest, drawing blood, a savage need to claim him, to mark him riding her hard. He repaid the pain with his own, kissing the column of her neck until he could mark her with his teeth. She mewled as pain mingled with and then was overtaken by pleasure. She was close again, his rough handling only sending her further over the edge. When at last he gave her what she sought, she screamed, stars bursting behind her eyes, her body alight with a pleasure so intense she felt it down to her toes. She pressed her forehead to his chest and whimpered in the aftermath, kissing the marks she'd left on him in apology. Theron swore, releasing a second time.

When it was done, the haze lifted and her mind returned to her. The animalistic desire ebbed from her body until she felt herself again. Aurora shivered. She dared look up to find Theron's eyes were gold once again.

They collapsed on the bed, faces flushed and eyes wide.

"It's done," Theron panted. "We're bound by Passion."

That was the sacred binding ceremony?

A laugh bubbled up inside her. If people knew the goddess Herself gave Her couples an extra, mind-numbingly good orgasm when they were wed, how many more would have signed up for a lifetime binding ritual? Aurora giggled.

"Do you think that happens every time?"

Theron's face lit in a smile. Her heart stuttered. He winked.

"Give me a few minutes and we'll test it out."

She grinned, feeling playful.

"It's an understudied aspect of temple rituals. We'll have to do it several times. For the sake of scholarship," she said, tracing circles on his chest and fluttering her lashes at him.

"Oh of course. Purely for academic reasons," he replied nobly, even though his gaze devoured her.

"Never doubt the rigour of my scholarly pursuits. I take these things very seriously," Aurora added, sidling closer.

"Do you, now? In that case, we should test it out in all of Passion's temples from here to Altanus. You know, to be thorough," he purred.

"I knew you'd see it my way."

"Was there any doubt?" he asked.

She leaned in to kiss him as happiness fizzed through her veins. He obliged, their kiss soft and playful. Her worries eased in her chest. It had been so long since she'd felt even a little bit mischievous. They could be silly together. Her heart pumped something warm and full of light through her body. Fate had taken so much from her, made her feel like she might never get even a slice of her former self back. But here she felt a tiny spark of her old self. Aurora could have wept with the magnitude of her relief, of her gratitude, of her hope. They'd made the right choice in each other.

Shouting in the temple halls interrupted them. They stood, Theron urging Aurora to stand behind him. The palace had discovered them.

CHAPTER 23
AURORA

Aurora's heart thundered in her ears. What would Flora do to her now that she'd so openly defied her?

"They risk Passion's wrath if they commit violence here. Remember that," Theron said.

But only if a priestess or the high priestess were attacked. The guards could certainly drag them from the temple and commit violence once they were free of sacred ground. Aurora pressed closer to Theron. Would the paladins intervene a second time? Aurora's gut clenched, and she was suddenly grateful they'd remained clothed. The shouting became more distinct. Flora. The queen tore open the door to their room, eyes glittering with rage.

"You!" she howled at Aurora. "Whore!"

Aurora glared back defiantly.

"That's my wife you're speaking to!" Theron snapped menacingly.

"You're both clothed. There's no proof! I demand you honour your vow and marry my daughter!" Flora screamed.

Theron chuckled.

"Oh, did Orithyia not tell you? I only vowed to wed before I left Boreas. I never once named *who* that person would be." Theron grinned.

Another set of footsteps echoed in the hall.

"Your Majesty, you cannot barge into my temple and disrupt sacred rites!" Myrina called angrily.

Myrina arrived at the door, glaring daggers at the queen.

"What sacred rites? Hmm? What proof is there that they've consummated the marriage?" Flora squawked.

Myrina's brows pinched in worry. She looked at them again, as if she could see through them, her hand to her heart. Her relief was palpable. Myrina sighed, a smile on her face.

"The proof is that I can sense that the bond has been forged. Theron and Aurora have been bound by Passion, until their last breaths," Myrina announced.

"And I'm to take the word of some disgraced Aurean royal, am I? I demand she be inspected by my royal physicians for proof of intercourse!"

Aurora suddenly felt ill. Flora couldn't demand such a thing, could she? Theron's hands clenched at his side.

"I will break them before they dare lay a hand on her," he threatened. Myrina's face darkened.

"Maybe Orithyia lets you get away with such disrespect in her goddess' house, but I am the high priestess of Passion and this is our temple. If you're not here to pray or ask for succour, you will leave or I will charge you with heresy."

"Heresy? Ha! For what? Calling your bluff?"

"For questioning the blessings of Passion!" Myrina thundered.

Divine magic suddenly choked the air, thick and heavy and menacing. The walls seemed to close in, like the gullet of a beast. Even Flora was affected, taking a half step away from the high priestess. Passion ruled over more than just lust within the bounds of Trisia. Wrath, too, was her purview.

Aurora had never felt divine magic so threatening in all her life. That it was directed not at her, but her enemy, gave her courage.

Myrina was right. They'd been blessed and bound by Passion Herself. She'd seen Passion's fire in Theron's eyes. How dare a mortal queen question the blessings bestowed by a goddess? How dare this wretched woman who had abused her daughter, neglected her sacred duties as queen, who planned sadistic tortures for any under her power and now insulted a high priestess, barge in here and ruin what should be one of the best days of Aurora's life? Rage boiled over, her magic seething inside her. Now that Aurora was bound to Theron, she was his queen. No longer a cowering prisoner—she was Flora's equal. Aurora would never have allowed anyone to treat her thus in her own time. Why should she countenance it now?

Theron was about to come to his aunt's defence when Aurora stepped in front of him. She urged him to stand aside as she marched over to Flora. How dare this woman question their marriage? How dare she come in here and treat them as if they were the dirt under her sandals? After all she'd done to torture them, to terrorise them? After all the things she'd put Epicasta through, she dared come here and make demands?

Aurora put all her strength into shoving the queen off-balance and out the door.

"How dare you—" She pushed Flora back. "Come in here—" She shoved harder as Flora stared at her, bewildered. "And make disgusting demands—" Aurora huffed, succeeding in pushing Flora back into the hall. "After *everything* you've done!"

"You promised my daughter would wed the king! Now you mean to steal him like the lowborn whore you are!" Flora raged back. "I offered you everything and you spit in my face!"

"You offered me chains and called them gifts! And you forced that vision out of me after you treated us like animals! You're not fit to lick the dirt off our sandals, much less make demands! But instead of begging for the forgiveness you clearly don't deserve, you question a goddess in Her temple! With every breath, you bring shame and ridicule to Viridis!"

Flora lunged. Myrina held her back.

"You want your proof?" Aurora rucked up her skirt so she could hook her fingers around her loincloth and shimmy out of it. She wiped her seed-coated fingers on the soaked fabric and tossed the sopping mess at the queen's feet. "Here." Aurora spat at Flora's feet for good measure. "I'm the queen of fucking Aureum now, and I know what you planned to do to us at your party, so I'd suggest you watch your back, you thrice-damned bitch!" She glared daggers at the queen, whose face was apoplectic with rage. Aurora looked back at Theron, leaning against the wall, a satisfied smirk turning his lips up at the corners. "Do you have anything to add?" she asked him.

"No, I think you summed it up nicely."

She turned back to the queen.

"He has nothing to say to you. Now leave my husband and I to enjoy the rest of our wedding."

Myrina looked deeply satisfied as Aurora slammed the door in the queen's stunned, horrified face. Aurora's ragged breaths echoed in the quiet of their chamber as Myrina's cheerful voice ordered Flora to immediately leave her temple. The queen stormed off. It was done. Her indignation left her almost as fast as it had come on.

Aurora turned around, eyes wide.

"Merciful Triad, I just threw my soaked loincloth at the queen of Viridis."

"Not the most tactful first act of diplomacy as a queen, but it was certainly memorable."

Aurora slid to the floor as her knees buckled.

"How badly did I fuck up?"

"On a scale of one to ten? Maybe a five." He shrugged, unconcerned.

"You know what? I don't even feel ashamed. Should I?"

"Not at all. I adored every minute of it. I hope they write songs about it."

Aurora snorted. Theron's eyes blazed with heat and good humour.

"Your anger is intoxicating. You're in charge of all our diplomatic efforts going forward. Though we may need to keep you well-stocked with undergarments if this is how you plan to handle foreign relations."

The laugh started in her belly and bubbled up until Aurora howled with laughter. She wiped tears of mirth from her eyes.

"Triad's tits," she giggled, "I thought her head was going to explode."

"Would that the Triad were so generous."

As her giggles died down, she sighed.

"Now what?"

"Now, we're going to clean off. And then I'm going to prove to you that I'm a man of my word."

"Oh?"

His gaze slid to the case.

"I promised to ruin you with each of them, one at a time, until you can take me inside you. And we're going to see how many blessings Passion is willing to bestow on us. For scholarship."

A shiver stole down her spine. He got off the bed and held out his hand for her. She took it as he helped her up. Theron opened the door she'd thought was the entrance to a closet. Instead, it opened into a small bathing chamber with a sunken pool of still-steaming water, big enough for two. He pulled her close, his eyes roving over her face.

His calloused finger trailed down her cheek and neck. He skimmed her collarbone until he met the clasp at her shoulder. He paused.

"May I?"

"Yes."

He dispatched it with a flick of his wrist, baring one breast and then the other. His hands trailed down her chest, skirting her nipples. But two could play at that game. Aurora urged his kilt down his hips. Powerful thighs bracketed his member. Goddess, just looking at it again made her insides feel like jelly. Lustful Aurora wanted nothing so much as to test the limits of her body's capabilities. Pragmatic Aurora doubted the logistics of their coupling.

"My eyes are up here, my fairy queen," he purred.

The grin on his lips was magnetic. She kept her eyes locked on his as she pressed a kiss to his chest. Aurora slipped from her gown, allowing it to pool at her feet. He took her hand as he backed into the pool. When the hot water embraced them both, he grabbed a nearby towel and soap and crooked his finger. He began with her face, wiping away the thick paint. When he was done, he smiled.

"There you are."

He tossed the towel aside and grabbed and soaped another, urging her to sit between his thighs on the sunken bench. He started with her fingers, kissing each after he was done, moved up, pressing his lips to her inner wrist, then her shoulder and neck. He repeated his care with her other hand, until he reached her neck, pressing his teeth to her neck and gently biting, asking forgiveness for the slight sting with a kiss.

"Do you want to play, Aurora?"

Anticipation was a drug pumping through her veins. Did he mean what she thought he meant? Heart in her throat she turned to look at him.

"What kind of play?" she asked, breathless.

"Control. Surrender."

Her next breath was shaky with need. He was doing it again, speaking fantasy into reality.

"Yes."

"And is there anything that would displease you?"

"Pain. I don't like pain."

"As you wish," he said.

"And I want to feel safe," she added.

"You're always safe with me, Aurora." He pulled her back between his legs, her back against his chest. "Arms around my neck," he whispered in her ear before he nipped it.

Aurora obeyed as best she could. Even with him seated and her standing, she only just latched her fingers around the back of his neck. He lathered the cloth once more and ran it down her chest, paying special attention to her nipples. Tracing around them in maddening circles until she was throbbing, he pinched them just enough to send little lightning sparks of pleasure through her body. The sight of huge hands on her only heightened the sensations. Only when her heart was racing and she was biting back a groan did he move lower, cleaning her belly, her thighs, and teasing her as he avoided the place that ached most.

"Please," she begged.

"Please, what?"

"Please touch me."

"I'm already touching you," he chuckled.

"Touch me here." She arched her hips, seeking his hand.

"Do you want to come again?"

"Yes," she hissed as he cleaned her with the cloth, teasing her slick folds.

"Only good girls get to come. Are you going to be a good girl, Aurora?"

"Yes," she gasped as he rewarded her with a firmer touch, the cloth abandoned. His rough fingers, softened by the water, brought her to the brink with only a few touches.

"Then dry off and wait for me on the bed."

She groaned with thwarted pleasure. Aurora left the warmth of the pool and grabbed the nearest cloth. But if she ached, so should he. She turned to face him, baring herself for him as she dried herself one inch at a time, her eyes on him the whole while. Gold bled to black as he watched her. When she dropped her towel, she backed away towards the bed, his grip on his own towel white-knuckled.

The moment she sat on the bed, he launched out of the water, dried off and prowled over to her. Droplets rained down from his dark crimson hair to his beautiful brown skin, from his strong jaw down his neck to his barrel chest. She traced their paths down his muscles, to his hips to where the very sight of his thick length thrilled her. She laid back as he neared, grinning at his eagerness. Already erect, he loomed over her. He raised his chin.

"Spread your legs."

Aurora swallowed, her neck heating. It was one thing to do so in the dark, but it was full daylight. He would be able to see everything. But this was the game they played. He commanded her to play out her fantasies and she obeyed. Slowly, Aurora spread herself for him.

Theron grabbed the case and set it by his side. He knelt between her thighs with another toe-curling smile. He jerked her close, surprising a gasp out of her. Hot breath on her curls, Aurora was ensnared by anticipation.

"Good girl," he said, rewarding her with a long, slow lick.

His tongue, hot and insistent, played with her mercilessly. Aurora's back arched, her hands twisted in the covers as she alternately pulled away from the overwhelming ecstasy and pushed closer, begging for release. He brought her to the brink of climax again and again, only to pull away, leaving her mindless with frustration. Just when she thought he would give her what she sought, he backed off. She grabbed his hair, trying to grind herself against his face without success. Whenever she got close, he peppered her inner thighs with kisses.

"Theron!" she cried when he tortured her again, leaving her wanting.

"Aurora," he warned. "Trust me."

"Please. I need...I need—"

"I know." He opened the case and pulled out the smallest glass rod. "I'm a man of my word."

He pressed it inside her, easing the ache, but only a fraction. Aurora bit her lip as he pressed his lips to her bud and sucked. When he pumped the rod inside her she came with a scream, bucking as she was finally rewarded with what she'd so desperately sought. As she was coming down from the high, her thighs trembling, he removed the first rod and slipped in the second, angling it to hit her just right.

"W-wait, Theron I need—"

"You need to come, Aurora, and you'll do as you're told," he growled.

The command sent a thrill through her. He pumped faster, teasing her bud with his tongue, sending her over the edge once more. A strangled sound escaped her lips as she arched against his tongue. Her inner walls clamped against the glass, but it wasn't enough.

"More," she moaned.

He pressed a hard kiss to her inner thigh.

"How could I refuse such pretty begging?"

Theron removed the second glass, kissing her curls as she shivered through the aftermath of her orgasm. He uncorked a bottle and poured some of the contents on the next toy. Just as before, without giving her time to recover, he slid the third rod inside her. It glided into her like silk. When he angled it though, it was more torture than ease. This time, he only used the rod, preferring instead to watch her as she gripped the sheets between her fists and met his every thrust with frantic need.

"So pretty when you're needy," he growled, increasing the pace of his thrusts.

The orgasm that hit her next left her breathless and more frustrated than before. It hadn't been enough. She threw her arms over her eyes as she shook, her heart racing. He pumped the rod inside her lazily as she rode the last waves of her orgasm.

"B-bigger," she croaked.

"That sounded like a demand," he chastised her, removing the third rod.

"Please," she begged.

"Better. Are you unsatisfied, my queen?"

"Mmm." She nodded.

"Well, we can't have that."

She could hear the smile in his voice. He ducked out from between her legs and rummaged through his discarded clothes, snatching up his gold belt. He returned, closed her legs and tied the belt around her thighs. Thus confined, he poured lubricant over the fourth rod. He pushed her knees against her chest, holding them there as he pressed the glass against her folds, teasing her with the head. When he pushed it inside her this time, she felt a delicious stretch for the first time. She moaned.

"But Aurora, you never apologised for making demands."

He withdrew the glass completely.

"I'm sorry," she gasped bereft.

"That's not going to be enough." He shook his head. "No, if you want to apologise," he began, pushing the fourth rod inside her with one brutal thrust, stealing her breath. "...you'll grip this rod inside you without my help and you won't let it move a single inch. If you can do that while I make you scream, I'll forgive you. Do you want my forgiveness?"

She nodded vigorously. Aurora reached down to take hold of the rod when he stopped her.

"Ah ah. No hands."

He wanted her to grip it with her inner muscles alone? Merciful Triad, she was going to fail. Without giving her a chance to think, he pressed his thumb to her bud, punishing her with slow, lazy circles, his eyes taunting her the whole while. She tried to concentrate on gripping the rod, but he'd made her wetter than she'd ever been in her life. Even with her knees belted together and pressed against her, it was already slipping. When her climax came moments later, she cried out his name.

"Oh, Aurora, I thought you wanted my forgiveness," he taunted her, taking the fourth rod from inside her. "Do you know what happens to bad girls?"

She shook her head. But she was dying to find out.

"They get punished. I'm afraid you don't get another orgasm until you've earned my forgiveness."

She liked the sound of that.

"P-please, Theron."

He removed the belt, his smile sending a shiver down her spine.

"Get into the middle of the bed and lay on your side."

She rushed to obey. When he joined her, he set the case by his side of the bed and withdrew the fifth rod. Aurora already knew this one would fill her the way she liked. Just as before, he coated it in lubricant. He sidled up behind her and hooked her leg over his.

"Kiss me like you want my forgiveness, Aurora."

She pressed pleading kisses to his lips, her tongue asking for permission to touch his. When he obliged, her tongue sought his. At the same time, he pressed the fifth rod inside her. She exhaled in pleasure as he pumped it inside her, hitting her in all the delicious ways she loved. They lay there like that for some time, exploring each other with kisses while he thrust the glass inside her. But the moment she tried to angle her hips for more, he withdrew the rod completely. She nipped his lip in protest.

His eyes flared with heat.

"That didn't feel like you wanted my forgiveness. And if you don't want that, then it can only be because you want to be more sternly punished instead," he purred.

Aurora shivered.

"Yes," she whispered.

"You want me to treat you like a bad girl, Aurora?"

She nodded.

"Then get the next rod and fit it inside your pussy. Once you've done that, you'll suck my cock until I'm satisfied that you've learned your lesson."

Aurora swallowed. She wanted more. She wanted him to conquer her. But in order for him to do that, she needed to fight him—and lose. Aurora took a steadying breath. Would he understand what she wanted?

"Make me."

His breath hitched, eyes darkening with lust. Theron grabbed her by the hair, never tight enough to cause her pain, but just enough to have control of her head. He delivered a punishing kiss. She twisted, her skin flush against his, her nails pressing into his chest. The harder her nails bit into the perfect skin there, the more brutal his kiss. Intoxicated by the violence, Aurora ground against his erection and bit his lower lip. He pulled her head away from his, breathing ragged.

He'd never looked more wild, more aroused. Theron touched his lower lip with his tongue. She'd stopped just short of drawing blood there, but even now, beads of it formed where her nails scored his skin.

"Do you know what I do to brats like you?"

She raised her chin defiantly as she panted.

"I tame them," he growled.

Theron released his hold on her head and grabbed the belt once more, this time pinning her hands behind her back. Aurora fought, trying half-heartedly to dislodge him as he bound her, her heart pounding in excitement. This was what she'd craved. As she scrambled to her knees, Theron was already pouring the liquid over the sixth glass rod. He pushed her onto her back, then grabbed her thighs and pulled her close to the edge of the bed. She tried to close her thighs, to deny him access, but he pressed his thighs between hers, forcing her to open wide. With one hand on her belly, he used the other to press the sixth rod inside her, inch by slow inch, his eyes on hers the whole while.

Aurora cried out as it stretched her taut. Once he'd fit it inside her, she was forced to catch her breath. She'd never felt so full, and she wasn't even ready to take him. But she loved this ruthless passion from him.

Heady with pleasure, she dared to demand more, even as he thrust the rod in and out in slow, small thrusts.

"F-fuck you," she whimpered.

"You have a filthy mouth," he retorted. "I think it's time we put it to good use."

He cupped her behind her head and levered her up, forcing her to splay her legs and sit on the rod. She moaned as it pressed further inside her. He stood in front of her, his erection pressed to her lips, one hand on her shoulder, the other behind her head. In this position, her every move was his to dictate. She was entirely under his control.

"You know what I want," he said.

It was so big, if he pushed even a little too hard, she would choke on it. Fear pierced the fog of lust.

"I'm scared," she whispered.

His hold instantly gentled.

"Why are you scared, my queen?"

"You're big and I'm afraid of choking," she whispered, ashamed.

After everything he'd given her, she was too afraid to do the one thing he'd asked of her for his own sake. And yet instead of disappointment, his expression was understanding. Theron traced a knuckle down her cheek, his eyes earnest.

"I can hold completely still, but do you want to end our play for today? Do you want to stop entirely? What would make you happy?"

With just a few words he cracked open that secret space inside her heart and filled her with hope and warmth. She'd never had a lover so considerate of her needs. If he could offer her that, then the least she could do was be fully honest.

"I wanted you to conquer me..." she muttered, heat creeping into her ears. It sounded ridiculous when she said it aloud. "I wanted to lose control and still be safe."

"And now? Do you still want that?"

"Yes."

"We can do this a different way. Gentler."

Her brows knit.

"But you like rougher, don't you?"

She'd not mistaken how he'd been filled with the greatest passion when she'd forced him to kiss and tease her into submission, when he'd been forced to fight her.

"I'm happiest when you're enjoying yourself, Aurora."

Aurora released a shaky breath.

"Then I think I'd like that. Gentler. This time. Maybe next time, we can play rougher."

He hummed in his throat approvingly, kneeling before her, his hands on her thighs, holding her in her seated position. Aurora's heart sank. She still wanted to please him as best she could. Had he decided to forgo his own pleasure just because she'd gotten frightened?

"But I still want to—"

"I know, but now you're going to please me with the larger dildo inside you," he purred. "After I reward you for telling me what you wanted."

It didn't take long before he had her dizzy with need, before he gave her another climax with his talented tongue. Her inner walls spasmed against the unyielding glass as his rough hands gripped her thighs. Another strangled cry escaped her lips. She was nearly at her limit for his special brand of torture.

Theron reached behind her, freeing her wrists from the hold of the belt and urged her to lie back, his hand stroking her belly as he removed the sixth rod. He poured the lubricant on his hand and stroked her inner walls with his calloused fingers. That done, he pressed a kiss to her belly and went to retrieve the seventh. Aurora swallowed. Goddess, it was enormous. How was she ever going to fit it inside her? How was she going to fit *him?* He generously poured the lubricant over it and returned to her.

But he must have seen her trepidation.

Theron kissed her, soft and slow. She shook with anticipation, waiting for him to begin. Instead, he deepened the kiss, distracting her with his clever tongue until she'd forgotten everything but his lips, the taste of him, the warmth of his breath on her. She wrapped her arms around his neck and pulled him close as the world drifted away. Only then did he press the head of the rod against her entrance, pulling back whenever he met resistance, stimulating and teasing her until she was the one pushing against the thickness he held in his grip. Between needy kisses and whimpers borne of desperation, it felt like it took hours before it was finally seated inside her, driving her mad with the pressure.

"Are you ready to earn my forgiveness?" he asked.

She shivered.

Her only response was a strangled groan and an insensate nod. He helped her sit again, legs splayed, the glass pressing even harder inside her than before. She cried out and shook, her nails digging into his hips as he stood before her. Her breaths were uneven as she inhaled the musk of him.

"Then put your beautiful lips on my cock," he said.

She was clumsy, her mind addled by the rod shifting inside her as she moved to run her tongue along his cock. Aurora grabbed it with one hand, her fingers not even meeting around the thick length as she angled it towards her mouth. As he promised, Theron held completely still, his breath leaving him in a hiss as she closed her mouth around the tip and sucked. But he was far too large to fit comfortably inside her mouth. Try as she might to take more of him, it was a losing proposition. She whimpered, forcing herself to give up. Instead, Aurora pressed kisses to his length, licking the sensitive underside of the head and pumping her fist along his silky shaft. But whenever she moved, shifted to get a better grip or place another kiss, the rod inside her moved, pressing on every over-sensitized spot inside her. She groaned against his cock, waiting for the jolts of pleasure to subside so she could concentrate on her task.

"Aurora," he growled. She looked up to him, half in a daze. "That's enough," he ground out.

She'd not noticed his galloping breaths, his white knuckles, the look of control one moment from snapping. He stilled the tremor in his hand, but only just, as he reached to cup her cheek.

"You've been a very good girl. Are you ready for me?"

"Yes. Please," she begged, mindless.

He laid her back on the bed and crouched on top of her, one arm outstretched to balance himself. He slid his free hand down to her bud, and with a single slide Aurora saw stars. She dug her nails into his arm and screamed his name like a prayer. As the aftershock sent delicious pleasure coursing through her veins, he slid the rod out of her. He put it aside and grabbed the liquid once more, his movements jerky as he coated his cock.

"Ride me."

Aurora, shaking mess that she was, scrambled atop his thick body and positioned her trembling thighs above his length. It felt impossible as she pushed down on the thick head of his shaft. But now was not the time for thoughts of impossibilities. Her lust had eroded good sense. She bore down on him, pushing him inside her, needy and reckless. Theron swore.

"So fucking tight," he cursed. "Slower, Aurora. We have time."

But she'd reached the end of her tether. Her patience had long since run out. She needed him fully inside her, and she needed it like she needed to breathe. Refusing to give into the sting of pain, she pushed harder, until he was inside her and she was collapsed on his chest, her breaths heaving. She was pinned in place, unable to move.

"T-Theron, I can't move. It hurts," she whimpered.

"Stay still," he groaned. His magic curled around her, finding her hurts and soothing them. "Better?"

"Mmm," she moaned.

"Just breathe," he said, panting. "Don't...don't move."

Goddess, she'd never felt anything so alarmingly divine. Cheek pressed to his chest, she could feel his racing heart, the quick rise and fall of his sweat-slicked skin. He burned inside her, hot and hard and gloriously thick. She was lucky he was a healer, for she'd never have been able to take him otherwise. She lifted her hips experimentally.

He gripped her hips in his hand and rocked into her, surprising a gasp out of her.

"Yes?" he asked, desperate.

"Yes!" she cried as he rocked again.

She didn't have the energy to take him in the way she wanted, so she let him take control of her hips, his rocking turning to thrusts, and his thrusts becoming more powerful the more enthusiastic her cries of pleasure. She scored his chest with her nails, her throat raw from crying out his name. Her mind was gone, her body his, her whole being remade by the pleasure he gave her. When he neared his limit, he ground against her overstimulated bud, bringing her to climax one last time as he pumped his release inside her with a roar.

They lay there, her on top of him, hearts galloping, breaths ragged. Where she ended and he began was anyone's guess. Aurora was utterly spent. A pleasant, sleepy fog descended on her as he pulled himself from her. She must have fallen asleep, because she woke when he pressed a warm, wet washcloth between her legs and kissed her forehead.

"Hold me?" she asked, her words slurred by sleep.

"Always," he murmured, pulling her close into his embrace.

Aurora fell asleep to sound of Theron's heartbeat, a smile on her lips and her heart full of hope.

Chapter 24
Theron

Theron watched as Aurora fell asleep in his arms. The gentle cadence of her breaths and the warmth of the late afternoon sun lulled him into deep relaxation. He'd never imagined Passion would dye his thread. Never could have conceived of a life like the one he now lived. He'd thought he would marry for politics, for his bloodline—for power.

His aunt and his parents had long been at odds over his eventual marriage. His aunt had instilled in him a need to find, if not a passionate love match, then at least a companionable one where emotional and sexual compatibility was given as much weight as political considerations. His parents had predictably told him that a match with a partner was about politics first and foremost, and finding someone he could respect or tolerate was a distant second. Theron hadn't had the chance to even contemplate marriage until his rebellious kingdom's nobles had been whipped into shape after his parents' passings. None could be trusted but Batea and Myrina back then. Once he had the nobles eating from the palm of his hand, he'd turned his mind to marrying one of King Enalos' daughters and refused to seek out any other. At the time it had felt like Fate was punishing him to make him wait until late in his third decade to take a wife, but it seemed She'd had other plans.

When Myrina had said Aurora was meant for him and he for her, his mind had gone numb as his whole world was turned on its head. Good kings didn't marry for anything approaching love. Not that what he felt could be called love, surely, but it was there—a whisper of a promise, a seed of what could grow between them. Theron wanted to protect that little seed with a ferocity that surprised him. He wanted to bask in her light, her soft touch, her demanding kisses, her sighs and her smiles. He liked her, craved the way she made his blood heat, wanted more of her mischief, her laughter. Theron wanted all of her.

His wife.

His fated.

She'd gifted him with her eager surrender and fiery defiance in equal measure. He didn't know which he craved more, but he was looking forward to finding out. Theron hadn't expected the pleasure they'd shared. In truth, he was shocked she'd managed to take him at all. He'd thought it would be days, maybe weeks, before she could comfortably seat him. To find a woman who shared his inclinations was already rare enough—to find one he could trust was rarer still. He pet her head, her blonde hair like silk in his rough hands. He trailed a knuckle down her forehead, her nose, lips, stubborn chin, enjoying the softness of her skin. She was soft sweetness in one moment, fiery in the next, all teeth and talons. Maybe next time she would gift him another glimpse of the fierce queen, demanding and indomitable. He did so enjoy it when her claws came out.

Theron pressed a hand to the red welts she'd left on his chest. The sting was a medal of honour, the memory of her disobedience, her goading, heating his blood. How had she known that he craved her violence? He'd never before wished for scars, but he hoped she left more of her marks on him.

A soft knock on the door interrupted his rest. Theron sat up and slipped from the bed, getting back into his kilt to answer the door. When he opened it, Myrina was there. He sighed.

"Aunty, if this can wait..."

Her lips twitched as she took in the sight of him.

"Don't be angry, I'm just playing messenger. None of your soldiers dared come up to disturb you, even though they had business with you."

Theron ran a hand down his face.

"Now?"

Myrina shrugged. He was about to leave the room when he stopped himself. He'd promised to stay by her side while she slept.

"Tell them they can come here if they must, but that if they wake her, they'll pay in blood."

Myrina's amber eyes sparkled. She kissed him on the cheek.

"I'm so happy for you, my little lion."

Unease stole through him. Nothing this good ever lasted. He wanted to be the man Aurora seemed to see when she looked at him, but in his heart of hearts, he knew he fell far short. What if he wasn't capable of being what she expected? Before Myrina left, he grabbed her wrist. He was a young man once again, lost and alone in a world that no longer made sense.

"Aunty, I don't know how to be a good man."

He didn't know anything about being a good husband. About nurturing something worth having between a man and a woman. He'd never expected to feel more than simple respect for his future wife, provided she proved herself to be an equally good queen. Those plans had gone up in smoke the moment Aurora had been named his fated. Now he felt adrift, new responsibilities he'd never prepared for suddenly thrust upon him, just as they had been when Tisander had died. What if he failed her the same way he'd failed his brother?

Her brows knit with concern.

"My sweet boy, you've always been a good man."

He shook his head. He wasn't. He was greedy and prideful, manipulative and petty, guarded and cruel. If Aurora had had anyone in all of Trisia to look after her wellbeing, they would have warned her off him. Myrina always wanted to see him in the best light, no matter what he did.

But Myrina knew of his flaws. She knew something of the horrible, cruel, calculating things he'd done as king. How could she call him a good man with a straight face?

"You know that's not true."

She smiled and took his hand in hers.

"Do you *want* to be a good man, a good husband, for her?"

Theron snuck a glance at Aurora, peaceful and trusting in sleep. His heart warmed unexpectedly. It alarmed him at the same time as it brought an ache in his chest. Love was a dangerous weakness for a king. She would be the target of all his enemies looking to destroy him. Could he really afford this feeling? If he loved, he would put a target on her back. If he loved, he could be hurt in ways he'd guarded against his whole adult life. But was it even possible to ignore it, now that they were bound? News of their union would soon be known throughout all of Trisia. If this was to work between them, to become something they treasured rather than regretted, he had to at least try—right?

"Yes," he answered.

"Then let yourself love her. Allow her to know you, so that she can love you in turn. Be brave, my little lion. I promise the rewards are worth the risks."

Was he even capable of the depth of trust and feeling his aunt spoke of? It always seemed like something only those less burdened with responsibility and power could indulge in. Even his parents, who had cared for each other after a fashion, had only truly loved Tisander. Just as he had. And look what good that had done them—their heartbreak had weakened their reign. Theron's own heartbreak had been a black cloud that he carried every day, locked in a box in his heart that he tried never to open. What if something happened to Aurora?

His throat tightened at the thought. He pushed it away.

"Thank you. It's not the answer I wanted but...thank you," Theron sighed.

She squeezed his hand.

"I'll let them know to attend you."

Theron found a red tunic in the room's wardrobe and stripped out of his kilt. Much as he loved her little marks, they were for his eyes only. No one else deserved to see the gifts she'd given him. Once he was newly attired, he sat beside Aurora on the bed, a hand on her shoulder. She shifted position, snaking her hand over his thigh, her little nails digging into him possessively. He smiled. Theron pulled the cover up to tuck it below her chin. She wouldn't like it if strangers saw her in this state.

The moment was interrupted by Nireus, commander of his soldiers, tip-toeing into the room when he saw Theron's scowl.

The commander bowed.

"Glory to the sun of Aureum."

Theron cleared his throat and tipped his head at Aurora. Nireus' dark eyes widened.

"And glory to the star of Aureum," he added.

Theron nodded.

"What news?"

"We are ready to depart to Aureum on your command, Your Majesty."

Aurora would need at least the rest of the day to recover from everything. And now that his people were here, he would have the funds on hand to outfit her as his queen. It was a shame that he would need to do business with the grasping merchants of Boreas, but some things couldn't be avoided.

"Then we leave tomorrow morning. And have someone acquire the appropriate trousseau for a queen of Aureum, or at least as close to one as can be had in this cursed queendom. The gown she wore today is in the bathroom. Use it to get her measurements."

"Yes, Your Majesty. I've also brought correspondence from home." Nireus presented him with several scrolls, as well as blank parchment, ink and sealing wax. "Is there anything I can do for you, Your Majesty?"

"Guard the temple. Ensure none of Flora's minions enter. And bring food and drink to the room. Return an hour after that for the letters being sent home."

"It will be done. Triad preserve the sun and star of Aureum."

As he read through the letters, all more of the same, pleading for his swift return, his mind wandered. His Aunt had counselled him to reveal himself to Aurora. Was it really wise to let Aurora know him fully? To see all his flaws? Wouldn't that just make her regret her choice? He was already playing with fire, given the existence of Batea's serpents. As far as Aurora knew, he'd never seen her Drakon or it's like. If she found out he'd kept them from her, she would be angry. Perhaps even angry enough not to forgive him.

A sense of disquiet settled on him. He knew it had taken the person she loved most from her. Had devastated her homeland. Had driven her to chase it across the world, no matter the danger. What chance did their nascent relationship have against the weight of her past? He didn't like his odds.

Maybe in this case, a small lie would save her from the greater hurt. Theron dipped the quill in the ink and scratched off the most important letter of the day. One to Batea, ordering her to slay her serpents. None of them were even close in size to the beast from Aurora's memory, or could fly, or even had the awesome destructive capabilities of the one that had nearly killed her. But it was better to be safe than sorry. He wanted to risk their relationship as much as he wanted to risk her life. If he presented their heads to Aurora when they returned to Altanus, she might be upset for a time, but by then the beasts would have been destroyed for good, and they could get on with their lives as king and queen. If he were exceptionally lucky, she might buy that he'd ordered their death the moment he'd seen Drakon through her eyes. She never needed to know how close he and his cousin had gotten to creating a beast just like it.

As for Drakon itself, he would question Batea in private about it. If it had escaped her kennels to cause trouble abroad, he needed to know how best to neutralize it, and putting that request to paper was simply too dangerous. The temples could accuse both he and Batea of being agents of chaos, and Aurora would truly never forgive him if they'd made Drakon in truth.

When the commander returned with food, drink, and another dress, this one in red and gold, as well as a sleeping gown made of silk, Theron nodded in pleasure. As Nireus retrieved the letters Theron wanted sent and saw himself out, Aurora roused.

"What time is it?" she asked, her words slurred by sleep.

"Late afternoon."

She groaned, pulling the covers over her head. Theron pulled them back.

"Here, have something to eat, refresh yourself and then rest."

She probably hadn't eaten much at all, and the day had already been long and strenuous.

"Mmm," Aurora replied, groggily sitting up.

He fed her bite-sized pieces of delicacies as she leaned on his chest, his arm around her. Skin to skin, he once again revelled in the softness of her. This felt warm, sweet, almost domestic. Was it safe to allow himself to sink into this? He'd never allowed such coziness with his past lovers. Suddenly, he was glad that this was something he and Aurora alone shared. Maybe the path towards love need not be fraught. Maybe it was filled with more tenderness than risk. As he was trying to decide if he should allow himself to like it or not, her eyes began to droop.

"Go wash up," he urged her.

"Tyrant," she grouched.

"But you love my tyranny."

She growled, leaving the comfort of the bed to waddle over to the bathroom, closing the door behind her. When she came out some time later, she leaned against the doorframe. Exhaustion had left her pale. She'd been through an ordeal today, and that was before he'd bedded her senseless. It was a wonder she could stand at all. She looked down at herself, blinking owlishly.

"Where did my clothes go?"

Theron held back a snort, getting her sleeping gown and helping her into it. Dressed in gold, she looked right. His.

"Oh, there they are," she said, plucking at the shimmery material. Aurora looked from him to the bed, to her shaking legs. "The bed is really far."

"Then I suppose it can't be helped," he said, pressing a kiss to her forehead.

He picked her up in his arms. She snuggled into him.

"This is nice," she mumbled.

As he settled her at his side, and she drifted back to sleep, he had to admit that holding her, caring for her, and luxuriating in her presence was very nice indeed. He hoped that they could have this together for many years to come.

Chapter 25

Aurora

When Aurora woke next, it was dark outside. She drank in the sound of Theron's steady breathing, the scent of his soap and skin, the comforting warmth of his presence. Would that she could spend every day like this, her greatest challenge deciding which dress she wanted him to divest her of and in what way he would make love to her.

"Oh goddess…" she groaned, remembering all the things they'd done, shame scalding her.

Aurora couldn't sit still. The memories of asking him to play out her deepest fantasies raced through her mind. She removed herself from his side and began pacing.

What if he'd only humoured her, and he didn't truly enjoy what they'd done? What if he thought her strange, unnatural? It was a common-enough reaction to her peculiar tastes. Few people were interested in such things. What if he regretted their bond, now that he'd glimpsed inside the part of her she'd kept hidden away? She should have approached it slowly, tactfully, sounding him out first. What if she spent the rest of her days wishing she'd kept it all buried deep, where no one would know of her shame or use it to hurt her? What a mess she'd mired herself in.

"You're going to wear a hole in the floor, Aurora. Come back to bed." Theron beckoned her sleepily.

She walked mechanically to his side, her gut churning. Theron took her hand in his and kissed her knuckles, looking up at her from the comfort of his pillow.

"What troubles you?"

"It's just…I've never…never done that before. P-play, I mean."

"Did you dislike it?"

"No! No, I…liked it."

"Then what's the problem?" he asked, amused.

"You're not…put off by me, are you?"

He raised a brow. Oh goddess, it was just as she'd feared.

"W-we don't have to do it again!" she reassured him, her heart in her throat. "If it's not to your liking, I don't want to force you to do anything that repels you. I didn't mean to—"

He pressed a finger to her lips.

"Hush. That's enough of that. Rest assured, I very much enjoyed what we shared, and I intend to indulge in our every fantasy—repeatedly, and at great length."

Aurora released a shaky breath and a quiet, relieved laugh as he cupped her cheek and stroked her face with his thumb.

"Thank you," she said, kissing his palm. "For everything."

"It's no easy thing to trust another with our most cherished desires. I'm grateful you proved worthy of that trust," he said solemnly.

"And I you, Theron."

"Now, are you coming back to bed? I want a few more hours of rest before we leave this thrice-damned city."

Aurora shook her head. There was no going back to sleep now that her anxiety had woken her.

"I slept for a whole day already."

"You ran yourself ragged, physically and emotionally, and that was before I brought you to the temple. You needed the rest. But if you can't sleep, feel free to wander the temple halls. The paladins and my people are on guard for any of Flora's minions. There's a dress for you there, in the wardrobe. It was all that could be crafted on such short notice. I'll have finer ones made as soon as possible."

Aurora smiled and kissed him on his forehead, changing into the dress and slipping from the room, Theron already asleep once more. She found her way to the courtyard and decided to enjoy the pre-dawn cool, wiping away the morning dew from the bench. Where the courtyards of Knowledge's temples were dedicated to rare and unusual plants meant for study, and Justice's were utilitarian, minimalist spaces meant to help clear the mind, Passion's were explosions of colour, scent and lush beauty.

Spices and florals mixed in the air. Even throughout millennia, some things remained the same. Though she couldn't identify all the different plant species, the blend reminded her of home. She alone amongst her family had chosen Knowledge as her patroness, despite being born under Passion's stars. Like most merchants, her family prayed most fervently to Passion. Her early childhood was filled with memories of incense and prayers in the ruby temple. Of racing through the halls and courtyard laughing and shrieking as she was chased by cheerful acolytes, and doted on by priestesses who pinched her chubby cheeks. Aspiring cooks would slip her confections when her parent's gazes were turned while complimenting her on her long ears.

Home felt so very close in that moment, here in the same temple where she would one day spend her childhood. And yet, she may never return. The cycle of calamity, Drakon, kept her here by necessity, but she had more than one destiny. The thread that bound her to Theron was as unexpected as it was precious. Already she felt herself pulled in two—the desire to go home, and the desire to stay. With Theron, a part of her was already home.

Aurora rested her head on the bark of the tree at her side.

She needn't think of such things. Those were decisions she didn't yet have the luxury of making. Drakon still needed to be destroyed. Theron's fate needed to be altered. After all, according to the histories, he was the first monarch to perish in the initial cycle of calamity. If she stayed, would she be able to alter his doomed course? She'd managed to alter it already, marrying him in place of the princess he was supposed to wed. But what if the histories had simply been incorrect all along and she'd changed nothing? What if, like her visions, she'd be forced to watch his death play out, no matter how hard she struggled against it?

Perhaps it was time to tell him everything. About who she really was, where—and when—she'd come from. About his ultimate fate, about the course of history. After all, the kind of love she wanted to share with him had no place for secrets. Aurora didn't know if what she felt for him was love yet, but it was achingly close. Even now, Passion's bond was like a tether between them. In this lifetime and in all her others, she was meant to find him. It was a comforting thought that though there was great evil meant for her, there was goodness too. She could only hope he would take the news of her origins half as well as Hyllus had. If he didn't... she didn't want to contemplate what her married life would look like.

Aurora chuckled softly to herself.

It would have been better to go back to bed, if staying awake was only going to make her morose. Just as she decided to seek her husband's warmth, the sound of a cane clicking on the mosaic floors of the temple caught her attention. There, in the gloom, Orithyia appeared like a wraith, draped in the deepest black of her high priestess' robes.

"I'd hoped I might find you here," she said, pulling back her veil to hang behind her, attached to the silver and black tiara atop her white, braided hair.

Aurora stood, squaring her shoulders and bracing for a fight. She was no longer the scared, lost girl who had come to her for aid. She was the queen of Aureum now, and she would not let this woman harm her again.

"I have nothing to say to you."

"If you're going to be a queen in more than name, you'll need to learn to lie better than that." Orithyia chuckled.

"What do you want?" Aurora seethed.

"I see his temper has rubbed off on you. But you have nothing to be cross about," Orithyia chided her.

"You left me to rot in the vivarium!"

"After you broke into my private chamber, raving like a madwoman." Orithyia raised a brow.

"Then what was your excuse to maim me?" She motioned to her eye.

Even now, Aurora feared the woman's switch. Her flesh had been fully healed and yet Aurora still remembered the panic, the agony. Invisible scars that would linger for a lifetime. She hated the fear this woman inspired in her, how now every crack of thunder brought her back to that horrid day.

"During the outbreak of plague? You dawdled while people died. Your reticence was costing lives I could have been saving. And in any case, you were seducing the Aurean king. I had every confidence you would be healed within the hour."

Aurora heart hammered with anger. She was so blasé about the suffering she'd caused.

"And what of your cruelties in Flora's throne room?"

At every juncture, Orithyia had chosen to harm her. Never once had she chosen kindness or compassion. Always she chose pain.

"You'd made it impossible to conceal your magic, screaming for days before the monstrosities had appeared what would occur. I held that demonstration to save your life. What would have been more believable—a worshipper of the sinister Triad receiving messages from their goddesses, or a true oracle? That demonstration proved what you are—and what you were not. Are you complaining because it hurt?"

Aurora swallowed her angry tears. It was quite rich for someone protected by a goddess from ever suffering more than a papercut to chide her for despising pain.

"And the princess? What excuse did you have to separate her from Hyllus?"

Orithyia laughed. Aurora reviled her in that moment. Aurora's hurts were but drops in an ocean of pain that Epicasta had suffered. Three unwanted marriages, her body used like a bargaining chip as the life of the man she loved was used as a cudgel to force her obedience. Years of agonizing heartbreak and horror. And for what?

"You mean the only other woman capable of keeping her mother in line? *That* princess? The same Epicasta who was wise beyond her years and intelligent enough to win the title of crown princess in spite of being the youngest of four? Why do you think, Aurora? Was it because I'm a cruel old bitch, or because the well-being of the queendom was more important than the heart of a single woman?"

She raised her brow, triumphant.

"So you don't deny it?"

"Did I help Flora imprison Hyllus far away from Epicasta? Yes. A prison he escaped soon after, never to darken the doors of the royal palace again—until recently. I allowed her to believe he was still in custody rather than let her know he'd abandoned her, because only one of those outcomes ensured she would stay in the palace. I did what had to be done to keep Epicasta where she was needed most."

Aurora glared at the high priestess.

"I don't believe that."

"You lived in the vivarium, Aurora. Yes, I know what it is called. I didn't realise how dreadful it was until after the attack. That is something I deeply regret." Orithyia sighed. "Flora is...unwell. She has always been unwell. I've spent a lifetime doing my utmost to keep her darkest impulses at bay, or at least mitigate them. I thought, with a strict and steady hand, I could help her overcome her character flaws—give Viridis the monarch it needed. Alas, her flaws ran so deep and were so destructive that all I could do was race from one fire to the next, putting them out as best I was able."

"None of that excuses the horrors you allowed Epicasta to suffer! That you allowed so many to suffer! You could have saved Epicasta from the harms done to her and Hyllus!"

Aurora stood her ground, her shouting no doubt rousing some of the sleeping clerics.

"If I had, it would have been at the expense of Viridis! When Epicasta demonstrated the ability to manage her mother, I knew she had to be encouraged to become the next queen—through any means necessary. Now Viridis' only hope has run away with a handsome nobody made avatar. You think you set her free? You allowed her to shirk the only duty she was born to, all so she can galivant across Trisia with a man whose divine mission puts him in harm's way. She's in constant jeopardy as long as she remains by his side. You were a fool, blinded by your naïve heart."

She felt the sting of guilt then. Had she actually done the wrong thing? How could causing suffering ever be the right thing to do?

"Is this what you came here for? To make excuses and insult me for having a heart at all?"

Orithyia stamped her cane on the floor in a fit of pique.

"I came here to give you the truth, and the chance to seize power. I'm giving you the opportunity to do the first intelligent thing you'll do since you were sent here. I'm offering you the chance to be more than just an ornamental queen bound to a lying king."

So now she sought to sow divisions between her and Theron? Aurora ground her teeth.

"I'm not interested in your slander. Theron is a good man who sacrificed his life for me! While you and Flora have thrown your worst at me, he was there to protect me! I won't stand here and listen to you insult his character!"

Aurora marched passed Orithyia, reining in the urge to throw the punch she so richly deserved. When Aurora was a few steps from the edge of the courtyard, Orithyia spoke.

"I found your beast, this bringer of calamity. Your Drakon."

Aurora stopped in her tracks, her breath hitching.

"Where?" Aurora spun around. "Where is he?" she asked, grabbing Orithyia's slender, bony wrists.

"In Aureum," she answered, pushing Aurora's hands off her. "And there is more than one." Orithyia dipped a hand into the pocket of her robe and withdrew a scroll, sealed with the insignia of Knowledge's temple. She pressed it into Aurora's greedy hands.

Aurora tore the seal and opened the scroll. Inside, detailed images of great serpents, each with a unique set of horns atop their scaly heads. The images were painted with colour, naming a few, notes on their size scribbled in the margins. Other details, like what they ate and how often, where they'd been spotted and more littered the pages. Except Drakon's image was not among them. Her heart sank as a cold sweat ran down her neck. Merciful Triad, there were so many of them. Was Drakon simply the last one of these beasts left standing at the end of the first cycle of calamity? Would she and Hyllus be forced to fight them all? One great serpent was bad enough. There were dozens detailed here.

"They're in Aureum. None of them can fly yet, as far as my informants are aware, but Batea is rumoured to be altering them for that purpose. Batea is your husband's cousin, by the way, and his most trusted general and acting queen of Aureum in his absence. Her magic allows her to create chimeras. She would not have been creating these creatures without the king's knowledge or express permission. He has lied to you, Aurora."

Aurora's knees gave out and she slumped to the ground, crumpling the scroll in her hand. Hot tears ran down her cheeks. Her heart threatened to shatter.

"No," she whispered, her voice cracking.

It wasn't possible. This must be some ruse, some trick.

"You can ask any of the Aurean soldiers staying here in the temple. They would have been selected from the ranks of your husband's most trusted. They will confirm that Batea's kennels contain these very same beasts."

Aurora spotted an acolyte wandering the halls.

"You!" she called.

"Yes, Your Majesty?"

"Bring one of the Aurean soldiers here, as quickly as you can."

The acolyte's eyes widened with alarm at her state. She bowed and raced off. Aurora held herself as still as she could. Theron wouldn't lie to her. Not about this. They were fated—meant to walk the path of life together. To find love in each other's arms. He knew how vital her mission was. He had some inkling of what Drakon had taken from her. And he'd promised to help her slay the beast. To put every resource of his kingdom at her disposal. This must be some mistake, some clever lie on Orithyia's part.

Aurora didn't even notice the soldier marching up towards her, so lost in her thoughts as she was. He knelt before her.

"Your Majesty? What's happened? Please, allow me to—"

Aurora pushed the scroll at the soldier.

"Do you recognise any of these beasts?" she asked, her voice brittle.

The soldier took the scroll from her and eyed it.

"Your Majesty, where did you get this?"

Aurora grabbed his tunic, her heart a moment from shattering and her voice hollow.

"Answer the question."

He looked from Orithyia to Aurora, his lips pursing.

"Yes, Your Majesty. These are some of Batea's beasts."

Her heart pounded in her ears.

"And Theron, he knows about these?"

"Of course, Your Majesty."

"How long?"

"Your Majesty?" the soldier asked, confused.

"How long has he known?" she asked, feeling ill.

"Since they were created, Your Majesty. Over a year now."

Whatever else the soldier said, Aurora couldn't hear it. She was mired in her mind, her thoughts coming slowly and too fast all at once. She'd been betrayed.

"Leave the scroll and go," she hissed, releasing him.

"As you wish, Your Majesty," the soldier bowed and left, concern swimming in his eyes.

It was a lie.

All of it.

He'd known this whole time. From the very first, Theron had been sheltering Drakon. All his promises to slay the beast, to give her an army to see the task through... How he must have laughed at her naïveté. What an easy mark she'd been! He'd never intended to help her. All this time, his only interest had been in using her—first for her knowledge, then for her magic, and finally as a way to escape marriage to a Viridian princess. Now she was irrevocably bound to the person who had used her in the cruellest way. In this lifetime and the next. A man she'd trusted with her heart, her body, her desires—her future. And not just her future, but the fate of Trisia itself.

If he was willing to create a multitude of great serpents to keep at his disposal, there was no telling what else he was capable of. And if Drakon was his creation, which seemed more and more likely, there could be no doubt—he was an agent of chaos at worst, and a monster at best.

Aurora wept, her tears staining the paper of the scroll, muddying the ink. Myrina had been wrong. Her dreadful fate would never be balanced with goodness—all that awaited her was death and suffering. All she was meant for was tragedy. All that had been good in her life had been obliterated by Drakon—and Theron.

"*Get up.*" Orithyia's whip-like command was punctuated by the crack of her cane against the ground.

Aurora gasped and looked up as disgust contorted the old woman's features.

"This is your first lesson as queen, Aurora. Remember it well. A queen does not have the luxury of tears. *You* do not have the luxury of falling into despair. Now, *get up.*"

Aurora struggled to her feet, wiping her red-rimmed eyes.

"As I said, I came to you with an opportunity. As you are, you'll become an ornamental queen. Without a noble lineage, allies, wealth or real power, your only recourse would have been to appeal to your husband's affections. I hope I don't have to remind you how fickle a man's heart is," she said, pulling another scroll from her pocket, this one sealed with the insignia of the Viridian throne. "I understand how you feel about Queen Flora, but I hope you'll see this for what it is—your only chance to be a queen in truth."

Aurora took the scroll from Orithyia, swallowing down bile as she tore the seal. But as many times as she read the words inscribed on the paper, her mind refused to encompass their meaning.

"You can't be serious."

"I am *quite* serious."

Aurora read it again. It must be a trick. Another trap. Queen Flora was offering to adopt her as a daughter, give her the status of a princess of Viridis, and send along a contingent of soldiers, servants, nobles and bureaucrats with her to Aureum to secure her position and help her destroy all of Batea's beasts.

But nothing the queen or high priestess ever did came without some cost.

"What's the catch?"

"Well, I doubt your husband will be too pleased," Orithyia laughed. "And I'll be coming along. I've not set foot in Aureum in some time. With the threat of Drakon looming over Trisia, you'll need every advantage," she said. When she saw the suspicion in Aurora's eyes, she sighed. "You don't have to accept this olive branch, but it was the best I could do on such short notice."

But would she be a queen, or just a puppet, beholden to the Viridian throne and Orithyia? Did she have a better option, given the circumstances? She'd allowed herself to be manipulated by Theron. Had bound herself to him to free him from his sacred vow. Reckless passion had doomed her now-shattered heart. All that was left—all that mattered—was destroying Drakon.

She laughed bitterly. At least she was no longer torn in two—her path was clear. Destroy Drakon by any means necessary. And if she survived, she would return home, leaving Theron to his loveless, lonely fate and his vicious battles with Viridis. She didn't need to remain here once her task was done, a pawn of two monarchs. Unlike him, she had people worthy of her love. What did it matter if she was broken? Once this was done, they could piece her back together. Phaedra. Silvanus. Her family. Her Orithyia. She could hold on a little longer, clutch the jagged shards of her heart close just long enough to see this through.

For them.

"I accept your offer," Aurora said.

Orithyia smiled.

"I thought you might."

Chapter 26
Theron

As the sun rose, Theron buried his head in his pillow. He wanted a few more hours of rest before the journey back to Aureum. And maybe a slow, leisurely roll in the sheets with his new wife. After all, beds as comfortable as these would be hard to come by on the road home, and he suspected that once they arrived in Altanus, they would be too busy for playful morning trysts. At least for a while. He dozed, daydreaming of what he would do to his delightful wife, until the doors to the room were flung open.

Theron smiled. Aurora had returned. Maybe he would get what he wanted after all.

But her expression was not at all suited for love-making.

Eyes red-rimmed, with the evidence of dried tears on her cheeks, she strode inside with wrath infused into her every step, rage blazing in her green eyes. Gone was the gold and red dress he'd prepared for her. In its place, a gown of Viridian green and silver, emeralds sparkling from her neck, her ears, her fingers, her hair. She was outfitted for court with a royal's tiara atop her brow—and kitted for war, with a blade at her hip. At her back, a number of Viridian royal guards poured in.

Bewilderment held him in its grip, his lust turning to ash as rage set it alight. The shock of betrayal, dark and ugly, pumped through his veins.

Aurora drew her sword and pressed the tip of it to his throat, her voice as cold as ice and as sharp as glass.

"Take me to my throne."

Thank you so much for reading The Oracle of Dusk! Did you know I offer a steamy bonus chapter of the wedding night from Theron's point of view? Read it by subscribing to my newsletter here: https://twolaurelspress.eo.page/zj5dk

I hope you've enjoyed Aurora and Theron's adventure so far, but their story is far from over. How will Theron retaliate for this betrayal? Will Aurora succeed in destroying Drakon? Find out in the next installment of the *Cycle of Calamity* series, *The Midnight King!* You can order your copy here: https://books2read.com/tmk

Eager for more epic fantasy romance with banter, magical mayhem, and court intrigues? Check out my other books here: https://www.elysethomson.com/

Don't forget to leave a review!

Afterword

Thank you so much for coming on this journey with me! *The Oracle of Dusk* was a labour of love and I hope it gave you a few hours of escapist fun. However, the story is far from over, and if you've made it this far and crave more, I have a treat in store for you. A steamy bonus chapter from Theron's point of view awaits any who sign up to my newsletter! You can also preorder the second book in the series, *The Midnight King!*

Enjoy, and remember to leave a review!

Book Links

Acknowledgements

No book is made without the love and support of a great many people. The Oracle of Dusk was no different. I have so many people to thank. Paulina and Sophia, for encouraging me. Juliette and Avie for reading my first draft. Alex, for being my rock through the whole whirlwind journey. My family; Mom, Dad, Sylvia, Ross, Kyle, Garrett and Jen for never doubting me. The best writing friends a girl could have (with a group name so lackluster, it doesn't bear repeating) Sophia, Rachel, Asha, Rebecca and Shirley. You kept me sane and gave me a place to belong. My life is richer for having known all of you. And finally, to my friends in FaRoFeb community, thank you for all your love and support.

Special thanks to my amazing editor, Rachel Le Mesurier, my talented map maker Catrin Russel and my lovely cover designer, Kostya Biletskiy.

About the Author

Elyse Thomson is the pen-name of author, bookbinder and self-proclaimed hermit residing in Canada's capital. She writes escapist fantasy with daring heroines, magical mayhem, swoon-worthy romance and court intrigue. Having graduated from University of Toronto with a Bachelors in History and Classics, she is delighted to bring her love of all things ancient to her work. When not writing, she's restoring antiquarian books for a select group of clients, gaming, or snuggling up with either her husband or her neurotic terrier, Freya.

If you would like to know about the author and the release of the next books, or be the first to get access to exclusive snippets and other goodies, visit the website or join the newsletter.

ALSO BY

Mages of Oblivion Series
The Firetongue Heir
Poisoned Empire
Conspirators' Kingdom
Isles of Corruption

Cycle of Calamity Series
The Starlight Princess
The Oracle of Dusk
The Midnight King
The Champion of Dawn
...and more to come.

Book Links